Also by Linda Lael Miller

THE
LAST
CHANCE
CAFÉ

LINDA LAEL MILLER

POCKET **STAR** BOOKS
New York   London   Toronto   Sydney   Singapore

A Pocket Star Book published by
POCKET BOOKS, a division of Simon & Schuster, Inc.
1230 Avenue of the Americas, New York, NY 10020

Copyright © 2002 by Linda Lael Miller

Originally published in hardcover in 2002 by Atria Books

ISBN: 978-1-4516-4628-3

First Pocket Books paperback printing May 2003

10 9 8 7 6 5 4 3 2 1

POCKET STAR BOOKS and colophon are registered trademarks
of Simon & Schuster, Inc.

For information regarding special discounts for bulk purchases,
please contact Simon & Schuster Special Sales at 1-800-456-6798
or business@simonandschuster.com

Cover art by Robert Hunt

Printed in the U.S.A.

For my beloved uncles:

Harry Bleecker
Hugh Bleecker
Ralph Bleecker
George Bleecker
Jess Bleecker
Clarence Bleecker

Jack Lael
Larry Lael
Otis "Wes" Lael

Raymond Wiley
Jack Wiley

Louie Paparich
Jack Bartol
Gordon Sly
Boyd Kramer
Joe Bass

1

SCOTTSDALE, ARIZONA

Joel Royer laid a hand on Hallie's forearm and cleared his throat in an effort to get her attention, but she couldn't look away from the body, the remnant, the wax figure that had once been her stepfather. Dear Lou, good cop, solid citizen, erstwhile knight in shining armor. He'd been at the core of her life since she was six, and his passing had left her scrambling for balance.

"It's over," Joel murmured, with undisguised relief. "Let's get out of here." His palm rested lightly on the small of her back, barely touching her and yet poised to administer one of those skillful, all but imperceptible shoves that always made her grind her back teeth a little. In that place, and in those circumstances, barely holding on the way she was, she wanted to whirl on him, spitting invectives.

"I'll meet you outside," she said instead. Her voice sounded moderate, even impassive, a strange state of affairs, given the maelstrom of angry grief raging inside her, a psychological firestorm that showed no signs of dissipating anytime soon.

Her resistance did not please Joel, but then, very little about her ever had. She was alternately too smart, then too stupid. Too ambitious, too lazy. Too strong, too weak.

He hesitated, as if preparing one of his brilliant arguments, then sighed and walked away to join the other mourners milling in the entryway and on the sidewalk outside the funeral home. There would be a wake at the Late Shift Tavern, a celebration of Lou's life and career, packed with cops, retired and active-duty, and their wives, but there was no graveside service on the schedule. Lou had left clear instructions that he was to be cremated, and he trusted Hallie to dispose of his ashes at her discretion—"wherever," as he'd put it. She smiled ever so slightly to recall that Lou-esque stipulation, specific, but leaving room for interpretation. Still reeling from the suddenness and violence of his death, she hadn't thought as far as potential ash-scattering locations yet.

She reached out, touched his right hand. The chill was hard, penetrating, and her first instinct was to recoil, but she didn't give in. She looked back, making sure the room was empty, and then turned to Lou again, squeezing his icy fingers once, lightly. Tears stung her eyes, and she sniffled, as jerky eight-millimeter images flashed through her mind: Lou, trying to pass himself off as Santa Claus that first Christmas after he joined the family, when Hallie was in first grade, and waxing skeptical where such things as sleigh-driving saints, elves and flying reindeer were concerned; Lou, proudly filming her dance-school recitals, drill team and cheerleading exploits and various graduation ceremonies, too: Cactus Ridge High, Scottsdale Community College, and culinary school. Lou, keeping a brave vigil at her mother's bedside, while Cheryl died a lingering and unjust death from cancer. He'd been a pillar for everybody, though even then Hallie had known he was crumbling inside, broken by the most profound loss of his life. He'd carried on, for Hallie's sake and his own, and that, too, was vintage Lou. His creed had been a simple one: show up, stick it out, never sit on the bench if you can be in the game.

"You were the best," Hallie whispered to him now, hoping his spirit was somewhere nearby, close enough to hear, and at peace now. God knew, he hadn't been himself the past few months; he'd been stressed out, and more than a little cranky. "You adored Mom. And you didn't just accept me, or tolerate me—I was *your kid*. You really, truly loved me. Thank you for that, Lou. Thank you for coming along just when we needed you and for hanging in there for all the ups and downs."

From behind her, probably in the open doorway, came more throat-clearing. She didn't have to turn around to know Joel was back, hovering, hurrying her along, mentally prodding her as if they were still married, instead of three-years divorced. She suppressed her irritation again, already on emotional overload. She needed to choose her battles, more now than ever before, and she simply didn't have the resources for an all-out skirmish with Joel.

She leaned down a little closer to Lou. "I know you'd tell me to walk away from all this and never look back, if you could," she told him softly, "and you'd be right, too. Still, I don't think it will come as any great surprise to you that I *can't* just let this go, because I'll never have another coherent thought if I do. I'll find out who shot you, and why, and I'll see them pay, if it's the last thing I ever do."

"Hallie?" Joel's voice was gruff. He was closing in, probably within prodding distance.

Hallie bit her lower lip and closed her eyes for a moment. When she opened them again, she thought she saw the barest suggestion of a smile touch one corner of Lou's mouth. Her imagination, of course. "Good-bye," she said gently. Then, spine straight, shoulders squared, she turned and walked back down the aisle, between the pews and the rows of folding chairs squeezed in to accommodate the sold-out crowd, toward the man she should never have married in the first place.

"You're going to the wake, right?" Joel wanted to know. Tall, with sleek brown hair, stylishly cut, he looked more like an uptown lawyer than a struggling assistant D.A. The twins, Kiera and Kiley, now seven, had inherited his distinctive blue-gray eyes. Kiley had his persistence, too, and his tendency to make a federal case out of everything.

It seemed to Hallie that her most sensitive nerves had migrated to the surface of her skin, jangling a discordant chorus there, and she was so tired she could barely focus her eyes, but the people gathering at the Late Shift were Lou's colleagues and friends, some of whom had known him since his days at the Academy. She owed it to them, and to Lou, to put in an appearance, although truly the last thing she felt like doing was hoisting a glass. Unless, of course, the glass contained white wine, to be consumed by candlelight while she soaked neck-deep in her old-fashioned bathtub at home.

There had to be some kind of informal send-off, of course. Lou had made the most of his time on the planet, but his passing was premature to say the least. He'd been fifty-eight years old, and in excellent health, with a lot of good living still ahead of him, and he'd died cruelly, in the very place he should have been safest, taking five shots in the chest when he'd surprised a burglar in his living room. That, at least, was the official position; Hallie couldn't quite square it all in her mind.

"Yes," Hallie answered, albeit belatedly. "I'll stop by for a little while."

"The kids are okay?" Joel was trying, she gave him credit for that. Although he paid support, and made all the appropriate father-noises, whenever she rattled his cage, anyway, she knew he wasn't really interested in their children. On some level, he was a child himself, unwilling, or perhaps unable, to share the nest.

"They're with Mrs. Draper, across the courtyard," Hallie answered, with a distracted nod. An odd numbness was beginning to roll in, like a fog, from the far edges of her consciousness. She should have welcomed any semblance of oblivion, she supposed, blessed and embraced any respite from the gnawing sorrow, and the wild, quiet fury; instead, she struggled to stay grounded. If she was going to keep her promise to Lou, and to herself—and she was, by God—she couldn't afford to lose her edge.

"You seem a little shaky to me."

Go away, Joel, she wanted to say, leave me alone, but again she held her tongue. "I'm fine," she lied. The truth was, in the five days since Lou's murder, she'd barely slept or eaten. Her stomach lining burned twenty-four-seven, probably eating a hole in itself, and a low-grade migraine pulsed at the base of her skull. She'd replayed old tapes from her answering machine over and over, fast-forwarding through countless mundane messages, seeking the unique timbre of Lou's voice, trying to find some hint there, some clue that he'd been in trouble. There hadn't been any red flags, and yet . . .

Oh, she was *anything* but fine.

The police were looking for a burglar, a cheap hood with a drug habit and a quick trigger finger. Hallie, meanwhile, was haunted by an inexplicable certainty that the killing had been about something else entirely, something a lot more complicated. The question was, what?

Outside, in the crisp October sunlight, fading now as the afternoon wore on toward another long night, Joel moved to touch Hallie's back again. She skirted him, offered a hand to Lou's captain, who was waiting on the sidewalk, next to the limo.

"Thanks for being here, Lenny," she said.

Genuine tears brimmed in Lenny Bennedetto's eyes. His wife, Rose, held his arm and leaned against him, offering silent comfort. "Lou was a decent guy," he said. For Lenny, notorious for understatement, this was unbridled praise. "It's a shame this had to happen."

Hallie nodded. Kissed Lenny's cheek, then Rose's.

"You're coming by the wake, of course?" Rose asked. Lou had liked her, said she looked out for other cops' wives.

"For a little while," Hallie agreed, suppressing a sigh. For Lou, she would do it, drink a glass of wine, say hello and thank you to his many friends, slip out as soon as she could.

"I'll make sure she gets there okay," Joel offered.

Once again, Hallie was annoyed. Once again, she stifled the feeling, kept her mouth shut. *Let this day be over,* was her mantra. *I just want to go home.*

Joel settled her in the back of the limo, then slipped in beside her, sitting a fraction of an inch too close on the sleek leather seat.

Hallie moved over a little. "How's Barbara?" she asked. She liked Joel's latest fiancée—he'd had several since their divorce—though she didn't know her well. She applied acrylics at Sue's Nailhouse, took an endearing pride in her work, and, best of all, she was nice to Kiera and Kiley.

Joel took her hand, and she didn't have the strength to pull away. "Never mind her," he said. "I've been thinking, Hallie—maybe we should try it again. You and me, I mean. After all, we have the kids—"

Hallie stared at her ex-husband, amazed. They'd done nothing but fight while they were married, and the divorce hadn't done a great deal to change that. She'd worked hard to build her reputation as a chef, then open her small restaurant, Princess and the Pea, and build it into a thriving concern. She'd pursued her goals single-mindedly, made a life for herself and the twins, put aside cash, paid off piles of old bills. She wasn't about to revisit her misguided past. "You can't be serious," she said.

"I know I made some mistakes," he allowed. Generous of him.

She reached the end of her rope with a painful yank, nearly strangled on the impact. "Right," she said. "You started sleeping with your secretary before our honeymoon was over. Then there was that girl who sold shoes at Nordstrom, followed by the law clerk who liked to leave her panties in your briefcase—"

"Hallie." He was scolding her. God, the nerve, the unmitigated *gall* of the man to even *think* there was a chance they could start over, let alone make the suggestion right to her face.

It came to her that he was still holding her hands and she wrenched free, as exasperated with herself as she was with him. "Don't, Joel," she said. "Don't say another word. Our marriage is over—heck, it was probably over before it started. Let's just leave it at that, because if this conversation doesn't stop right here, right now, I'll say something I'll regret, and I don't want to do that."

"Of course you don't." He smiled fondly, certain of his irresistibility.

"Because of Lou," she clarified.

He gazed soulfully into her eyes for a long moment, injured. "Because of Lou," he echoed.

Hallie simply shook her head.

Within fifteen minutes, the limo was purring at the curb in front of the Late Shift, where Lou had played darts and billiards and swapped stories with old pals. After her mother's death, the place had been a second home for him, a congenial refuge where there was always light, music and good beer.

The bar was packed, and people seemed to surge toward her from every direction, kissing her cheek, patting her hand, telling her what a great guy Lou had been. Swamping her with emotions that nearly took her breath away. She smiled resolutely, listening and nodding at intervals, trying hard not to cry. For the better part of two hours, she kept up the front, avoiding Joel to the best of her ability, listening to tall tales about Lou's exploits as a vice cop, tucking them away in her heart like matchbook covers and postcards in a scrapbook.

There was only one customer in the Late Shift whom

she didn't recognize, an older man, with a long face and deep pouches under his eyes. He'd probably been hand-some once, maybe even athletic, given his tall, rangy frame, but time had extracted its full measure, moment by moment, year by year. She might have thought he was there by accident, and not a mourner at all, the way he sat keeping his own counsel and nursing a cup of coffee at the far end of the bar, talking to no one, except that every time her glance strayed in his direction, she caught him looking right back at her. He wasn't even trying to be subtle about it.

Prompted by a certain distracted curiosity, she made her way toward him, perched on the edge of the empty stool next to his.

He managed a lugubrious smile as he took in her trim dark suit and pearls, raised his coffee cup slightly off the saucer, as if to toast her. "Hello, Hallie," he said.

She studied him, tilting her head to one side. Maybe he was a member of Lou's bowling league or something, and she'd encountered him at one of her stepfather's boisterous backyard barbeques. "Have we met?"

"Once or twice," he said. "It's not important." He put out a hand. "Name's Charlie Long," he explained. "Lou and I were buddies, and business associates, after a fash-ion."

Hallie felt a strange quickening, deep in her middle, in that place where gut instincts hang out, as she shook his hand. "I didn't see you at the service," she said.

"I try to avoid funerals." Charlie took a pack of ciga-rettes from the inside pocket of his tobacco-scented suit jacket, shook one out, offered it halfheartedly to Hallie. As he'd probably expected, she refused, and he lit up,

drew deeply on the smoke, exhaled across the wide surface of the bar.

"Well, thank you for coming to the wake," Hallie said.
The brief silence that had fallen between them, a little
void in the center of chaos, was untenable. "Lou would
have appreciated that."

Charlie gave a raspy chuckle that Hallie might have
read as contempt if she hadn't caught a glimpse of sad
amusement in his hound-dog eyes. "Lou and me, we said
all that needed to be said, before the fact. I'm here for two
reasons, Mrs. Royer—one, I wanted to talk to you, and
two, I believe in hiding in plain sight." She didn't correct
him, though she hadn't used her married name since the
divorce. In her mind, she was Hallie Waitlin, Lou and
Cheryl's daughter.

A little shiver moved up her spine. Here it came, the
news she'd expected, suspected, and dreaded, all at once,
from the moment she'd learned of Lou's death. She
braced herself, waited.

"These guys," Charlie said, cocking a thumb over one
slumped shoulder, apparently to indicate not just Lou's
friends, but the police department itself, "will tell you
that the perp was a small-time thug, just somebody who
didn't expect to get caught tossing a house, and panicked
when he did." He paused, studied her face, made a visible
decision to trust her. "It's bullshit, pure and simple." He
took a very small manila packet from the same pocket
where he'd stashed his cigarettes earlier, laid it on the
bar, nodded his approval when she automatically palmed
the item and slid it into her purse. "Lou Waitlin could
have handled any fruitcake cat burglar. This was a professional hit. Company business."

Hallie's mouth fell open, and her stomach dropped, spinning. She wanted to protest that Charlie's theory was crazy, something out of a movie or a bad detective novel, but she knew it wasn't. The idea resonated only too well with her own admittedly nebulous suspicions.

Charlie looked around casually, spotted Joel making his way through the crowd, just as Hallie did.

"I'd better get out of here," he said.

Hallie nodded. She wanted to take out the packet he'd given her then and there, see what it contained, but she didn't move. She watched as Charlie Long laid a five-dollar bill on the bar and shouldered his way through the crowd of cops toward the door.

Joel reached her side. "Who was that?"

"No idea," Hallie said, frowning.

"Are you ready to go home?"

"Yes," she replied, secure in the truth of that single word, if nothing else.

He peered through the front window at the street, squinting a little. "The limo is gone."

"I'll get a cab," she said, and hurried away before he could offer to join her. All she could think about, in that moment, was the packet Charlie had given her; whatever was inside would change her life, probably irrevocably. A sensible person would toss the thing into the nearest trash bin and forget about it. Hallie wasn't sensible, not where Lou Waitlin's murder was concerned.

Outside, the night breeze was picking up and there was no sign of Charlie. Maybe, Hallie thought, with grim fancy, she'd imagined him, along with their brief but patently disturbing conversation. By some miracle, a cab was passing; she raised one hand, well aware that Joel was probably headed in her direction at that very moment, and the car rattled to a stop at the curb.

She jumped in, spouted her address, and felt a dizzying sense of relief as she looked back through the rear window. Joel was on the sidewalk, hands stuffed into the pockets of his stylish overcoat, watching the car pull away.

Within twenty minutes, she was home. She tipped the driver generously and dashed up the walk to her own door, fumbling a little with the key. Inside, she flipped on the hall lights, paused beside the telephone table in the hallway—the light on the answering machine was blinking—debated her options for a moment, wanting to open the packet, wanting *not* to open it, then pressed the play button. Mrs. Draper might have called with some concern about Kiley and Kiera.

The voice she heard was totally unfamiliar, the tone quietly callous, and somehow insinuating. "I saw you at the bar, Hallie," the man said. "What was in the package?"

Hallie laid a hand to her heart, her breathing rapid and shallow, her eyes wide with alarm. The message ended with the click of a receiver being replaced, and she knew, even before she checked the caller ID screen, that the effort was wasted. *Unknown name, unknown number,* it read.

She turned around, locked and bolted the door behind her, then walked through the dining room to the spacious kitchen. Through the window over the sink, she could see the courtyard, still riotous with summer roses, and the lights of Nora Draper's townhouse. She fumbled for the phone hanging near the stove, speed-dialed the number.

Her neighbor answered immediately, and the cheerful

sound of her voice nearly made Hallie's knees buckle with relief. She freed her shoulder-length hair from its clip at the back of her head and ran the fingers of her right hand through it. She would shed pearls, suit and pantyhose as soon as it was feasible.

"It's me, Hallie," she said. "I'm back. Are Kiera and Kiley okay?"

"Why, bless your heart," Nora replied, "they're just fine. We're having a slumber party."

Hallie swallowed in an effort to rein in her emotions a little. "You're sure you don't mind keeping the girls overnight?"

"Mind? I'm enjoying every moment." There was a gentle pause. "Are you all right, dear? Do you need anything? I just hate to think of you over there all alone, trying to cope with a loss like this. You could sleep here, you know. I'd fold out the hide-a-bed."

Hallie smiled, blinking back tears. "I really just need to rest," she said quietly. She would examine the contents of the little manila envelope now, have that private glass of wine she'd been promising herself, that long, hot bath, and then slip between the sheets, close her eyes and, please God, step outside her life, however temporarily, into sweet oblivion. Time enough to think about the phone message when the daylight returned. "I'll come and get the girls in the morning."

"You're exhausted," Nora said kindly. "Get a good night's sleep."

"I will," Hallie promised, missing her long-dead mother sorely, missing Lou. She had her daughters and a few friends—acquaintances, really, since her long work days hadn't left much time for socializing—and she was

used to being independent, but she'd never felt more profoundly alone, or more vulnerable.

She hung up, checked the front and back locks again,
then sat down at the dining room table, opened her
purse, and took out the small envelope. Her fingers trembled slightly as she lifted the flap and turned the package
upside down.

There was a little brass key inside, with a paper tag
attached, on which Lou had written, *Virgin Mary*. Hallie
smiled and shook her head, immediately breaking the
code.

She held the key against her heart for a long moment,
then carried it into her bedroom and set it carefully on
her nightstand. She proceeded to the adjoining bathroom, where she lit candles and started water running in
the tub, then backtracked to the kitchen for a glass of
Chardonnay. After a long, restorative soak, she put on a
cotton nightshirt and crawled into bed, where, to her
great surprise, she slept soundly until the twins awakened
her the next morning, leaping on the mattress and
bouncing with their usual exuberance.

Hallie groaned, then laughed, then got out of bed. At
the start of that day, so innocent and so ordinary, she
could not have imagined how it would end.

"We're going to Grampa's place," she said, when she
was dressed, and the three of them had had cereal and
fruit at the breakfast bar.

Two sets of blue-gray eyes regarded her solemnly.

"Grampa's dead," Kiley said, as though that dispensed
with any need to set foot in the man's house.

"Don't say that," Kiera protested.

"It's true."

"Enough," Hallie said, and poured herself a second cup of coffee. She was stalling. Lou's place, without Lou. It would be like a body without a heart. The girls missed him terribly; he'd been a surrogate father to them, since Joel wasn't interested. "If you'd rather stay with Mrs. Draper, I'm sure it can be arranged."

"I want to go with you," Kiera said.

"Me, too," Kiley decided.

Hallie went into her room, collected the key, slipped it into the hip pocket of her jeans. Then, taking her coffee along, she collected her car keys, locked up the condo, and loaded the kids into the backseat of her navy blue BMW. When the seatbelts were fastened and the engine was humming, they started across town.

Lou's split-level rancher was in a modest section of Phoenix, on a tree-lined street. While many houses in the Valley of the Sun boasted stucco walls and tile roofs, with courtyards and rock gardens instead of lawns, Lou's was a simple brick affair with green shutters. There were flower beds and green grass in the front yard, though it was starting to look a little overgrown.

Hallie hesitated for a few moments, just sitting there in the driveway with the BMW still running, then switched off the ignition, pocketed the keys, and got out. *Virgin Mary*, she thought, remembering the scrawled letters on the key tag, and headed for the storage shed in the backyard. The door was padlocked, but Hallie knew the combination, and she opened it easily. Kiera and Kiley, having no interest in the shed where their grandfather had kept his lawnmower, an assortment of tools, and boxes of Christmas paraphernalia, among other things, raced toward the tire swing Lou had put up years before, for

Hallie, and left their mother to her mysterious pursuits.

It took half an hour of dusty exploration, but Hallie finally located the nearly life-size plastic Nativity set that had graced the front yard every holiday season, from the Friday after Thanksgiving until the second of January. Each piece was swaddled in newspaper, and she unwrapped Joseph, a shepherd, and one of the Wise Men before coming at last to Mary.

Upending the statue on the cement floor, she found a metal cashbox wedged into the base. Stomach fluttering, she pulled it out, rewrapped Mary, and put her back with the other decorations. Then, after running her hands down the thighs of her jeans, she brought out the tagged key and turned the lock.

At first, the contents seemed innocuous—documents, printouts downloaded from the Internet, newspaper clippings, a few murky Polaroid shots, their subjects not immediately discernible. Hallie closed the box, held it protectively in both hands as she stepped outside into the fresh air and sunlight.

Kiera and Kiley were playing on the tire swing, getting along for once, laughing. Hallie looked around, the hairs rising on the back of her neck, then made her way to the relative privacy of the covered patio, where Lou had probably grilled a million hot dogs and hamburgers over the years. She sat down at the picnic table, feeling weak in the knees, the box before her, and raised the lid again.

The computer printouts were maps to places in the desert, campgrounds mostly, and parks. Some were marked, in Lou's handwriting, with small, indented X's. The snapshots showed men in various bars, and other dark places, exchanging things, or just talking in earnest. Hallie recognized several of the men, and her flesh prickled.

She unfolded a document, smoothed it on the surface of the picnic table, and scanned the first page. It was a transcript, probably of a telephone conversation, and the subject was some kind of shipment, being brought in from Mexico. Hallie felt another sick quiver in the pit of her stomach. This was stuff she didn't want to know, and the names, many of them all-too-familiar, were ones she didn't want to recognize.

She looked over her shoulder, and was startled to see Joel standing by the swing, hands in the pockets of his chinos, chatting with the girls. Their faces were upturned, adoring. Hallie felt a sudden urge to race across the lawn, gather her children close, hustle them away. Instead, she froze, there where Lou had served so many summer meals, watching as her ex-husband looked up, met her gaze, and ambled toward her. His hands were still in his pockets.

He was just a few feet away when she found her voice. "What are you doing here?" she asked. Stupid question. His face was in some of the pictures, his name in the transcript. *Jesus God, Lou,* she thought, *if you knew this stuff, why didn't you warn me?*

She knew the answer, of course. Lou had been pursuing a major investigation, and he hadn't expected to die before it was completed. He wouldn't have compromised the case by discussing it with a civilian, even if that civilian was his stepdaughter, with children sired by one of the suspects.

"Just thought I'd see how you're doing this morning," Joel said. He was trying not to look at the open cash-box and the papers, but he didn't succeed. "What have we here?"

Hallie was surprised at how easily the lie sprang to her lips. She even managed a cordial smile. "Stocks, bonds, some appraisal photographs," she said. "It seems Lou left me something besides this house and his pension fund."

"Let's have a look," Joel suggested, as if he had every right.

Hallie shuffled everything back into the box, smoothly, and drew it toward her. "It's all pretty straightforward," she said. "I can handle it."

He frowned, and she got to her feet, cradling the box. Smiling.

"Why don't you and Barbara stop by the restaurant Saturday night?" she said, talking too fast, too eagerly. "I've got a new dish you might like to try. On the house, of course."

Joel arched an eyebrow, still watching the box. "Okay," he said, uncertainly. Then he rustled up a smile of his own. "I could take the kids for the day. Give you a little break."

A chill danced up Hallie's spine. "We have plans," she replied lightly. "Stop by the restaurant Saturday night, Joel."

He got to his feet.

"Girls!" Hallie called. "Come on. Time to go."

"Let me have the box, Hallie," Joel insisted, in a monotone.

"Another time," Hallie chimed. She'd never make it to the BMW, still parked in the driveway in front of the house, but Lou's old pickup was behind the shed, facing the alley fence, and the keys were probably in the ignition. Nobody in their right mind, Lou had always maintained, would steal that worthless truck, but he could always hope.

She started toward the girls, and the pickup truck, her strides long, her heart pounding in her throat. She shuffled her surprised daughters into the front seat of the old rig, tossed the box in after them, and scrambled behind the wheel. Joel was several yards behind her, but he was taller, and intent on the chase. Hallie had passed easily under the clotheslines, but Joel had gotten himself entangled, affording her precious moments to start the sputtering motor and push down the locks on the doors.

"Mommy," Kiera piped up. "What are you—?"

Hallie stepped on the clutch, shifted into first gear, and drove right into the board fence, knocking it down, jostling into the alley.

"Daddy is chasing us!" Kiley announced, looking back through the oval window. "Mommy, *stop!*"

Hallie shifted again, and barreled toward the end of the alley, picking up speed with every jostle and bump. A glance at the rearview mirror showed Joel standing in the alley, glaring after her and swearing. It wouldn't be long until he regained his senses and came after them, but Hallie had grown up in that neighborhood, and she knew every side street, every shortcut, and every dead end. By the time he got back to his car, she and the girls and the evidence Lou had gathered would be long gone.

Kiley tried again. "Mommy?"

Hallie took the corner on two wheels, tires screeching. "Fasten your seat belts, girls," she said. "We're going on a little trip."

The first thing she did, once they had left Phoenix far behind, was hide the cashbox.

2

The tiny brass bell above the door tinkled in the same annoyingly cheerful way it always did, that night when the whole slow and sleepy course of his life did a sudden 180. Chance Qualtrough probably wouldn't even have bothered to give his stool at the counter a quarter turn and take a look, if it hadn't been for the odd sliver of heat that caught somewhere in the innermost regions of his heart and took a tight stitch there.

He glanced over his shoulder, and there she was, coated in snow, skinny and scared, with a little kid clasping either hand. He squinted, taking in the rugrats—girls, judging by their small pink jackets, fuzzy mittens and the pom-poms on their knitted hats, and no older than six or seven. Despite an instinctive reluctance, Chance raised his gaze to the woman's face.

Her eyes were brown, and there were strands of blond hair—that dishwater shade that's invariably natural—peeking out from under her snow-crusted baseball cap. She was a stranger to Primrose Creek, Chance was sure of that, and yet, as he looked at her, he had a peculiar feeling that they'd been acquainted once, long ago, and parted unwillingly.

He was still chewing on that fanciful insight when Madge Beardsley, who owned the Last Chance Café in partnership with her brother, an ex-rodeo clown and one-time convict named Bear, rushed over to greet the new crew of refugees. Bear came out of the kitchen, wiping his hands on his apron, to get a better look. "Why, just look at you," Madge fussed, fluttery as an old hen. "Half frozen to death!" She was caught in a time warp, Madge was, circa 1955. She wore her drugstore-red hair high and hard, and her lipstick was vampire-crimson. Her pink dress was right out of an early episode of *I Love Lucy*, as were the oversize pearl baubles clipped to her earlobes and the saddle shoes on her feet.

The blonde shivered visibly and finally released her hold on the little girls' hands. She nodded to Bear. "My . . . my truck broke down, out on the highway—"

"Good heavens," Madge exclaimed, herding her charges toward the one empty booth remaining. There were a lot of folks stranded at the Last Chance that night, most of them locals, though a few were just passing through, and the place was pretty lively. "You don't mean to tell me you were all alone out there, in this weather—"

She smiled warily and nodded, and Chance was chagrined to realize that he was still watching her. She must have sensed that, for she glanced briefly in his direction, and the smile faded. Fumbling a little, she concentrated on unbundling the kids, then herself. Madge draped their coats and hats over the old-fashioned soda cooler, since the pegs on the wall were already bulging, and poured three big mugs of hot cocoa, with extra whipped cream on top, without even being asked.

"What's your name, honey?" Madge demanded of the stranger, setting out the mugs. Both kids stared at the mounds of sweet froth on top, their eyes wide and luminous, like their mother's, but light instead of dark, and one of them hooked a finger in the stuff and slipped it into her mouth.

"Hallie," the woman answered, a little hesitantly. "Hallie . . . O'Rourke. These are my daughters, Kiley and Kiera."

Madge beamed at the kids. "Twins," she remarked, delighted. "How old are you?"

"Seven," said the one who'd swiped a taste of whipped cream. "I'm Kiley, and that's Kiera. I was born first, so that means I'm bigger, even if it doesn't show." She paused, as though mulling over some private secret, debating whether or not to share it, then added, "We're gifted, you know."

Kiera tossed her sister a long-suffering look, but offered no comment.

Still embroiled in a drama that was, any way you looked at it, none of his damn business, Chance wondered where *Mister* O'Rourke was, and what the hell had possessed the man to let his family go traipsing all over the countryside in weather like this. He turned back to his coffee and pie, trying in vain to set Hallie O'Rourke aside in his thoughts, like a newspaper article he'd already read. In spite of that effort, he remained aware of her in every cell of his body, and all the spaces in between, and that scared the hell out of him. He took a few moments to recover, and when he had, a vague sense of suspicion still nudged at him. Maybe it was something he'd glimpsed in her eyes, maybe it was his own need to be cautious, but the possibility that she was on the run from somebody or something definitely crossed his mind.

He tried not to eavesdrop on the new arrivals—God knew, there was plenty of noise in the café to distract him, what with the jukebox cranked up and the Ladies Aid Society over there in the far corner, playing cut-throat canasta—but he might as well have been sitting right at Hallie's table. It was as if the conversation were being beamed to a transmitter behind his right ear.

One of the kids spoke up. "Hallie? Can I have a cheese-burger?"

Chance shook his head and took another sip of his coffee. What was this world coming to? he wondered. Families out joy-riding in the middle of a blinding snow-storm. Little kids calling their mothers by her first name, as if she were a playmate and not a parent. Madge gave Hallie a vinyl-covered menu, then trotted off to refill cups along the length of the counter and cut slices of banana cream pie for a flock of truckers over by the pin-ball machines.

"That's 'Mom' to you," Hallie said, unruffled, "and you can split a burger with Kiera. You wouldn't be able to eat a whole one anyway."

"I want my *own* cheeseburger. All to myself."

Hallie tried another tack. "We have to be careful with our money, sweetheart. You know that."

"I think we should go home. We'd have lots of money if we just went home."

Hallie couldn't have been much more than thirty, but the way she sighed, she might've lived through a century since breakfast, and a turbulent one at that. "We can't go back," she said patiently, and she sounded like she was about to burst into tears. "We'll find a new place to live. A wonderful place, I promise."

"I need to piddle," the other child interjected. Chance sensed that, small as she was, Kiera was used to heading up domestic peace-keeping missions. It seemed to him that kids had to grow up too fast these days.

"Let's go, then," Hallie said, and they all trooped down the hall to the rest rooms.

When they returned, Madge was just setting three plates on their table. Cheeseburgers and French fries, full orders all around. Chance watched Hallie's reflection in the age-streaked mirror behind the cash register.

"I didn't order all this," she said, sounding a little desperate.

Madge glanced in Chance's direction, probably blowing his cover. He'd offered to pay for the food, though he didn't want anybody else to know it. "Don't worry about it, honey," Madge told the young mother. "It's covered."

The kids were already tucking into the food in a way that made Chance wonder how long it had been since they'd had a decent meal, but Hallie stood stiffly beside the booth, her chin high. She spoke in an agitated whisper. "I wasn't looking for charity!"

Madge recovered her aplomb, gestured to take in the crowd of customers filling the café to the baseboards, then smiled at Hallie again. "You ever wait tables, kiddo? I could use some help right now, tonight. I've about run my feet off, the last six hours, and that snow doesn't show any signs of letting up." As if to lend veracity to her story, a sudden wind shook the front door and made the fan rattle in the ventilator behind the big cookstove in back. The storm had begun in the early afternoon, as a mere skiff, not an unusual phenomenon in the high country of Nevada in mid-October, and worked itself into a hissy-fit of apocalyptic proportions. "You'd be doing me a favor," Madge finished.

Silently, Chance blessed Madge and her kindly heart, and took another sip of his coffee. She might have told Hallie that he'd staked her and the kids to the cheese-burgers and let it go at that, but she'd chosen instead to respect the other woman's pride. When Hallie didn't say anything, Madge leaped back into the breach.

"You just have yourself some supper and quit your worrying. You can work off the bill by pouring coffee and helping me clean up later."

Hallie sighed again, gave a brisk little nod of agreement, then sank gratefully into the booth and started to eat. Madge rounded the counter, picked up the coffeepot, and gave Chance a long wink as she topped off his cup. He glared at her for almost giving him away, though he knew there was a smile lurking in his eyes, and she chuckled and shook her head. There were people he could intimidate with hardly any effort at all, but Madge wasn't one of them.

The weather got worse over the next hour, but the crowd began to dwindle all the same. Sheriff Jase Stratton, a distant relation of Chance's, being descended from the original McQuarry bunch, same as he was, and a former best friend at that, showed up with his four-wheel drive and, without so much as a howdy-do for Chance, began squiring the members of the Ladies Aid Society to their various homes, four at a time. The truckers went on down the road, their rigs equipped for hell and high water, and young Ben Pratt, a budding entrepreneur, started a little taxi service with his snowmobile, charging two bucks a passenger for every trip.

Chance, who drove a good-size truck himself, remained where he was, on his usual stool at the Last Chance Café, nursing what must have been his eighteenth cup of coffee and watching surreptitiously as Hallie O'Rourke showed herself to be a diligent worker. The kids, full of cheese-burgers and fries, were asleep on the vinyl seats in their booth, Madge having covered them with an old sweater and a raggedy afghan she kept in the rear storeroom.

When Hallie came to a stop across the counter from Chance, coffee carafe in hand, he started a little, caught off guard, and she favored him with an attempt at a smile. "Too much of this stuff is toxic, you know," she said.

He gave his cup a little shove in her direction, to indi-cate that he wanted more poison. He'd head for home soon, try to get a few hours of sleep. No need to hurry, though, since there was nobody there waiting except the dogs and the horses, and they had each other for com-pany. "Thanks," he said, when she broke down and poured the java. It was bottom-of-the-pot stuff, potent enough to fuel a tractor.

She put the pot back on its burner and started wiping down the counter with a cloth. Chance didn't flatter himself that she was lingering on his account. The café was warm and bright with light, and her kids were asleep. She had no place else to go, except back out into the storm.

He thought about Jessie Shaw's log house, standing

empty across the creek from his own place, and inspiration struck. It seemed sudden, but he reckoned the idea had been sneaking up on him right along. "You need somewhere to stay for a few days?" he asked.

She froze, right where she stood, Hallie did, and her eyes narrowed. He was glad she'd set the pot down, because she looked like she wanted to douse him with something, and scalding-hot coffee would not have been his first choice.

Chance laughed, held up a hand. "Hold it, ma'am," he said. "You just jumped to a wrong conclusion. Jessie's a relative of mine, and she's been away on a business trip for the last week or so. I've been keeping up the chores over at her place. You know, making sure the pipes don't freeze, and feeding her livestock, stuff like that. Fact is, I've got enough to do on my own spread, without spending half the day on the other side of the creek." He watched as Hallie's brown eyes widened out again, this time with cautious interest. "She'll be back shortly, but in the meantime—well—do you know anything about horses?"

She hesitated, and he knew, without knowing *how* he knew, that she wanted to lie, to say she knew all there was to know about equine management, but couldn't bring herself to do it. He weighed the small insight, filed it away. "Not a thing," she admitted, with a little sigh.

"Well, it's not too hard to learn," he allowed. Was he crazy? He knew next to nothing about this woman, and there was a good chance that she was trouble. Here he was, all the same, offering to let her stay in Jessie's house, unsupervised. She could strip the place bare, burn the furniture for firewood, for all he knew. Set up a drug-running operation, or hide a body under the floorboards. Hell, he thought, he'd been watching too much satellite TV—he needed to get himself a life. "I could show you the basics." He paused. "Of looking after horses, I mean."

Hallie bit her lower lip, and eagerness flared in her face, like a flash of muted light. She glanced at her sleeping kids. "No strings?" she ventured. Her meaning was clear enough, and she hadn't wasted many words getting it across.

Chance met her gaze squarely. "No strings," he promised.

She hesitated again, then nodded. "Okay, then," she said, and went back to her counter-wiping with a spurt of fresh energy.

—

Madge, a guardian angel clad in pink nylon, stood in her tiny office, with her hands resting on her ample hips, smiling at Hallie. "Chance Qualtrough?" she said, dropping her voice to a virtual whisper, even though the door was closed, and somebody had just cranked up the jukebox out front. "He's all right. His people have been out there on Primrose Creek since pioneer days. They done all right for themselves, all of them. Jessie, she's a famous artist, a weaver. Shows her work all over the world. And the sheriff—he came in a while ago—that's Jase Stratton. He's one of them, too. There's a fourth one, Sara Vigil, she lives in Hollywood and produces movies. Chance leases her share of the land."

Hallie ran her hands down the thighs of her worn jeans, thought of the cowboy, probably still parked on the same stool at the counter. He was good-looking, with his dark blond hair and blue eyes, and he didn't seem dangerous, but Hallie had learned to be careful. Learned it the hard way. She tried to ignore the little twinge of envy she felt, hearing that he had a family, and that his roots ran deep into the Nevada soil. "Does he hang around here a lot?"

Madge chuckled, a fond, raspy sound. "No more than any of the other regulars," she said. "He likes to take his breakfast here, and I've never seen a body that could hold more coffee. He's got himself a nice little ranch and a few cattle. Raises horses, too. The fancy kind. He's got a Thoroughbred stud over there that's worth a wad of money."

"That's impressive," Hallie admitted, a bit grudgingly. She *was* impressed, but not because Mr. Qualtrough was well-off. She knew only too well that money and possessions were small comfort when the proverbial chips were down.

"Anyway," Madge sighed, "I got an opening here, if you want a few days' work to tide you over. Bear's girlfriend, Wynona, is supposed to be coming in on the bus sometime next week to lend a hand, but she isn't very dependable, and if you make a good showing in the meantime, you might get on permanent."

Hallie swallowed. "Thanks," she said, wondering how long she dared hang around Primrose Creek. She'd need a place to stay, once this Jessie came back, even if she succeeded at waitressing, and two hundred and twenty-eight dollars was nowhere near enough to rent a house or an apartment, even in a little town like that one. Maybe there was a motel, and she could pay for a room by the week.

Madge didn't miss much, that was evident by the expression of kindly speculation in her eyes. She took one of Hallie's hands and gave it a motherly pat. "Take things one step at a time," she said. "A few days looking after Jessie's place, that'll give you a chance to catch your breath, get your bearings and the like. You can earn a little money here—it's just minimum wage, but the tips are decent. Maybe enough to get your rig fixed."

Hallie couldn't speak for a few moments. She was in big trouble, no question about it, but there were blessings, too. Just a couple of hours ago, she'd been stranded on a snowy highway, essentially homeless, with two children, one cheap suitcase stuffed with equally cheap clothes, chosen by size and price in a discount store. When the truck gave out, she'd laid her forehead on the steering wheel and breathed deeply until she was sure she wouldn't cry, and offered a desperate, silent prayer for help. Now, after a two-mile walk in the cold, half-carrying one or both of the twins the whole way, she'd stumbled into this place, met these people. Kiley and Kiera had eaten their fill, and they were warm now, and safe, dreaming little-girl dreams as they slept. For now, for tonight and tomorrow and a few precious days beyond, everything was all right.

"Well?" Madge prompted. "Have I got me a waitress, or not?"

Hallie smiled and put out a hand to seal the bargain. "You've got a waitress," she said. "Thanks again, Madge. I swear I won't let you down."

Madge was all business, hustling her out of the little office, back to the main part of the café. "Good," she said. "I'll expect you around eleven-thirty tomorrow morning, weather permitting. You can work lunch and supper." She paused, briefly worried. "I don't mind tellin' you, it makes for a long day. We don't get out of here till midnight sometimes, me and Bear, but you can knock off around eight o'clock. Meals are included, of course, and you can bring the kids with you as long as need be. They seem well-behaved."

Hallie felt a little rush of pride. Maybe she wasn't such a bad mother, after all. Okay, she wasn't exactly rising out of the ashes of her life, phoenix-like, not just yet anyway, but she could see a glimmer of light, faint as a distant star, through the wreckage. There was reason to hope. "They're the best kids in the world," she said.

Madge smiled. "Let me just fix you up a little care package to take out to Jessie's place. Lord, she'd be relieved to know somebody was actually staying there, holding down the fort." The older woman peered through the kitchen doorway, hands braced on the framework. "You better fire up that truck of yours, Chance," she called to the handsome cowboy. "Get the heater going. Don't want Hallie or those little girls coming down with pneumonia before they even get out there to Jessie's."

He nodded, pulled on his battered hat, and tugged at the brim, a real gent. Hallie felt a stir, part anticipation, part fear, as she digested the fact that she and her children were about to ride God knew how far, to God knew what kind of place, with a total stranger. Under normal circumstances, she wouldn't even have considered taking a risk like that, but now, on this snowy October night, she was fresh out of choices.

Madge put together a box of provisions—bread, milk,

cheese, a small can of coffee, eggs, a package of breakfast sausage and half a pecan pie—while Hallie woke the twins and shuffled them back into their coats.

"Where are we going?" Kiley wanted to know.

"Is there a bed?" Kiera added. "With covers?"

Before Hallie could come up with an answer to either question, Madge was right in there. "You're headed for a real nice place, with lots of beds and blankets. There's a hill for sledding, and a barn, too. In the summer, you can swim and fish for trout in the creek."

Hallie bit back a protest. By summer, they'd be long gone, she and the twins, miles from Primrose Creek, Nevada, with new identities and new lives, or back in Scottsdale, if they were unbelievably lucky. Of course, she wasn't ready to reveal that, as kind as Madge had been. "There are horses, too," she offered, a little tightly. "We're going to help take care of them."

The look in Kiera's eyes made her wish she hadn't mentioned the horses. *"Really?"* the child whispered, in sleepy awe.

"Wow," Kiley said, pushing Hallie's hands aside to zip up her own jacket. "Do we know how to take care of horses?"

"We'll learn," Hallie answered, and then Mr. Qualtrough was back from the parking lot, snow-dappled and bringing a chill wind along with him.

He led the way out, carrying Kiley in one arm and the groceries in the other, while Hallie, having donned her own coat, followed with Kiera. His truck was parked a few yards from the door, humming with power, spewing white vapor from the tailpipe. The headlights turned the steadily falling snow into a shower of golden coins.

With a sort of rangy grace, the cowboy put down the box, opened the passenger door, hoisted Kiley inside, then helped Kiera and Hallie in after her. When Hallie had buckled the appropriate seat belts, he set the provisions behind the seat, shut the door again, and went around to the driver's side. A few seconds later, they were pulling out onto the still-unplowed highway, headed away from town.

Hallie held Kiera on her lap and slipped an arm around Kiley, who was huddled beside her. "You're sure your friend won't mind?" she asked, mostly to make conversation. She was a person who appreciated solitude, but right now she couldn't deal with silence. It made the world seem too vast, too dangerous.

Chance fiddled with the radio, found a country oldies station, and settled back to concentrate on his driving while the voice of Johnny Cash joined them in the warm darkness, a familiar, rumbling bass.

"I think Jessie will be pleased," Chance said.

"She's away on business?"

Chance nodded, squinted as he navigated the nearly invisible road. "Jessie's a textile artist. She's been visiting galleries, most of them back East. Schmoozing and delivering new pieces."

"I'd like to see her work." She searched her mind for something else to say, to keep the conversation rolling. "Is Jessie married?"

Chance shook his head. "She's the independent type," he said, with neither admiration nor scorn. They crept over a wooden bridge, the same one Hallie and the kids had crossed on foot on their way into town earlier. "What about you, Hallie? Do you have a husband?"

"Nope," she answered, smiling a little. "Independent type."

He chuckled. "Me, too," he said. They traveled on in silence for several minutes. Johnny Cash finished walking the line, and Marty Robbins came on, crooning "El Paso." A shape loomed, snow-mounded, at the side of the road. "That your truck?" Chance asked.

Hallie nodded. She'd left her things behind, after the breakdown, having her hands full with the children. She shivered, remembering how scared she'd been, and how cold.

Chance pulled in behind the battered pickup without any suggestion from her. "I suppose you have some stuff in there?"

"A suitcase," she said.

"That's all?"

Kiley spoke up. "Elmo's there, too," she said. "I bet he's cold."

Yes, Hallie thought. *Elmo.* She'd splurged on the toy, when she raided Wal-Mart for clothes for herself and the girls. After all, Kiera and Kiley had had to leave everything they owned behind.

"Bet he is," Chance agreed. He grinned, got out of the truck, slogged through the blizzard to the other rig, and pulled open the door. He was back within a few moments, bringing Elmo and the pitiful plastic suitcase.

"I'll come back and have a look at the engine in the morning," he said, after handing Elmo to Kiley and stowing the suitcase in the space behind the seat. "Maybe I can get it running again."

Hallie knew zero about mechanics, but she figured the truck was a hopeless case, remembering some of the remarks Lou had made while puttering with the engine, but she was too tired to say so, and she didn't want to worry the twins any more than necessary. They'd already had their world turned upside down.

"Okay," she said. Then, hastily, she added, "I don't have money for parts, though. Or labor, either."

He shifted his own truck back into gear, and rolled out onto the highway. "It might not be anything serious," he said.

The windshield looked almost opaque to Hallie, as the snow was coming down even harder than before. "How can you see?" she marveled, squinting.

"I could drive this road in a coma," Chance replied. "Lived here all my life."

A row of mailboxes appeared in the white gloom, and they turned onto a bumpy road. Hallie sensed, rather than heard, the sluggish burble of the creek flowing alongside. At last, they stopped in front of what looked like a two-story log house.

"Wait here," Chance said. "I'll switch on some lights and turn the furnace up a notch or two."

Hallie waited, holding tightly to her daughters, relishing the delicious heat flowing from under the sleek dashboard. A light winked on inside the house, then another, and something awakened in Hallie's heart, bittersweet and hopeful. Unconsciously, she laid a hand to her chest, as if to keep the feeling from escaping.

"Where's the horse?" Kiley asked, all business.

Hallie chuckled. "In the barn, probably," she said.

"Can I ride him?" Kiera put in.

"No promises," Hallie answered.

Kiley sighed with temporary resignation, settled

against Hallie's side, and nestled there. Hallie relished having her close, having both her children safe within the circle of her arms. She'd learned, in the last two days, to appreciate the simple things.

In due time, after the radio had pumped out two more of Johnny Cash's ballads and a Patsy Cline medley, Chance returned from the house and opened the door on Hallie's side.

"It's still pretty cold in there," he said, "but the furnace has kicked in, so the place will warm up pretty quickly, I think. I laid a fire for morning."

Hallie's throat tightened a little, with gratitude and relief. "Thanks," she managed.

He reached in, taking Kiley in one arm and Kiera in the other, and favored Hallie with a brief grin. "We'll see if you're still singing the same tune after you've met Trojan," he said.

"Trojan?" Hallie queried, literally following in Chance's footsteps as they trudged toward the house.

"He's a miniature horse. Known in some quarters as Jessie's Folly," he said, pausing on the roughhewn porch. "She's got a couple of full-size ones, too. A mare named Dolly, and an old gelding she calls Sweet Pea. Wonder the poor fella doesn't die of embarrassment, hung with a moniker like that."

Hallie tried to imagine herself feeding these animals, cleaning up after them, grooming them. The prospect was overwhelming, considering that she'd never even looked after a goldfish.

Then they were inside the house, with its two-story rock fireplace, its hooked rugs and rustic furniture. Colorful weavings graced several of the otherwise plain log walls, intricate portraits of Indian women, exquisitely depicted. There was a desk across from the fireplace, with a plastic-covered computer on its surface.

The floor was fashioned of gleaming pine planks, mellowed with age, and a gigantic loom, surely antique, stood in one corner, framed on all sides by windows. A set of stairs led to a mezzanine of sorts, lined with a total of six doors.

"The kitchen's that way," Chance said, pointing to an archway to their right, "and that's the downstairs bathroom there, at the base of the steps. The bedrooms are all on the second floor, and there's another bath up there, too. You'll find sheets and towels and all that in the linen cupboard, and you should have hot water by morning."

Hallie turned in a slow circle, there in the middle of the floor, trying to take it all in. The very threads in the weavings seemed to vibrate with an energy all their own, and even though the heat was just beginning to kick in, the atmosphere in that house felt like an embrace.

Kiera headed for the bay windows overlooking the front yard. "This," she said, with authority, spreading her tiny arms wide and twirling with sudden exuberance, "is where the Christmas tree goes."

Hallie's heart ached. "This isn't our house, honey," she reminded the child. "We're just visiting."

Out of the corner of her eye, she caught a glimpse of Chance. He was turning his hat in his hands and looking somber, but if he wanted to say something, he held it back.

"No," Kiera insisted. "We *belong* here."

Hallie was too tired to argue the point. She turned to

Chance. "You'll show me what needs to be done?" she asked. "For the animals, I mean?"

"First thing in the morning," he agreed, a little gruffly. "I'll be over as soon as I finish my chores."

"Good," she said, walking with him to the door. "And thanks." She nearly choked on the word, and on the emotions that came with it. "Thanks for everything."

He smiled. "Lock the door behind me," he said, and she nodded, and he was gone.

She fastened the latch, went to the nearest window, and watched as Chance became a shadow, and finally disappeared, leaving no trace except for the faint gleam of taillights and the whir of his truck's engine. Then she turned to face her children, summoning up another smile.

"Well," she said, "what do you say we make up a bed and get some sleep?"

The girls, wide-awake again, would probably have preferred to stay up all night, exploring, but by the time Hallie had chosen a bedroom for the three of them to share, made up the large four-poster bed, seen to the brushing of teeth, the washing of faces, the putting on of pajamas, and the saying of prayers, they were both exhausted again.

They crawled between the cool, crispy sheets, the three of them, cosseted by mounds of quilts, Hallie lying in the middle, with a child cuddled against either side. Soon, both Kiera and Kiley were sound asleep, but Hallie, weary though she was, stared up at the rafters and wondered. Had her luck finally turned, or was this run of good fortune just a cruel prelude to yet another disappointment, another battle, another headlong rush for safety?

Joel had friends in high places, friends with as much

to lose as he had, and more, if Hallie turned Lou's evidence over to the proper authorities. How long would it be until they found her, found her children?

—

Chance parked the truck in the aisle of his barn, and the dogs came out to meet him, barking a jubilant greeting. The border collies, Smoke and Magic, could be counted on to throw him a welcome-home party, whether he'd been gone for an hour or a week, and he laughed, glad to see them, scuffling with them a little before he looked in on the horses.

Rookie, the Palomino yearling who'd tangled with a cougar two weeks before, and gotten the worst of the bargain, was huddled in a corner of his stall, head down, ears askew.

"Hey, Buddy," Chance said quietly. "How's it going?"

Cocoa, the bay mare across the way, nickered conversationally, as if to comment on the colt's progress, which seemed minimal to Chance. The outer wounds, savage as they were, were healing nicely, but for Rookie, the hurt went deeper. It seemed he'd given up, decided to sit out the rest of his life.

Chance acknowledged the mare's input with a few cordial words, opened the gate, and stepped inside Rookie's twelve-by-twelve-foot quarters. The floor was thick with cedar shavings, the automatic waterer was working just fine, and the feed Chance had put out earlier was untouched.

He stood at a little distance from the small horse, calm and quiet. Rookie tried to melt into the cinder block wall behind him.

Chance remained where he was, unmoving except for the hand he extended to the animal, in unspoken invitation. Rookie began to pace frantically, caught in his corner.

Chance took a step backward. Something about that little critter put him in mind of Hallie O'Rourke, though he couldn't have said why—it was just a feeling, really. He lingered for a few more moments, then left the stall, taking time to scrawl a note to himself on the dry-erase board next to the tack room door. *Call Doc Whitman.*

After that, the dogs tagging at his heels, he spoke to each of the twenty-odd horses in his keeping and then, lifting his collar and pulling his hat down, he fastened the barn doors for the night and headed for the house.

It was old, but solid, a lot like Jessie's place, only bigger. Trace Qualtrough and his wife, Bridget, from whom Chance was directly descended, had built the house themselves, way back in the eighteen-hundreds, and it had stood the test of time. He was the only Qualtrough left, though there were McQuarrys aplenty, all claiming Bridget's son, Noah, as an ancestor, and there were Shaws and Strattons, too, along with one or two Vigils. The original tract of land, left by one Gideon McQuarry to his four granddaughters after the Civil War, was still in the family, though considerable acreage had been added along the way. Chance's chunk was the largest, at nearly 2,000 acres, followed by Jessie's spread, which added up to about 1,500. Jase had rented out his share, and moved to town when he married Katie, right out of college. Chance leased the plot that had originally been settled by Skye and Jake Vigil, mailing away a check every six months to some outfit in Hollywood.

Entering the house through the kitchen, Smoke and Magic keeping him company, he flipped on a light, brewed coffee and set the timer for morning, then refilled the dogs' dishes and headed upstairs. His office adjoined his bedroom, and he stopped there, watching the red light blink on his answering machine, hesitating for a long moment before pressing the play button.

Katie's voice filled the room. She sounded weary. "Hi, Chance. Obviously, I was hoping you'd be there. I need to talk to you about Jase. Call me, or stop by the bookstore tomorrow if you can. Thanks."

The next call was from the vet he'd made a note to contact in the morning. "Hey, Chance. It's Doc. Just wanted to find out how the Rookie's doing. I'll catch up with you later."

Chance sighed, waited for the third and last message to play. "Hi. This is Hallie O'Rourke. Your number was on the blackboard by the kitchen phone, so I decided to call and tell you—well—thanks. For finding the girls and me a place to stay and giving us a ride out here and everything, I mean." A long silence followed, while she tried to figure out what else to say. "I guess I'll see you in the morning. Bye."

Click.

Chance erased the first two messages, and let the third one play over again, smiling a little as he listened. Half an hour later, when he stretched out in bed, he cupped his hands behind his head and reflected on Jessie's firm belief that every house ought to have a woman living in it. There were times, like right then, when the idea seemed to have uncommon merit.

3

Hallie was jolted awake by the sound of knocking and, for several fevered seconds, she couldn't remember where she was. She tensed in a spasm of fear, relaxed again when she felt her children curled against her sides, and memories of the night before seeped slowly into her mind. She scrambled out of bed—Kiera and Kiley stirred, but did not awaken—wrenched on jeans and a flannel shirt, and hurried down the back stairs.

It was barely light outside, and Chance Qualtrough was standing on the porch, peering in through the frosted oval of glass in the door. He wore an expression of good-natured irritation, and she wondered how long he'd been waiting out there.

Hallie shoved a hand through her tangled hair, in a futile effort to make herself presentable, undid the bolt, and let him in.

"You must be a city girl," he said, with a grin, whisking off his hat and hanging it on a peg close at hand. He didn't remove the long gunslinger's coat he wore. In that getup, he looked like the real thing, a trail boss, or an old-time outlaw. "Bet you haven't even put the coffee on."

Hallie stifled a yawn and closed the door. A glance at the bay windows revealed a pristine, icy-white world. The snow had stopped, the sun was out, and it was probably cold enough to give a polar bear chilblains. "I've been called a lot worse than a 'city girl,' " she said. *Truer words had never been spoken*, she reflected, thinking of some of the fights she'd had with Joel, before and after the divorce. "What time is it?"

Chance chuckled, made for the kitchen, started the process of brewing. Watching him, Hallie felt as if she'd stepped back in time. The man, the coat, the cocky grin and the banter—all of it was oddly familiar, a memory of something that had never actually happened. "Hell, it must be *six o'clock* by now," he said, eyes dancing. "I've got half a day's work done already." He looked her over. "You got a decent pair of boots?"

She glanced down at her bare feet, wriggled her toes. "Just sneakers," she said.

He left the coffee-maker to do its magic, went out onto some kind of porch back of the kitchen, and rummaged audibly for a few minutes. He returned with a pair of lace-ups and an old jacket of red plaid wool. "These are Jessie's," he said, holding up the boots. "They might fit you. You'll probably find some work socks upstairs in her room." He glanced at the window over the sink, the early-morning light playing over the strong planes and angles of his face. "Better get a move on. We're burning daylight."

Hallie nodded. "I'll be right back," she said, and headed for the stairs.

The twins, sound asleep when she left the room minutes earlier, were already out of bed and fully dressed, their curly brown hair uncombed, their eyes wide with excitement. "Is it time to take care of the horses?" Kiera wanted to know.

Hallie laughed. "Yes," she said. She scrounged a pair of heavy woolen socks from a dresser drawer, sat down on the edge of the bed, and pulled them on. Jessie's boots were a snug fit, but they would do for the time being. This was, after all, not a permanent arrangement.

In the bathroom, she splashed water on her face, ran a brush through her hair, and pinned it up in back with a plastic clasp. "You two can watch, but you have to stay out of the way. Horses can be dangerous."

Kiley gave Hallie one of those looks that always made her feel as though their roles had been suddenly reversed, Kiley the mother, herself the child. "Not if you whisper to them," the child said, with authority.

Hallie didn't roll her eyes until she'd turned her back and started out of the bedroom. A few hours spent watching *Animal Planet* and the Discovery Channel and the kid thought she was Monty Roberts. You had to admire that kind of confidence, though.

The scent of strong coffee filled the downstairs rooms and lifted Hallie's spirits a little. Chance had poured himself a mug, though the pot was still brewing, and he stood leaning casually against the counter, in front of the sink, sipping. Seeing Hallie, he set his cup aside, reached for a second one, and filled that, while coffee dripped onto the burner and sizzled there, making a cheerful morning sound.

She thought of the message she'd left on his answering machine the night before, thanking him for the help he'd given, and hoped she hadn't sounded needy.

"You'll have to doctor it yourself," he said, holding out the cup with one hand. "There's probably some sugar around here somewhere, but if you need cream, you're out of luck."

She couldn't help smiling, even though the man made her nervous, and she reached out to accept his offering. "Black is fine," she told him, and sipped.

He looked past her, to the girls, who were getting into their coats. "Mornin', ladies," he said gravely. "Are you planning to lend us a hand out in the barn?"

Both girls nodded.

"*She* thinks we're too little," Kiley confided, cocking a thumb at Hallie.

Chance favored Hallie with an amused look, though the expression in his eyes was a measuring one. "Does she, now?" he replied. Then he turned and headed for the door.

Moments later, they were all slogging through the deep, hard-crusted snow, headed toward the large red and white barn, set well back from the house. There was a spacious corral surrounded by a rustic rail fence, and even as they approached, Hallie keeping to Chance's boot prints, Kiley and Kiera goose-stepping along after her, the horses began to nicker and whinny inside. It was a chorus of impatience.

The sky was a bright, high-country blue, and the pungent scent of pine trees roused a festive feeling in Hallie, reminding her of long-ago Christmases with her mother and Lou. Her heart, heavy for so long, rose a little.

The barn doors were tall, and secured with a wooden bar. Chance raised the latch and swung them open. They creaked on their hinges. "You'll want to be careful about closing these at night," he said. "We've had some trouble with cougars."

Hallie stopped in her tracks. "Cougars?" she echoed.

"Wildcats," Chance explained, quite unnecessarily, looking back at her over one shoulder.

Cougars. Instinctively, she groped for her children, pulled them against her sides, much as she had done before going to sleep the night before. Kiera clung to her blue-jeaned thigh, while Kiley, typically, tried to pull away.

"They don't attack people, right?" Hallie managed, in a small voice. "The wildcats, I mean?"

Chance met and held her gaze. "They've been known to," he said. "In general, though, they're more likely to go after livestock—especially foals and calves."

Hallie looked from side to side, half-expecting to see a big, slavering cat slinking toward her and her children, moving soundlessly over the diamond-scattered snow. Remembering the long walk she and the girls had made into town after the truck finally gave out, she shuddered. Suddenly Scottsdale and Phoenix, with their singular perils, didn't seem quite so frightening. "Oh," she said, sounding lame.

You can do this, insisted the voice of her better self. *You have to do this.*

It wasn't as if she had a whole lot of choice. She gave the girls a shoulder-squeeze and started moving again, following Chance into the barn. Her cash on hand was severely limited, her truck was in critical condition, if not dead, and if she failed to make things work here and at the café, the three of them would literally be home-less, sooner rather than later. She didn't dare access her bank accounts; Joel would find her within hours if she did.

Jessie Shaw's barn was a spacious structure, with lofts, a large tack room, and an area for storing bags of feed—alfalfa, bran, some kind of sweetened oats mixture. Bales of hay or grass filled one end of the building, and there were six large stalls at the other.

The twins headed straight for the stalls.

"Look," Kiley crowed, peering through the rails at the smallest horse Hallie had ever seen, "he's *little*. Is he still growing?"

Chance joined the kids, grinning. "That's Trojan," he said. "He's about as big as he's ever going to get. He's a miniature."

Hallie approached, hands in the pockets of her borrowed coat, and took a closer look. Trojan, a buckskin with a dark mane and tail, was barely thirty-six inches high at the shoulders, and when he leveled a glance at Hallie, he conveyed enough attitude for a herd of Mustangs. Stallions, no less.

"Can we ride him?" Kiley demanded, addressing the question to Chance, not Hallie.

Chance shook his head. "He's a knot-head," he said, with a philosophical sigh. "Trojan's won a lot of ribbons and trophies in his time, though. Jessie used to enter him in shows all over the country."

Kiera reached a hand between the rails to touch the animal, and Hallie tensed, barely stopped herself from blurting out a warning. *Watch out!*

Chance met her gaze, and she saw understanding in his blue eyes, and questions. Questions she didn't dare answer.

Trojan nickered, sniffed Kiera's mittened fingers, and tossed his head, wanting breakfast.

"Here's what you do," Chance said easily, and then he showed Hallie how to fill the feed pans and set them in the stalls. Using a knife drawn from the worn leather case on his belt, he cut the twine binding a bale of hay and carried the bristly stuff to the feeding troughs. "Don't give them too much," he said, as he worked, "or they'll get colic and die."

"Colic?" Kiley asked. "What's that?"

"They get bad stomachaches," Chance answered, as he worked, "and bloat up."

"Like Grandpa did last Thanksgiving," Kiera told her sister, very seriously.

Chance and Hallie exchanged glances. She knew he was curious about her background, that was only natural, given that he'd trusted her with a family member's house, and that he'd catch every clue she or the children let slip—like Kiera's innocent reference to Lou. She felt a rush of panic, and thought about ditching that rattletrap truck once and for all, turning her back on the job at the aptly named Last Chance Café, as well as the blessed refuge of Jessie Shaw's log house, and catching the next bus out of town, her and the girls.

"That's different, silly," Kiley informed Kiera. "You can't die from eating too much turkey."

"I've felt like it a time or two," Chance confided, and Hallie smiled again. He proceeded to the next stall, introducing the mare, Dolly, an aging pinto, and Sweet Pea, an enormous bay gelding. He measured out their feed, then fetched a pair of pitchforks and a wheelbarrow from the tack room, handing one of the forks to Hallie.

She stood there for a moment, rather like the old woman in Grant Wood's *American Gothic*, and then realized that looking after horses involved manure removal. She swallowed hard.

Chance chuckled. "Okay, Dale Evans," he said, his mouth crooking up at one corner when he smiled, "start pitching."

He demonstrated, stepping into Trojan's stall, and Hallie took a deep breath, squared her shoulders, and let herself in with Dolly, who regarded her tolerantly, chomping happily on her feed.

"She won't kick me, right?" she asked.

"Not if you don't surprise her," Chance answered.

Hallie bit her lip and began to pitch manure over the stall door and into the waiting wheelbarrow. Once she found a rhythm, the work wasn't too bad. In fact, there was a soothing aspect to it that felt almost like meditation. When the wheelbarrow was full, Chance emptied it into an industrial-size garbage bin behind the barn. While the girls played in the stacks of hay, Chance and Hallie finished the chores.

"That's it," Chance said, hanging up his pitchfork. "Until this evening, that is."

Hallie did some quick mental calculations. She wouldn't get out of the Last Chance Café until after eight, according to what Madge had told her the night before, which meant it would be dark when she got back. She'd be working alone, too, with a cougar prowling the countryside.

"Do you know how to use a gun?" Chance asked, evidently reading her mind.

"It wouldn't be a bad idea to carry a pistol."

An image flashed into Hallie's mind, Lou, felled by a nine-millimeter, in his own living room. She felt her knees go weak, but before she could think of a response, she heard a fragile mew, and Kiera cried out with glee. "Kittens!"

"Four of them," Kiley confirmed, equally pleased. "There's a yellow one, and a white one . . . where do you suppose their mama is?"

"She's probably hunting up some breakfast," Chance told them. "Speaking of that, I'm pretty hungry myself. What do you say we head into town for some grub and then see about that truck of yours? I might be able to get it running again."

Hallie bit her lower lip, hesitating, then nodded. "As long as I'm not late for work." She was still looking at Chance, but she addressed her next words to the twins. "Leave the kittens alone for now," she said. "It isn't good to handle them when they're so new."

"Their eyes are still squinched shut," Kiera said, jumping off a hay bale and starting toward Hallie. Kiley, who usually led the way, followed thoughtfully.

"What if the cougar eats them all up?" she fretted.

Chance ruffled Kiley's hair. "They're pretty safe in here," he said, with a sort of gruff tenderness.

Hallie's heart constricted; once again, against her will, she thought of Joel. He'd sired the twins, but he'd never been a real father, like Lou had been to her, never reassured them in that ordinary way. She tried to put the past out of her mind as she followed Chance and the girls toward the huge truck waiting in the driveway next to the house, but it wasn't easy to do. She was as skittish as a deer, jumping at every sound.

Hallie's own decrepit vehicle was right where she'd left it the night before, all but buried in snow. She shivered, reliving the long, cold walk to town, and scanned the hillside beyond for signs of cat tracks as they drove past.

The Last Chance Café stood at the edge of town, and in the glare of a blue and white day, the place showed its age. It reminded her a little of Edward Hopper's diner painting, *Nighthawks*, though of course the ambience was a lot cheerier. There were seven or eight cars in the parking lot, which had been plowed since the night before, and a rush of warm, bacon-scented air met Hallie when she stepped over the threshold. The twins had raced ahead, staking out stools at the counter, and Chance brought up the rear.

Madge greeted them with a smile that somehow took in everybody. "Mornin'!"

Hallie smiled back, though tentatively. "Good morning," she said.

Chance waited beside one of the booths until Hallie took a seat, then sat down across from her. He didn't reach for a menu.

Hallie consulted the blackboard behind the counter, where the specials were listed, and settled on oatmeal and orange juice. Kiera and Kiley were seated primly at the counter, and she grinned a little at their independence.

"They're great kids," Chance observed quietly.

She nodded. It gave her an illusion of safety, of happiness, being in this place, in the company of this man she barely knew, and she wanted to warm herself at those feelings, like a fire. Instead, she reminded herself not to let her guard slip. *They* were certainly still out there, searching for

her, and they had the means to track her this far and further. Her life and, more importantly, the lives of her children, depended on her vigilance, and on her ability to
make the right contact with the right law enforcement
agency. Because of the identity of the men she'd seen in
Lou's photos, she was still afraid to trust anyone.

"Thanks," she said.

Chance waited until Madge had taken their orders,
looking smug the whole time, as if he had discerned some
sweet secret that was hers alone, before leaning in a little. "What are you running from, Hallie?" he asked, his
voice low.

She felt the color drain from her face, looked away,
looked back. Defiantly. "Nothing," she lied, her tone curt.
But she wished she could tell him about Lou, and the cashbox, and the men in the pictures.

"You're a bad liar," he replied, with a sigh.

She didn't answer, *couldn't* answer, and Madge returned
in the silent interim to set cups of coffee and glasses of
juice before them. Chance held Hallie's gaze throughout,
quite against her will.

"If you're running from the law, you'd better tell me,"
he went on quietly.

She stiffened, but before she answered, she glanced
toward the twins, to make sure they weren't listening.
Madge had given them a box of crayons, and they were
coloring on paper place mats.

"I have problems, just like everybody else," Hallie
whispered furiously, "but I am *not* a criminal." That much,
at least, was true—she was living a lie, but she hadn't
broken any laws.

He took a leisurely sip of coffee, watching her over the

brim of his cup. "Seems to me that your troubles must be a little worse than average. If they weren't, you probably wouldn't have ended up stranded beside the road in a snowstorm, in the middle of the night, with two little kids and no place to stay."

She lowered her eyes, regrouping. When she looked up, she knew her cheeks were charged with color, and her chin was jutting out. "I was on my way somewhere," she said. She was bluffing, and he clearly knew it, but pride compelled her to make an effort. "I just ran into some bad luck, that's all."

"I'd like to help you," he said quietly. "If you'll let me."

She looked away. She had defenses against every-thing—except kindness.

He reached across the table, laid one of his hands over hers. His fingers and palm were callused from years of hard work, and his strength, as much a part of him as any organ or limb, seemed to flow into her. He didn't urge her to speak, he simply waited.

At last, she met his gaze again, and shook her head.

"Okay," he said.

Madge appeared with their food. She glanced from Chance to Hallie and back again. A grin quirked her bright red lips. "You wouldn't be tryin' to do me out of a waitress, now would you, Chance Qualtrough?"

He spread his hands, the picture of innocence, though those blue eyes of his were full of sweet evil. "Just being neighborly," he said.

Madge laughed and turned her attention on Hallie. "You want to watch out for this fella," she warned good-naturedly. "He's been lassoed a couple of times, but he always manages to slip the rope."

Chance's smile went high-beam, and Hallie was at once glad and sorry that it was trained on Madge, not her. "Nobody measures up to you, Madge," he said. "That's the trouble. Come on, say you'll marry me . . ."

Delighted, Madge laughed again, uproariously this time, snatched Chance's hat from its place on the booth seat beside him, and swatted him with it. He raised both hands, as if to shield himself. Madge whacked him a few more times for good measure, then plopped the hat on his head, sideways. "Now," she said. "You just behave yourself, or I'll throw you out of here."

Chance removed his hat, set it aside, this time on the inside of his seat, next to the wall.

"You've known Madge a long time," Hallie observed somewhat wistfully, as the other woman bustled away to greet some new arrivals.

"All my life," Chance answered, watching Madge with quiet affection. "I'd do anything for her."

Hallie felt a knot rise into her throat, thicken there. Her stepfather had been the one person on earth who would have gone to the wall for her and the kids, and he was gone forever. They'd killed him, Joel and those men in the pictures, she was sure of it, just the way she was equally sure they would kill her, and maybe her babies, if they got the chance.

"Tell me," Chance urged, his expression solemn, watchful. He simply saw too much, this man.

Tears stung her eyes. She wanted to tell him everything—the burden was buckling her very soul—but she didn't dare. Oh, he was well-intentioned, she had no doubt of that, but he had no idea what he was asking her to do. Besides, she didn't know the whole story;

Lou had left her only bits and pieces of evidence.

She pressed a hand to her mouth, remembering. She squeezed her eyes shut, but the images were still there, imprinted on her mind for all time. Lou, lying stone cold in his coffin, forever lost to her and to her children.

She pushed her oatmeal away and glanced up to see a woman approaching the table, looking at once purposeful and pleasant. She had a cap of short, dark hair, and her eyes were indigo blue. She wore black slacks, boots, and a peacoat over a turtleneck sweater. She smiled questioningly at Hallie, then batted Chance's shoulder with one hip. The distraction was a blessed relief.

"Scoot over, Cowboy," she ordered.

He grinned and slid to make room, and Hallie quelled an embarrassing stab of jealousy. "Hello, Katie," he said, and then indicated Hallie with a toss of his head. "Meet Madge's new waitress and Jessie's new house-sitter, Hallie O'Rourke. Hallie, this is Katie Stratton."

Katie assessed her frankly, but her smile was genuine. "Hi, Hallie."

Hallie nodded. "Hello," she said.

Katie turned her attention on Chance. "I need to have a word with you," she told him.

"I know," he replied. "I got your phone message last night."

There was some kind of dynamic at work between these two, Hallie thought, but she couldn't quite figure out what it was. Or maybe, she reflected wryly, she just didn't *want* to recognize it. She sat back against the booth, arms folded, and watched them watching each other.

Just then, Madge hurried over. *"Incoming!"* she warned, like a soldier on lookout.

The café door *whooshed* open, and cold air flooded the place. Hallie looked up, saw Jase Stratton entering, and nearly had a heart attack then and there. He was on *somebody's* trail, that was obvious. Had Joel gotten to him, turned the tables somehow, convinced Stratton that she, Hallie, had done something wrong?

"Good morning, Jase," Katie said mildly.

He acknowledged a stricken Hallie with a brisk nod and leaned down, his large hands grasping the edges of the table. "What are you doing here?" he demanded of Katie, who looked up at him without flinching.

"I was planning to have coffee," she replied evenly. "Is there a law against that?"

Chance was stuck in the corner of the booth, which was probably a good thing, because he looked as though he might have gone for the lawman's throat if the way had been unobstructed. His face had gone hard, his blue eyes had turned gray as slate; there was one hell of a storm brewing. "Not now," he warned, glaring at the other man. "I mean it, Jase."

Hallie glanced toward her children, saw with relief that they were still absorbed in their coloring project, though they'd both done justice to the cereal and fruit Madge had served them earlier. *Maybe they'd witnessed so many angry scenes in their young lives,* she thought ruefully, *that another one was of no great consequence to them.*

"I wasn't talking to you," Jase drawled, glaring at Chance.

Hallie bit down on her lower lip, wishing she could take her children and disappear into thin air.

Jase moved to take hold of Katie's forearm; she

stopped him with a quiet, "Don't even think about grabbing me."

"Amen to that," Chance warned. His tone was low, and dangerous.

Jase straightened, heaved an exasperated sigh. Although fury flashed in his eyes, Hallie saw pain there, too, and something else that she hadn't immediately recognized. Decency. "Christ, Katie," he breathed. "You know I'd never manhandle you."

She didn't look away from his face. "Do I?" she countered. A charge passed between the two of them then, Katie and Jase, and Hallie glanced at Chance. He still looked as though he wanted to climb over the table and rip the officer a new one, but he was making an effort at restraint.

"Hallie O'Rourke," Katie said, "this is my husband, Jase Stratton. He's sheriff—not of Nottingham, as you might think from his behavior—but of this very county. Jase, this is Hallie. If you bother to look, you'll probably notice that you've just scared the hell out of her."

Jase sighed again. He was handsome, broad-shouldered and square-jawed. He took off his hat and made an honest attempt at a smile. "Welcome to Primrose Creek," he said, and he sounded sheepish.

By then, Hallie had sized him up. He wasn't mean, and he wasn't dangerous. But he was hurting in a big way. Over Katie. Obviously, Chance figured into the equation somewhere, too, but she wasn't ready to think about that. "Thanks," she said.

Jase let out another great sigh. "Look," he said to Katie, "I admit I overreacted. I'm sorry. But we were supposed to meet this morning, remember? For the conference with Janie's teacher?"

Katie responded with a sigh of her own. "Jase," she replied, "that was *yesterday*. You didn't show, so I talked with Mrs. Carter myself." Her tone said she did a lot of things by herself, and hated it.

Jase looked as though he'd been struck in the belly with a ramrod. "Yesterday?" he echoed, sounding horrified.

"Yesterday," Katie confirmed. Her lips were tight, and her blue eyes snapped as she regarded her husband. "Ellie's dance recital was last night. You missed that, too."

"Oh, God," Jase muttered.

Although she was much smaller than Jase, she somehow claimed the space he was standing in, rising to her feet, forcing him to step back. "Nice to meet you, Hallie," she said. "Stop by the bookstore and I'll try to convince you that there *are* a few sane people in this town. It's just down the street, across from the feed and grain." She didn't spare a look for Jase, but spoke, instead, to Chance. "Thanks for being there last night. It meant a lot to Ellie, and to me."

Chance nodded a reply, but didn't elaborate; he was on his feet almost as soon as Katie gave him room. He and Jase glared at each other, like a pair of stallions claiming the same territory. Hallie felt a twinge of unfounded, inexplicable heartache as she looked on.

"I'd like a word with you, Stratton," Chance growled.

A white line edged Jase's jaw, and his eyes flashed with fire. "That's fine by me," he growled back. "Let's just step outside, shall we?"

Katie closed her eyes, engaged in a visible struggle with her temper, and then opened them again, speaking calmly. "That's enough," she said. "From both of you. This isn't the old days, when you used to strip the hide off each other out behind Jessie's barn. You're grown men, and you're family, and I'll thank you to act like it."

Jase raised an index finger, as if to shake it under Katie's nose, thought better of the idea when he saw the look in her eyes, and let his hand fall to his side. "I'm sorry about missing Janie's school meeting," he told his wife, "and Ellie's dance program, too."

"Tell it to your daughters," Katie said, and pushed past him to leave.

"Katie—" he reached for her, and missed. After shooting one ferocious glance in Chance's direction, Jase followed Katie out of the café and into the parking lot. It seemed fitting to Hallie that the snow was beginning to melt; tempers ran hot in Primrose Creek.

"Let's go see about your truck," Chance grumbled, watching the retreating couple with an expression Hallie couldn't read.

For a moment, she didn't know what he was talking about, she'd been so absorbed in the drama playing out between him and Jase and Katie. "Oh . . . yeah," she agreed. "Right."

He looked at her and she saw an old sorrow in his eyes.

Tell me, she wanted to say, just as he had done earlier. But she knew she didn't have the right to ask, especially when she wasn't willing to give up her own secrets in return.

"I'll look after the kids," Madge volunteered. The

breakfast crowd had thinned out, Hallie noticed, once again aware of her surroundings. "You go on with Chance and get your business taken care of."

"We'll be good," Kiley said, in a pleading voice, obviously afraid Hallie would refuse to leave them, even in such a safe and cozy place as the Last Chance.

"Please," Kiera added.

Hallie hesitated for a moment, then worked up a smile, and nodded. "Okay," she said. "Thanks, Madge."

Madge grinned, a blue crayon in hand, working on a place mat of her own. "No problem," she said. "Just be back here by eleven or so, so we can get ready for the lunch rush."

Hallie, once the owner and operator of one of the most popular restaurants in Scottsdale, Arizona—no small accomplishment in a town where trendy eateries were plentiful—was pleased at the prospect of slinging hash in a high-country greasy spoon, even on a trial basis; work was therapy for her. "Any particular dress code?"

Madge exchanged the blue crayon for a yellow one. "Jeans and a blouse are all right," she said. "If Wynona doesn't blow in on schedule, we'll order you a couple of uniforms from the supply house. Their sales rep is due sometime next week."

Hallie pictured herself in a pink nylon number like Madge's, and had to smile. "Great," she said. "See you in a little while." She spoke to the girls again, as Chance held her coat for her. The small, ordinary courtesy surprised her, though she didn't let it show. "You behave yourselves while I'm gone."

Kiera beamed, Kiley rolled her eyes. "We will," Kiley promised. "Okay," Kiera said, at the same time.

Outside, Chance got behind the wheel of his pickup, fired up the engine, and leaned across to push the passenger door open for Hallie. She climbed in, settled herself, fastened her seat belt. Through the windshield, she could see what must have been Katie's bookstore. The sheriff's car was parked out front, and he stood on the sidewalk, gazing into the shop. He seemed, to Hallie, the very personification of loneliness.

"Poor guy," Hallie murmured, and winced inwardly when she realized she'd been thinking aloud.

Chance made a derisive huffing sound. "Don't waste your sympathy on him. He's got women all over the county looking to cheer him up."

Hallie was stung, on Katie's account. "He doesn't look like the type to run around," she said.

Chance kept his eyes on the road. "Looks," he replied, "can be deceiving."

4

Chance drew his truck to a stop behind Hallie's, shifting into neutral and yanking the handle of the emergency brake. "Wait here," he said. It was bitterly cold, even though the sun was out; no sense in both of them freezing their asses off.

Hallie ignored him, pushed open her door, and jumped to the ground. Her hands were stuffed into the pockets of her coat and her chin was set at an obstinate angle that made him want to laugh out loud. Passing the rear wheel of her own rig, she stopped and kicked it, hard.

Grinning to himself, Chance went around to the front of the truck, unhooked the latch with a curved finger, and raised the hood. He knew at a glance that there was no saving that old engine; it had thrown a rod, and that was the least of its problems. He let out a long sigh. Closed the hood again.

Hallie was hugging herself against the cold. Stubborn woman. She could have stayed in his truck, where the heater was blasting, but no. That would have been too easy, he supposed. "It's not good, is it?" she asked, in a small voice that said she was unaccustomed to trouble, at least in large doses.

"No," he said. "I'd say that old truck has seen its day. You could probably sell it for scrap, though. Get a few hundred, if you're lucky."

She sucked in a breath big enough to seriously deplete the atmosphere, then gave a hissing sigh and threw her head back, gazing up at the cold sky, absorbing the news. "Great," she said, at some length. "*Now* what do I do?"

He figured it must be a rhetorical question; she certainly wasn't asking *him* for suggestions. So he waited, raising the truck's hood again and fiddling with the carburetor, just for something to do. Talk about beating a dead horse. It was a miracle, in his view, that she'd covered any real distance at all in that wreck-on-wheels.

She stomped one sneakered foot. "Damn."

He closed the hood again, dusted his gloved hands together, then rested them on his hips. "I take it you don't have the money for another car."

She glared at him. "Not much gets by you, does it, Cowboy?" she snapped. Then she bit her lower lip, and her expression was pained. "I'm sorry," she sighed, spreading her hands, letting them fall against her sides. In a way, he'd liked it better when she showed some fight. He'd been less afraid for her then.

He swept his hat off, put it on again. Shrugged. "That's okay," he said. "I've got a thick hide."

"What about a new engine?" she asked, hope flaring in her eyes. He felt a proportionate rise in his own spirits. "How much would that cost?"

He sighed. Gave a speculative figure.

Her face fell. "Shit," she said.

He bit the inside of his lower lip to keep from laughing again, guessing she might fling herself at him in a fury if he did. "Shit" was a minor-league curse word, but hearing her say it was encouraging. For a few moments there, he'd been sure she was going to give up, maybe, or at least break down and cry. He never could abide a woman's tears.

He waited.

She continued to pace. "How am I going to get to work?" she demanded.

Chance didn't reply; she still wasn't talking to him— she was confronting the universe. A good sign.

She slammed one fist into her palm. "You'd think just one thing would go right, wouldn't you?" she expounded. Then she stopped, and her face changed again. A sort of woeful humor quirked at the corner of her mouth. "Okay, so maybe a *couple* of things have gone right."

He wanted to help her, to make *everything* all right, but he didn't need a season of *Oprah* episodes to know he couldn't fix Hallie O'Rourke, that they'd both be worse off for the effort if he tried. Still, he had to do something. "Jessie has a Jeep, under a tarp in her shed. You could drive that."

"I'm already living in the woman's house," Hallie protested, looking exasperated now, as well as a little frenzied. "I can't just help myself to her car!"

"I don't think she'd mind," he said, folding his arms because *damn*, it was cold. Couldn't they have this conversation in the truck, where there was heat? "We'll go to her place and call her, if that will make you feel better. Believe me when I say, Jessie will be so grateful to have somebody staying right there on the place, she'll probably want to adopt you."

She scraped her upper lip with her teeth. "We can't just leave this pile of junk sitting here," she said, gesturing toward her dead truck.

"I'll call Bob Riley when we get to the house. He'll tow it to his junkyard. At least you'll get a few bucks out of the deal. If you've got a clear title, that is."

He saw the flicker of alarm in her eyes, there and gone, in less than a moment. She went around to the passenger side, wrenched open the door, flipped the latch on the glove compartment, and rummaged. Her blue-jeaned butt looked good from where Chance was standing.

Soon enough, she produced a piece of paper. After examining it with squinty intensity, she thrust the document in his direction, grinning. "It's been signed over."

Chance read the title. Sure enough, there was a scrawled signature on the proper line. Legally, the vehicle was up for grabs, the property of whoever paid the fees and filed for ownership. He deciphered the name. "Who's Lou Waitlin?" he asked. He'd automatically registered the Phoenix address.

For a long time, she just looked at him. Then she shoved a hand through her chin-length hair and gnawed at her lower lip again. "Just a guy. I bought the truck from him a few weeks ago."

She'd taken too long to answer. He let her know, with a look, that he didn't believe her. "Whatever," he said. He gestured toward his own rig. "Hop in. I'll take you back to Jessie's."

She strode over, opened the door, and climbed up into

the seat. She was gazing straight ahead when he got in and started the engine.

"Do you want me to call the tow truck?"

She didn't look at him. Just leaned against the window on her side, the fingers of one hand splayed in her hair.

Once they were rolling, he took his cell phone from his shirt pocket and got Information on the line. A few moments later, he was talking to Bob at the junkyard. He asked the other man to pick up the truck and promised to check in with him later.

"This is taking up a lot of your time," she said, when they turned in through Jessie's gate and started up the driveway.

"Yeah," he agreed.

"Don't you have to earn a living?"

He chuckled. "No," he said. "I guess I'm what you'd call a gentleman farmer."

She smiled at the term, though the threat of tears glinted in her eyes. "Must be nice," she said. She glanced at her watch, a thin gold one, out of sync with her discount-store clothing. He knew she was worried about being late for work.

They hit the rutted part of the road—he'd been after Jessie for years to have it graded and then paved—and the truck bounced on its springs. "It has its good points."

Watching him, she simply raised an eyebrow. Her right elbow was propped on the lower part of the window, fingers curled against her cheek.

He wanted to tell her a lot of things about himself, both mundane and profound, and that surprised him. How he'd been a rodeo champion in college, for instance, and how he'd yearned for this place all the time he was away. He was generally inclined to play his cards close to the vest, operating on the old saying that everybody's business is nobody's business. They pulled into Jessie's driveway, came to a stop in front of the shed where her Jeep was stored.

Inside the house, Hallie immediately started a pot of coffee. Chance noticed that she glanced at the clock over the sink periodically, agitated at being separated from her children and probably still fretting to herself about getting to work on time, though she still had an hour.

Chance took the cordless phone from its hook on the wall and ran a mental finger down the list of numbers on the typewritten itinerary Jessie had pinned up nearby. He punched the appropriate buttons and waited while the call rang through to her hotel in Kansas City.

Jessie answered immediately, and there was an eager note in her voice, as though she was hoping to hear from one particular person. "Hello?"

"Jessie, it's Chance. I'm calling from your place."

He heard her catch her breath. "Is everything all right?"

Chance wasted no time reassuring her. "Things are fine out here," he said quickly. "Fact is, I called to introduce you to your new house-sitter. Her name is Hallie O'Rourke. Want to say hello?"

Jessie sounded surprised, and full of questions. She tried to get more details out of him, then sighed. "Put her on," she said cautiously.

Chance handed the receiver to Hallie, who hastily smoothed her hair, as though trying to make herself more presentable. It was, he thought, amused, a little like dressing up to sing on the radio.

"Hello?" Hallie said.

While the conversation continued, Chance poured two cups of coffee, set one out for Hallie, and wandered into the front room, sipping from his own mug as he went. He crossed to the desk where Jessie's computer stood, lifted off the dust cover and, for no particular reason, flipped the On switch. Hallie's voice trailed in from the kitchen, and he knew from her tone that Jessie was giving her the third degree, in that gracious way of hers. He doubted that she'd have any better luck in that department than he had. Hallie O'Rourke—if that was her real name—wasn't giving anything away, not when it came to her past, at least.

Reaching for the mouse, he zeroed in on the icon for Jessie's Internet server and clicked twice. Her password was stored, and he got online with no more effort than that. Within a few moments, he was logging on to a familiar Web site. He clicked Search and a name box came up, and he filled it in without hesitation.

Lou Waitlin.

~

Jessie Shaw's voice was quiet, but vibrant with life. She seemed thrilled to have a perfect stranger living in her house. Hallie took an occasional sip of the coffee Chance had poured for her, and got a word in edgewise when she could.

"You just make yourself at home," Jessie said, while Hallie stood in the kitchen doorway, watching Chance, who had switched on the computer. "There's food in the freezer out on the back porch—help yourself. If you've got a valid driver's license, you can use my Jeep, too. It's not good for any machine to just sit around gathering dust that way. And I suppose Chance has shown you how to look after the horses?" She didn't wait for an answer. "You'll want to be careful around Trojan. He's a caution, that one. But he's got a good heart."

Hallie's eyes narrowed a little as she watched Chance, typing busily at the computer. The click of words was rapid and steady; no two-finger cadence for him. She waited for Jessie to ask for references—that would be the end of her short career as a house-sitter and horse-tender—but the question never came. No doubt Jessie thought Chance had already gotten the pertinent information, and was willing to trust his instincts.

"I have twin daughters," Hallie heard herself telling the woman on the other end of the line. "They're seven." She dared reveal little or nothing of her past, but she needed to offer *something* in return for all this trust.

There was a smile in Jessie's voice. "The house must be so pleased," she said.

"Pardon?" Hallie had been watching Chance, wondering what he was up to, and it took her a moment or two longer than normal to absorb Jessie's words.

Jessie laughed. "That place has a heart and a soul," she said, and made the idea sound rational. "For several generations, it was filled to the rafters with noisy children. I never married, never had a family of my own, so it's been mighty quiet around there—except for when Chance and Jase were boys, of course." She paused, sighed. "It's been a lonely house."

Chance swiveled in the desk chair, tossed Hallie a thoughtful glance, and went back to what he was doing. Her stomach churned with anxiety. What was he up to? Was he checking her story? She knew he'd seen Lou's name on the truck title earlier. If he ran a search, he might find out about the murder . . .

"Of course you can use my computer, too, if you want to," Jessie was saying. "You could e-mail me, keep me up on all the gossip around Primrose Creek, while I'm traveling. I carry a laptop everywhere I go. I'm working on a family history."

Somehow, Hallie managed a smile. If the phone had had a cord, she might have twisted it around her neck and hanged herself, she felt so guilty for deceiving this good, generous woman in any way.

She leaned against the framework of the door that led into the kitchen, still watching Chance. "I imagine I'll hear plenty of that, working at the Last Chance Café," she said. She couldn't help thinking of the scene she'd witnessed just that morning, between Jase and Katie Stratton, with Chance on the fringes. There was a story *there*, that was for sure. Briefly, she wished she knew Jessie Shaw well enough to ask.

Jessie chuckled. "In Primrose Creek," she observed, "all roads lead to the Last Chance Café."

Chance pushed back from the computer, turned to face Hallie. Although she saw questions in his eyes, she was reassured by the slight smile curving his lips.

"Jessie?" Hallie said sincerely, "Thank you. Thank you for giving the twins and me a place to stay. I promise I'll take good care of your horses and the house, too."

"I'll be home soon," Jessie replied. "Just briefly, though,

I'm afraid. My agent has booked a whole new batch of gallery tours for me."

It was more than Hallie could take in, the thought of Jessie returning to Primrose Creek, for however short a time. She was simply too frazzled to think about what she'd do then, where she and the children would go. "Here's Chance," she said, a little too quickly, and held out the receiver to him.

He accepted it. Listened. Said good-bye, and pushed the button to disconnect.

Hallie followed him into the kitchen. He opened the broom closet and took a set of keys from a hook inside, jangled them at her. "The house key is on this ring, and there's one here for the Jeep, too." He glanced up at the clock. "You'll want to get back to the café soon," he said. "I'll make sure the rig starts before I go home, if you want me to."

She ran her hands down the thighs of her jeans. Something about this man made her palms sweat, and other things were happening inside her, too, none of them ordinary. "You've done enough," she said. "Thanks for everything."

He nodded, and for one brief moment, she thought he was going to confront her, ask her point blank about Phoenix, and Lou, and all the rest of it. "I'll see you around," he said instead. And then he was gone.

Hallie watched through the oval window in the kitchen door as he backed the truck out, turned around, and drove away. When he was gone, she locked the house, hurried upstairs, and took a hasty shower in Jessie's bathroom.

She ironed a blouse from her suitcase, put on clean

jeans, applied minimal makeup, blow-dried her hair, and caught it up in a clasp. Then she moved her things into another bedroom, one adjoined by a smaller one, with twin beds. Kiera and Kiley could stay there, close enough to her to feel safe, but far enough away to begin establishing some degree of normalcy. Their lives, like her own, had been turned upside down in the space of an afternoon, but they were at an extra disadvantage, because they had no way of comprehending the reasons for what had happened. They'd been thrust into a maelstrom of change, taken from the only home they'd ever known, with the clothes on their backs and the image of their father running after the truck.

Tears rose in her eyes, and she blinked them away. No time to fall apart now. She had a job to do and besides, there was no use in looking back. She had to reinvent herself, move on, leave the past behind.

She could do it.

She went downstairs, switched off the coffeepot, paused in the living room, before the computer, unconsciously flexing her fingers. A few key strokes, and she would know what Chance had been doing while she was talking with Jessie on the telephone. The question was, did she *want* to know?

At last, she turned away, headed outside, locking the door of the house behind her. The snow was melting, lying in wet, ragged patches upon the muddy ground. The nearby creek was visible through the trees, sparkling in the thin autumn sunlight, making music as it went on its way.

She headed for the barn first, to look in on the horses, then made her way to the shed. The Jeep was parked inside, dark blue and dusty, and when she turned the key in the ignition, the motor roared to life. She was almost jubilant with relief.

A few minutes later, she pulled into the parking lot at the Last Chance Café, which was empty except for a yellow Volkswagen and a big SUV, emblazoned with a gold badge and the word "Sheriff." She parked the Jeep, got out, and made her way to the door, projecting a confidence she didn't really feel. Although she'd been telling the truth when she told Chance that she wasn't a criminal, she had ample reason to be wary of the police.

Jase Stratton was sitting at the counter, on the stool Hallie already thought of as Chance's, drinking coffee. Kiley and Kiera were dancing with each other, while the jukebox poured out a lively tune.

"Mommy!" they chorused, when they saw her. They ran into her arms, and she gathered them close, as if to push them all the way into her heart and lock them away there.

Jase turned on the stool, looked at her curiously, then smiled. "Looks like you've got your very own welcoming committee," he said.

She laughed and nodded, ruffling her daughters' hair. "We're a team, all right," she said, and then focused on the small faces turned up to her. "So. Were you good?"

"I was," Kiera said.

"There was a lady here," Kiley added excitedly, tugging at the hem of Hallie's coat. "She invited us to play-group, after school. There's going to be a costume contest at the Harvest Carnival, with lots of prizes—"

"Can we go to play-group?" Kiley asked.

"Please?" Kiera pleaded.

"We'll see," Hallie hedged. She couldn't promise, not before she'd done some research, found out how much it cost. The days when she could afford a lot of extras were gone, possibly forever. "The first order of business is to get you signed up for school." That task would have to wait until tomorrow, for better or worse, since she couldn't ask for time off on her first day.

"The teacher is Ms. Callahan," Kiera persisted, ignoring her mother's reference to elementary school. "She has bells on her ankles."

Jase, who had been looking on, chuckled at that observation.

"Bells on her ankles?" Hallie echoed, surprised. And intrigued.

"Evie Callahan," explained the sheriff, "is Primrose Creek's resident free spirit. She teaches belly dancing over at the Grange Hall, and reads palms and tarot cards, too. Besides running the play-group."

Hallie raised both eyebrows and smiled.

"Evie is great with kids," he added. "Both my daughters attend her after-school dance and art classes. They love every minute."

Just then, Madge came out of the kitchen, looking weary. She smiled warmly at Hallie. "Well, girl," she began, "you ready to run your feet off? Bear's made up a batch of his beef stew for today's special, and everybody in town comes in for either lunch or supper whenever he does that."

Hallie drew a long, appreciative breath. The very air of the café was savory. "It smells delicious," she said.

"It is," Jase put in. He stood up, laid a dollar bill on the counter. "Guess I'd better get back to fighting crime," he said, with a wink at Madge. "I'll be back for some of that stew, though."

Madge beamed, maybe with affection for Jase Stratton, maybe with pride over the stew. "We'll be watching for you," she said.

He executed a teasing salute and left the restaurant.

"My dogs are barking," Madge announced, and sank into a chair at one of the Formica-topped tables.

Kiera looked around, puzzled. "They are?"

"I don't hear any dogs," Kiley said.

Madge laughed, pointed at her crepe-soled shoes. "It means that my feet hurt," she said.

Kiera and Kiley looked at each other and shrugged. A young couple, probably the owners of the yellow Volkswagen Hallie had seen in the parking lot, left their booth to study the selection of tunes on the jukebox. When they'd dropped in a few coins and made their choices, the café brimmed with lively music again, and the twins once again occupied themselves with their version of dancing.

"Can you handle the lunch crowd on your own?" Madge asked Hallie. The older woman was still sitting, though now she'd propped both feet on the seat of the chair across from hers. "I was planning on hanging around, you being new and all, but the bone spurs on my heels are really acting up. I need to go home, plop down in my recliner, and watch soap operas until my eyes cross."

Hallie grinned sympathetically. "I can handle it," she confirmed. "It might take me a while to learn the prices. You want me to work through supper?"

Madge's expression was touchingly hopeful. "If you're up to it. It'll mean a long day for the kids, as well as for you."

"They're good at entertaining themselves," Hallie said.

Madge heaved an enormous sigh. "Well, bless your heart," she said. "You're the answer to an old lady's prayers, Hallie O'Rourke, I'll tell you that. That brother of mine, he was born to be a fry cook, and he can work eighteen hours without even slowing down, but I'm just plain pooped. Why, I haven't been to Bingo in three months, and I can't remember the last time I read anything longer than a magazine article."

"Go home and put your feet up," Hallie said gently. "Bear and I will hold down the fort here."

Madge sighed. "Who knows? Maybe Wynona will put in an appearance, and actually help out around here." She paused, gave a huff of weary laughter. "The Tooth Fairy will probably show up before Wynona does." She hoisted herself to her aching feet. "Bear!" she called to the man in the kitchen, who was scraping the grill industriously. "Hallie's here. She's taking over for me. Don't you run her off, you hear me?"

Bear, a homely man with kind eyes, smiled at Hallie through the pass-through window. "You're the one with the contrary nature," he told his sister. "I'm real easy to get along with."

Madge shuffled across the linoleum floor and took her coat, a camel-colored woolen garment with a hood, down from a hook. "You call me if it gets to be too much," she said. "My number is on speed-dial. Just press zero-two."

Hallie sincerely hoped she wouldn't have cause to summon Madge back to the café. The woman was obviously exhausted, and in considerable pain. "Zero-two," she repeated dutifully.

Madge put on her coat, fastened the loops around the large buttons. She took a hand-knitted scarf from one pocket and draped it over her head, tossing one generously fringed end over each shoulder. Then she pulled on her gloves. "All right, then," she said. "I'm going." She seemed to expect someone to stop her, and she was clearly relieved, and a little disappointed, when no one tried.

Finally, after casting one long look around the place, Madge opened the door and went out.

Hallie busied herself refilling salt and pepper shakers and napkin holders, wiping tables, sponging off the vinyl-covered menus. The couple with the Volkswagen paid their check and left, and she cleared their table. The twins got tired of dancing and settled in one of the booths again, reading stories to each other from a battered copy of *Field and Stream*. Thanks to an accelerated learning program at their school in Scottsdale, Kiera and Kiley had both been reading at a near-adult level for the past year.

At eleven o'clock, a man in greasy clothes came in, announced that he owned the junkyard, and offered Hallie seven hundred dollars for her dead truck. It sounded like a fortune, in her current circumstances, and she accepted readily, signed the title, which he'd brought along, and he promised to drop off a check later in the day. He tarried long enough to consume two bowls of Bear's stew, and left a good tip.

Hallie was in a cheerful mood when the lunch rush started; she enjoyed the work and the social interaction, such as it was. She'd missed her own restaurant sorely, and the idea of it standing closed up and empty, bothered her a great deal. There hadn't been time to tie up any loose ends before leaving, and she'd left several good people without jobs or explanations. She hadn't dared to call them, for fear Joel or some of the rogue cops in Lou's photographs might have tapped the line.

Why didn't you go to the FBI, Lou? she thought for the hundredth time. *Did you really mean to dump this on me?* She'd tried repeatedly to reach Charlie Long, but without success.

There she went again, she scolded herself. Dwelling on things she couldn't change, mysteries she might never solve. She put the whole grim situation out of her mind, for the time being, and concentrated on waitressing.

During a brief lull, she fed the twins, who were beginning to squabble, and grabbed a bite or two for herself, and by the time Katie Stratton came in, business was slowing down. Hostilities between Kiera and Kiley, however, were beginning to heat up in earnest.

Katie's smile was genuine, though there was a subtle sadness in her eyes. She greeted Hallie, who was wiping down the counter, and the several older people dining on the "Senior Special," then approached the twins, who were glaring at each other like two miniature gunfighters preparing to slap leather.

"Looks like somebody's coming down with cabin fever," Katie remarked. From her tone, a person would have thought she was addressing adults, not children.

"She called me booger-face," Kiera said.

Hallie had long since given up on reprimanding the children; she had her hands full with restaurant work and was willing to settle for quiet mayhem.

"You must have misunderstood," Katie said, in all seriousness, turning an appraising gaze on Kiley, the likely offender. "You wouldn't say a thing like that about your sister, would you? Not when she looks so much like you, and everything?"

Kiley had obviously not considered the booger-face question from that particular angle. She didn't back down—that wouldn't have been like her—but she did toss Kiera a glance that said she'd be willing to suspend hostilities for a while, if the price was right.

Hallie decided she liked Katie very much, watching this small interaction. "Hi," she said. "Can I get you something?"

Katie shook her head. "I really came by to apologize," she told Hallie quietly. "Jase and I must have made a pretty poor impression on you this morning."

"There's no need," Hallie answered.

"There is," Katie insisted good-naturedly. "I'm a card-carrying people-pleaser, and I want you to like me."

Hallie chuckled. "No problem there," she said.

"Good," Katie replied. She looked back at the twins for a moment, then smiled at Hallie again. "Actually, I have another motive as well," she admitted. "It's story day at the bookstore. Adele Denny, the librarian, will be in to read a chapter of *Harry Potter*, and afterward the kids will have cookies and juice. I came to invite your daughters. They could play with my kids afterward—we have two girls, too."

Kiera and Kiley had tuned in to the conversation right away, and now they were at Hallie's sides, jumping up and down. "Please," they chanted, "please let us go— please, please, *please!*"

"How can I refuse?" Hallie asked, though a part of her

wanted to do just that. She'd always been overprotective where the twins were concerned, and she was worse than ever now, but there was one thing greater than her fear for her children, and that was her love for them. They would never learn to function in the real world, or feel safe in their own care, if she didn't loosen her grip. Besides, they had to be going crazy, penned up in the café all day.

Katie's eyes reflected understanding. "Story time starts in fifteen minutes," she said. "We'll be back in an hour and a half."

Hallie nodded, a little choked up. The twins were dizzy with excitement, and they'd scrambled into their coats before their mother had a chance to help them. Like a swirl of leaves in an autumn breeze, they seemed to soar for a moment, all energy and bright colors, and then they blew out the door, closely followed by Katie.

At three o'clock, the high school let out, and the café filled with exuberant teenagers, consuming hamburgers, French fries, milk shakes and Cokes and making the jukebox jump. Their laughter and talk restored Hallie, rather than wore her out, and when customers started showing up looking for supper, she was ready for them. The twins, back from their visit to Katie's book store, were pink-cheeked and bright-eyed. They had grilled cheese sandwiches and milk, and promptly fell asleep in the corner booth.

Madge called three times, over the course of the evening, checking up. Was everything okay? Did Hallie want her to come back and help? Was the stew selling? Would she tell Bear that he should plan on making a batch of chicken and dumplings for tomorrow's special?

When eight o'clock came, Bear stepped out of the kitchen, something he rarely did, as far as Hallie could tell, and turned off the neon "Open" sign in the window. "You'd better get those kids on home now," he said to Hallie, his voice as kind as his eyes. "It's been a long day for all of you."

Hallie looked around. There were still a few customers, finishing up their pie and coffee, and the floor needed to be damp-mopped. The sugar and ketchup containers at the tables had to be refilled, and there was a stack of dishes in the sink. "There's still a lot of work to do—"

"It'll keep," Bear interrupted gently. "Go on, get the girls bundled up. Looks like we might get some more snow tonight, so you'd best hurry."

Hallie smiled. "Thanks," she said.

She'd made good tips that day, and the check for her truck was in her pocket. She didn't dare open a bank account, she'd still have to pay cash for things, but in the morning, she could stock up at the supermarket without holding her breath when the bill was totaled. She would buy each of the girls a toy, and get them signed up at school, though the prospect of that worried her a lot. Primrose Creek Elementary was sure to ask for inoculation records, among other things, and they'd certainly be in contact with the girls' old school in Scottsdale. The Phoenix police might well have asked to be alerted if Hallie got in touch, directly or indirectly.

Perhaps home schooling was the best solution, she concluded, with a flutter in her stomach. No questions asked, that way.

Bear watched from the café window and waved when

Hallie started the Jeep's engine. She waved back, then headed out, driving slowly, carefully, over the country roads that led to Jessie Shaw's house, the kids sitting sleepily in the backseat. Silently, Hallie went over her options.

She mustn't get complacent, or careless, mustn't allow herself to pretend, even for a moment, that she belonged in Primrose Creek. There was no future for her here; it was a stopping-off place, a pit stop on the way to Somewhere Safe, and she couldn't afford to forget that. They were still out there, Joel and the others, and they'd want to make sure she stayed silent about what she knew— whatever that took. Her children could either be caught in the crossfire, or taken back to Arizona to live with their father, the crook.

She shivered, heard a childhood phrase in her mind. *Somebody step on your grave?*

Reaching the log house facing the creek, she woke the kids, helped them out of their seat belts. They came wide awake in the cool, fresh night air, looking up at a magical sky, counting the stars.

"Let's make a wish," Kiera suggested to her sister.

"Okay," Kiley answered. "I wish we could see Daddy."

Tears stung Hallie's eyes, but she made no comment. Whatever her own feelings about Joel, he was the twins' father, the only one they knew, and it was natural for them to miss him.

Kiera spoke quietly, intent upon whatever star she'd chosen to hang her dreams upon. "I wish we could stay right here at Primrose Creek, forever and ever, with Trojan and Madge and Chance."

Hallie blinked, and invisible fingers tightened around

her heart. She knew only too well that neither child's wish would be granted, but nothing would have made her shatter their hopes. She wanted them to believe in good things.

Kiera caught her off guard. "What's your wish, Mommy?" she asked.

Hallie's throat clenched, the way her heart had, moments before. *To be safe*, she thought, but she kept that to herself, too. "I just want the three of us to be together, and happy, for always and always," she managed, at some length.

"Me, too," Kiera agreed.

Kiley was plodding toward the back door, her small shoulders stooped. "Where do you suppose Daddy is tonight?" she asked, almost whispering. The sad thing was, she clearly didn't expect an answer.

5

Hallie was washing her hands at the kitchen sink that night after supper when she saw a truck pull in, and immediately recognized the vehicle as Chance's. He parked near the corral, climbed out, glanced toward the house once, and then headed for the darkened barn. She saw the lights go on inside, and wondered at the little thrill of agitated delight the man's arrival had stirred in her. She was at once glad he was there, and anxious to assure him that she'd been planning to feed the animals as soon as she'd gotten the girls to bed. It was important that he didn't think she was irresponsible.

She reached for her jacket, told the girls to put on their pajamas and brush their teeth, that she'd be back in a few minutes, and hurried out. Just as she reached the spill of light flowing from the open barn doors, she heard the distant cry of something fierce and wild, and a chill sprinted up her spine. She thrust her hands into her pockets and glanced back at the house, instinctively making sure her children were safe. It would be just like them to follow her, with or without their coats, in spite of her instructions that they stay put.

Chance was pouring a bucket of oats and alfalfa pellets into one of the horse feeders. "Howdy," he said, with a light touch to the brim of his hat.

She stood still, just inside the doorway, shoulders straight. "You don't have to do my work," she said carefully.

Chance grinned and went back to refill the bucket. "Just being neighborly," he said. He looked, and sounded, like a cowboy in a Western movie. Hallie was charmed, in spite of herself.

Get a grip, she thought. *You're just passing through, remember?*

The chilling animal sound, a bone-numbing shriek, came again, before she could think of a reply, and she stiffened in fear. "What is that?" she whispered.

Chance's expression had turned serious. "Cougar," he said.

She swallowed hard. "Is it close?"

"Hard to tell," he replied. "It could be as far off as a mile, or as close as the other side of the creek."

"My God," she said. In the near distance, she heard the kitchen door open and close, and was instantly on high-alert. She turned to run back to the house, but the girls were already trundling toward her, through the deep, crusted snow, laughing gleefully as they came.

"It's all right," Chance said quietly, and she realized he was beside her, that he'd taken a light but firm grip on her arm. A rifle had materialized in his free hand; he held it loosely, an expert. Hallie realized distractedly that the gun must have been leaning against the wall, just inside the barn door, since his arrival. "Don't scare them."

The cougar screamed again, farther away this time, thank God, and the twins heard it, freezing halfway between the barn and the house, stiff as ice sculptures.

"Here," Chance said, and shoved the rifle into Hallie's hands. "I'll get them. Keep your finger away from the trigger unless you see the cat."

With that, Chance strode off toward the kids. Hallie waited for a moment, still in shock, then hurried after him. He scooped Kiera up in one arm, and Kiley in the other, and both of them clung to him, their little arms wound around his neck.

He spoke gently, with a smile in his voice. "You're okay," he said.

Hallie stood trembling, rifle in hand. She caught herself wanting to lean on this man, if only in a very small way, and resisted the feeling for all she was worth.

"I thought I told you two to stay inside," she said, looking from Kiera's face to Kiley's.

"What was that noise?" Kiera asked, addressing the question to Chance. It probably seemed the safer course, given that Hallie was obviously upset.

Chance linked gazes with Hallie. "It was a cougar," he said. "Let's get you inside, where it's warm."

They trooped into the house, Chance and the girls in the lead. Hallie brought the gun, terrified the whole way that it would go off on its own.

Kiera and Kiley hurried off to get ready for bed the moment Chance had set them on their feet, and he turned to face Hallie. He grinned and relieved her of the rifle.

"I'll finish the chores," he said.

Her pride, temporarily routed by fear, kicked in again.

"I'm accustomed to hard work, Mr. Qualtrough," she said. At Princess and the Pea, she'd often put in fourteen-hour stints on site, then spent even more time going over spread sheets and invoices at home. She was a worka-holic, according to everybody she knew.

Chance shook his head, took off his hat, put it on again, plainly exasperated. She knew he thought she was being stiff-necked; she also knew his assessment was dead right. She wanted so much to tell him everything then, about Joel, and the cashbox hidden in the plastic Virgin Mary, and the cops she'd seen in the Polaroids, but she simply could not afford to risk opening her heart to this man, even by a crack. There was simply too much at stake.

"You'd better keep this," he said, ignoring her words, indicating the rifle.

"No," she said. "I don't know how to use it." She was still fighting a singular yearning to extend some sort of olive branch, invite him in for coffee at the kitchen table, even tell him a little of her story. It was hard, knowing all that she knew, and being so very alone in that knowing, too frightened to share the burden with someone else. "I don't mean to seem ungrateful," she said, at last.

"I could teach you," he said.

"I'm scared," she confessed, hugging herself.

"All the more reason to learn," he answered.

She backtracked, started over, after drawing a deep breath and letting it out very slowly. "I agreed to look after Jessie's house and animals," she said, "in return for a place to stay. I just want to keep my end of the bargain, that's all."

He took off his hat again, shoved splayed fingers through his hair. Then he grinned at her, and because her defenses were down, because she hadn't had a chance to steady herself after the last onslaught of emotion, her knees nearly buckled with the impact. "I understand that," he said. "You can start tomorrow." Then, after hanging the rifle above the door, utilizing two hooks Hallie hadn't noticed before, he went out.

Hallie took a few moments to recover her composure, then locked the door and went up the rear stairs to find her daughters.

They were both in the bathtub, up to their chests in bubbles.

"Are we in trouble?" Kiley asked.

Hallie sat down on the toilet seat lid, sighed. "Should you be?"

The twins exchanged glances. "Maybe," Kiera allowed.

Hallie bit back a smile. "Next time I tell you to do something," she said, "I expect you to obey me. Is that clear?"

Both children nodded, their expressions solemn. Then Kiley piped up. "Mr. Qualtrough had a gun," she said.

Hallie waited, unsure what to say. The children had never been around firearms before, except for seeing Lou's service revolver, always from a safe distance, and it was hard to know what conclusions they'd drawn about Chance's rifle. She didn't want to plant any ideas, so she merely nodded.

"If the cougar tried to eat us," Kiley said, "he would have shot it."

"The cougar was a long way off," Hallie said. Her voice sounded hollow, and odd, like it was being piped in from somewhere other than her own throat. She had a sense, a brief flash, of what it must have been like to be one of the women who had originally settled this land alongside Primrose Creek, far from familiar places and people, virtually on her own in a beautiful, treacherous frontier, with loved ones to protect. Maybe she *would* learn to shoot.

"Are we going to school tomorrow?" Kiera asked.

Hallie reached for a washcloth and soap, knelt beside the large tub, and began scrubbing their small backs. "I was thinking we might do lessons right here at home, in the evenings," she said. "Maybe you could go to Evie's play-group some afternoons."

Both children seemed delighted. "You'd be our teacher?" Kiera asked.

"Yes," Hallie said. "We can try it, anyhow."

"Wow," Kiley commented.

When their bath was finished, and they'd both dried off with towels and gotten into their pajamas, Hallie oversaw the ritual of brushing and flossing, then tucked her daughters into their twin beds and read them an article from an old issue of *Farm Journal*, that being the first thing that came to hand. Halfway through the discourse on tractor maintenance, they were both asleep.

Hallie smiled, closed the magazine, kissed both Kiera and Kiley on the forehead, and sneaked out of the room.

Downstairs, she went immediately to the window over the kitchen sink, looking for Chance. He'd finished his work and gone, for the barn was dark, and there was no sign of the truck.

Letting the curtain fall back into place, Hallie walked away from the window, made double-sure the doors were locked, and shut off the kitchen lights.

Curiosity, not to mention a deep instinct for self-preservation, sent her to the computer instead of back upstairs, to her bed. She switched the machine on, then clicked the icon that would link her with Jessie's server.

While the program was loading—she'd used the same service herself, and it could be slower than the Second Coming when there was a lot of traffic on the Web—she went into the kitchen again, rummaged through the cupboards until she found tea bags and a mug, and brewed herself a pick-me-up in Jessie's microwave. By the time she returned to the living room, the computer was ready to roll.

She rested her fingers lightly on the keys, her heart racing a little, and went over everything she knew about computers and the Internet, which was comparatively little. She was paranoid when it came to giving away her location, and it would be all too easy to do just that, if she wasn't careful about every single thing she did. Still, she needed to know if there were any new developments.

Jessie's server allowed for a total of seven screen names, and only one was in use. Anybody who might try to trace an e-mail back to its source—and she wasn't about to connect with any of her friends back in Arizona in any event—would get only as far as Jessie's electronic mailbox. Wouldn't they? Besides, she wasn't going to stay around Primrose Creek all that long. She mustn't allow herself to get too comfortable, mustn't come to care too much for the town or the people.

She bit her lip, flexing her fingers above the keyboard, considering potential screen names. Finally, she chose "Primrose," and composed a short message for Jessie. *Hello from Primrose Creek. This is Hallie.* She paused to think, uncertain how to go on. How to establish a relationship with her benefactor, without revealing too much. *The horses seem to be okay, and Chance is sort of overseeing things. The Jeep runs fine. I guess that's all for now, except to say thanks. You can't imagine what your kindness, trust and generosity mean to me. I won't let you down, I promise. Hallie.*

She hit Send, and waggled her fingers again. She sucked in a breath, held it in puffed cheeks, let it out with a *whoosh*. She was thinking of Chance, sitting in that same chair the night before, checking . . . what? Her name? There were a surprising number of Hallie O'Rourkes in the world, living and dead; she'd found dozens of them online when she'd done the research in a northern California library, having decided to take back the surname she'd had at birth, and helped herself to a defunct Social Security number.

Of course, she knew exactly what Chance had been doing. Trying to find out more about her background, and her connection with Lou, whose name he'd seen on the truck title. Irrational panic swept over her and for a few moments she had to battle a purely adrenal urge to jump up, snatch her children from their beds, and race off into the night.

She closed her eyes, breathed deeply. Calmed herself.

Then, hands shaking, she started a search of her own, typing Lou's name into the small box. A great many Lou Waitlins came up, with various spellings, but even with her limited experience, she was soon gazing, in horrified disbelief, at an archived newspaper article, bearing the headline, FORMER PHOENIX POLICEMAN KILLED IN ROBBERY.

Nausea roiled in Hallie's stomach. She clasped the

bridge of her nose between a thumb and forefinger, rub-bing hard. She didn't need to read the piece; she knew the gruesome details by heart, and the image of Lou, lying in his coffin, would never leave her. Dear God in heaven, how she wished she could forget. . . .

Elbows braced on the edges of Jessie's compact com-puter desk, Hallie covered her face with both hands and pushed past the sad memories, into the sweet sanction of earlier times. She went back to her first meeting with Lou—she'd been a year younger than the twins were now—and felt a sense of calmness seeping into her spirit.

It was a week before Christmas, and her mother, Cheryl, divorced since Hallie was a baby, and working as a teller at a bank, had begun dating a man she'd met at work, a young beat cop named Lou Waitlin. When he'd come to pick Cheryl up that evening, for dinner and a movie, he'd brought along a take-out pizza for Hallie and her baby-sitter, a teenager who lived in the apartment across the hall.

Hallie smiled a little, remembering. Pizza had been a rare treat in those days, money being in very short sup-ply. She'd liked Lou immediately, and hoped he would stick around, though even then she'd been a little jaded where things like that were concerned. Kiley was like her in that way, trying to protect herself from disap-pointment by looking at the world through narrowed eyes.

Lou had come back, of course. By the following Christmas, he and Hallie's mother were married, and the three of them had moved into that modest but cozy brick house in Phoenix. They were a family.

Hallie came back to herself, back to the present

moment, and found that there were tears on her cheeks. She dashed them away with the heel of one palm, straightened her spine, reached for her cup. Its contents were lukewarm, but she sipped anyway, and felt at least partly restored. *Ah,* she thought, *the marvels of ordinary tea.* She printed out the article, and after a little more deep breathing and tea-sipping, forced herself to read it. No mention of her name, but she wasn't out of the proverbial woods yet. Leaning in slightly, she ran a search for Lou's obituary, which had been published in the *Arizona Republic* a few days after his death, and it came up almost instantly.

> Louis W. Waitlin, 58, died Tuesday of gunshot wounds. Waitlin, a Phoenix police officer with a twenty-year record of exemplary service to his credit . . . will be buried on Saturday, with full honors. . . . He is survived by his daughter, Helene Waitlin Royer, and two grandchildren. . . . In lieu of flowers, the family requests that donations be made to the Phoenix Police Department's Victims' Fund. . . .

"Okay," Hallie whispered, almost sick with relief. "Okay." Sure, she was mentioned, but not by the name she was using. It wasn't likely that Chance Qualtrough, or anyone else in Primrose Creek, would connect her with the woman mentioned in the obituary. Helene was her legal name, but she'd always been called Hallie.

The musical sound of an Instant Message startled her so much that she nearly spilled her tea. She blinked, thinking the sender might be some random Web surfer, trying to strike up a conversation, then realized who it was.

Hi, Hallie. Jessie here. I'm on my laptop computer. I went online a few minutes ago, and got that "your account is in use" report, so I'm using a different screen name.

A little dizzy, Hallie hesitated briefly before typing her response. *How are you?*

The answer was slow in coming. *Tired. Homesick. Eager to get back to my weaving projects.*

I've been admiring your work, Hallie wrote quickly, and in all truth. The weavings hung throughout the house were as intricately worked as medieval tapestries, although their subjects were always Indian women, performing various tasks. *You have an amazing talent.*

Thank you, came the eventual reply. *But enough about me. Tell me about you.*

Hallie caught her breath. She had to say something, but what? *I'm thirty-two,* she typed, *and I have two daughters, as you know. I used to run a restaurant, and I'm divorced.*

Chance must like you, Jessie answered. *He doesn't usually take to strangers.*

Hallie scraped her lower lip with her teeth. There didn't seem to be anything else to say, at least, nothing safe. *He's been kind,* she replied.

Guess I'd better get myself to bed, Jessie went on. *Big day tomorrow. Oh, and there's room service with my midnight snack.*

Hallie smiled, rested her fingers on the keys. *Good night,* she wrote. *And thank you.*

Good night, and you're welcome. Jessie was gone, and Hallie's aloneness seemed deeper, more profound. She exited the online server, then shut down the computer and covered it neatly. She rinsed out her cup in the kitchen sink, checked the locks yet again, turned off various lights, and headed upstairs.

She was tired, but she dreaded sleeping. She felt all the more vulnerable when she closed her eyes, as though she were letting down her guard. She took a bath, looked in on the girls, who were resting well, and then crawled into bed. She started to read a mystery novel she'd borrowed from Jessie's bookshelves downstairs, but her eyes wouldn't focus. With a yawn, she switched off the bedside lamp, slid down between the sheets, and told herself everything would be all right. She would see to it.

She stretched, getting comfortable, thinking she might actually get some rest. She closed her eyes and, at that moment, somewhere in the chilly autumn night, the animal she'd heard earlier—Chance had said it was a cougar—gave a long, keening screech, as if in torment.

Hallie's stomach jumped, and her heart wedged itself into her throat. Too distraught to formulate a prayer of her own, she used the one that came to mind, the one Lou had taught her when she was small. *Now I lay me down to sleep, I pray the Lord my soul to keep . . .*

Doc Whitman, still a ladies' man at seventy-something, with his shock of white hair, rangy frame, and eyes full of both humor and sorrow, drew his truck to a stop in front of Chance's barn and got out. He was pulling a small horse trailer behind him, and from the sounds of things, the devil himself was tied up inside.

"Mornin'," the older man said, with a pull at the brim

of his misshapen hat. Like Chance, Doc wasn't inclined to spend good money on fancy headgear.

Chance, who had just finished working a three-year-old filly in the round pen back of the barn, frowned. "Mornin'," he answered, and if he sounded a little suspicious, well, he was just going by past experience.

"I brought you a hard case," Doc said, going back to unlatch the trailer and cautiously open the door.

Chance approached reluctantly. "Mighty generous of you," he said, with a marked lack of enthusiasm.

Doc laughed, a raucous, guffaw of a sound, but the expression in his eyes was grim. Even bleak. "Stay back," he said. "I tranquilized this poor critter, but she's still ready to turn inside out."

"Let me get her," Chance insisted, approaching.

"You always were a smooth talker," the vet said, in sporting acquiescence, and stepped back out of the way. The cold morning sunlight struck his oversize belt buckle, the one set with the biggest chunk of turquoise Chance had ever seen. Jessie had brought that buckle back from one of her gallery tours, though both she and the Doc thought nobody knew it.

Chance peered into the trailer, saw a good-looking black mare with three white stockings. "Easy," he said, and laid a light hand on her flank. In his mind, he saw energy coursing through her, and she calmed a little. He slipped in beside her, untied her lead rope, and eased her backward, out of the trailer. "One of these days," he told Doc Whitman, "you're going to get me killed."

Whitman rubbed his chin, admiring the animal. "She's a beauty, isn't she? Her registered name's Winslow's Risk of Flight, but she's called Sugar."

Chance had to agree that Sugar was a fine specimen, but she'd been out to pasture for a while. Her coat was shaggy, and her hooves needed work. She'd thrown a shoe, too, but it was the shivering in her flanks and the frantic roll of her eyes that garnered his attention. "What happened to her?" He knew the Winslows; they had a ranch down near Carson City. They were absentee owners, richer than God, and Chance had never warmed up to them.

For a moment, the doc looked as though he might break down and cry. "Cougar got her foal a few days ago. Dragged it off. She's been in a state ever since, I'm told, though nobody called me until last night. The straight of it is, as far as I can tell, this horse is having a nervous breakdown."

Chance swallowed the bile that surged into the back of his throat at the images playing in his mind—he'd seen what a bear or a wildcat could do to another animal—took the mare's halter in his left hand, and ran his right down the length of her neck. She shrieked as if she'd been branded, and reared. *Easy*, he said again, this time silently. He saw the scene, as if through her eyes, heard and felt the terror she'd known and, worse, the terror of her foal. "Jesus," he breathed aloud.

"You can see she put up a fight," Doc said, coming closer now that Sugar was out of the confined space of the trailer. Chance had already noticed the deep, recently treated wounds on her chest and forelegs.

"What do you want me to do?" he asked. He was a strong man, he'd had to be, but when it came to the suffering of animals or children, his heart turned to glass.

"Bring her back," the doctor answered. "She's the

daughter's horse. The kid's been through hell with lupus this past year, according to the caretaker over there at the Winslow place, and the loss of this animal might just finish her off. Guess she lives for visits to the ranch, and spends just about all her time with Sugar when she's there."

"I'm a rancher, not a horse whisperer," Chance reminded his old friend. "What makes you think I can help?"

"I've seen you straighten out a lot of messed-up horses, that's what," Doc answered shortly.

Chance did know horses. He'd lost both his parents when his dad's small plane crashed, back when he was seventeen, raised himself after that, with considerable help from Jessie, and spent every spare moment either in the barn or out in the pasture, with the animals. That passion had saved his sanity more than once. Except for a few years at the University of Nevada, and some rodeo-ing, he'd rarely left home.

When he didn't speak, Doc took up the slack. "What do you hear from Jessie?" He and Jessie had been an item for as long as Chance could remember, and they seemed to believe it was a big secret from the rest of the world. Rumor had it they'd had some kind of falling out before she went to off to sell the latest batch of weavings.

"She's fine, as far as I know," Chance said. He found himself leading Sugar slowly toward the barn; mentally he'd already assigned her a stall. He would put her next to Rookie, and catty-corner from Cocoa, the sweet-natured bay mare.

"I hear you rounded up a house-sitter for her."

Sugar balked, and Chance paused to reason with her,

stroke her neck again. Even though it was cold outside, she was sweating and radiating heat like an old stove burning dry wood.

"Hallie O'Rourke," he answered, in due time, and in a casual tone. *Or so she says,* he thought.

"Madge told me she's filling in at the Last Chance. Where'd she come from?"

"Phoenix, I think," Chance replied distractedly, concentrating on the silent exchange he was having with the horse, and then wished he hadn't revealed even that small scrap of information. Doc Whitman was a good man, through and through, but he got around, being the only large-animal vet in the immediate area, and he was gossipy when the mood took him.

"She tell you that?"

Chance wooed Sugar through the doorway of the barn and down the aisle toward the stall he'd chosen. There was a long, hard haul ahead, when it came to reaching the mare, but he was committed now, just as Doc had probably figured he would be. He'd never been able to resist a woman in trouble, whether she had two legs or four. "No," Chance answered, "she didn't say."

"Then how do you know she's from Phoenix?"

"I don't," he said, opening the stall gate, stirring the fresh cedar shavings on the floor with his boots as he stepped inside, willing the horse to follow. He'd seen a Phoenix address on the truck title she'd shown him, and guessed the rest, but he wasn't about to go into detail. Hallie was scared, scared half out of her mind, and she probably had good reason for it. Until he knew for certain what she was dealing with, he intended to keep speculation to a minimum.

Doc leaned against the stall door, after Chance and the mare were inside, his woebegone, craggy face wearing a wry expression. "You're taken with her, aren't you? This woman from Phoenix?"

"I'm not sure she's from Phoenix," Chance said, feeling a little testy. He unfastened the lead rope from Sugar's halter and stepped back to give her a little space.

"You mentioned the place yourself." Doc could be like a dog with a bone, when he was in his nosy mode.

"I was just guessing, that's all."

Doc let the subject drop. "This is a valuable animal," he said, assessing the mare with bleak admiration. "The Winslows will pay handsomely if you can bring her around so their girl can ride her again. They figure they'll have to put her down otherwise, and they're probably right. I don't need to tell you that an animal like this is unpredictable—which makes her dangerous."

"I'll see what I can do," Chance agreed. He didn't feel very confident at the moment, but he kept that to himself, like he did most things.

"Their lawyer will fax you a contract sometime today," said Doc, sounding relieved.

"You were pretty damn sure of yourself, weren't you?"

Doc chuckled, shook his head. "On the contrary, Chance, it was you I was sure of, not me."

Chance eased backward to the stall gate, never taking his eyes off the mare until he was clear. He wouldn't be any good to anybody if he let himself get careless. He'd seen better horsemen than he killed or injured by tame animals as well as wild ones, in all sorts of circumstances, and he wasn't going that route if he could help it. He planned to die an old man, warm in his bed, with a flock of grandchildren fighting over his estate. "You explained to these people, I trust," he said, "that this is just a hobby with me, and I don't offer any guarantees?"

"They're clear on that," Doc agreed, more mildly now. He'd turned his attention to Rookie, the little Palomino colt, who was shaping up to be a real knot-head. He belonged to a lady judge down in Reno, and she'd gotten him from some kind of animal rescue outfit. He was moving along about as fast as your average glacier, when it came to recovery, and the judge called every day for a progress report. "How's the lad here?"

Chance sighed. Rookie was out of the corner, but he had his head down and his ears pinned back, ready to kick the living shit out of anybody fool enough to get close to him. "I was going to call you, and I forgot, what with everything that's been going on lately," he said, missing the light that flickered briefly in the doctor's eyes. "I think this little fella's problem might be something internal."

Doc resettled his hat. Sighed. "Besides his attitude, you mean?"

"Yeah. You X-rayed him, didn't you? Ran all the usual tests?"

Doc just looked at him, eyebrows raised. An old-fashioned country practitioner with a steady, modest practice, he was as thorough as they came. Chance would have taken his veterinary trade elsewhere if he hadn't been as good as he was, a lifetime of friendship notwithstanding, but he trusted Whitman with all his animals.

Chance shook his head, studying the colt. He felt a headache taking shape at the base of his neck. He'd missed breakfast, and he had to stop by Jessie's place, whether he was so inclined or not, to look in on the live-stock over there. Her protests aside, Hallie O'Rourke didn't know jack-shit about ranch life, and he wasn't going to trust her with the whole responsibility until he was sure she could handle it. Whether she liked that arrangement or not, that was the way it was.

Doc startled him out of his reflections with a hard slap on the back. "You get a halter on Sport, here," he said, indicating the Palomino, "and I'll give him another going over. Draw some blood, feel around a little."

They had their own private rodeo of sorts, Chance and the doc, but between them they managed to subdue Rookie, at least partially, so that he could be examined.

At one point in the struggle, Doc laughed out loud. "You ever think about getting yourself a real job?" he joked.

Chance chuckled, shook his head. "Nope," he answered. "How about you?"

Hallie looked around the barn, early that October morning, pitchfork in hand, pleased with herself. She'd fed the horses, loaded the inevitable manure into a wheelbarrow, and pitched it into the huge disposal bin behind Jessie's barn, all without getting trampled, bitten or slobbered on. Kiera and Kiley, ready for a new day, looked on from the stacks of hay, the former kneeling, with four kittens in her lap, the latter perched on the edge of a bale, feet swinging. She beamed her approval, and Hallie felt ridiculously proud of her accomplishment.

"Okay," she said, hanging the pitchfork in its proper

place, "I'll just rinse out the wheelbarrow with the hose, and we'll be done."

"Are we going to work at the café now?" Kiera asked, getting into the spirit of the "we" thing.

Hallie consulted her watch, then shook her head, smiling. Things seemed a lot less hopeless than they had the night before. "Not yet. We've got a little time. I'll get cleaned up, and we'll have some breakfast, and run some errands in town. We'll do lessons tonight."

"What kind of errands?" Kiley wanted to know.

"The kind where I buy you a brand-new, never-been-read-before book," Hallie replied, with a bit of a flourish. Not so long ago, she'd thought nothing of virtually cleaning out Toys "Я" Us or FAO Schwarz, and now she was looking forward to buying her daughters one small gift, something they would share. It felt good, this new approach. The simpler and more down-to-earth their lives were, the better.

Both twins hooted and clapped their hands. "Can we get *Harry Potter?*"

"Maybe," Hallie said, and turning, stopped short. The joy drained from her heart, and the smile fell from her lips.

Jase Stratton had just pulled into the driveway, behind the wheel of his sheriff's car. Even without the official rig, she would have known by the expression on his face that he'd come on business.

6

Sheriff Jase Stratton removed his hat as he walked toward Hallie, who stood still as a fence post in the doorway of the barn, watching, waiting. The moment seemed surreal, time out of time, as though it were happening in a void, or some kind of mystical tunnel. His smile was brief and grim, and it fell just short of his eyes.

"Mornin'," he said.

Hallie heard the simple greeting through a pounding haze, and tried hard to hide the fact that she was rattled. Had Joel or the others set her up somehow, persuaded a fellow cop that *she* was the guilty party? She had no doubt that the men Lou had been pursuing were capable of that and a lot more.

"Good morning," she managed. The twins had drawn close to her sides; she was aware of them in every corner of her being, though she could see them only at the periphery of her vision.

Jase was a fine-looking man, with dark hair and a powerful build. He stood now with his hat in his hand, his expression still solemn. The collar of his coat was crooked, and Hallie suppressed an oddly maternal urge to straighten it. "I was wondering," he began gruffly, "if you and I could talk." The poor man looked so extraordinarily uncomfortable that Hallie almost felt sorry for him. "There's some news about the cougar problem."

Hallie felt a chill at the mention of the cat. She hadn't encountered the creature face-to-face, thank God, but she'd heard it screaming in the night, and if she lived another hundred years, she would never forget that sound. She nodded, a little stiffly. "Would you like to come inside?"

He shook his head. "It won't take long," he said, with a nervous glance at Kiera and Kiley. "I'm on duty," he said. "And I don't want to keep you from anything."

Inwardly, Hallie gave a deep sigh. He hadn't come to take her into custody, then, send her back to Phoenix, where she'd be at the mercy of her ex-husband and a lot of other bad people. She relaxed, and he must have noticed, because after that he seemed a little more at ease, too. "What can I do for you, Sheriff?"

"Call me Jase," he urged, still twiddling with his hat.

Kiera and Kiley were bored by then, and began chasing each other between ragged patches of dirty snow. The sun was bright, though there was a nip in the air, and the twins' laughter was like music.

"You'll want to keep the kids close to the house when they're playing. A family up the road had a mountain lion come right into the yard yesterday, in the middle of the afternoon. Tried to attack their dog—chased him under the porch."

"My God," Hallie breathed, laying a hand to her chest. She was a city girl, and knew next to nothing about cougars, but even she was aware that this was bold, even desperate behavior for a wild animal.

"Luckily, Jim heard the carrying on and ran the cat off with a shotgun. The dog's all right." He paused, sighed. "The thing is, if that cat would come in that close to a house, he'd go after a human being the same way he did the dog. A foal was killed up at the Winslow ranch, too."

Hallie felt as though an arctic wind had spiraled down the center of her spine, like a miniature tornado, and she shivered violently, then automatically scanned the horizon, looking for any threat to her children.

Jase sighed. "I wouldn't have blamed Jim if he'd shot that critter on the spot," he said. "He and Trisha have four kids to look out for, after all."

"I'll be careful," Hallie vowed to herself, to Jase, and to the universe, thinking of the rifle Chance had left the night before, wondering if she could actually fire a gun at a living creature, and deciding that she definitely could, if her children were threatened.

"Good," he said. He straightened his collar. Inside his vehicle, the police radio crackled. "I'd better get back to work."

"Thanks for stopping by," she said.

He nodded, got into his rig, and drove away.

Half an hour later, Hallie stepped into Katie's shop, called the Book Shelf, setting the bell over the door jingling. It was a cozy place, though small, with carpeted floors, several overstuffed sofas and chairs, and an old-fashioned wood-burning stove, where a cheerful fire crackled. There was a coffeepot on a table against one wall, surrounded by cups, spoons, napkins, and the like. A second pot was marked "hot water," and a selection of teas awaited nearby. Katie had set out packets of cocoa and apple cider mix, as well, for the children.

Kiera and Kiley headed immediately for the bookshelves, no doubt looking for *Harry Potter*, and Hallie let them go. There were no other shoppers in the store at the moment.

"I'll be with you in a minute!" Katie's voice called from beyond the pink and white beaded curtain covering a doorway behind the counter.

Hallie approached the "new titles" shelf, spotted a romance novel by a favorite author, and felt a pang at not being able to buy it. For the time being, she would borrow her reading material from Jessie's sizable collection, and continue to keep her spending to a minimum. Later, she'd stop by the tiny local branch of the county library, spotted just that morning, and check out a stack of books on home schooling. Sometime in the future, when she and the twins were settled in a new place, a *safe* place, she would be able to splurge once in a while.

Katie appeared, wearing jeans and a white sweater. She was smiling, but there were shadows in the backs of her eyes. "Hallie," she said cheerfully. "Hi."

"Hello," Hallie answered, smiling back. "I promised Kiera and Kiley a book, so they're busy shopping."

"Good. Have some coffee or tea," Katie urged, indicating the refreshment table. "I usually put out some cookies, but I didn't get a chance to stop by the supermarket this morning. I never seem to have time to bake anymore."

Hallie offered no comment on that, though baking had been one of her favorite tasks at Princess and the Pea. Instead, she nodded in cheerful commiseration, and helped herself to coffee. "I wanted to ask you about Evie Callahan and her play-group," she said.

Katie warmed to the subject immediately. "Evie is a wonder," she answered. "I've known her since she was a little girl—I used to be her baby-sitter, in fact. She's always had a way with kids, and of course she's got a degree in Early Childhood Education, as well as all the licenses and permits. She runs her operation out of the old Grange Hall down at the end of Main Street, and tuition is pretty reasonable."

"I'll go and talk to her first chance I get," Hallie mused aloud. "The kids are used to—" She stopped. She'd been about to say that they were used to the stimulation and social interaction they'd enjoyed at school in Scottsdale, but there was unacceptable risk in revealing even that much. It would be too easy to slip, and bring the sky down around her ears.

Katie was watching her closely, a quizzical expression in her eyes, but she didn't pry. Kiera ran up to the counter just then, waving the book she and Kiley had chosen. Hallie smiled, unzipped her fanny pack, and took out the money to pay.

Katie rang up the purchase at the cash register, put the book into a bag, along with the receipt, and made change. "Thank you," she said. Then she handed the bag to Kiera, who took it with pride. Hallie's heart swelled with love for her daughters and, once again, she renewed her vow to keep them out of harm's way, no matter what she had to do to accomplish that purpose.

"I'll talk to Evie this morning, if I have time," she said. "I need to get to the supermarket and the library, and then back home in time to get ready for work."

Katie smiled sympathetically. "It's hard sometimes, isn't it, doing everything on your own?"

Hallie's throat squeezed tightly and, for one difficult moment, she thought she might actually break down and cry. Some conversationalist she was. The perfect opening, a chance to strike up a meaningful friendship with Katie, and did she take it? Certainly not. She felt shy, cautious, even tongue-tied. She did manage a nod, however.

Katie reached out, laid a hand on her arm. "If you ever need to talk," she said quietly, "I'm here. I'm usually at the shop in the daytime. My home number's in the book, and our house is the white colonial with green trim, at the end of McQuarry Road. Stop by if you get the chance."

"I'd like that," she heard herself say. It was as though her voice came from the other end of a long tunnel, instead of her own throat.

The bell over the shop door chimed again, and a group of women came in, talking among themselves, all of them carrying copies of the same book. The latest Oprah selection, no doubt. Hallie recognized several of the elderly canasta players who'd been hanging out at the café the night she and the girls arrived in Primrose Creek.

"It's the Speedy Readies," Katie confided, with an amused smile. "They call themselves that because they go through a new book every week. Most of my groups meet just once a month."

Hallie nodded to the blue-haired, pin-curled contingent. "I'd better get to the supermarket," she said, with a glance at the clock behind the counter.

Katie smiled in farewell, then went over to help the group get squared away for their discussion. They had gathered around the wood stove, talking and shedding their coats, and they watched with friendly interest as Hallie and the girls left the store.

They crossed the street to the bank, where Hallie cashed the check for Lou's old truck with relative ease. She politely skirted the teller's suggestion that she open an account and hurried back to the Jeep. The twins scrambled into the backseat, fastened their seat belts without being told, and began poring over their new book. She heard them reading from it, and marveled.

She felt a now-familiar pang of guilt. They were exceptional children, and they needed mental challenges. Back in Arizona, they'd attended a special program at school. Now, they were little vagabonds, essentially, with one toy and one book to their names, about to be home-schooled by their mother. Hallie was an intelligent woman, but she knew that, by virtue of her inexperience, if nothing else, she was not going to be able to give her daughters the kind of education they deserved, not on her own.

The supermarket was at the opposite end of town from the Last Chance Café, and when Hallie stepped through the whooshing automatic door and took a shopping cart, she was once again struck by the importance of ordinary things. She'd taken so much for granted—buying groceries, for instance—for so long. Hard times had given her a new sense of appreciation for such simple blessings as being able to feed her children.

She made her selections carefully, ever mindful of limited funds, choosing sugar-free cereals, milk, bread, fruit, cheese, hamburger, and the like. She was wheeling her cart into the checkout line when a flyer on the bulletin board beyond caught her eye. Even from that distance, she could make out Evie Callahan's name.

When she'd finished checking out, she read the blurb, then tore off one of the fringe of telephone numbers at the bottom of the flyer and tucked it into the pocket of her jacket. She'd call Evie on her break, maybe, and find out if it would be feasible to enroll the twins in class.

At the library, she found a number of books on the subject of home schooling, and borrowed three, after applying for a card.

Back home, she checked on the animals in the barn, keeping the girls close all the while, in case the mountain lion was prowling around somewhere nearby, then the three of them carried in the groceries and put them away.

When that was done, it was time to get ready for work. She sat the twins down at the kitchen table for a midmorning snack of apple slices, crackers, and cheese, and then dashed upstairs to shower and put on fresh clothes. She was humming when she came down again, after half an hour, feeling as though she could handle anything.

She found Chance Qualtrough in the kitchen, sipping coffee he must have brewed himself, and looking damnably appealing in his jeans, boots and blue chambray work shirt.

Hallie stopped on the threshold, so suddenly that she nearly lost her balance and pitched forward, face-first onto the linoleum. There it was again, that battering-ram sensation in her midsection, a distinct and apparently involuntary overreaction to the presence of this one particular man. Evidently it didn't matter whether the encounter was unexpected or not; she suspected she would have felt exactly the same way if she'd seen him coming from a mile away.

"The girls let me in," he explained, with a twinkle.

She ran her hands down the thighs of her jeans and came up with a wobbly little smile. "I can see that," she replied. "What can I do for you?"

He was leaning against the counter, and now he shifted, mildly uncomfortable. It was reassuring to Hallie to know she wasn't the only one who felt awkward. "I was hoping we could have dinner Sunday night, and maybe take in a movie."

It was no big deal, Hallie told herself. Just a restaurant meal and a show. So why did she feel as though she'd just been asked to take a sunset, champagne-and-violin balloon ride over the Loire Valley? She'd gotten out of practice when it came to dating.

"Can we go too?" Kiley piped up, from the table. She and Kiera had finished their snacks and had been taking turns reading aloud from the book. "Please?" This was in chorus. "Please, please—"

Hallie was about to refuse, make some excuse, when Chance grinned at the kids' upturned faces, which were glowing with anticipation. "Sure," he said.

Kiera and Kiley began to cheer. When had they been to a movie last? At the moment, she couldn't recall. Neither could she bring herself to disappoint them.

"I guess it would be all right," she said, guessing no such thing. Hadn't she already made up her mind to be extra-careful where this man was concerned, to keep her distance as much as possible, both physically and emotionally? "If I don't have to work, I mean."

"The café closes at six o'clock on Sundays," Chance said. He'd set aside his coffee, and folded his arms. He had good biceps, straining a little at the sleeves of his shirt, probably the kind that come from hard ranch work rather than some gym. "Besides, Madge likes to work that day. It's her idea of a social event." He grinned again. And, again, that simple motion of his mouth had the effect of a sucker punch.

"Ummm, okay," she said.

He seemed to be looking deep into the shadowy corners of her heart, though his expression was gentle, and a flicker of amusement moved in his eyes. "You seem a little edgy," he said. "I don't make you nervous, do I?"

"No," she lied.

He laughed.

"Maybe a little," she allowed.

The blue eyes danced. His hat was resting on the counter top, and he reached for it, letting her admission pass without further comment. "How are Jessie's horses?" he asked.

She smiled. "Are you going to try and tell me that you haven't already looked in on them?"

He laughed again. "No," he said. "That was the first thing I did. They look pretty good. You'll call me, though, if you run into trouble?"

There was a promise she wouldn't hesitate to make, on behalf of the livestock, anyway. Or if she saw the cougar. She didn't look up at the rifle hanging over the door, but she was conscious of it, all the same. "You bet," she told him.

He nodded, turned with that rolling, loose-hipped
ease that said *cowboy*, and headed for the door. Before
opening it, he crooked a finger.

She followed him out onto the porch without a
thought, and then could have kicked herself for being so
deferential.

He stood in a way that sheltered her from the crisp
autumn breeze, though she couldn't be sure whether it
was a deliberate courtesy, or a simple accident. He
exuded the good, earthy scents of hay and fresh air and
sun-dried laundry. "Did Jase warn you about the cougar?"
he asked.

Alarm wriggled in the pit of her stomach, and she
nodded, hugging herself tightly against the sense of elemental fear that arose within her. "Yes," she said.

"And have you decided whether or not you want to
learn to use a gun?"

She shuddered hard. She'd grown up in a cop's household, and she'd developed a healthy respect for Lou's
service revolver in the process. The only time her stepfather had ever punished her, in fact, was when she was
nine, and she climbed up and took the pistol from the
top of a high bookshelf, in order to show it to a friend.
When Lou found out, he not only grounded her for a full
month, he cut off her allowance, revoked her television
privileges, and assigned her extra chores around the
house. She'd never gone near the thing again.

"I hate guns," she said, at some length. Imagined
images of Lou's bullet wounds flooded her mind and, for a
moment, she thought she would have to bend over the
porch rail and throw up. Deep breathing saved her from
that humiliation, but barely.

Chance saw too much in her face, in her countenance; he took her upper arms firmly but gently into his hands. "Hallie," he ground out, "look at me."

She looked. She couldn't help it. Nor could she find the impetus to break free of his grasp.

"Tell me about Lou Waitlin," he said.

Her knees went weak, and her vision shrank, in the space of a second or two, to a pinpoint, then expanded again so rapidly that she nearly fainted. She couldn't find words; merely shook her head.

Chance sighed. "Listen, I know he was a retired cop. I know he was murdered in his own living room, in Phoenix. What I don't know is, who was he to you?"

"Don't," she pleaded. He knew too much as it was. If she explained about Lou, the dam would burst. She'd be forced to flee Primrose Creek before she was ready.

He cupped her chin in one hand. "All right," he said gruffly. Reluctantly. "All right. I'll let it go for now, but we've got to talk about this, sooner rather than later."

She gazed up at him, tears stinging along her lower lashes, and that was when it happened. That was when the earth shifted on its axis, when all of creation changed, starting at a point square in the center of Hallie O'Rourke's battered heart.

He kissed her.

She felt a surge of aching energy rise through her center like a shaft of light. Her breath caught, and something turned over inside her, and she put her arms around Chance Qualtrough's neck and kissed him back, hard. Right there on Jessie Shaw's porch.

The contact ended of its own accord; neither Chance nor Hallie pulled away on purpose.

"Uh-oh," Chance growled, after a short interval of stricken silence. His hands were resting lightly on the sides of her waist.

"It didn't mean anything," she said quickly.

He looked at her with a sort of wry annoyance. "Whatever," he replied. He waited a few beats, then added, "I'm going to teach you to use a rifle. No arguments." With that, he was walking away from her, crossing the yard, striding toward his waiting truck, looking back at her over one shoulder. "When's your next day off?"

Hallie gripped the porch railing. She was freezing, and deeply, deliciously shaken, and she didn't have the good sense, evidently, to go into the house. "I don't know," she said.

"Find out," he replied, and then he was inside the truck, shutting the door, grinding the motor to life.

Hallie watched him drive away.

~

"I'll need your Social Security number," Madge announced, as an aside, when Hallie arrived at the café some fifteen minutes after her encounter with Chance.

She'd left Phoenix in a hurry, but that was one contingency she'd covered, thanks to one of a number of fringe Web sites devoted to such topics as the fine art of disappearing without a trace. She'd found another Hallie O'Rourke, one close to her own age, who had died in an auto accident at seventeen, and simply appropriated the necessary statistics. If Madge asked for references, though, she'd be in trouble.

"Sure," Hallie said, busily wiping down the tables in preparation for the lunch rush. "I'll write it down for you.

Do you want me to fill out an application of some kind?" She held her breath, and her smile, waiting for the answer.

"No need of an application," Madge replied. She was restocking the pie cabinet with several fresh examples of Bear's baking wizardry. "You're already hired. Just need the number—you know, for Uncle Sam."

Hallie nodded. "Right," she said.

Madge was untying her apron, getting ready to leave. "I was just wondering," she mused. "Would you rather work the breakfast shift? You'd start at seven and get off at two in the afternoon. Might be better for you, since you've got the kids and all."

Hallie stopped, watched Madge, who wore her usual benign expression. It *was* hard, trying to put in a day's work and keep an eye on her children at the same time. For the moment, hanging out at the café was a novelty to them, but soon they'd start getting bored and restless. "It would be easier," she said, very carefully. Maybe she could find good part-time daycare for Kiera and Kiley, and enroll them in Evie Callahan's school for the rest of the day. That left the evenings for their schoolwork and her farm chores.

"Fine, then," Madge said. "You can start the new shift tomorrow. And we haven't talked about your days off. Would Sunday and Monday work for you?"

"Perfectly," Hallie said, thinking of her date with Chance, for the following Sunday evening. Of course, she assured herself quickly, it wasn't really a *date*, not with the kids going along. More of a friendly outing. Or a field trip. "No sign of Wynona, huh?" She couldn't help thinking of Bear's girlfriend, due to arrive on the bus at any time; when Wynona got there, she would probably be out of work.

Madge rolled her eyes. "Must have been abducted by aliens," she breathed. "God help the poor devils." She peered at the feed store calendar on the wall next to the kitchen doorway. "What's tomorrow? Friday?"

"Saturday," Bear boomed, from behind the grill. Hallie wondered if he'd heard his sister's remark about Wynona and the aliens.

"Saturday," Madge marveled, in a tone of disbelief. She shook her head as she turned away from the calendar. "Where does the time go?"

Hallie sighed. That was a question she couldn't begin to answer, and it had been rhetorical, anyway. Barely a week ago, she'd been another person entirely—a successful businesswoman with a beautiful condo, a nifty BMW sedan, and several bank accounts. Her children had attended a good school, taken dance classes, and enjoyed play dates with their friends. They'd had plenty of toys and clothes, and no cause to be afraid. True, she'd had a difficult divorce to cope with, but lots of people dealt with worse. Then Lou had been killed, and from then on, the pillars of her life had collapsed in rapid sequence, like so many dominoes.

Madge broke Hallie's reverie with a cheerful cluck of her tongue and a shake of her bright-red head. "If I stand around here yammering for another minute, I'll be late for my manicure," she fussed, grabbing her purse from behind the counter and trundling toward the door. "I've got my soaps to watch—I tape them all, you know—and there's bingo tonight at the Knights of Columbus. Five-hundred-dollar blackout."

Bear and Hallie exchanged glances, and Bear made a comical face, but he was obviously pleased that Madge had wasted no time in going out and getting herself a life, once she'd been relieved of some of her duties at the café.

As she stepped outside, she almost collided with a long-legged young woman in tights, a gold sweater, and a short green skirt. Her hair was the color of polished copper, and cut in an attractive layered style. For a moment, Hallie was afraid this was Wynona.

"Hi, Evie," Madge said, with a smile.

Evie smiled back. "Hi, Madge," she replied. Then she crossed the floor, reached across the counter, and caught one of Hallie's hands in hers. She turned it palm up, and bent to study the lines with all the intensity of a brain surgeon peering into an open skull. After a few moments, she lifted round brown eyes to Hallie's face. "Oh, my," she breathed.

Hallie withdrew her hand, a little unnerved. "What?" she whispered.

"Your life is a train wreck," Evie said succinctly, and plunked down on a stool. She instigated a handshake, which Hallie returned by rote, and smiled, lowering her voice a little. "Don't worry, though. It's all temporary. You're going to be married within a few months. You've been together in other lifetimes, you and this guy. Happy every time."

Hallie was practically speechless.

"I'm Evie Callahan," the other woman finished. "And you're—?"

"Hallie O'Rourke," Hallie said, wondering if Evie could tell, with her psychic abilities, that she hadn't legally been an O'Rourke since before her mother married Lou Waitlin. He'd adopted her within a few months.

Evie turned on the stool, admiring Kiera and Kiley, who were coloring at a nearby table. There was no other word for the expression on her face; this was a woman who not only adored children, but understood them on a very fundamental level. "Are those your little girls?"

"Yes," she said. "They're seven."

Evie nodded. "I suppose you've heard about my playschool."

Hallie smiled, glad the café was empty of customers. She could spare a few minutes to talk about enrolling the twins. "I have," she affirmed. "Katie Stratton told me about it. She says you do a great job."

Evie blew on her fingernails and polished them against the front of her sweater, then grinned engagingly. "It's true," she said.

Hallie chuckled. "How many students do you have now?"

"Ten," Evie answered.

"That's a lot of kids for one person to handle," Hallie said, imagining a herd of children running amok, sloshing finger-paints in every direction, pulling each other's hair, jumping up and down on top of desks. Sometimes—more often than not, actually—her imagination got out of hand.

"I have assistants—Polly and Clarissa. And, of course, the angels help out." Evie's expression was absolutely serious.

Hallie swallowed. "The angels?"

"Oh, yes," Evie said. Then her eyes were shining with mischief, and her face broke into a glorious smile. "You think I'm crazy, don't you? Don't you believe in angels?"

She thought it over. "I guess I do. But I didn't know they were in the child-care business."

"Can you think of a better one?"

Hallie smiled, shook her head. "Now that you mention it, I can't."

Evie laughed again. "Well, of course you'll want to see the school for yourself, check things out. What about Primrose Elementary? Have you signed them up?"

"I'm planning to home school, for the time being," she replied, "but I'll definitely stop in at your place as soon as I can." She was intrigued by this woman who read palms and had angels on staff. She liked her immensely, and she knew the kids would, too. "About the tuition—"

"It's doable," she said, and named a figure that seemed within the realm of possibility, even on Hallie's strangulated budget.

Hallie remembered that she was a waitress. "Can I get you something? Coffee? Tea?" *Eye of newt?*

Evie was on her feet again, shaking her head, smiling. "No, thanks. I just came in to look at your palm and invite you to check out the school. I've got to get back— it's almost time for our afternoon left-and-right-brain-integration exercises."

Hallie squinted at the other woman.

Evie nodded, then crossed to the twins, leaving a trail of sparkling fairy dust in her wake. "Most children are geniuses, you know." She smiled winningly at Kiera and Kiley, who were gazing up at her in rapt adoration, and cast her singular spell. "Hi," she told them. "I'm Ms. Callahan."

They chatted for a few minutes, Evie and the twins, and then Evie breezed out the same way she'd breezed in.

"What an amazing person," Hallie remarked, and started when she realized that Bear was standing virtually at her elbow.

"She's that, all right," Bear agreed quietly, and with something more than fondness, something decent and good. "One of our own, Evie is. She went away to college, came back and taught at the elementary school for a while, then decided they were holding the kids back. She got herself a charter from the state and started her own school, just like that."

Hallie wasn't really listening; at that moment, she was thinking about Joel and the people who probably wanted to kill her, while staring down at her own palm and trying to find her lifeline.

7

Chance leaned against the chest-high door, watching as Sugar and the little colt, Rookie, rubbed noses over the cinder-block divider between their stalls. Further proof, he reflected wearily, that misery really does love company. He'd spent all day Saturday and most of Sunday morning working with the pair, separately of course, and hadn't gotten to square one with either of them. Normally, he could get inside a horse's head, inside its heart, but these two were hard cases, blocking him out at every turn. Maybe, though, if he couldn't reach them, they could reach each other.

He straightened, turned. He'd finished the day's chores, except for the second feeding, which he would take care of when he got back from taking Hallie O'Rourke and her daughters to dinner and a movie. He intended to put his concerns—the cougar; the tense situation between Jase and Katie, whose marriage seemed to be falling apart; the horses; and a seemingly irresistible urge to run where angels feared to tread—and simply enjoy the evening.

The plain black wall phone near the tack room rang just as he passed it on his way back to the house. He still needed to shower, shave, and put on clean clothes. He snatched up the receiver. "Hullo," he said, hoping it wasn't Hallie calling to cancel their plans.

The answering voice was Katie's. "Hi, Chance," she said, sounding apologetic and pretty well worn out. In a flash, he saw her at sixteen, shiny-eyed and elfin, queen of the prom. God, he'd been so crazy about her back then, he couldn't see straight. "I hope I'm not interrupting anything."

Chance suppressed a sigh as he leaned against the wall. He was over Katie, had been for a long, long time, but the damage between him and Jase had been done, and there was no going back. "What's up?"

"That woman called again."

Chance consciously relaxed his jaw. "What woman?"

"You know the one. The cocktail waitress in Carson City." Katie began to cry. "Oh, Chance, she says he's still seeing her. Claims she can prove it."

The fingers of Chance's right hand clenched into a fist; he barely kept himself from slamming it through the wall and bloodying his knuckles up good. If Jase had been right there, he probably would have lost it entirely. "Have you talked to him?"

She struggled to gain some control. "No," she said finally. "I told her I had nothing to say to her, and that she ought to call Jase directly if she wanted to talk to him."

"Do you want me to come over?" He couldn't see how his being there would change things—hell, it might even complicate matters—but Katie was his friend and he couldn't just leave her hanging. She'd called him, after all, and that meant she was pretty shaken up.

Katie was silent for a long time. "I don't know what I want, Chance. For all this to be over, I guess. Better yet, for none of it ever to have happened in the first place."

He shoved a hand through his hair. "Okay. Suppose I find Jase and have a word with him?"

"No!" Katie cried. No ambivalence there. "The two of you will just get into a fistfight and kill each other."

He drew a deep breath, let it out slowly. At the moment, he did feel like tracking the sheriff down and beating the last hallelujah out of him, but Katie was right. It wouldn't solve anything in the long run, and one or both of them would end up in a world of hurt. On top of that, he'd have to change his plans for the rest of the day. "Listen, Katie—" he began slowly, awkwardly.

"I know," she broke in. "This is my problem, and I shouldn't be dragging you into it. It's just that, with Jessie gone, well—"

"You think you don't have anyone to talk to," he said kindly. "But you do, Katie. You have Jase. The best thing would be for the two of you to sit down and hash this out, once and for all."

She gave a bitter, broken cry, meant, he supposed, as a laugh. "Do you really think we haven't tried?"

"Then divorce him." It was a challenge, a bluff. He knew it, and so did she, but she bit anyway.

"You know I can't."

"Then I guess you'll have to find some way to work things out, won't you?"

"What is this?" she demanded, but with a smile in her voice, a real one. "Tough love?"

"Something like that. You don't need to me to tell you—or maybe you do—that this isn't good for the kids. They probably feel like they're living in a cement mixer."

Katie was quiet for a long time. "You're different somehow, Chance." The comment didn't sound like a complaint, just an observation. "I don't know, more open or something. What's going on with you?"

"I'm the same guy I've always been," he said, but then he felt the burn of Hallie's mouth beneath his, hot as a fresh brand, and he knew Katie was right. He *was* different. Once, he'd been in total control of his emotions and his life, and now it was as if he'd been hijacked to another planet, where all the rules were different. And it scared him shitless.

"It's Hallie, isn't it?" Katie pressed. At times, usually the worst ones, she could be damned near as perceptive as Evie Callahan. "You like her."

"Yeah, I like her. So what? I like lots of people."

She sniffled, obviously cheering up a little. "Chance, that's great!"

"Now don't go making some big thing out of this. We're going to supper and a movie, that's all. And we're taking her kids."

"You have a date with Hallie?" The tone of her voice made Chance picture Katie all but clapping her hands.

"It's not a date," he insisted.

"What is it, then?"

"It's . . . supper and a movie."

"Why didn't I think of this? She's perfect for you—"

"You don't know a thing about her," Chance pointed out, getting a mite testy. Hell, for that matter, he didn't know squat about Hallie either. Unfortunately, he'd already reached the point where that didn't matter.

"Evie read her palm. She's an old soul."

Chance rolled his eyes. "Oh, well," he drawled, "in *that* case—"

She waited, and he could sense her laughter in the silence.

"At this rate, Hallie'll get a little older, just waiting for me to pick her up. I've got to shower and change clothes, Katie, so if you don't need me for anything—"

"A friend," she said softly. "I'll always need you for a friend."

Funny. She'd said those words to him once before, and they'd broken his heart. Now, years later, they sounded, well, *right*. "You know I'll be here," he replied.

"Good-bye, Chance. Have a nice time."

He smiled, said a good-bye of his own, and hung up. In his mind, he was back on Jessie's doorstep, kissing Hallie, only this time, the kids were nowhere around, and he carried her inside, up the rear stairway, along the hall . . .

He reined in his thoughts, closed and fastened the barn doors, and sprinted toward the house.

———

Chance Qualtrough looked good in his clean, creased blue-jeans, white Western shirt, polished boots, and denim jacket. He'd left his hat at home, and his blond hair, which curled against his collar in back, glinted in the late-afternoon sunshine. He tugged at the nonexistent hat brim. "Howdy, ma'am," he drawled, his eyes full of laughter.

Hallie's defenses were flimsy where this man was concerned, and as she looked at him, she felt them wobble precariously. She stepped back to admit him, felt the heat as well as the impact of his presence, even though they were standing a few feet apart. It was like the aftermath of an earthquake. "Come in," she said belatedly. Stupidly.

He stepped across the threshold. Kiley and Kiera burst into the room, ready to go. As a unit, they launched themselves at Chance, and he caught them, one in each arm, with a chuckle, then carried them around in a big circle, like schoolbooks. They squealed with delight, and Hallie looked away, blinking, her eyes hot and wet. Their longing for a father's presence in their lives was pure and poignant, and Hallie nearly couldn't bear it.

There was a brief silence, and when she turned her head, she saw that Chance was watching her. He set the girls down gently. "Get your coats," he said, and they ran off to do his bidding.

He and Hallie stood there, alone in the kitchen, looking at each other.

"They're starting play-group tomorrow," Hallie said, knowing the remark was out of context, but desperate for something to say. The silence had seemed magnetic somehow, pulling her toward him; she'd had to break it.

"At Evie's place?"

She nodded. "I went over there yesterday, after work, and looked at some of the other children's work. I was impressed."

"It will be good for them."

She nodded again, fresh out of small talk and quite unable to look away from Chance Qualtrough's face. She felt his kiss again, not just on her lips, but as a hot echo that ran throughout her body. Fortunately, Kiera and Kiley returned just then, wearing their coats.

"I never saw a truck with a backseat before this one," Kiera said, when she and Kiley were both buckled in.

"Yes, you have, silly," Kiley retorted. "Daddy's friend Mike has one. We went to Sedona in it once."

Chance and Hallie, settling themselves in the front, exchanged a long look. Hallie was the first to glance away.

"Mommy," Kiera protested, "she called me 'silly.'"

Hallie didn't answer. She was looking out the passenger window, watching the waters of Primrose Creek roll by, sun-dappled and shimmery-clear. She realized then that she wanted to stay in this place, for always. And that, of course, it was impossible. She felt the last shards of her dreams fall, tinkling, to the ground, and her spine sagged a little.

When Chance's hand came to rest on her shoulder, a reassuring touch, demanding nothing, she couldn't bring herself to look at him.

Less than an hour later, they were in Carson City, standing in line to buy movie tickets. Looking around at the other people waiting, families mostly, Hallie was stricken with a sense of loneliness so profound, so elemental, that it nearly brought her to her knees. When she stole a glance out of the corner of her eye, she discovered that Chance was watching her again.

He bought four tickets, and they went in.

"Popcorn, anybody?" Chance asked, addressing the question to the girls.

"Yes!" cried Kiley, stabbing the air with her fist like an

athlete after a score. "Me, too, me, too!" Kiera joined in.

"You'll spoil your dinner," Hallie said.

All three of them looked at her as if she'd just confessed to a long history of alien abductions.

"All right!" she conceded, outvoted, and heard herself laugh, as if from a little distance.

The movie was a comedy about talking dogs and cats, and the twins enjoyed it enormously. When the four of them left the theater, Kiera and Kiley were still wired.

Hallie didn't shush them; she loved the sound of their voices, and Chance was smiling to himself as he watched their antics.

"You guys like Chinese food?" he asked.

A chorus of yeses was his answer, and Hallie joined right in.

They went to a cafeteria-style place, crowded with Sunday evening diners, and got into line behind a man in a clown suit, much to Kiera and Kiley's delight. Just as they reached the cash register, a merry tune sounded, and the fellow produced a cell phone from the depths of his oversize yellow and blue polka-dot pocket. He looked serious, even dour, as he barked, *"Yes?"*

"Clown emergency?" Chance whispered to Hallie, in a tone of mock urgency, and she laughed. In a way, sharing a silly joke made her feel even more vulnerable than the infamous kiss.

The clown glared at her, snapped his phone shut, paid his bill, and took his big floppy feet over to a small table, where he was dining alone. Hallie rolled her eyes at him, then immediately felt foolish. She saw Chance grinning at her, and blushed.

"What a cranky clown," Kiera said.

"I bet he didn't get a nap," Kiley added.

They took a table in a corner, Chance and Hallie on one side, the twins on the other. The clown was forgotten as they discussed the movie, with most of the observations coming from Kiera and Kiley.

When they'd finished eating, Chance tossed them each a cellophane-wrapped fortune cookie, from the little pile on his tray.

"You like Chinese food,'" Kiley read exultantly. Then she made a face. "Well, duh!"

Chance and Hallie laughed. "What does yours say, honey?" Hallie asked Kiera, who was studying the tiny strip of paper with a perplexed expression.

"Be–ware–of–strangers–bearing–gifts,'" she recited.

Hallie bit her lip, looked down at her plate, reminded of the danger she and her children were in. How could she have forgotten, even for a moment?

"Hey," Chance said, elbowing her gently. "It's just a fortune cookie."

She smiled. "You're right," she said, and opened her own packet, pulling out the fortune with a flourish. " 'Your true love is near at hand,'" she read, and then blushed again.

Mercifully, Chance made no comment. His was the only fortune still unread. He held it up with some ceremony, studied it ponderously, as though it contained holy writ, and said, " 'You will meet three beautiful women.'"

The twins' eyes were round.

"Does it really say that?" Kiera asked, in awe.

"Truly?" Kiley added.

Chance folded the slip of paper and tucked it into his shirt pocket, where he tapped it once with the palm of his hand, as if to imprint its message on his heart. "Absolutely," he said.

"What did it really say?" Hallie asked, forty minutes later, when they were all in the truck, headed for Primrose Creek. Kiera and Kiley were sound asleep in back.

"What?" Chance asked, tossing her a sidelong grin. The dim light inside the cab only accentuated his fair hair and white teeth.

"You know what," she pressed. "The fortune."

He smiled. "Why do you ask?"

She swatted at him lightly, then wished she hadn't, because her hand wanted to linger on his shoulder. She pulled it back. "Because I want to know."

"Do you always get what you want, Hallie O'Rourke?" he asked.

She turned her head, looked out at the moon and stars and the dark, towering pines fringing the mountainsides. "Once," she answered, surprising herself, "I had it all."

He waited, but she didn't go on. She'd said too much already.

A few minutes passed. "Seems to me, you've got everything that matters," Chance said, indicating the girls with a slight motion of his head.

She nodded. Smiled. "Yes," she agreed softly. "I know."

He reached over, patted her hand. It was an innocent motion, companionable, rather than romantic, and yet it set off tiny fireworks under Hallie's skin. Her every instinct compelled her to yank it away, but for some reason she didn't. He closed his fingers around hers, squeezed, then took a proper hold on the steering wheel again.

"We had a nice time tonight, Chance," Hallie said. "Thank you."

"I enjoyed it, too," he replied.

She thought again of the families they'd seen at the movies, and later, in the restaurant. Most of them would go home, in groups, to the same houses. The kids would hear a story, say a prayer, slip off to sleep. The mothers and fathers would talk awhile, about bills and Chinese food and clowns with cell phones, and then they would go to bed, and some of them, the lucky ones, would go into each other's arms, and make slow, sweet love.

Hallie ached with a sort of benign envy. She'd been divorced from Joel Royer for a long time, and while she had never really missed the man himself, she'd certainly yearned for the feel of strong arms around her, deep in the night, and for the sound of a masculine voice. She would do just fine if she never had another relationship; even in her current straits, she knew she was complete, in and of herself. Still, the thought of being alone forever made life seem awfully, well, *long*. She sighed.

"Are you married, Hallie?" Chance asked, out of the blue.

The question caught her so off guard that she answered it. "No," she said.

His grin flashed, and he flipped on the turn signal as they pulled off the main road toward Jessie's place. The big trees, ponderosas mostly, seemed to be dancing in the night wind. "Good," he said.

"I'm divorced," she said. What was this, she asked herself. Truth or Dare? "What about you?"

He shrugged. "Never met the right woman, I guess."

"Katie wasn't the right woman?" Now what made her ask a personal question like that? She wouldn't blame him if he told her to mind her own business.

Chance's sigh was heavy. "All that happened a long time ago," he said, pulling into Jessie's driveway. The truck jolted over the rutted road. He grinned again, this time sheepishly, and there was something hollow in his eyes. "I see the gossip mill is oiled and running."

Hallie wished she'd kept her big mouth shut. Not only was this a painful subject for him, it was his private concern. She had no right to meddle. "I'm sorry," she said.

He drew the truck to a stop near the barn. The animals still needed to be fed, and their stalls would have to be mucked out. Hallie looked forward to the physical work, instead of dreading it. She needed the outlet.

"It's okay," Chance said quietly. "After that scene at the Last Chance the other day, you'd have to be an idiot not to figure out that *something* was going on."

She looked at him steadily. "*Is* something going on?" she asked, and was appalled. Maybe she was moonstruck, she decided. Maybe she was possessed. *Something* was making her ask personal questions.

"No," he said, without hesitation. "Not that Jase would believe it."

Hallie heard the kids stirring in the backseat, and got ready to hustle them inside, where it was warm, before starting the barn chores. She had another few moments.

"What happened? Between Jase and Katie?"

"Mommy?" Kiera asked sleepily, from the backseat. "Are we home?"

"You're home," Chance confirmed. "Come on, let's get you inside, where it's warm."

Hallie unlocked the back door, and paused for a moment on the threshold before stepping inside. Maybe she would always do that, when entering a dark house. You never knew what—or who—might be waiting.

Chance reached around her to switch on the lights and, though she knew he had noticed her hesitation— how could he help it—he offered no comment.

"I'll just put the children to bed now," Hallie said, somewhat hurriedly. "Thank you for everything."

He wasn't ready to leave, not quite yet. His expression said as much, and so did the set of his shoulders. She was glad the kids were there, because if they hadn't been, and he'd given her another of those nuclear kisses of his . . .

"I'll see to the horses," he said. "You look after the girls."

She didn't have the strength to argue that she had to pay her own way, depend on herself, even when it was late and she had sleepy babies to look after. She simply nodded, and shooed Kiera and Kiley up the back stairs.

They called good-byes and thank-you's to Chance all the way to the second floor, and he answered with a jovial "you're welcome" before going outside.

Kiley and Kiera each gave their teeth a slapdash brushing, and Hallie helped them into their pajamas. By the time they stretched out in their twin beds, they were already nodding off. Hallie kissed one forehead, then the other, then hurried down the stairs. In the kitchen, she snatched her coat off the back of a chair and pulled it on.

She nearly collided with Chance on the porch, and he grabbed her, steadied her. Her heart did a strange little flip, and electricity surged into the softest and most secret parts of her anatomy. She waited for him to kiss her again, as he had done that other time, when they were standing in exactly this place.

He didn't. He set her away from him, in fact, with a slight thrust of his hands. "No," he said hoarsely, and from the sound of it, he was talking to himself, not her.

She searched frantically for her voice, and found a version of it. "You're—you're finished in the barn?"

He nodded.

"Come in," she said. "I'll make coffee." Hallie had an unusual immunity to caffeine. She could drink half a pot by herself, and drift off to sleep the moment she closed her eyes. In fact, the stuff calmed her.

Chance hesitated, then followed her into the kitchen, took off his coat and hung it from one of the pegs by the door, and pulled back a chair at the table. He sat in silence while Hallie brewed the coffee, apparently lost in his own thoughts.

"You must have a lot of good memories of this place," she said.

He smiled, nodded. "I remember coming here in footed pajamas, when I was three or four. The whole family would gather, McQuarrys, Shaws, Strattons, Qualtroughs and Vigils, and the grown-ups would sit around this same table, drinking coffee and solving the problems of the world. Jase and I and the others would fall asleep on blankets on the floor, and those familiar voices were the last things we heard."

Hallie was touched by this glimpse into Chance's past, and a little envious of it, as well. "Do you have any brothers or sisters?"

Chance shook his head. "Cousins aplenty, though."

"I'm an only child, too," Hallie confided, sitting down across from him, cupping her chin in her hands. "But I didn't have cousins. It was just the three of us."

"Sounds lonesome," Chance commented.

"I guess it was," she recalled, "some of the time, at least. We were a pretty tight unit, Mom and Lou and me—" Too late, she realized what she'd given away. She felt the color drain from her face. A fool. She'd been a *fool* to think she could chat about her past without tripping up.

"So he was your dad," Chance said.

She moistened her lips, looked away, looked back. "Yes," she said.

"And he was murdered."

She nodded. The coffee was finished, and she leaped to her feet, nearly overturning her chair, to get away from the table.

"Hallie."

She stood frozen at the counter, with her back to Chance, her spine as stiff and cold as a spear of ice dangling from a roof in winter. "I didn't kill him."

"But you know who did, don't you?" he asked easily. "And you know why. And you're scared."

"There's so much more to it than that!" Her hand shook as she reached for the coffee carafe; she nearly spilled the stuff when she attempted to pour.

Chance was beside her in a moment, taking the pot from her. "Are you sure you want a jolt of caffeine, in the state you're in?"

"Yes," she said, in a sort of whispering wail. She put both her hands to her mouth and turned her back to him again, fighting to regain her composure. It was, for the most part, a hopeless effort.

He filled the cups, set them on the table, squired her back to her chair, sat her down. "Talk to me," he said.

She shook her head, cupped both hands around her mug, blessed the heat that warmed her icy flesh. "I can't." A burst of frenetic energy surged through her; she should pack, get the girls, leave!

But how? She had no vehicle of her own, and she couldn't steal Jessie's Jeep. The nearest bus station was probably miles away, maybe as far as Reno, and that meant a drive down the mountain, over treacherous, winding roads, in the darkness. She couldn't take a chance like that with her children's safety. On the other hand, were they in any less danger right here, on the banks of Primrose Creek?

Chance caught her hand in his, held it tightly. "Listen to me," he said. "I know what you're thinking, but it won't help to run from this, whatever it is. It's time to stop, Hallie. It's time to stand and fight."

She took a sip of her coffee, then another. Chance got up, went to a cupboard, came back with a bottle of Jack Daniel's. He poured a generous dollop into each of their mugs, and Hallie offered no protest. A delicious, soothing heat raced through her blood with the first taste, and she began to relax a little. Power of suggestion, she figured. She was sure the alcohol hadn't had time to really kick in. "You don't fight these people," she went on, after some time. "Lou tried that, and look what happened to him."

"Were you there when he was killed?"

Hallie shook her head. "If I had been," she whispered, "I'd probably be dead, too." She stared into the middle distance, took another hit of whiskey-laced coffee. "He was shot in the chest."

Chance waited, still holding her hand. He didn't urge her on, didn't speak at all, just rubbed the callused pad of his thumb slowly and soothingly back and forth, back and forth, across her knuckles.

"Have you ever seen a dead person?"

He nodded.

"Somebody you loved?"

"A few," he said.

"Lou wasn't even old," Hallie replied. "He was only fifty-eight."

"That's rough," Chance said. "I'm sorry, Hallie. What about your mother?"

"She died when I was thirteen. Cancer."

He sighed, shook his head, as if to say that the universe was an unfair place. Which, of course, it was.

Hallie realized she was crying and, for once, she didn't try to stop. "Lou was such a good guy," she said. "Decent, through and through. He loved my mother, and he loved me, just as if I were his own. He and Mom tried to have more kids, but after her third miscarriage, they gave it up." She sniffled powerfully. "He must have been disappointed—every man wants a son or daughter of his own blood—but bless his heart, he never let on, never let me think I wasn't enough. Not once."

Chance's smile was slight and crooked and more than a little sad, but it was real. *He* was real, in the same basic, nearly inexplicable way that Lou had been. "I'll bet he was proud of you."

She remembered her coffee, took a big gulp, and nearly choked. She'd forgotten the whiskey.

Chance stood, and patted her back until she caught her breath.

"What did it really say?" she asked hoarsely when he'd gone back to his chair.

"What?" he asked, frowning.

"The fortune," she said. "The one you put in your shirt pocket."

He leaned forward, waggled his eyebrows. "It's private."

"I told you my secret," she pointed out, miffed. "And it was pretty heavy-duty, too. So why all the mystery—it's just a fortune cookie!"

He sighed philosophically. "My point exactly," he said.

She blew out a breath, and he laughed.

"All right," he said. "All right." He reached into his shirt pocket, took out the scrap of paper, and laid it on the table.

She picked it up, read it, read it again. Frowned. " 'You are turning a corner, from new to old,' " she murmured. "That doesn't make sense."

Chance reclaimed the fortune, put it back into his pocket, patted it in the same way he had earlier, in the restaurant. "Maybe to you it doesn't," he said.

She leaned forward. "Now, what the heck is that supposed to mean?"

He chuckled. "You figure it out." He pushed back his chair, with a deep sigh, and got to his feet. "I'd better get home. The new day starts early." He was quiet for a few moments, studying her. "You'll be all right?"

She bit her lower lip, then nodded. "I'll be fine," she said, but she wasn't so sure.

"You won't go running off someplace, in the middle of the night?"

"How would I do that?"

"I can think of several possibilities."

"I'll just bet you can. Well, for your information, I'm

no thief. I wouldn't take Jessie's car, or any of her horses."

He smiled, probably at the image of Hallie trying to escape the high country on horseback, with two kids and her discount-store suitcase. Then he bent, kissed the top of her head, and left. Hallie was still sitting right where he'd left her when she heard his truck start, then drive away.

She waited until the sound of the engine faded to silence. Then she folded her arms on top of the table, laid her head down, and cried. She cried for Lou, and her long-dead mother, and for the kids. She cried for herself, and even for Joel. After that, she stood, went to the sink, and splashed her face with cold water.

She locked the doors, made sure all the latches on the windows were fastened, and went upstairs. She took a long bath, brushed her teeth, slathered on moisturizer, and looked in on Kiera and Kiley. They resembled angels, lying there, smiling innocently in their sleep.

She kissed her fingertips and touched them to Kiera's cheek, then did the same with Kiley.

In her own room, between Jessie Shaw's crisp sheets, she thought of Chance, of the way it felt when he kissed her, and the heat of recollection took her breath away, and kept her awake for a long time, dreaming with her eyes open.

8

The animals were waiting none-too-patiently for their supper when Chance got back to his own place, after leaving Hallie sitting at her kitchen table with tears on her face, and he was grateful for the distraction hard work afforded him, however temporary its effects. Smoke and Magic were there to keep him company while he did the chores, and they stuck to his heels when he went into the house, their toenails clicking rhythmically on the kitchen linoleum. They'd had kibble outside, but he refilled their water dishes before heading for the stairs.

He took a long, hot shower, and when he came out of the bathroom, the mutts were sitting in the hallway, like a pair of sentinels, waiting for him, ears perked. He listened, following their cue, and heard the piteous lament of coyotes somewhere nearby. Although the critters usually howled melodically in the movies, in real life they made a screaming sound, fit to raise the hairs on the back of a man's neck.

The dogs following, he walked into his room, sat down on the edge of his bed, and gazed out the window at the full, chilly moon. For a long time, he'd been content in his mostly solitary life, but that night, he felt downright lonely. Maybe it was the call of the coyotes, but he doubted it. While he was with Hallie and the kids, he'd felt connected, a part of things, Now, he was as melancholy as a stray calf.

He wasn't a religious man, not in the formal sense of the word, but for some reason he thought of the old McQuarry Bible, which had been printed in Boston before the Revolution. He'd borrowed it from Jessie, who was the official keeper of heirlooms, as well as the self-appointed genealogist for the clan, several weeks before she left on her trip. He'd wanted some solid connection to the distant past, because even though he'd lived at Primrose Creek all his life, he sometimes felt rootless.

Jessie was passionate about family memorabilia; she had a large collection of journals, murky photographs, and the like, and she'd offered to let him look those over too, make copies if he wanted, as long as he promised to guard the stuff with his life. They were stored in file cabinets over at her house, near the computer.

He smiled to himself. Damn the luck. Now he'd have to impose on Hallie O'Rourke, getting underfoot on a fairly regular basis, in order to check out all that material. No sense moving the stuff to his place, risking damage or loss. Hadn't Jessie told him, straight out, that she'd take a horsewhip to him if he didn't take proper care of the family papers?

He pulled on a pair of boxer shorts, then went back downstairs to fetch the tattered Bible. The dogs followed, sighing, and plunked themselves down near his desk, eyeing him balefully.

He took the Bible from its place on the shelf and slowly raised the heavy leather cover. There were dozens of names inscribed on the parchment pages allotted to the purpose, the earliest entries in faded copperplate, all sweeping loops and flourishes, with *f*'s where there should have been *s*'s. He turned the page, marveling at the parade of generations, spanning more than two hundred years of one family's history. He found Trace Qualtrough's name, linked with that of Bridget McQuarry, and smiled. He'd come from these people; their blood flowed in his veins and—sometimes he could have sworn to it—their recollections of life as they'd lived it lingered in the back corners of his brain, intermingling with his own memories. He rubbed his forehead with the fingers of his right hand, and thought of Hallie once more, over there at Jessie's place, alone except for the kids, fighting off what seemed like a whole platoon of private demons.

He wished he could bring her here, lie down with her upstairs, in the old bed that had been Trace and Bridget's, so long ago, hold her in his arms, and, yes, make love to her. God, he wanted her so badly that he got as hard and heavy as an anvil every time the notion sneaked into his head. He knew, without having seen her naked, that her skin would be taut, faintly golden with the ripe glow of late summer apricots. And soft. Oh, Lord, she would be soft.

He knew, too, because of the way she'd returned his kiss, that she'd respond, fiercely, vibrantly, to every caress, every nibble, every whispered word. He ached with the need of her—and yet the fantasy wasn't entirely lascivious, for there was an element of deep tenderness in his desire for Hallie O'Rourke. Oh, yes, he planned to carry her to the heights, to drape those shapely legs of hers over his shoulders and work her until they were both shouting, both soaring. But when it was over, he wanted to soothe her, reassure her, cherish her. Slay dragons for her.

He groaned. If he kept thinking along those lines, he'd have to take a cold shower, and that was not a prospect he favored. He closed the Bible, got into bed, snapped off the light and waited for sleep.

It was elusive. Whatever his fantasies might be, he knew that Hallie was just passing through, that she had a life someplace else, one she'd go back to if she had the opportunity. All appearances to the contrary, she wasn't the type to leave a lot of loose ends.

Best not let himself care too much.

—

Hallie felt as though she'd been dragged backward through an emotional knothole. "Get a grip," she told herself aloud. She got up, brewed herself a cup of microwave tea, then headed for the living room, and the computer.

She logged on, found a message waiting from Jessie, smiled when she read it.

Hi, Hallie. I'm in Dayton, Ohio. How is everything in Primrose Creek? Don't forget to use up that food out in the freezer. I don't want it to go to waste. I meant to caution you about Trojan, my miniature horse, too. He can be testy with men, when he's bonded with a female of any species; I guess it's a territorial thing. One time, he bit Doc Whitman, the vet, right in the gluteus maximus. Here, Hallie paused, and chuckled in spite of sympathy for the unfortunate doctor. *Doc had a bruise the size of South Dakota. By the way, call him immediately if any of the animals get sick. His number's on the kitchen blackboard, along with Chance's. Better go, as this is running on. Best, Jessie. P.S. How IS Chance? I haven't heard from him in a few days.*

Hallie hit the reply button, then took a few moments to think, sipping tea as she mused. Her reply was brief. *So far, Trojan is behaving himself. I appreciate your generosity; we'll use what we can from the freezer. As of this evening, Chance appeared to be fine.* She didn't mention the movie they'd gone to together, or supper at the Chinese buffet. It wouldn't do to give Jessie any wrong ideas.

"You've got mail!" announced a cyber-voice, startling Hallie so that she sloshed some of her tea down the front of her shirt. Frowning, she clicked on the appropriate icon, and a whole list of messages came up. Most were junk, with subject lines like *Live Naked Men* and *Triple Your Income in 30 Days.* Hallie deleted those, weeding them out until only two remained. One read *Thanks for the Memory*, while the other simply said *Let's Do Lunch.*

Holding her breath, Hallie opened the first message. *I can't sleep. Can you? I had a great time today. Chance.*

Warmth spilled through Hallie's heart, and she was too tired, too vulnerable, to resist replying. *So did I. Had a good time, I mean. Thanks. Sleep is overrated anyway. How did you get my e-mail address? Hallie.* She hit Send, then opened the remaining message.

Hi, Hallie. It's Katie. I was hoping we could have lunch together tomorrow. Let me know.

I'd like that, Hallie typed, in response to the lunch invitation. She had Monday off, and the girls would be starting afternoon classes at Evie's school, though she planned to map out some lessons for them to work on, too. The home schooling was a temporary arrangement, a means of avoiding Joel's notice, since she would be leaving Primrose Creek and settling somewhere else in the near future, but she took the task seriously. *What time?* With that, she signed off, went upstairs, and started a bath.

She was just sinking down into the hot water when she heard a shrill snarling sound, practically beneath her window, followed by a high-pitched scream that plunged into her middle like a knife. She bolted out of the tub, grabbed a robe off the hook behind the bathroom door, and yanked it on. Her children were safe in their beds—she checked to make sure—their sleep undisturbed. She heard the shriek again, a death cry she would never forget, and rushed down the back stairs.

She was outside, in the moonlight, the grass cold beneath her bare feet, before it occurred to her that she'd acted rashly.

A mountain lion bigger than any she'd ever imagined crouched beneath the clotheslines, devouring a rabbit. Stricken, maybe even a little mesmerized, Hallie stood perfectly still, her heart pounding in her throat, bile roiling in her stomach. The cougar wasn't more than twenty feet away—a couple of good bounds and it would be on her—and when it lifted its bloody face to peer at her, she figured she was next on the menu. She managed a step backward, conscious of the open door behind her. Every primitive instinct she possessed, and she realized now that there were many, compelled her toward that blessed space.

The cougar growled, stretched, haunch muscles poised to spring. Hallie stood still again, thinking of Chance's insistence that she learn to use a rifle. Repellent as the idea had been at the time, it had a certain appeal now, when she found herself face-to-face with an obviously hungry cat. She loved animals, though she had only a nodding acquaintance with most of them, but this was no house pet.

"Mommy?" the voice was Kiley's. Hallie knew, though she didn't dare turn and look, that her daughter was standing on the threshold of the kitchen, a silhouette, a clear target, with the light glowing behind her. "Is that the cougar?"

"Yes," Hallie said, as calmly as she could. "Stay back, baby. Whatever you do, don't come out here."

"But the cougar might eat you!" There was a note of hysteria in the child's tone, and a little awe as well.

"Close the door," Hallie insisted quietly. Evenly.

"But—"

"Kiley Anne Royer, *close the door.*"

"You're supposed to call me Kiley Anne O'Rourke, remember?"

"*Kiley.*"

Several charged moments passed, and then Hallie heard a soft *click.* She let out her breath. She was still in danger, but at least the twins were safe inside the house. The cat would not be able to get at them as long as they stayed where they were.

The cougar continued to study her, still as a snowy morning, and she stared back. Waited. The cat stretched again, languorously, and took a step toward her. Hallie felt a thrill of fear and thought she'd be sick, right there on the ground.

"Go away," she said.

She heard the horses in the barn, kicking up a fuss, and realized they'd been carrying on like that all along. She'd simply been too mired in fear to realize it. Her gaze strayed in that direction. *Was there another cougar? Did these creatures hunt in pairs?* Hallie couldn't have said. In point of fact, she was so scared, she could barely think straight. Her palms were sweating, and she felt light-headed. She risked another step back, and the cat took another step toward her.

A scream rose into the back of her throat, raw and spiky, and she swallowed it. By that time, her heart was beating so fast, and so loudly, that she barely heard the bleating sound of a car horn. The cat perked up its ears, sniffed the air, sized Hallie up once more, and then turned and trotted off into the darkness just as a vehicle came to a gravel-flinging stop somewhere nearby. She felt the small stones strike her, and her knees gave out.

Only seconds later, Chance, carrying a rifle in one arm, scooped her up in the other and half-carried, half-dragged her into the house, lowering her into a chair at the kitchen table.

Kiley and Kiera rushed to her, and she took them into her arms, nearly blind with shock, and held them close.

"Kiley called 911!" Kiera cried.

Hallie chuckled, though she still felt like vomiting, and lifted her eyes to Chance. He was wearing blue jeans, a misbuttoned chambray shirt, boots, and a jean-jacket. She wanted to crawl into his lap and cling to his neck, but of course that wasn't going to happen. She couldn't afford the luxury of letting go like that.

"Thank you," she murmured, addressing him, her brave little daughters, and the universe, all at once.

Chance filled a glass at the sink, his motions angry, and fairly shoved it at her. "Drink that," he ordered. "All of it."

Under any other circumstances, she would have tossed it in his face for having the nerve to talk to her in that tone, but he'd just saved her life, after all. And besides, she felt as though every cell in her body had been freeze-dried. She consumed the water, reconstituting herself.

"You girls did a good job," Chance told the kids. "Why don't you go upstairs and find your mom some slippers and maybe a blanket?"

Kiley and Kiera scampered off to obey, and Hallie was perversely irritated by that. She often had to cajole the twins to mind her, but one word from Chance Qualtrough, and they were rushing to comply.

"What the *hell* were you thinking of?" he demanded, in a husky whisper, the instant they were alone.

Hallie set the empty glass down, her hand shaking visibly as she did so. "If Kiley dialed 911," she stalled, "how come we got you?"

"Jase took the call, and he called me because I live close by," Chance answered, the model of grim impatience. "Jesus, Hallie, do you have any idea what almost happened out there?"

She laid one hand to her chest, willing her heart to slow down to a reasonable rate. "Oh, yeah," she answered, with a flippancy she didn't feel, "pretty much."

He crouched in front of her, took her hands in his. Her gaze strayed to the rifle, which he'd left lying on the kitchen counter, then to the one over the door, and she shivered. His tone was calmer now, and kinder. "Are you all right?" he asked.

Hallie bit her lower lip, nodded. "I heard it scream—"

"The cat?"

She shook her head, her eyes clenched shut, and

shuddered again. "The rabbit. Oh, Chance, it was a terrible sound—"

"You went out there to save a *rabbit?*"

"I *went* because I heard a scream. I didn't think beyond that." She strained, but could no longer hear the horses kicking and neighing in the barn. "Trojan and Sweet Pea and Dolly—"

Chance laid a finger to her lips. "I'll look in on the horses in a few minutes. Right now, I want to make sure you're not going to keel over from shock."

"I'm all right," she insisted, but her eyes stung with tears, and every tiny muscle in her body seemed to be twitching.

Kiera and Kiley returned, bringing the requested items. Chance, still crouching, put the slippers on Hallie's feet, Prince Charming style, and then wrapped her in the blanket and sat down on a chair, settling her on his lap. His arms were strong and warm around her, and though she knew she shouldn't let him hold her, there was nowhere else she wanted to be, just then, but inside his embrace. She let her head rest on his shoulder.

"Is my mommy okay?" Kiera asked, her voice very small.

Kiley elbowed her. "She's my mommy, too!"

Chance's tone was calm, quiet, fatherly. As soothing as Lou's had been, when she was a child, frightened by a bad dream. "Your mother is just fine," he said, "and she's got two of the bravest, smartest little kids in the world, bar none."

The twins' eyes were wide and luminous, and they basked in the compliment. How resilient children were, Hallie marveled. A few minutes ago, they'd been terrified, and no doubt they would have a nightmare or two because of the cougar incident, but for the most part, they seemed to have taken everything in stride. Hallie herself wasn't sure she'd *ever* get the image of that slavering mountain lion out of her mind.

"What you probably ought to do now," Chance went on, still talking to the kids, "is go back to bed. Agreed?"

Kiera and Kiley both nodded solemnly.

"What about our mommy?" Kiera wanted to know.

"I'll take care of her," Chance promised. His arms tightened around her, just a little and, against her better judgment, Hallie allowed herself to be held.

"You won't let her go outside?" Kiley persisted.

"Absolutely not," Chance replied.

The twins looked at each other in consultation, communicating silently, as they often did, then kissed Hallie on either cheek and trundled back up the rear stairway.

"How do you do that?" Hallie asked.

Chance patted her rear end, through the blanket. "What?"

"Get them to obey like that."

"Charm," he answered. And he hooked a finger under her chin, lifted her face, kissed her. It was a light kiss, and brief, probably intended to comfort rather than arouse, but it did both.

She whimpered, stirred a little.

"I'm spending the night," he announced.

She didn't answer. In fact, they sat in silence for some time. Then, still holding her, the blanket trailing like a bridal train, he stood.

"There's a spare bedroom through that doorway," he said, with a nod to indicate the direction.

"I know," she replied.

He didn't put her down. "What I'm thinking is, I want to take you in there, lay you down on the bed, and make love to you."

She trembled in his arms, nodded under his neck. She was a fool, and she knew it, but she'd just come so very close to dying, and everything within her, body and soul, clamored for celebration. She was *alive*, and that was reason enough.

He flicked off the kitchen lights with his elbow as they passed the switch and entered a faintly musty hallway. The door of the small bedroom was open, and he closed it with one foot, once they were over the threshold. The latch made a faint metallic sound as it caught.

The bed, an antique with a white chenille spread, was awash in moonlight. Chance pulled back the covers and laid Hallie down. She didn't resist when he unwrapped her from the blanket, then divested her of her bathrobe, too.

"I knew it," he breathed.

She felt ravishing, lying there, naked and willing. "What?"

"You're beautiful," he replied, unfastening his jeans, slipping them down, kicking them aside. Somewhat to her surprise, he was wearing underwear, as well, though she couldn't see it clearly in the poor light.

He stretched out beside her, making the bed sag in a soft, portentous squeak of springs, and threw the covers off the end of the mattress. That done, he lay on his back, and rolled Hallie on top of him, and kissed her.

She was lost, even then. The kiss sent fire streaking through her, and the size of his erection, pressed between their bellies, took her breath away. She wanted him inside her, without further delay, and wriggled to indicate the fact.

He broke the kiss, chuckling. "Oh, no," he said. "Not yet."

She whimpered, and he moved again, on top of her now. He kissed her eyes, her ears, the line of her jaw, the length of her neck. Despite the chill in that little room, a fine sheen of perspiration broke out all over Hallie's body.

He found her breast, teased the nipple with the tip of his tongue.

"Oh, God," she moaned, pressing him closer with both hands.

He enjoyed her with an exuberance that made her hips dance on the mattress, then reached down to tease her into an even greater frenzy. She had gone a long time without sex—much too long, her senses said—and when he put two fingers inside her, all the while caressing her most sensitive place with the pad of his thumb, she came, in a quick, dizzying spin. When she'd stopped gasping and crying out, she tugged at his hips with both hands, urging him to enter her.

"You're going to have to do a lot better than that," he told her in a rumbling voice, and he began kissing his way down over her rib cage.

A sense of delicious dread overtook Hallie. With Joel, lovemaking had always been over quickly. Chance's approach was clearly different. "You mean—you're not—"

He reached her belly button, and explored it with the tip of his tongue. She knew for sure, then, that things were going to get a whole lot more intense, and she trembled with reluctant anticipation. "I mean," he drawled, "that you're going to give up a lot more than one little squeak before I get through with you. That was"—he moved lower, tasted her—"just the beginning . . ."

He parted her, touched her with his tongue, and she jumped as if she'd just straddled an electric fence. "Chance—" she gasped.

He tongued her, holding her hips, positioning her for pleasure. *Her* pleasure.

By now, satisfied that she'd had a climax, Joel would have been mounting her, rocking on her, his husbandly duty fulfilled, pleasing himself. Chance, on the other hand, seemed committed to driving her crazy, brain cell by brain cell, and he was in no hurry to accomplish the purpose.

"Oh, God," she said again.

He pushed her knees apart, and fell to her in earnest, suckling, now softly, now demandingly. She began to toss her head back and forth on the pillow, breathless, dazed with sensation. A senseless, urging litany fell from her lips, and he cupped his hands under her, and lifted her, the way he might make a chalice of his hands beside a stream. "Sweet," he murmured, between forays, "sweet and warm and wet—"

She sobbed as another orgasm seized her, deep inside, fairly tearing her asunder. She knew she was shouting, knew also that Chance had laid a gentle hand over her mouth, catching her cries, absorbing them into his own flesh.

It seemed an eternity before he allowed her to settle, shivering, to the blanket underneath them, the one he'd cosseted her in earlier.

"N-Now?" she asked, eager to have him inside her.

Desperate for it. She was sure she couldn't bear any more waiting.

"No way," he answered, and began, methodically, to kiss her all over. He kissed the backs of her knees, the arches and insteps of her feet. He turned her over and kissed her shoulder blades, and the small of her back. Then he lay back on the pillows and settled her astride him, not of his hips, but his head. When she felt his tongue again, she grasped the headboard in both hands, threw back her head, and gave herself up to the wildest ride of her life. If she cried out, she had no memory of it.

Finally, when she was utterly spent, or thought she was, Chance relented. He arranged her in the middle of the bed, with two pillows propped beneath her backside, and gently lifted her legs, laying one over each of his shoulders. His erection was huge against the inside of her thigh, and she was amazed to find herself climbing the peak again, from the moment he slipped inside her.

"Yes," she whispered raggedly, as he took her, inch by jubilant inch. "Oh, God, yes—*yes*—"

Even now, when she knew he'd nearly reached the limits of his control, Chance moved slowly, deliberately, every stroke long and hard and hot. Only when she tightened her legs around him, and raised herself, pleading, did he finally let go. He was fierce then, slamming into her, and she gave a low, keening sound as he sent her soaring, once again, over yet another pinnacle. Then, at last, at last, she felt him stiffen, pouring his seed into her. She hoped, wildly, foolishly, that they'd conceived a child, even as she prayed they hadn't.

When it was over, they lay holding each other, their breathing fast and shallow, their bodies wet with perspiration. Even when he rolled onto his back, he kept an arm around her, pulling her close against his side.

A long, long time had passed when he gave a raucous chuckle. "Were you trying to kill me, or what?" he asked.

Hallie twirled an index finger in the rich nest of hair matting his chest. "Me?" she countered. "You were the one who—"

He turned onto his side, grinned wolfishly when she fell silent, suddenly overcome with a strange, virginal shyness. "Yes?" he prompted.

Her face was hot. "Nothing."

"It didn't sound like nothing to me."

Her eyes widened with alarm. "Oh, my God, do you think the girls heard?"

"No," he said. "They're clear upstairs."

"How do you *know* they didn't hear?"

"Because I used to sleep in this room once in a while, when I was a kid. Sometimes, very early in the morning, a certain male friend of Jessie's would sneak out, whistling under his breath and grinning like an idiot."

"Your point is?"

He began caressing one of her breasts, idly. She trembled.

He bent, tasted her nipple. "The point is, Miss Hallie, that I never heard a thing, the whole night through."

She wasn't entirely reassured. "What are you doing?"

He took the time to suckle. "Based on prior experience," he teased, "what do you *think* I'm doing?"

Hallie was already responding, her blood heating, her body writhing a little. She was exhausted, spent. She had nothing to offer. "Not again?" she whispered, her breath catching as she spoke.

He moved to her other breast, had his way with the nipple until Hallie was half delirious. "And again," he promised.

Her protest was lame, and she knew it, but pride compelled her to take some kind of stand, even if it was a hopeless one, utterly lacking in conviction. "We need to sleep."

"We need this a lot more," he said.

Damned if he wasn't right. Within five minutes, she was bucking beneath his tongue again, like some shameless tramp, and then under his hips, and then his tongue again. He was relentless, wringing every last sigh and sob and gasp of response out of her. The sky was turning pink before he kissed her, one last time, dragged himself out of bed, pulled on his jeans, and left the house.

She lay boneless, right where he'd left her, smiling up at the ceiling.

In time, she heard his truck start, knew he was driving away, going home. She missed him sorely, but she was relieved, too. One more sky-splitting orgasm and she would probably have lapsed into a coma.

When she heard the twins in the kitchen, she sat up, pulled the robe around her, and stepped on a pair of boxer shorts. She kicked them under the bed, with one graceful motion of her foot, and joined her daughters.

"You slept downstairs?" Kiera asked, when she appeared in the kitchen.

Apparently, her darling daughters had been planning to make breakfast on their own. They'd gotten out the flour and a dozen eggs, and now they were scrounging for pans.

Hallie nodded.

"How come?" Kiley wanted to know.

She shrugged, looked away, through the window over the sink. The sun was high, and there was a feeling of fall in the air, crisp and somehow festive. "I guess I was too tired to climb the stairs," she said. In a way, it was the truth. Her knees *had* turned to water after the encounter with the cougar, and she probably wouldn't have been able to make it to her second floor bedroom under her own power.

The answer satisfied the girls, thank God. They didn't ask about Chance, and Hallie, who had sorrowed when he left the bed and, subsequently, the house, blessed him for it now. It would have been impossible to explain his presence, had he remained.

"What are we making?" she asked, indicating the flour and sugar with a nod while she started the coffee brewing. Lord, she needed a little tension, a little starch in her muscles and bones; Chance had all but melted her in bed the night before.

"Pancakes," the twins answered, in chorus.

"I was really scared last night," Kiera confided, a few minutes later.

"Me, too," Kiley said. Both twins were covered in flour.

"Hmmm? Why?" Hallie asked, taking over the pancake-making, praying they hadn't heard her carrying on while Chance made love to her.

"Because of the cougar," Kiley said, with exaggerated patience. "He almost ate you."

Hallie let out her breath. "Yeah," she said, knowing it would do no good to minimize the experience. After all, the twins had witnessed most of the drama. "That was pretty scary, all right," she admitted. "But it's over now, and we're safe. All of us."

"What if it comes back?" Kiera asked.

"What if it comes in the house?" Kiley added.

Hallie glanced at the gun Chance had left behind, still resting on the rack over the door. "If it comes back," she answered calmly, "we'll deal with it. It won't come inside the house."

Reassured, at least for the moment, the girls ate quickly, and made a joint project, with their mother, of the cleaning up. Hallie donned jeans and a T-shirt, along with Jessie's coat and barn boots, and went out to feed the animals.

It wouldn't take long; the stalls were pretty clean, and the feeders were nearly full of hay. Hallie took a moment to chat with each of the horses, stroking their necks. Trojan, the miniature, seemed to need extra attention, so she opened his gate and took a step inside.

Rearing, Trigger-like, the little bugger made a run for it, practically trampling her in the process. She leaped to one side, landed in a pile of horse poop, and came up shouting the only horse-word she could think of, which was, "Whoa!"

Trojan loped around the yard, like Seabiscuit taking the track for exercise before a big race, and then stopped, tossed his shaggy head, and nickered, for all the world as if he were laughing at her.

Hallie was frustrated, bruised and smelling of manure, thanks to her crash landing in the stall, but she couldn't help laughing back. The sweet fog Chance had left her in was a thing of the past—*this* was real life. She held out a hand and walked slowly toward Trojan.

"Come on, Snippet," she said. "Your excellent adventure is over for now, but I get the message. You need some range time, even if it's just pretend. So I'll put a lead rope on you later, and walk you like a big dog."

Trojan appeared to be considering the proposition, withholding judgment.

Hallie spread her hands. "I know, I know," she cajoled. "You're *not* a dog, you're a horse, and you ought to be treated like one. But there's a cougar out there." She paused, gestured for emphasis toward the fields and the timber in the distance. "You don't want to end up as an appetizer, do you?"

"Mommy?" It was Kiera, standing a few feet away, without her coat. "Are you talking to the horse?"

Hallie smiled, shrugged, slapped her hands against her sides. "Yes," she said.

"You need a halter if you want to lead him," Kiley put in. She wasn't wearing a coat, either.

"Feel free to fetch one," Hallie said cheerfully, carrying on her stare-down with Trojan while her daughters ran to fetch a pony-size halter from the barn. She took it, moved slowly toward the horse, chattering all the way, and managed to slip the thing onto his head and fasten the buckle. "Bet you shop in the petite section of the tack store, don't you, buddy?" she asked conversationally, as she led the runaway back to his stall.

Later, while taking a hasty shower, she remembered that she'd promised to have lunch with Katie Stratton. She and the girls would stop by the library first, and she'd get them started on a reading project. They'd have to go along on the lunch date, but that shouldn't be a big problem, since they were usually well behaved.

Looking forward to a busy day, Hallie was able to put the events of the night before out of her mind.

Mostly.

9

Feeling a little daring, even reckless, Hallie made an impulsive stop at the Corner Thrift Shop, in town, settling the twins on the couch at the front of the shop, with their coloring books, while she flipped through the racks of consigned clothes. She found two gossamer skirts, one in aquas and darker blues, one in earth colors, accented in crimson, and tops to match. The garments were in good condition, and clean, but it was the price that pleased Hallie most. She'd left behind all but the clothes she was wearing at the time when she fled Arizona, and bought as little as possible for herself in the subsequent Wal-Mart foray, choosing to outfit the kids instead. Now, she found herself craving something cheerful, something *pretty* to wear, and it was no mystery why. Making love with Chance Qualtrough the night before had awakened parts of her spirit that she hadn't known were sleeping.

"Good choices," remarked the woman behind the counter, indicating the clothes in Hallie's arms. She was short, definitely a "plus" size, and wore tiny half-glasses on the end of her nose. Hallie remembered her vaguely as a member of the canasta group stranded at the Last Chance the night of the blizzard, and a plastic tag pinned to her ample bosom read, Hello, My Name Is Doris.

Doris dropped her voice, although she and Hallie were apparently the only people in the shop. "We get a lot of things in from wealthy ladies up at Lake Tahoe, since we're a nonprofit organization. Some of them are even famous. And *they* spend a pretty penny on their clothes, let me tell you. They like to get a tax write-off." Doris fluttered a plump hand. "Rich people!"

Hallie smiled, certain that nobody ever had to "let" Doris tell them anything; it was a verbal flash-flood. She rummaged in her fanny pack for cash.

"Don't you want to try those things on?" Doris asked.

"They'll fit," Hallie answered. Some women are born with curly hair, some with fast metabolisms or a talent for piano. *She* could buy her size off the rack, and always get it right.

The saleslady seemed disappointed, as if she'd hoped to keep the transaction rolling a while longer. "You're the new waitress, over to the Last Chance Café, aren't you?"

Hallie nodded, resisting an urge to glance at her watch. The girls, still seated on the couch, were behaving themselves. "Sort of," she clarified. "I'm just filling in until Bear's girlfriend gets here." It wouldn't hurt to say that out loud every once in a while, so she wouldn't forget and get too comfortable in Primrose Creek.

"Well, Bear and Madge can sure use the help," Doris said, folding each item as though it were *haute couture*, worthy of tissue and gold seals. She dropped her voice to a confidential whisper, shooting a glance at Kiera and

Kiley before she went on. "You know about Bear, don't you?"

Bear was a fry cook, and part owner of the Last Chance Café. That was the extent of Hallie's knowledge where he was concerned. "Bear?" she echoed, and then wished she hadn't left an opening.

Doris jumped right in, a little flushed with the importance of the revelation she was about to make. "Killed a man. Bashed in his head with a crowbar."

Hallie needed to sit down, but that would mean staying longer, so she gripped the edge of the counter instead. Bear, a murderer? It wasn't possible. She glanced back at her children, to see if they'd heard, but they were still coloring industriously. "No," she said.

Doris bagged her purchase and reluctantly surrendered it. "Yes," she insisted.

"Why?" Hallie asked. After all, she spent time around Bear almost every day, and so did her daughters. "Why did he kill the man?"

Doris was on a roll. "He did fifteen years in the state penitentiary for it, too. I don't mind saying, there were those of us who figured that old coot *needed* killing."

Hallie waited, bracing herself against the counter. A conversation with Doris was like one of those wild carnival rides; no matter how scared you were, once it got rolling, all you could do was hang on until it was over.

"I've said too much," Doris announced, leaving Hallie hanging, and clammed up just like that.

Hallie suppressed an urge to lean across, get the woman by the throat, and shake her until she agreed to finish the story. "Is he dangerous?" she asked. "Bear, I mean?"

"Depends on who you ask," Doris replied. Her mouth was in a tight line, as if Hallie had been prying, and she was having none of her gossipmongering.

Thoroughly alarmed, as Doris must have intended her to be, Hallie headed for the front of the store, beckoning to the girls. At the door, she waved as cheerfully as she could and fled, shooing Kiera and Kiley ahead of her.

Doc showed up just as Chance finished grooming the Thoroughbred stud. Smoke and Magic greeted the newcomer with a chorus of cheerful yips, and Doc spoke to them as lovingly as if they were children, stopping to pat each of their heads as he came down the center aisle of the barn.

"Well," Chance commented, with a half grin, "look who came calling. Business most be slow."

Doc sighed and shook his head. "Unfortunately, business is anything *but* slow. I just came from the Rogers place—they lost a cow to that damn cougar last night."

Chance winced, stepped out of the stall, carrying the brush and curry comb he'd used to spruce up the horse after a long morning ride. "Shit," he said. "They need to put a bounty on that cat."

"You know how it is," Doc said ruefully. "There are those who want to see the cougars protected."

It was an old argument, with the ranchers and farmers on one side, and the animal rights people on the other. Chance could see both sides of the controversy, but in this particular instance, he sided with the stockowners. "It's only a matter of time before that cat takes down a human being," he said. "But that isn't what you came here to talk to me about, is it?"

Doc cleared his throat. "No," he admitted finally, with a shake of his head. He took off his worn-out hat, put it on again. "It's about Jessie."

Chance stopped putting away gear until then, and went still. "What about her?"

"She's coming back. Asked me to pick her up at the airport tonight, down in Reno."

Chance's first thought was of Hallie; he wondered if she would leave town now, rather than look for another place to stay. He felt a painful little stab in the pit of his stomach. "And?" he prompted, when Doc just stood there, looking tongue-tied and flustered.

"She said she'd come to an important decision," Doc managed to say, never looking at Chance once the whole time he was talking. "About us. Her and me, I mean."

Chance grinned, slapped his friend's shoulder with a pair of work gloves as he passed, headed for the next stall. He planned to work with the Winslow mare, Sugar, for an hour, then find some excuse to go and find Hallie. Memories of the night before were still thrumming through his bloodstream like drumbeats. He wondered how he'd survive it if she left. "And you figure it's something bad? Maybe she wants to marry you."

There was a *harrumph* in Doc's voice, though he didn't actually make the sound. "More likely, she'll send me packing. We had a hell of a tiff before she left." He paused, searched Chance's face. "I was thinking maybe you could go and get her. Smooth the way for me a little."

Chance rested his hands on his hips and tried to look

stern. "I'm not about to play go-between," he said, and glared at Doc with plain impatience. "Good Lord, the two of you have been carrying on for thirty years, at least. Didn't you and Jessie learn how to talk to each other in all that time?"

Now it was Doc who went crimson, and his jaw clamped down like an old-fashioned bear trap. His eyes, usually twinkling with mischief, were shot with blue fire, reminiscent of heat lightning. " 'Carrying on'? Is that what you think we've been doing?"

Chance chuckled, stood, and ran his hand along Sugar's long neck. "I remember a storm one summer night, when I was eight or nine, and staying at Jessie's place because my folks were away on a trip. I had a nasty dream and, with all the thunder and lightning, I was scared half out of my skin. I ran up the back stairs to tell Jessie about it and son of a gun if you weren't right there in her bed, naked as a jaybird and snoring fit to make the wallpaper come loose."

Doc opened his mouth, closed it again.

Chance laughed. "Now, don't go having a stroke or something. I never told anybody." He paused, frowning. "What I can't figure out is why it has to be such a deep, dark secret. Everybody in the county knows about you and Jessie anyhow."

"They do?"

"Hell," Chance drawled, "of *course* they do. It's such old news, nobody even talks about it anymore."

"Fat lot of help you've been," Doc muttered, flushed. "You just remember, if things go sour between Jessie and me, it's at least partly your fault."

"How do you figure?" Chance retorted, but the old

coot was done talking. He stormed out of the barn and, presently, Chance heard his rig start up.

He chuckled and went to fetch a halter for Sugar, so he could lead her out of the stall and work with her in the corral for a while. He'd just begun when Jase pulled in.

"I just met Doc at the turnoff from the bridge," the sheriff said. "We damn near collided. What's got *his* shorts in a bunch?"

Chance sighed. Shrugged. "Who knows?"

Jase gave the horse a quick once-over. "That's a nice-looking animal, but skittish as hell."

Chance nodded, waited for his onetime best friend to get to the point. He and Jase had been out of the habit of making small talk for a long time. Once, they'd been pals, swimming in the creek, riding all over their combined properties, sharing kid-secrets and big plans for the future. Then they'd reached their mid-teens, and they'd both fallen hard for Katie Robinson, the new girl at Primrose Creek High School. That had been the beginning of the end.

Jase sighed, and his shoulders drooped a little under his official sheriff's jacket. His badge was a cold gleam in the sunlight of that autumn morning. "I came to ask you about the run-in with the cat, over at Jessie's place last night? Did you shoot it?"

"No," Chance answered, recalling that it had been Jase who had called him, after receiving a mayday from one of the twins. "It got away." Hell, he'd forgotten all about the mountain lion, once he'd carried Hallie into that back bedroom and peeled away the blanket and that bathrobe she'd been wearing. . . .

Abruptly, he steered his thoughts in another direction, but the memory of Hallie lingered in his loins, like a molten weight.

Jase took off his hat, shoved a hand through his hair. Chance noticed he was in need of a shave, and he wasn't projecting his usual cock-of-the-walk attitude, either. "We're going to have to put up a bounty, I guess," he said. "Hallie wasn't hurt, was she?"

"She's all right," Chance said carefully. "She was a little scared, that's all. As for the bounty, well, it's about time."

Jase looked uncomfortable. "Listen, Chance—"

"What?" Chance asked, maybe a little too quickly, and too sharply.

Jase narrowed his eyes. "What is it with you? Hell, I know you wanted Katie, and she chose me, but hell, all that happened *years* ago. Don't you think it's about time we worked things out, you and me?"

Chance smiled, keeping his manner and his voice easy. "If you're in the mood to 'work things out,'" he said, "I'd suggest you start with your wife. If it isn't too late. She told me she got a call from your girlfriend the other day. Seems like you need to make some choices and stick by them."

Jase looked ready to bite the top rail of the corral fence right in half. "Damnation," he rasped. "I *have* made my choice—I chose Katie."

"Maybe you ought to tell the girlfriend that."

"I did. And she's not my girlfriend. I made a mistake, all right?"

"You sure as shit did," Chance agreed, beginning to feel a little sympathetic in spite of himself.

"I love Katie."

"You need to convince her of that, not me." First Doc had come around, spilling his guts, now Jase. Hell, who did they think he was—Dear Abby?

Jase was flushed, and one of his hands kept closing into a fist at his side. "You could talk to her. She listens to you."

Chance gave a long, ragged sigh. "Not where you're concerned," he said.

Jase calmed down a little. "What am I going to do?" he asked.

Chance actually felt sorry for him. During Jase's brief but torrid affair with a secretary down in Carson City, a few months back, he'd wanted nothing so much as to knock his teeth out for being stupid enough to throw away a beautiful wife and a loving family. Jessie had maintained all along that Jase would come to his senses and make things right, and she'd counseled Katie not to file for divorce without thinking long and hard first.

Chance reached out, laid a hand on Jase's shoulder. "Park the kids with Katie's folks for a few days," he heard himself say, and wondered where the words were coming from. He wasn't normally one to give advice. "Take Katie away somewhere. Walk on the beach. Look at the stars. Talk to her, and listen to what she has to say."

Jase squinted at him. "You think that would work?"

"It's worth a try," Chance said. He hoped he wasn't turning into one of those sensitive types, always yammering about getting in touch with their inner child. To his way of thinking, most of them would do better to hook up with their inner adult instead.

"She'll never agree to go anywhere with me."

"Have you asked her?" Hell, next he'd be composing

greeting card verses and taking up needlepoint. Was it possible that one night of stupendous sex could change a man's basic personality? Chance shuddered at the prospect.

"Well," Jase allowed. "No."

"Start with that," Chance advised.

"What if she says no?"

"I guess that might mean she thinks you're still involved with the other woman. In which case, nothing would satisfy her except your bringing the two of them together, and making it clear to both of them where you stand."

Jase stared at him. "Bring them together? Are you out of your *mind?*"

Chance shrugged. "What else can you do?"

Jase shook his head. "I don't know. Jump off a bridge, maybe."

Chance laughed, slapped Jase's shoulder again. "That's a little drastic," he said. "However, a bulletproof vest might be in order."

Jase chuckled at that, albeit ruefully, and hearing it felt good to Chance, who'd missed their friendship more than he could have admitted, even to himself. "Right," he agreed, and shook his head again. "I'd better get back to town. This cougar thing is shaping up to be a powder keg."

"See you," Chance replied. He leaned against the corral fence, watched until Jase had disappeared around the bend. Then he turned back to his work, though his thoughts were still with the sheriff. It might be time to stop acting like they had forever to mend their fences.

When Hallie pulled into a parking space in front of the bookstore, Katie waved through the window, turned the Open sign around to Closed, and hurried out, pulling on a jean jacket as she crossed the sidewalk. She smiled when she saw Kiera and Kiley.

"Hi, everybody," Katie said, pausing by Hallie's open window. "Do you want to take my car?"

"We might as well take Jessie's," Hallie answered. "Just point me in the right direction."

Katie nodded and got in on the passenger side, fastened her seat belt, then turned to greet the twins, who were bouncing with excitement in the backseat.

"Sorry," Hallie said. "No baby-sitter."

"It's okay," Katie said. Then she pointed. "Go that way." They drove out of Primrose Creek, past the high school, past the Last Chance Café, onto the state highway.

Katie explained that the restaurant they were headed for was a little roadside place, owned by a woman from San Francisco. They had great pasta salads, and the best chilled avocado soup Katie had ever tasted.

Within fifteen minutes, they had arrived, pulling into a gravel parking lot. There were several cars out front, as well as an RV and a semi. Hallie stopped to study the menu, which was posted outside, and felt a pang of longing, as she did so, for the old days, before the calamity, when she'd still had Princess and the Pea. She missed planning the menus, greeting the customers, trying new dishes.

"Get us a table, will you?" Katie asked hurriedly. "I need to visit the rest room."

"Me, too," said Kiera.

"Me, three," added Kiley.

Hallie nodded, and they all went inside. She stood next to the Please Wait to Be Seated sign, taking in the country French decor, while Katie and the girls vanished down a nearby hallway.

"How many?" the hostess asked, smiling.

"Four," Hallie answered, a little distracted. She'd noticed a middle-aged couple seated at a corner table, and something about the woman seemed familiar.

As she was following the hostess to her and Katie's table, the woman looked up. The jolt of recognition was instant. Margaret Gibbons, her mother's old friend. Cheryl and Margaret had worked together, in the banking field, for years.

"Why, Hallie!" Margaret beamed. "Isn't this a marvelous coincidence! How *are* you?"

Hallie, taken entirely off guard, received Margaret's exuberant hug and tried to smile. If she remembered correctly, the other woman had moved to Denver or Santa Fe or somewhere, when Hallie was still in high school. There had been a going-away party, given by mutual friends, and Lou and Hallie had been invited, though they hadn't gone. Lou had been busy with some big case, and Hallie had avoided the occasion, along with many others, simply because she didn't want to face the empty space where her mother should have been.

"I'm—I'm fine," Hallie managed. "How are you?"

"Wonderful!" Margaret said, gesturing toward the nice-looking gray-haired man seated across the table from her. He was standing now, in gentlemanly fashion, one hand out. "This is my husband, Edward. We're newlyweds, and this is our honeymoon."

"Congratulations," Hallie said. *Stay calm*, she told herself sternly. *They couldn't possibly know that you're hiding out from Joel and his cronies in the police department.* She shook Edward's large, age-spotted hand. "It's nice to meet you."

"What are you *doing* here?" Margaret asked. Then her face fell, and sadness came into her eyes. "We read about Lou. Awful, just awful. I'm so sorry, dear. You've certainly had more than your share of grief for one lifetime, it seems to me."

Hallie felt as though her airway had been cut off. She nodded. "Thanks," she said. She was trying to think of something to add, anything coherent would have done, when Katie and the girls reappeared. Introductions were made—that couldn't be avoided—then Edward, bless him, interceded.

"We'd better get back on the road if we want to make Sacramento before dark, sweetheart," he reminded his bride kindly.

Margaret was plundering her purse. "Here," she said, coming up with a business card, which she thrust at Hallie. "My address and telephone number are both there. E-mail, too. Give me a call, and we'll catch up." She looked at the twins, as if memorizing their faces, then glanced at Hallie expectantly, probably expecting a card in return.

Hallie nodded again—it seemed that was all she could do—and saw, out of the corner of her eye, that the hostess was standing impatiently beside the table she'd chosen for them, tapping the vinyl-covered menus against the palm of one hand. "I will," she lied.

She and Katie and the twins sat down, and Hallie pretended to study the menu, though in reality she was simply waiting for Margaret and Edward to leave. Only then would she be able to breathe again. She was dizzy with adrenaline, forcing herself to sit still when she wanted to leap to her feet and run like a madwoman.

"They're gone," said Katie, who was facing the door.

"Who were those people?" Kiera asked, frowning.

Hallie looked up, surprised. She'd thought she was doing a pretty good job of hiding her agitation, despite the hurricane of emotion raging inside her. "Okay," she said, addressing Katie. Then, to Kiera and Kiley, "I knew the lady when I was younger."

"Can we sit at that table?" Kiley asked, pointing to the empty one across the aisle. "Me and Kiera?"

Hallie smiled. Her girls loved to play "grown-up." "If it's all right with the hostess," she said.

It was, and the twins were soon ensconced at their own table.

Katie leaned forward, lowered her voice. "Are you okay, Hallie? You look ready to jump out of your skin."

Hallie sighed. She couldn't explain in detail, of course, but she didn't want to lie, either. Not to Katie, whom she already regarded as a friend. If she were going to stay at Primrose Creek—which, of course, she wasn't—she was sure the two of them would have bonded for life. "My mother and Margaret used to work together. They were close, and seeing her again—well, it stirred up a lot of old stuff." That was certainly true. She still felt as if she'd swallowed a beehive.

"And Lou?"

So, Katie had heard the reference to Lou. Hallie had hoped her friend was still out of earshot when Margaret mentioned him. "He was my stepfather."

Katie studied her somberly for a long moment, then flipped open her menu. "Well, obviously, you don't want to talk about him," she said, "and that's okay."

Hallie's relief was exceeded only by her gratitude. She thought she might even be able to eat, if she proceeded slowly. She pretended to read her own menu, although in reality she was still too scattered to focus on the tiny, elegant print.

In the end, Katie chose a grilled veggie sandwich, the girls shared a giant cheeseburger, and Hallie opted for the chilled avocado soup her friend had mentioned earlier. Although she'd been starving when they arrived, her appetite had all but deserted her since the encounter with Margaret. She would make a project of the meal, try out the soup, see how it compared to her own recipe.

The food was delicious, as it turned out, though Hallie thought her Princess and the Pea version of the soup was better. She used real cream in hers, and this was made with the fat-free stuff.

Midway through the meal, Hallie was taken aback to see that Katie's eyes were bright with tears.

"I'm sorry!" the other woman whispered, her voice wobbly, rubbing angrily at both cheeks with the heels of her palms. She glanced over at the twins, but they were engrossed in their game of ladies-who-lunch.

Hallie reached across the table and touched her friend's wrist. "What is it?" she asked gently.

The story tumbled out of Katie in a rush, held back for too long, punctuated by soft sobs and hiccoughs, and Hallie listened intently. Jase had had an affair with somebody named Crystal, and he and Katie had been separated since it all came out. Katie loved Jase, she was miserable apart from him, and she'd been hoping they might be able to reconcile, with some marriage counseling, once the emotional dust had settled a little. Then Crystal had called the Stratton house, claiming that she and Jase were still seeing each other.

When Katie paused, Hallie plucked a handful of napkins from the metal holder and offered them. "Men," she muttered. For two cents, she would have told Katie her own horror story, about Joel and his various exploits during their marriage, just so Katie would know she wasn't alone in trusting the wrong man, but of course she didn't dare.

Katie wiped at her face, completely smearing her mascara. "But Jase isn't like most men," she said. "Or, at least, I always *thought* he was different."

"What are you going to do?"

"File for divorce," Katie said, with fierce resolution. Her chin wobbled.

"Are you sure that's what you want?" Hallie presented the question softly. Katie was a strong woman, but she was obviously in pain. A decision made in haste might be repented at leisure.

Katie bit her lip. Her eyes bloomed with tears again, and she shook her head. "I'm not sure of anything anymore," she replied brokenly.

"Well, then you need to wait. If there's even a ghost of a chance that you and Jase can resolve this, and make a new start—"

"I'm tired of playing the fool," Katie interrupted. "What if it's true, what this woman says? What if Jase is still involved with her?"

"Have you asked him about it?"

Katie was silent.

"Have you?" Hallie pressed. Across the aisle, Kiera and Kiley were still chattering away, caught up in an exchange of their own, and paying no attention to the adult drama unfolding at the other table.

"There just hasn't been a good time," Katie fretted. "Jase and I strike sparks whenever we get together. He's jealous, because Chance and I are good friends and—"

Hallie said nothing.

Katie's cheeks glowed with a faint tinge of pink. "Not that there's anything more to it," she said. "Chance and I were an item in high school, and then we broke up. There's never been anybody for me but Jase."

Hallie hoped her relief didn't show. Her body was still buzzing from Chance's attentions the night before, and she definitely had feelings for the man, even though their relationship, if that's what it was, was on a greased track to nowhere. Still, if she'd learned that Chance and Katie really *were* involved, she'd have been devastated, as little sense as that made.

"You need to talk to him," Hallie said. "Maybe the two of you could go away somewhere for a couple of days."

Katie's eyes lit up. "I guess I could close the bookstore briefly, and my mother would keep the girls."

Hallie spread her hands and smiled. "There you have it."

"What if he tells me he loves this other woman?"

"Then at least you'll know the truth," Hallie said.

Katie nodded. "I'm going in and wash my face." She laid a bill on the table. "Here's my half of the check." With that, she was scurrying back to the rest room, purse in hand.

Hallie waited until Katie was out of sight, then took Margaret's business card out of her skirt pocket and studied it. Her mother's old friend was in real estate, and she lived in Colorado Springs.

She let out a long breath and then slowly tore the card into confetti.

Kiera and Kiley finished their shared cheeseburger and glasses of milk, crossed the aisle, and squeezed in beside Hallie.

"Did you like that lady?" Kiera asked.

"You said you were going to call her," Kiley pointed out.

Who needed a conscience, Hallie wondered, when they had seven-year-old twins watching their every move. "I was just being polite," she said, at once defiant and ashamed.

"How come Katie was crying?" This was Kiera.

Kiley rolled her eyes. "She's not going to tell you," she said. "It's a grown-up secret."

Hallie was spared from making a comment on that by the arrival of the hostess, bringing the check. Hallie settled up, left a tip on the table, and headed for the Jeep. By the time she'd unlocked the door on the driver's side, Katie was back, red-eyed, but smiling bravely.

"There's another story-time at the bookstore this afternoon," she said, addressing Kiera and Kiley. "Would you girls like to join us?"

"Can we?" Kiera asked, as Hallie opened the back doors, helping her daughters to scramble in and snap their seat belts.

"Please?" Kiley added.

Hallie chuckled. "Yes, already!" she said, but she was

thinking back to her conversation with Doris that morning, at the consignment shop. Bear had been in prison, the woman had said, convicted of murder. Apparently, a good many people saw the crime as justifiable, or so Doris had implied, but Hallie's children spent a lot of time at the café, as did she. She had to know whether or not Bear represented a threat. She couldn't ask Katie, with the twins right there, and she couldn't work up the courage to approach Bear himself—*pardon me*, she imagined herself saying, *but I heard you were a murderer and I was just wondering if my children and I are safe around you*—nor did she want to question Madge or Jase. Madge, after all, was Bear's sister, and might be defensive. She was uneasy around Jase, for the simple reason that he was a cop, and might have some connection, however remote, with Joel or someone in the Phoenix Police Department.

Everyone else in Primrose Creek seemed to like and trust Bear. For the time being, she would follow their lead.

10

When Hallie stopped by Jessie's place to change her clothes—she didn't want Chance to think she'd dressed up to impress him—she was only mildly surprised to find that his truck was parked in front of the barn.

She shut off the Jeep and, after a moment's hesitation—the pull of him was strong—hurried into the house to change out of her going-to-town outfit and into jeans and a fleece top. When she reached the barn, she'd gotten her racing heart under some semblance of control, though her stomach was doing small leaps.

Chance was busy grooming Sweet Pea, the big gelding, with a stiff-bristled brush. The memory of the night before, imprinted on her cells for all time, shimmered through her, and even as she told herself she mustn't ever let it happen again, an elemental, aching need rose within her. She fought it down.

The wry look in his eyes assured her that he knew what she was thinking, and that mortified her. She felt her face go hot.

"Where are the kids?" he asked, coming out of Sweet Pea's stall and setting the brush aside.

She knew she ought to take a step back, but she'd grown roots, it seemed. "In town," she said weakly. "They're with Katie, at the bookstore."

"Good," he said, and now, all of a sudden, he looked rueful. "We need to talk."

"About last night?" She was filled with dread. Did he regret what they'd done? It was one thing for *her* to be remorseful, but quite another for him.

He sighed, and though his expression was still mostly solemn, there was a sparkle in his eyes. "About Jessie. She's on her way home."

"Oh," she said. It came as a shock, even though Jessie had certainly mentioned the possibility. She'd also said she'd be home only briefly, before going out on another gallery tour, which meant she'd still need a house-sitter. Nevertheless, the reminder that she and the girls were essentially homeless left her feeling bereft. "When— when will she be here? I need to vacuum—"

He came to her, took her hands in his. "Hallie," he said. "Hold on a minute. I don't think she's planning to hold an inspection. I just didn't want you to be taken by surprise, that's all. Doc Whitman is picking Jessie up at the airport in Reno sometime tonight."

Only when Hallie sat down on a hay bale did she realize Chance had maneuvered her into it. He crouched in front of her, still holding her hands.

"What's going on?" he asked reasonably. Quietly.

Hallie shook her head. "I'm okay," she said.

Chance didn't look as if he believed her.

She remembered her original intention. "I wanted to

ask you about something. Today, a woman told me that Bear was in prison for murder. Is that true?"

Chance's jawline tightened. "Yeah," he said. "It's true."

Hallie sucked in a breath, let it out slowly. "He k-killed someone, with a crowbar?"

"Madge's first husband," he said, calm as you please.

Hallie stared at him, stunned.

Chance sat beside her on the hay bale, still holding one of her hands, and stared into the shadows of the barn. The scent of dried sweet grass came to her. "Seth—that was Madge's husband—had beaten her up pretty badly. She was in the hospital, in fact, and the doctors weren't sure she'd ever regain consciousness. Bear lost it, and he found Seth before the cops did. The story was, Seth came at him with the crowbar, bad-mouthing Madge the whole time. Bear got the crowbar away, and next thing he knew, his brother-in-law was lying at his feet, dead. He shouldn't have handled things that way, but most folks tended to sympathize more with Bear than Seth. On account of Madge being hurt and everything."

Hallie ached, picturing the tragedies, one after the other—Madge, suffering at the hands of a man who had promised to love her. Seth, dead. Bear, spending fifteen years of his life behind bars. She put a hand to her mouth, thinking she'd be sick. "Oh, God," she whispered.

Chance put an arm around her waist, held her loosely, but close against his side. He smelled good, felt good.

She barely kept herself from resting her head on his shoulder. God knew where that would have led. "Poor Madge. Poor Bear."

"They've made the best of things," Chance said. "Are you okay?"

She nodded, turned her head, looked into his eyes. "I guess I should have asked Bear, but—"

"I can understand why you wouldn't," Chance said. His arm was still around her, and she didn't want him to move away.

Just then, they heard the sound of a car engine, a door shutting.

Kiley appeared in the doorway of the barn, fuming, closely followed by her sister. Katie was behind them, looking rueful. "Kiera called me Ugly-Buggly Booger Face!" Kiley burst out.

"I'm afraid there's trouble in paradise," Katie said. "They got into it in the car."

Hallie stood, suppressed a smile, gave her daughters a stern look and an exasperated sigh, her hands resting on her hips. Chance was beside her.

"What's this?" Hallie demanded of her children.

"She *is* an Ugly-Buggly Booger Face!" Kiera insisted. Kiera, usually the more manageable of the pair, looked downright recalcitrant.

Kate, standing behind the children, could afford to smile. "Well, I guess I'd better be getting back to town," she said. "Hi, Chance."

"Thank you for bringing them home, Katie," Hallie said, still looking at Kiera and Kiley. "As for you two—"

"I'll walk you back to your car," Chance told Katie, and then they were both gone.

"What's going on here?" Hallie asked her daughters.

"She—" Kiley began again.

Hallie held up a hand. "I know, I know. Kiera called you a name. How did it get started?"

Both kids clammed up, though they wouldn't look at

each other. Their lips were rolled inward and their eyes were narrowed.

Great, Hallie reflected. Jessie would arrive in a few hours, and be greeted by two angst-ridden seven-year-olds. What a fine impression that would make. "We'll talk about this later," she said. "In the meantime, I would like you both to go out there and apologize to Mrs. Stratton for arguing in her car. Then you will go inside, get your spelling books, and work on your lessons before supper."

The twins turned on their heels, in almost perfect syncopation, and headed for the barn door. "Big Baby Butt Face," one of them murmured.

"Tattletale," replied the other.

Hallie rolled her eyes, followed them out, and supervised the apology. Chance, who had been talking quietly with Katie, smiled and squired the girls into the house.

"Sorry," Hallie said to her friend. "They can be bratniks."

Katie, already behind the wheel, chuckled. "I know—I have two of my own."

"Have you spoken with Jase?"

Katie sighed, and her hands tightened slightly on the steering wheel. The engine was running, heater cranked. "I paged him. He's been pretty busy with this cougar thing."

"He'll be in touch," Hallie said gently. "Keep the faith."

Katie nodded, good-byes were exchanged, and then Katie drove away, and Hallie went inside the house.

The girls were at the table, poring over their library

spelling books as though they'd been at it for hours. Chance was at the sink, running water into the coffeepot.

"I was an underachiever, compared to these two," he confided, when Hallie stood facing him, shaken by his presence and at the same time wanting him to stay and stay. "Since when are 'laborious' and 'retinue' second grade spelling words?"

Hallie just shrugged.

Chance reached out, hooked a finger in the waistband of her jeans, and tugged her playfully into his arms. He chuckled when she blushed.

She pulled back, though her heart was hammering in her throat and a slow heat was building between her hip bones. If she wasn't careful around this man, she thought, she'd end up in a segment on one of those TV reality shows, a case of spontaneous human combustion. She went into the living room, started picking up, straightening, fluffing sofa pillows.

"Last night was good, Chance," she said, very quietly, and without looking at him, "but it was also a little premature. We hardly know each other."

He sighed. "All right," he said. "We'll step back a little. But don't expect me to pretend it never happened, because I can't."

"We didn't even use protection," she fretted, barely whispering, but meeting his unwavering gaze. "That was really stupid."

"It *was* a little sudden," Chance allowed. "But I don't have any diseases, if that's what you're worried about."

"Neither do I, but we'd be fools to take each other's word for something like that at this stage, wouldn't we?"

He let the comment pass, since there was no denying it. Unprotected sex was for idiots. "Next time, we'll be ready," he said, and he sounded damnably sure that there would *be* a next time. "Do you think you could have gotten pregnant?"

She felt a rush of sweet sadness, and shrugged. When she'd told Joel she was expecting the twins, he'd said they couldn't afford children, and asked her to get an abortion. She braced herself for a similar reaction from Chance, who was, after all, a virtual stranger and not a husband, doting or otherwise. "Maybe, maybe not. I'm not very regular, so it's hard to tell."

Chance surprised her by putting out a hand to cup her chin, gazing down into her face for a long moment, and then placing a light kiss on the tip of her nose. "If there is a child," he said gruffly, "I want to know, Hallie. I want to be part of his or her life, whatever happens between you and me."

She blinked. "You do?"

A light danced in his eyes. "Oh, yeah," he drawled. "If I ever get that lucky, I might even break down and buy a lottery ticket."

Hallie didn't know what to say. In fact, she was afraid she'd cry if she tried to speak at all. Suddenly, she was reminded of Lou, seeking her out after he and her mother were married, telling her he was a lucky man, getting a beautiful wife *and* a daughter, all in the same day.

Chance smiled and ran the backs of his fingers down her cheeks. "Maybe one of these days, you'll trust me enough to tell me what's going on in that head of yours."

Hallie felt a delicious tension, drawing her insides taut. She was flushed, not just in her face, but from her hairline to her feet, and it was literally all she could do to keep herself from telling Chance everything. She remembered, though, that she was leaving Primrose Creek, sooner or later, and lowered her head. "I'm just passing through, Chance," she reminded him, when she was able to meet his eyes again, some moments later. "What's the point in exchanging a lot of confidences?"

He frowned. "What was the point of last night?" he asked.

She lifted her chin, trying to find level ground. She pretended she hadn't heard the question. "Will you stay for supper?" she heard herself ask, and was astounded. Jessie would be back that night; she had cleaning to do, plans to make.

He grinned, as if he were reading her mind. "I'd like that," he said. "Are you a good cook?"

"If only you knew," she said, and sighed a little.

"Yeah," he agreed. "If only I knew."

She went around him, headed for the kitchen. Took a package of chicken out of the freezer compartment above the refrigerator. "Peel some potatoes," she instructed and, to her surprise, Chance did as he was told.

Later, when the four of them, Chance and Hallie and the twins, were seated around the kitchen table, enjoying fried chicken, mashed potatoes, and green beans from Jessie's pantry, he told her about the McQuarry Bible and the various genealogy projects Jessie was working on, among other things.

After supper, he cleared the table and did the dishes while Hallie went through the upstairs like a cyclone, dusting, changing sheets, putting fresh towels in Jessie's bathroom. The twins, grumbling, went back to their mom-imposed spelling lesson.

Presently, Hallie came downstairs again, helped herself to a cup of Chance's coffee, and went over her daughters' work. They'd done a good job, and she told them so, but when she sent them to bed early, because of their earlier row in Katie's car, the little faces looking back at her were dark with impending rebellion. Hallie stood her ground and, in the end, the twins excused themselves and slogged up the back stairs like a pair of slaves headed for the salt mines.

Chance was smiling when she looked at him. "They're quite a pair," he said.

"Quite," Hallie agreed.

"Why don't you enroll them in school in Primrose Creek, instead of teaching them yourself?"

She set her hands on her hips. "Sometimes—no, most times—you ask too many questions, Chance Qualtrough."

"Part of my charm," he replied, unruffled.

"I have my reasons," she said, flustered.

"I'll just bet you do."

"What is that supposed to mean?"

"You're not going to drive me off by picking a fight, Hallie," he said. "So give it up."

She sat down at the table with a plop, holding her coffee mug in both hands.

"You're beautiful when you're being put-upon," he teased. He took in her face, breasts and hips in an impudent sweep of his eyes. "But then, you're pretty hot the rest of the time, too."

"Go home, Chance," she said, but she didn't mean it, and he obviously knew.

"And leave you to face Jessie by yourself?" he asked, with mock horror. "No way." He turned to get the coffeepot from the counter, and she picked up the dish towel lying on the table and flicked his tight cowboy butt with it, then was appalled with herself. What had she been thinking?

He pulled her to her feet with one hand, snatched the towel from her with the other, slipped it around her hips, and hauled her against him. She leaned back slightly, and he increased the delicious pressure.

"Best not to start something," he rumbled, "if you don't plan on finishing."

Heat surged through her. Her nipples tightened, and she thought the ache between her legs would never go away. But she didn't try to move out of his embrace.

Chance bent his head, tasted the peak of her right breast through her shirt, then her left, and she moaned. When he loosened his hold on the dish towel, she nearly fell on her backside.

"Maybe you'd better go upstairs and tuck the kids in for the night," he said, his eyes laughing. "I'll look in on the horses."

Because she didn't know what she'd do if she stayed, Hallie turned, without a word, and fled up the stairs. She heard Chance's deep, wholly masculine chuckle behind her, and smiled in spite of herself.

He was playing with fire, Chance admitted to himself, as he pulled on his jacket and headed for the barn. The cold wind, buffeting his face, restored some, but not all, of his good sense. He had no business getting involved with Hallie O'Rourke. She was just passing through, she'd said so herself, and one of these days she was going to be gone for good.

He tilted his head back, looked up at a sky full of stars. The sight made him feel reverent, gave him a deep sense of the sacred, even as he lusted after Hallie O'Rourke. He'd have given just about anything, right then, to be alone with her, to take her down in some pri-vate place and feed the fire that was consuming both of them until it raged out of control and slowly, slowly burned itself out.

He was just letting himself into the kitchen again, twenty minutes later, when Hallie came down the stairs, looking frazzled and moist and utterly delectable.

"They're in bed," she said, with relief. "Any sign of Jessie?"

"Are they sleeping?" he asked, and wriggled his eye-brows.

She tilted her head to one side. "Don't get any ideas," she told him, but there was a sparkle in her eyes, and a little smile lingered at the corner of her sweet, soft mouth.

"Too late," he ground out. Truer words had never been spoken, God help him.

She laughed. "I'll make another pot of coffee," she said. "This might be a long night."

He nodded, sighed again. He was going to suffer the tortures of the damned before it was over, unless he 1) made love to Hallie, or 2) threw himself into the creek to cool off. Since the second scenario seemed much more likely to happen than the first, for the time being at least, and likely to give him pneumonia into the bargain, he elected to endure. Hell, he'd never known a hard-on to last more than, say, six weeks.

There was nothing to do, once the place was tidy and the kids were asleep, but wait for Jessie to arrive. Chance got out some of the family memorabilia Jessie kept, and they looked at photographs.

Bridget and Trace Qualtrough, and their children, posed in front of the house Chance lived in now. These were Chance's people, his ancestors. How amazing and wonderful that he could link himself, generation by generation, to these pioneers.

A dark-haired woman, imperiously beautiful, with her handsome blond lawman-husband. That was Christy and Zachary Shaw. Jessie was descended from them, and they'd lived right here, in these very rooms.

A third likeness showed a lovely, slender vixen, probably a redhead, with a handsome man who resembled Jase. The back of the picture was inscribed "Megan and Webb Stratton. Our honeymoon."

Yet another photograph revealed another lovely woman, with brown hair and wide-set, expressive eyes, standing beside a tall, powerfully built man with a square jaw and an attitude. "Skye and Jake Vigil," Hallie read aloud.

"Quite a crew," Chance observed. He was in a chair near the fire, reading old letters.

Hallie nodded, set the pictures carefully aside, and reached for a slender volume resting on the coffee table.

The diary had a cloth cover, partially eaten away, but the handwriting inside was still bold and strong, even after the passing of well over a century. Hallie handled the volume with careful awe.

On the first page of yellowed vellum, she read, "The Remembrance Book of Bridget McQuarry, State of Virginia, Christmastide, Year of Our Lord, 1859." A shiver of anticipation and something else, something almost mystical, went through Hallie. She glanced up at Chance, who was still bent over his letters.

Hallie turned to the opening entry in the journal of Bridget McQuarry, one of the first settlers at Primrose Creek.

> Granddaddy left this book beside my plate this morning, at the breakfast table, with a snow white ribbon tied around it. I shall keep all my secrets in these pages, all my joys and sorrows. . . .

She closed the book with a small sigh. A diary was a private thing, even if the woman who'd written in it was long dead. Perhaps it was a violation for her, a stranger, to read young Bridget's most private thoughts.

Chance looked up—perhaps he'd heard her sigh—and gave her a questioning smile. "What?" he asked.

She took a few moments to sort through her thoughts and emotions. "Do you have any idea how blessed you are?"

He didn't speak, but his expression was a questioning one.

"You're part of a—well, a *lineage*—you have a history. A connection." And, she added to herself, he obviously *appreciated* that connection, valued it, sought to sustain it, if he was at all interested in old pictures, diaries and letters. Which, of course, he was.

As far as Hallie was concerned, that said a great deal about his character and his capacity for commitment, all of it good.

"So do you," he pointed out. "Everybody has ancestors, Hallie."

"But with me, with most people, it's simply biological. My mother was a single parent when she met my stepfather. I never knew anything about her family, or my father's. It didn't seem important for a long time, but now that I have children of my own, I wish—"

He left his chair, came to perch on the arm of hers. "You didn't know your real father?"

"Lou was my real father," she said. "He raised me. He loved my mom, and he loved me. He supported us both, in every way." She bit her lower lip. "The sperm donor, as Mom always called him, was some guy named Michael O'Rourke. She didn't like talking about him, and if she had so much as a photograph of the man, she never showed it to me. There must have been some kind of scandal attached—maybe they weren't married when she got pregnant. In those days, that was a big deal. Maybe her mother and father, my grandparents, just cut her out of their lives."

"And maybe it was the reverse. Maybe they're out there somewhere, your mother's folks, wondering about you. Have you ever tried to find out?"

How could she tell him that she'd been in survival mode for most of her life, dealing with the early loss of her mother, meeting and marrying Joel, having babies, building a successful business, coping with a divorce? Now, on the run as she was, she could hardly go poking around in her past, leaving a paper trail and perhaps drawing unwanted attention to herself. "It wouldn't do any good," she said, at some length.

He watched her in silence for a long moment, then answered, "It's your decision. But maybe you're going to go on feeling as if there's a piece missing until you figure out who you are, where you came from."

She studied him, trying to imagine what it would be like to be a Qualtrough, with pictures of your forebears, journals and correspondence written in their own hand-writing. She couldn't even imagine it, and she felt set adrift, like a boat with its mooring line cut. Finding no words to say, she shrugged again.

Chance leaned down and kissed the top of her head. "Jessie's taking her sweet time," he said, after a few moments. "Maybe I'd better just go home, and try to get some sleep." His tone indicated that he didn't hold out much hope for that, and Hallie could empathize. They'd been doing innocent things all evening, but the air between them was charged, practically striking sparks.

Then they heard the engine outside, in the crisp, cold darkness.

Hallie set the diary aside, as tenderly as if it were a living thing, with nerves and senses, and walked with Chance to the kitchen door. He took his hat and coat down from the pegs and put them on. She hugged herself and stepped out after him.

Jessie, a tall woman with a long, silver-black braid, got out of a pickup truck, assisted by a handsome gray-haired man. The legend on the truck door clued Hallie in to his identity—Hal Whitman, DVM. He went around, after opening Jessie's door, and hoisted two suitcases out from under a tarp in the back of the rig.

Chance hugged Jessie, then took the bags from Dr. Whitman. When he turned back toward the house, Hallie could see that Chance was smiling to himself, and she wondered why.

"I'm Hallie O'Rourke," she said, putting her hand out to Jessie.

Jessie beamed. She was wearing slacks, a beautifully woven poncho in shades of turquoise, sand and rose, and boots. "And I'm Jessie Shaw."

"Hal Whitman," the man said, and shook Hallie's hand. "Folks just call me Doc."

"Come in," Hallie said, and then felt foolish. Of course they'd come in—this was Jessie's house. *She* was the visitor here, not them.

Inside, there was a hubbub as Jessie's things were carried to her room, and when she came downstairs, they all sat down at the kitchen table to drink coffee, despite the late hour.

"What a day," Jessie sighed, reaching for her coffee cup. "Please tell me this isn't decaf."

Chance laughed. "It's high-octane," he assured her, "just the way you like it."

They talked for a while, all of them, but it was soon apparent that, caffeine or none, Jessie was exhausted. Chance and Doc said good night, and left together, and there were Jessie and Hallie, standing there in the kitchen, looking at each other.

"The place looks wonderful," Jessie said. "Let's get some rest. We can talk in the morning."

Hallie only nodded. Tired as she was, she was a long time getting to sleep that night. Maybe she'd been rash, running away from Joel, hiding the cashbox full of evidence Lou had probably spent months, if not years, gathering. Maybe there was some sort of misunderstanding, something easily explained, and she and the girls could go home for good. Back to Scottsdale, where they had friends, a comfortable condominium, money.

Except that, for some strange reason, Arizona didn't seem like home anymore, even though she'd lived there all her life.

Now, wasn't that a strange thing?

Very early the next morning, before it was even light outside, Hallie awakened to a distant, rhythmic sound. After a few moments, she recognized it as the song of a loom. Jessie was weaving.

Hastily, Hallie scrambled out of bed, pulled on an old robe of threadbare chenille, and went downstairs.

Jessie, looking magnificent in jeans and a simple, long-sleeved white blouse, her salt-and-pepper braid resting over one shoulder, smiled at her. "I hope I didn't disturb you," she said. "The coffee's made."

Staggering a little, Hallie made her way into the kitchen, poured a cup, came back. "You must miss this place when you're away," she said to Jessie. "I know I would."

"Do you like it here?" Jessie asked, looking down at her weaving for a few moments. A pattern was already taking shape, though Hallie couldn't recognize any images yet.

"Yes," Hallie answered. "Very much. I appreciate your letting the girls and me stay here while you were away."

Jessie frowned prettily. "You sound as though you're planning to leave soon."

Hallie shrugged one shoulder, took a steadying sip of her coffee, holding the mug in both hands. "I understood that it was a temporary arrangement."

"Where would you go?"

The question filled Hallie with bleak contemplation. "I'm not sure," she finally admitted.

"Just away?"

"Pretty much, yes."

"I wish you could stay."

"So do I," Hallie answered, before she could catch herself.

Jessie raised one dark eyebrow. "Then why don't you? I'm on the road a lot, and I could really use somebody to help out around here. Chance is good about it, but he's got a lot to do on his own place."

Hallie was at once pleased and chagrined. On the one hand, she wanted to stay, wanted to be a part of the Primrose Creek community. On the other, well, it would be wrong to make Jessie think she was going to be around for a long time, somebody she could depend upon, when she would probably be gone in a matter of weeks, if not days.

"You could keep your job at the Last Chance Café, of course," Jessie said, when the silence grew long.

"For now," Hallie said, very carefully, "I'd like to stay. As for the job in town . . ."

"You can go on using my Jeep to get there," Jessie

helped out when Hallie ran out of steam. "I usually walk or ride a horse when I want to go somewhere."

Hallie couldn't help being struck by the woman's kindness, and by her trust. "You don't know very much about me," she reminded Jessie.

Jessie smiled. "I'm a good judge of character," she said, and turned her full attention to her weaving.

Hallie lingered for a few moments, basking in Jessie's easy acceptance, then went upstairs to get ready for a new day.

11

A row of empty dog food cans lined the rickety saw-horse Chance had set up at the far end of Jessie's pasture. Beyond the barbed wire fence rose a high, stony dirt bank, perfect for absorbing stray bullets. It was late afternoon, and Hallie had finished her shift at the café early, since business was slow. The animals at both Chance's place and her own had been taken care of, and Kiley and Kiera were at Evie Callahan's school. Jessie, home just three days, was already packing for a second gallery tour, this one aimed at the West Coast.

Hallie stood stiffly as Chance handed her a .32-caliber hunting rifle. The thing weighed heavy in her damp hands, and she wanted to throw it down, turn on her heel, and simply *run*, with arm-pumping, heart-pounding speed. It was the memory of facing a mountain lion in Jessie's backyard, with no way to protect herself and her children, that kept her standing still. She had a choice here. She could go on being afraid, feeling helpless, and running away, or she could prepare to fight back. She could stand her ground.

"You're making a big deal out of this shooting thing," Chance told her. "There's no need to do that. It can be easy, if you'll let it."

"Maybe it's easy for *you*," Hallie said. "It just so happens that guns are dangerous." Now *there* was a flash; trust her to offer a penetrating insight.

"That's the whole idea," Chance responded patiently. He stood behind her, set her hands in place on the rifle, covered them lightly with his own. His breath was warm on the side of her neck, his torso hard against her back and bottom. "What good would they be if they fired cotton balls?"

It would be a different, better world, that's what—not that there was any use in saying so. Hallie moistened her lips. Her arms felt weak, and when she slipped a finger into the trigger guard, she shuddered. "I'm not sure I can do this," she said. She was in serious danger of losing her lunch.

"You can," Chance replied, "and you will."

She sighed. She wasn't going to mention it, of course, but she couldn't help recalling, with him standing so close and all, the glorious night they'd passed together, in Jessie's spare room bed. Nervous as she was, she felt a stab of heat and thought she smelled ozone.

He showed her how to site in, bracing the butt of the rifle in the hollow of her shoulder, and when she fired, the recoil threw her back against him with startling force. She knew she'd have a bruise where the gunstock struck her flesh; the impact rattled through her bones. Meanwhile, the hard contours of Chance's body were practically fused to hers. It was as if every cell in her body had its own runaway heartbeat.

For all this, the cans on the sawhorse stood untouched, as if taunting her, but there was a hell of a chink in the trunk of the venerable ponderosa pine just on the other side of the fence.

I'm sorry, Hallie told the tree silently.

Chance steadied her, though belatedly, it seemed to her. "Try again," he said.

"No," she replied. It was part rebellion, part plea, that one small word.

"Yes," he answered.

She'd made a choice: running away—or even *walking* away—was no longer an option. Her knees had turned to butter. Resigned, she cocked the rifle, guided by Chance's hands like before, set the stock against her sore shoulder, and fired again. There was a pinging sound, and a sharp, metallic smell. Small stones rolled down the dirt bank in a mini-avalanche.

It was hopeless. *She* was hopeless. "This is hopeless!"

He took a playful nip at her earlobe, and she was uncomfortably reminded of wild horses she'd seen on TV, the stallion moving in on a mare in similar fashion, with mating in mind. The parallel all but took her breath away. New energy surged through her. "You're a woman, Hallie, and that's a magical thing. Show me your power."

Fire roared through her, partly sexual, partly pride, all but scorching the earth at her feet. She fired, and missed, reloaded, and fired again. She'd made nine shots before she managed to nick one of the tin cans—it teetered on the sawhorse, and finally fell into the grass. The whole thing seemed to happen in slow motion.

The shooting lesson continued until twilight began to

gather around them. Then they got into Chance's truck, and headed back to Jessie's house.

Evie was just arriving, behind the wheel of a small green Toyota with a bumper sticker that read, I Brake for Gnomes. The twins were buckled into the backseat, and though Evie waved cheerfully as she got out of the car, Kiera and Kiley stayed put.

Grateful that she and Chance were no longer alone— it wasn't him she didn't trust, but herself—Hallie hurried to greet her visitor. Evie had told her earlier that she would bring the girls home after play-group.

"Hi," Hallie said, waiting for Kiera and Kiley to jump out of the Toyota and steamroll her in their usual fashion, all giggles and hugs and waving papers. She was puzzled that they hadn't already done so.

"We're decorating the Grange for the Harvest Festival," Evie explained. "It's sort of a tradition. There's chili and cornbread—lots going on. I was hoping Kiera and Kiley could join in. And you're invited, too, of course."

Hallie's tendency to be overprotective surged to the fore, but she contained it. Her situation required constant vigilance but, at the same time, she did not want the children to grow up in constant fear. They'd been through more than their share already, thanks to the odyssey she'd taken them on. "Okay," she said carefully. "I guess that's all right."

Evie nodded, clearly pleased, and favored Chance with a bright smile. "Hi," she said, eyes twinkling. "I hear Jessie's back."

"Hello, Evie," he responded cordially, with a nod in his voice. His tone was that of a fond older brother. "Jessie's home, but she's just passing through."

Evie shook her head. "She must hate being away from her loom and her horses so much. Not to mention Doc."

Chance laughed. "Doc's a sticking point, all right," he agreed.

Hallie looked toward her daughters, who waved through the windows of Evie's little car, their faces wreathed in hopeful smiles. They wanted to go back to town and join the decorating party, there was no doubt of that. She nodded slightly, to signal that she'd given her permission, and they bounced and applauded, eyes alight.

Hallie walked over to the Toyota, as casually as she could, and leaned in through the open window on the driver's side.

The twins greeted her with a chorus of "hi's."

"Hi," Hallie said, smiling. God, they were so beautiful, so precious. Her love for them was a consuming, desperate thing, bigger than anything else in her life, bigger than she was.

"You're not going to change your mind, are you?" Kiley fretted, and Hallie felt a deep pang. "All the other kids get to be there. We're going to have chili for supper, and put up all kinds of neat decorations—"

Hallie smiled. "Sounds like too much fun to miss. Maybe I'll join you."

Kiera squealed with delight at this, Kiley beamed, and the two of them high-fived each other. It was a plan.

"Good idea," Chance said, when Hallie told him that she'd decided to accept Evie's invitation to help out with the festival preparations.

Hallie gazed toward the house, where Jessie had been weaving at her loom, almost nonstop, since her return to Primrose Creek a few days before. It would do the other woman good to get out for a few hours, see some of her friends, relax a little.

Evie read her mind, or so it seemed. "Bring Jessie," she said. "What about you, Chance? Will you be there, too?"

He hesitated, but only briefly. "Sure," he said. He was looking down into Hallie's face, though he spoke to Evie. "We'll be along in a little while."

Evie nodded and got back into her car, honking the horn once as she drove away. The twins waved exuberantly from the back window.

"You're freezing," Chance said, and steered Hallie toward the porch, up the back steps, into the kitchen. The steady *thunkety-thunk* of Jessie's loom filled the house with a low, comforting rhythm.

Chance closed the door, and leaned against it, at the same time pulling Hallie into his arms. He wedged his hands into the back pockets of her jeans and pressed her close again. His warm breath touched her mouth, played there, causing her flesh to tingle. "If we were alone," he teased, filling her senses with his scent and substance, "I do believe I'd make an effort to seduce you right about now."

It wouldn't take much of an effort, Hallie thought, but she wasn't about to make an admission like that aloud, obvious as it probably was. Instead, she heaved a great sigh. "Ah," she said, "but we're not alone."

The loom stopped. "Hallie?" Jessie called. "Chance? Is that you?" A moment later, she was standing in the kitchen doorway, elegant in her jeans, loose-fitting shirt of dark green silk, and custom-made boots. A brilliant smile set her classic features alight. "How did shooting practice go?"

Chance frowned at her, ignoring the question. "You're working too hard," he replied.

Hallie realized that she was standing very close to Chance and stepped back too quickly, and too late. Jessie's eyes danced with sweet, weary mischief.

"It runs in the family," Jessie answered.

"We're going to town for the evening," Chance replied. "And you're coming with us."

"That," Jessie told Hallie, "runs in the family, too. Bull-headed stubborn bossiness, I mean."

Chance laughed. "So it does," he agreed.

Jessie sighed philosophically. "I'd better get a wrap," she said.

Five minutes later, they were all in Chance's truck, headed for town.

There were a lot of vehicles parked outside the Grange Hall and inside, the place was jumping. High school students were hanging orange, yellow and crimson streamers from the ceiling. Members of the canasta crowd, clad in colorful sweatshirts and double-knit slacks, stirred enormous pots of chili in the old-fashioned kitchen. Children arranged cornstalks in corners while others, in stocking feet, chased each other between bales of hay and goofy-looking scarecrows, and slid like skaters on ice.

Hallie took it all in, delighted by the festive atmosphere and the homespun simplicity of the celebration. She'd spotted her daughters first thing, seated at a table with a flock of other children, helping to make a chain by interlocking small loops of autumn-colored construction paper. Sensing Hallie's presence, they looked up, waggled their fingers briefly, and then turned back to their work.

Meanwhile, cries of delight greeted Jessie's arrival.

Men, women and children embraced her by turns, asked about her trip, expressed the fervent hope that she wouldn't stay away so long next time. Hallie noticed Doc Whitman standing to one side, watching Jessie with his heart in his eyes, and something turned over inside her, made her look up at Chance.

He was looking right back, his expression humorously solemn, in that way that was his alone. "Let's get some chili," he said quietly. He laid a light hand to her lower back, and she didn't flinch the way she always had with Joel, didn't feel the slightest urge to move away. Instead, she let him squire her toward the long counter between the main part of the community hall and the kitchen. Bowls rose in teetering stacks, soup spoons stood upright in decorated coffee cans. There were paper napkins, too, along with packets of saltine crackers, plates of fresh cornbread, and pats of butter molded into small, smiling moons. A card table had been set up at the end of the obstacle course, and an older woman in a flowered muumuu sat behind it, taking money, stashing it in a metal cashbox.

Seeing the box, Hallie flashed momentarily on her adventure at Lou's house, that last afternoon in Phoenix, and she sank her teeth into her lower lip. She'd stashed the evidence in a place where Joel and the others would never find it, but if they were to find her first, or the children . . .

"What is it?" Chance asked, putting his wallet away. He carried a bowl brimming with chili in his hand, with a big slice of cornbread perched on top, and Hallie realized, with some surprise, that she'd dished up a bowl for herself without ever noticing.

"Nothing," she lied, and tried to smile. That night, when she got back to Jessie's place, she'd go online, check the Web for news from Phoenix, something she hadn't been able to bring herself to do, until now. Maybe there had been some break in the case, some development that would set her free.

Some tables had been set up near the small stage at the other end of the hall, and they sat, Chance and Hallie, eating and chatting with fellow diners. Kiera and Kiley put in a brief appearance to tell Hallie that they'd eaten when they arrived, then rushed back to help with the paper chain.

"They're great kids," Chance said, when he and Hallie found themselves alone. It wouldn't last, this solitude— the food line was getting longer, and people were headed that way with bowls of chili and plates of cornbread and cups of steaming coffee.

Hallie laid down her spoon, smiled. "Thanks," she said. "I think so, too."

An awkward silence descended then; Hallie wanted to ask Chance if he'd ever thought about having a family of his own, but she couldn't think of a way to phrase the question without sounding as if she were in the market for a husband.

Chance was watching someone over near the door; she followed his gaze and saw Kate and Jase step inside, accompanied by their two daughters, Ellen and Janie, pretty little girls in matching blue coats. Their parents seemed shy with each other, as if they were teenagers on a first date.

"Looks like they're speaking again," Hallie commented. She would have given anything to know what was going through Chance's mind at that moment.

"Let's hope it lasts," Chance replied. He turned back to her, gave her his full attention.

Madge approached, beaming, wearing a sweatshirt with a smiling pumpkin painted on the front. Battery-operated lights flashed on and off all over the front of her torso. "All right, you two," she joked, "enough of your lollygagging around. I'm in charge of making popcorn balls to sell at the festival, and I need all the helping hands I can get."

Thus drafted, Hallie and Chance dutifully trooped into the kitchen, washed their hands at the big steel sink, and commenced shaping sticky gobs of popcorn and syrup into large balls. Someone else wrapped each one in colored cellophane and attached a bit of ribbon, while Madge ran the popper on top of the stove. Out in the main hall, an impromptu band assembled itself; there were two guitar players, and someone sat down at the keyboard of the town's ancient, out-of-tune piano.

After almost two hours, a new crew was conscripted, and Hallie and Chance were released from their duties. Kiera and Kiley were with the Stratton girls and some other children, playing hide and seek. Jase and Katie were dancing, along with a few other couples, waltzing and staring into each other's eyes while everyone else jitterbugged.

Chance pulled Hallie into his arms and swept her out onto the floor, into a waltz all their own.

"If I kissed you right now," Chance whispered into her ear, "you'd probably taste like a popcorn ball."

She laughed. "Are you insinuating that I ate some of the product?"

"No," he replied, "I'm saying so, straight out. I was right there, remember? I saw you."

"You did a little pilfering yourself, if I remember correctly," Hallie pointed out, her tone prim. She caught sight of a flurry of movement at the edge of the dance floor, recognized Jessie and Doc Whitman. They were jitterbugging. "Well, will you look at that?"

Chance looked, chuckled. "They've never been able to keep away from each other for very long," he said.

"They're in love?"

"Oh, yeah," Chance replied, "I'd say so. Trouble is, they're both so damned stubborn and independent that they can't agree on what to have for supper, let alone how to make a relationship work."

"That's sad," Hallie said.

Chance's gaze was direct. "But not all that uncommon."

She realized that he could have been, and probably was, talking about her, and about himself. The insight made her so uncomfortable that she had to change the subject. "I suppose I should be heading for home," she said. "I've got work tomorrow, and lessons with the girls—"

Chance sighed. "Any time you're ready," he said, but he didn't sound happy about leaving.

They said good-bye to Madge, greeted Katie and Jase, exchanged pleasantries with a few other people, then corralled the kids, got them into their coats, and made for the door. Jessie, reluctant to leave her weaving earlier, was still dancing with Doc Whitman. Chance had already checked in with her, and reported back that Jessie would be home later.

"Or not," he added, with a twinkle in his eyes.

Hallie smiled and shook her head.

At home, Chance saw Hallie, Kiley and Kiera safely inside the house, said good night, and looked in on the horses before driving away in his truck. Hallie watched through the kitchen window until the taillights disappeared into the darkness, then went upstairs to help the girls get ready for bed.

Kiley and Kiera had already brushed their teeth, washed their faces and hands, and put on their pajamas. It was model behavior, and that made Hallie suspicious.

"What are you two up to?" she demanded, as she tucked them into their beds.

Both her daughters were the very personification of innocence. "We're just trying to be good," Kiley said.

"Ah," Hallie said, and kissed one small forehead, then the other.

"Do we still have a daddy?" Kiera asked.

Hallie's heart cracked. No way out of this one. "Yes, sweetheart," she said softly, "but you might not see him for a while."

"Does he want to hurt us?" Kiley asked. Her voice was very small.

Hallie couldn't help it. She started to cry, sitting there on the side of her daughter's bed, and both children scrambled into her arms, clinging.

"No," Hallie managed, after a very long time. "No, honey. Daddy doesn't want to hurt you." She prayed it was the truth.

"He was chasing our car," Kiley reasoned.

"He was yelling," Kiera added.

"And you were scared, Mommy," Kiley went on. "You

wouldn't have drove so fast if you weren't scared."

Hallie hugged her daughters tightly for a long moment, then stood them at her knees, so she could look straight into their small, earnest faces. "Listen to me," she said, very gently. "There's a lot happening right now, and I can't really explain it. Not until you're older."

Both the twins looked unconvinced, but for the moment, it was all Hallie had to offer. They kissed her cheeks, then climbed into their beds.

"Can we talk about Daddy?" Kiera's small voice piped, when Hallie shut off the light, lingering in the doorway. "Or is he a secret?"

Hallie wanted to curl up in a fetal position and block out the world, at least for a little while, but of course she couldn't afford that luxury. Her life, as well as the lives of her children, was at stake. "Both," she heard herself say. "We can talk about Daddy anytime, the three of us. The rest of the time, we need to keep things secret."

"Does he love us, Mommy?" Kiley asked.

Hallie hugged them both. "Yes," she said, and she knew it was true. In his own way, as best he knew how, Joel loved his daughters. He had to.

"What about you?" Kiera pressed. "Does he love you?"

She ruffled the child's hair, shook her head. "No, sweetie, I don't think so. But we were close once—we made you two—so it was good that we were together."

The girls seemed satisfied with that answer, at least for the time being, and nestled into their blankets.

Hallie moved off down the corridor, down the stairs, through the front room. She made tea in the kitchen and helped herself to Jessie's computer in the living room.

She flipped the proper switch, logged on to the Internet, hooked up with a news site, then narrowed her search to Arizona. Time for another update on what was happening in Phoenix.

The newspaper story broadsided her, took her breath away.

Charles Long, 66, a native of Phoenix, was found dead in his garage, inside his car on Tuesday evening, by a concerned neighbor. Long was a victim of suicide, according to Metro police . . .

"Charlie," Hallie whispered, the image of the man sitting next to her at the bar, the night of Lou's wake, filled her mind. She saw him handing over the packet with the key to her stepfather's cashbox, heard his voice. And she was as sure as she'd ever been of anything that he hadn't killed himself.

She pushed back from the computer, shaken and sick, and sipped her rapidly cooling tea until she began to feel a little better. When the phone rang beside her, she was so startled that she nearly fell out of her chair.

She answered on the second ring. "Shaw residence."

"Very professional," Jessie said warmly, from the other end of the line.

Hallie chuckled. Just the sound of another adult voice helped. "Thanks," she said. "I try."

Jessie hesitated, went on. "I'm not coming home tonight," she said, all in a rush.

Hallie smiled to herself. "Okay," she said.

"I didn't want you to worry."

"I would have," Hallie replied. "I appreciate your letting me know."

After that, there wasn't much to say. Jessie and Hallie exchanged good-nights, and then Hallie hung up the receiver and made the rounds of all the doors and windows, setting the locks wherever necessary.

She went upstairs, looked in on the girls, then took a quick shower, washing away traces of syrup from the popcorn balls and quietly mourning Charlie Long. She needed to tell someone what had really happened to Charlie, someone with the power and authority to help her face down Joel and the others, once and for all. Someone who could take the evidence Lou had gathered and use it as he'd intended, to bring a mob of rogue cops and corrupt officials to justice.

There were lots of people in the Phoenix Police Department whom she could trust—the problem was, she didn't know who they were.

The next morning, after she'd fed the horses and returned to the house to make breakfast for her daughters, now squabbling in the living room, Hallie made her first attempt to ask for help. She called information, asked to be connected with the nearest field office of the FBI.

The moment the line was picked up, however, she slammed the receiver down in a fit of cowardice.

Minutes after that, Jessie arrived, looking fresh and mysterious and very cheerful. Doc Whitman had dropped her off; Hallie caught a glimpse of his truck through a new snowfall as he drove away.

"Morning," Jessie said, pulling her poncho off over her head and hanging it from a peg next to the door.

"Morning," Hallie answered, spatula in hand. She nodded toward the percolator on the counter. "There's fresh coffee."

"Just what I need," Jessie answered, taking down a mug and filling it, adding plenty of sugar and cream before taking that first restorative sip.

"Breakfast will be ready in a few minutes," Hallie said.

"I could eat a whole side of pork," Jessie admitted, and both women laughed. It was easy to get along with Jessie, easy to relate. Maybe Hallie ought to confide in her, about Joel, and Lou's murder, and Charlie's . . . and endanger her life? No. Very bad idea.

Hallie smiled, glanced up at the clock. She was due at the Last Chance Café in just over an hour, and the girls were dawdling in their room. They were getting bored with spending their days at the restaurant with her—who could blame them?—and her attempts at home-schooling bordered on pitiful. Both Kiera and Kiley would be much happier in a real school, with other children, and they would learn faster, too, but registering them would be tricky.

"Hallie?"

She started slightly, looked at her friend, who was seated at the table, sipping coffee. Jessie's eyes were luminous with compassion, experience and wisdom, and Hallie had to blink and look away.

"Why don't your children go to school?"

Hallie swallowed, dished up a plate for her friend, carried it to the table. It was impossible to lie to Jessie, and yet she didn't dare answer honestly. She sighed. "It's complicated."

"I imagine so," Jessie agreed. "Maybe I can be of some assistance."

Hallie's eyes smarted with tears. All her adult life, she'd been pretty self-reliant, solving most of her own problems, paying her own way. Now, she truly needed help, and didn't dare ask for it. It was dangerous enough, just accepting a temporary job and a place to live. "You've done plenty by letting us stay here. Lending me your car almost every day."

Jessie smiled a gentle, knowing smile. "Let me keep the girls here today, with me," she said. "I'll show them how the loom works. You can call it an art lesson."

Hallie bit her lower lip, considering. Then she shook her head. "We're already imposing. I simply can't ask you to baby-sit, too."

"You're not asking," Jessie pointed out, resting her elbows on either side of her plate and making a steeple with her long, slender fingers. "I'm the one doing the asking, Hallie. I love children. It would be a joy for me to have Kiera and Kiley here."

Before Hallie could think of another objection, her daughters came clattering down the back stairs and hurtling into the kitchen. It soon became obvious that they knew what was going on.

"Please, let us stay here today!" Kiera begged.

"I think I'm getting a cold," Kiley added, for effect. Hallie automatically felt the child's forehead for fever anyway, and found her flesh cool.

"You wouldn't want to make everybody at the Last Chance sick, would you?" Jessie put in, grinning.

Hallie sighed. "All right," she said, fixing her gaze on the girls and shaking a warning finger at them. "You mustn't go outside alone, for any reason. Do you hear me?"

"Because of the cougar," Kiera explained sagely.

Kiley folded her arms. "We *aren't* babies."

"I'll take good care of them, Hallie," Jessie said seriously. "I promise. You just go to work."

Hallie sighed again, gave the twins their breakfast, and picked at her own. When she arrived at the café, forty-five minutes later, Bear was there alone. He'd started the coffee and switched on the Open sign, but so far there were no takers.

"Where's Madge?" Hallie asked, wiping the counter. All the while, she was thinking of the man Bear had killed, the time he'd spent in prison. She supposed she should have been afraid of him, but she wasn't.

"Feeling peaked today," Bear said. "I think it's the flu."

Hallie made a sympathetic face. "She seemed fine at the Grange Hall last night."

Bear shrugged a large shoulder. "You know how that stuff is. Creeps up on you, knocks you flat before you see it coming."

The metaphor was disturbing, coming from a person who had beaten a man to death with a crowbar. "Is she planning to see her doctor?"

Before Bear could reply, the bell over the front door jingled, and cold air surged into the café in a rush. Hallie turned to see a woman wearing heart-shaped sunglasses, big hair, and a faux-leopard coat. She didn't need a formal introduction to tell her that the elusive Wynona, Bear's legendary girlfriend, had finally arrived.

12

~

Bear came out of the kitchen and stood behind the counter, his brawny hands braced against the edge. His eyes seemed as big as his biceps.

"Wynona," Bear said.

"Bear," Wynona said.

"Uh-oh," Hallie said. So much for her brief period of gainful employment.

"What kept you?" Bear asked, voice vibrating with quiet passion. They might have been alone in the universe, let alone the café, for all the notice they gave Hallie. She was afraid they'd start tearing off their clothes.

"Oh, baby," Wynona whispered. Hallie edged toward the door.

"Do you two want to be alone?" She didn't want to walk off the job, even if she *was* about to be replaced, but her choices were narrowing by the moment.

Deaf to any other voice but Wynona's, blind to any other face, Bear wrenched off his cook's apron, tossed it aside. The veins in his neck were bulging, but he exuded a strange, sweet tenderness.

"Oh, Lord," Hallie whispered, almost to the door now, expecting the atmosphere itself to ignite at any moment.

"My motor home is outside," Wynona told Bear. "Right back there in the alley."

That was all it took. Bear rushed Wynona, swept her up like a leaf in a storm, and carried her out the front door, nearly trampling Hallie in the process. Through the front window, she saw them round the side of the building, and she dropped onto a booth seat, totally spent.

"What the devil is going on around here?" asked Jase, taking off his hat as he pushed open the door and came inside. Hallie hadn't seen him drive up, and she jumped a foot.

"Wynona is back," she said, at once pleased and despairing.

Jase gave a long, low whistle, and approached the counter. "How about a cup of coffee?" he said, and proceeded to pour it himself.

Hallie immediately got to her feet and rushed behind the counter. "Cream?" she asked automatically.

"Black," Jase said, and sat down. He was the only customer in the café, and Hallie hoped it would stay that way for a little while, just until she could get her equilibrium back. She had no idea when—or if—Bear and Wynona would be back from their motor-home rendezvous. For all she knew, they meant to hit the road, take off for parts unknown.

Hallie poured coffee for herself, still standing behind the counter, and was surprised to find that her hand was trembling a little.

"You worried about something?" Jase put the question

casually, but Hallie caught some nuance in his tone that set her nerves hopping all over again.

"Losing my job," she said. It was a partial truth, at least, and thus might have the appropriate ring to it.

"Why would you lose your job?" Jase asked, frowning. "They need you around here. Madge is no spring chicken anymore, and Bear spends so much time at that grill back there, he hasn't got a life." He paused, grinned. "Or, at least, he didn't, until Wy got back."

Hallie was cataloging information on one level, carrying on the conversation on another. On a third, she was going over the logistics of another fast getaway, because her instincts insisted that Sheriff Stratton hadn't come to the café just for coffee. He had questions to ask, questions she might not be able to answer.

" 'Wy'?" she asked, belatedly. For some reason, she'd thought Wynona was an outsider, but Jase's use of a fond diminutive suggested that he knew the woman rather well.

He raised a dark eyebrow, assessing Hallie for a moment before he spoke. "You knew about the murder, right?"

"Bear and the crowbar," she said, and shivered a little.

"Well," Jase said, "Wy's father owned the Texaco station at the time, and Bear worked there. They were already an item, Bear and Wynona, though she was still in high school. Pretty little thing, full of the dickens. Anyway, somebody came to the station and told Bear that Madge's husband had beaten her half to death, and she'd been taken to Reno by ambulance. Bear headed out looking for the bastard, with blood in his eye. Wy went after him, saw the whole thing. It was her testimony that put Bear away, though he never denied that he'd done the crime."

Hallie was breathless. Bear and Wynona's story was at least as dramatic as her own and, as such, it was something of a relief. "He wasn't mad at her—Bear, I mean—for testifying against him?"

Jase chuckled, shook his head. "Nope. It's true love on both sides, with those two. Wy had to tell the court what she knew, and Bear understood that."

"Then what?" Hallie prompted.

"Well, Wynona waited, as best she could. Got a job down in Reno, dealing Black Jack. Visited Bear as often as possible while he was in prison."

"I got the impression from Madge that Wynona sort of—well—comes and goes."

Jase smiled. "She's a gypsy, all right, like her mother was. Can't seem to stay put for very long. Like as not, she'll be out of here again, in a day or two. One of these days, Bear will go with her."

Hallie sighed, completely forgetting, for the moment, her certainty that Jase Stratton had come to the café for something other than coffee and gossip. "Crazy as it seems, it's kind of romantic."

Jase chuckled. "That kind of romance, I can do without," he said.

Hallie refilled his coffee cup. She was hoping for positive news about him and Katie, after seeing them together on decoration night at the Grange, but he didn't seem to be leaning that way, either.

In the next instant, he confirmed her suspicions. "It's about your kids, Hallie," he said. "You need to get them in school. It's the law."

"I'm home-schooling them," she said. The truth was, she was botching that, big-time, but she was feeling cornered, so she didn't clarify.

"That's fine if that's what you want to do," Jase allowed. "But you've got to make arrangements with the school system all the same. You have to lay out some kind of curriculum to keep the state happy."

"Okay," Hallie said. What was she going to do now? To hell with keeping the state happy, she was trying to keep her children and herself alive.

The bell sounded over the door, and two truckers came in, took seats side by side at the counter, exchanged good-natured greetings with Jase, gave Hallie shy, mannerly nods.

Hallie served them coffee, took their orders, and went back into the kitchen to prepare French toast and eggs. It was good to be cooking again, even if she was about to jump out of her skin, and she made short work of the task, adding a garnish of lime slices to give the plates a little panache.

The food was a hit. "This is better than anything old Bear ever slapped together," commented the older of the two men.

"Amen," said the other. "They ought to put you on steady, Miss."

Hallie smiled, a little sadly. Even if Wynona didn't stay on and take over her job, she, Hallie, might as well be twenty miles down the highway already, she was that gone. She had a feeling that Joel was catching up to her, a gut-grinding certainty that she didn't dare ignore. Her fear had been rising ever since she came across the article about Charlie Long's death.

Yes, she was going to have to pack up the kids and hit the road, ASAP. Tricky, when she didn't have a car. The bus was such an obvious choice that she probably wouldn't get to the next town before someone came after her, and the train wasn't any better.

"Thanks," she told the truckers, distracted by her musings.

"Stop by Primrose Creek Elementary as soon as you can," Jase said to her, standing up, laying payment for the coffee, plus a small tip, beside his saucer. "They'll get you squared away with that home-schooling thing."

Hallie nodded. She wished she were a better, quicker liar, that she'd come up with a valid reason for teaching the girls herself, instead of enrolling them in the school system. Jase was no fool, and he was surely pondering her resistance in some part of his mind. It wouldn't be long until he decided to sit down at his computer, or pick up his telephone, and start asking questions about Hallie O'Rourke.

Hallie was profoundly grateful when the café filled with customers, because she was too busy to fret. Two full hours passed before Bear and Wynona returned to the café. Bear was freshly showered, wearing an expression of obstinate sheepishness, while Wynona, who was probably Hallie's age, looked essentially unruffled. She wore her auburn hair big, and her makeup, though skillfully applied, was heavy.

"Sorry to run off and leave you that way," Bear said. Well, Hallie reflected wryly, at least she was visible again.

Wynona merely smiled.

Hallie waited to be fired.

"Looks like you've done a good job of holding down the fort," Bear said instead, noting the lunch rush. Everyone was munching away contentedly, and Hallie had obviously done the cooking, as well as waiting tables, without a problem.

"No big deal," Hallie demurred, though her feet were hurting and trouble was closing in and it looked like she had no way to escape it. She was going to have to leave this place, these people—and Chance. Just by caring for him, she'd put him in danger, too. The criminals she was running from wouldn't hesitate to mow down anyone who got in their way—Lou and Charlie were proof of that.

"You could take the rest of the day off if you wanted," Bear said magnanimously. "Wy can wait tables while I sling hash."

Hallie felt another pang. There would be no sense in coming back; she was history. "Sure," she said, and felt her chin wobble slightly.

"Just make sure you're back in time to serve breakfast," Bear added, smiling beatifically at his girlfriend. "Wy doesn't do mornings."

Wynona giggled and inspected her acrylic nails. "You can say that again," she commented.

Hallie got her coat and bag, rummaged for the keys to Jessie's Jeep, and left the café. She had no idea where to go, or what to do, and drove aimlessly for some time, before coming to a decision. Jessie was scheduled to leave on her next tour in the morning. Hallie would "borrow" her Jeep, then drive herself and the kids to Reno, where they could hop a bus for somewhere far, far away. Once they were at a safe distance, she would simply go into a library or an Internet café, log on to a computer using a fake address, and send Jessie an e-mail, thanking her for her kindness, explaining where the car was and apologizing for any trouble she'd caused.

Once she'd gained some distance, so that Joel couldn't get to her as quickly as he would in Primrose Creek, which wasn't all that far from Phoenix, she would call the FBI, tell them her story, retrieve the cashbox from its hiding place, and hand it over. They could take it from there. Heck, maybe they'd even put her and Kiera and Kiley in the Witness Protection Program, or at least help them establish new identities. Hallie had no illusions that she would ever be truly safe, no matter how many people went to jail. In a big operation like the one Lou had been investigating, somebody always slipped through the cracks, and one "somebody" was all it took.

She drove back to Jessie's in a virtual haze, never so much as glancing toward Chance's place when she passed it. Saying good-bye to him would be impossible, for a number of reasons. She would simply leave.

Like a sleepwalker, she fed the horses in Jessie's barn, taking the time to pet each one for a few minutes. Being near the animals soothed her a little, made her feel more centered.

Inside the house, Jessie was at the loom, and Kiera and Kiley were seated on high stools on either side of her, watching with rapt attention as designs took shape. It must have seemed magical to them, the colors, the pattern appearing, row by row, thread by thread.

"You're back early," Jessie observed, looking up, but never breaking the ancient rhythm. *Thunkety-thunk*, sang the loom. *Thunkety-thunk*.

"Slow day," Hallie said. She'd washed her hands in the kitchen sink, but she was anxious for a shower and a change of clothes. "All packed?"

Jessie sighed. "Yes," she said. "I'd give anything to stay home and keep working on this piece. I'm going to lose my momentum, I just know it."

Hallie smiled, a little sadly. When Jessie returned to this warm, wonderful, refuge of a house, she and the twins would be long gone, never to return. Why did it seem that they would be losing so much more, she and the girls, than they had by leaving Arizona?

Jessie stopped working, helped Kiera down from her stool, and Kiley from hers. "You girls need a break," she said. "We've done enough weaving for today."

"Can we go look at the horses?" Kiley wanted to know.

Hallie thought of the cougar. "In a little while. Why don't you color, or watch TV for a few minutes. I'll take a shower, then we'll say hello to the horses together."

"Okay," Kiley agreed, spokesperson for the group. Then she and Kiera hugged Hallie hastily and bounded up the stairs.

"They're wonderful children," Jessie said softly, watching them go.

"Yes," Hallie agreed.

Jessie studied her closely. "Something is terribly wrong, isn't it?"

A painful lump rose in Hallie's throat. "Yes," she said, in a raspy whisper, "but I can't tell you what it is, so please, don't ask."

"Fair enough," Jessie said, surprising Hallie with her ready acquiescence. "Do you need money?"

Hallie bit her lower lip, thinking of her own substantial bank accounts, languishing in Phoenix, of her car and her clothes and her credit cards. All of those things were as inaccessible as if they'd been on another planet. "Yes," she said. "But I'm not sure when—or if—I'll be able to pay you back, so please don't offer."

"When are you planning to leave?"

Hallie glanced toward the stairs to make sure the twins weren't there, eavesdropping. "Tomorrow," she said.

"Ah," Jessie said.

Hallie, rolling now, couldn't seem to put on the brakes. "I need to use your Jeep, Jessie," she blurted out. "I'll leave it somewhere safe, I promise, as soon as we're far enough away, and send you an e-mail, telling you where it is."

"Okay," Jessie replied, to Hallie's utter surprise.

"That's it? Just 'okay,' and no questions asked?"

"That's it," Jessie said. "I have good instincts about people, Hallie. I know you're not a criminal. You must be in very big trouble, though, and I'd like to help you if you'd let me. For your sake and the girls'."

Tears sprang to Hallie's eyes. There were still good people in the world, Jessie was proof of that, people who believed in others, and were willing to trust them even when trusting was a stretch. Knowing that made everything a little easier. "Just let me use the Jeep," she said. "That's all I really need."

Jessie got up from her stool in front of the loom, walked to a far wall, moved aside a picture of two little boys, one fair-haired, one dark. Hallie had seen the photo a number of times, but never registered, until then, that the subjects were Chance and Jase.

A small safe was revealed, and Jessie turned the knob without hesitation, or any visible effort to keep Hallie from seeing the combination. She removed a fat envelope, plucked out a handful of bills, put the envelope back, closed the safe, replaced the picture.

"Here," Jessie said, approaching Hallie and holding out the money.

Hallie knew, without touching the crisp currency, still lying in Jessie's palm, that there were several thousand dollars there. Unless she could tap her own funds, and it didn't look as if that would be an option in the very near future, thanks to the official strings Joel had surely tied to everything, she would never be able to repay her friend. She took a step back.

"Take it," Jessie urged. "I've done well, Hallie. It won't be a hardship for me."

Hallie sighed. Accepted the cash reluctantly. "Thank you," she said.

"Maybe you should drive me to the airport tomorrow," Jessie mused. "That way, you'd have the Jeep. You could just keep going."

It was settled, then. She was really leaving. Hallie nodded, temporarily unable to speak.

"Are you going to say good-bye to Chance?"

Hallie swallowed, shook her head. "I can't," she whispered, and headed for the stairs. It was the beginning of a long evening.

—

A skiff of snow had fallen during the night, leaving everything covered with a cloak of velvety white, studded with diamond chips. Hallie could see her breath as she hurried toward the barn, carrying Chance's rifle in one hand lest she encounter the mountain lion. Jessie's horses were waiting patiently, as if they were aware that she was new at equine relations, and allowances must be made.

She greeted each of the animals by name, pausing to stroke their long faces, their necks, their sides. She hated leaving them, hated the thought that she would never see them again.

She refilled their feed pans, checked to make sure the automatic waterers in each stall were working, and broke open a new bale of grass.

Jessie's plane was leaving at one that afternoon, and Hallie had packed her things and the girls' before going to bed. Everything was ready, and in place—except her heart. She'd be leaving big chunks of that behind, scattered over the countryside like the fallout from a meteor.

She was dumping the last of the manure into the large metal bin behind the barn when Chance's truck rolled in, leaving broad tracks in the snow. A flash of betrayal ached in her chest—had Jessie told him what was going on?

But Chance seemed to suspect nothing. He glanced approvingly at the rifle, leaning against a stack of bales, as he got out of the rig and came toward her. "It's nice to know you listen to *some* of what I say," he told her. "Any sign of the cat?"

She shook her head. "No, thank God. I think I'm just feeling a little—well—exposed. Now that I know how to use a gun, it seemed sensible to carry it to and from the barn."

Chance nodded. There were shadows in his eyes, and he needed to shave, but other than that, he looked damnably attractive. He took the rifle out of her hand and started toward the house, and she kept pace.

"What brings you here?" she asked, trying to give the question a light touch.

He glanced at her, probably seeing more than she cared to reveal. "Doc's in kind of a snit because Jessie won't let him take her to the airport today. I came by to see if she wanted me to drive her."

"I'm doing that," Hallie said quietly.

"Ah," Chance said. "You don't have to work?"

"Not this morning," she answered, hoping Chance wouldn't stop by the café and find out that Bear was expecting her to cover the breakfast shift. That would surely clue him in, and Hallie wanted to be far away before anybody realized that she was gone for good.

Inside, she pulled off her coat, hung it up, went to the sink to wash her hands. She felt Chance's gaze move from her barn boots, over her jeans and long-john shirt, to her face and then her hair, which was escaping the plastic clasp she'd used to restrain it. She smiled sadly as she snapped a paper towel off the roll. "Stay for breakfast?" she asked. It was selfish of her, she knew, but she needed this last, brief time with Chance. Soon, memories would be all she had of him.

"I'd like that," he replied, drawing back a chair.

Within minutes, Kiera and Kiley were pounding down the steps, in their footed pajamas, crowing, "It snowed! It snowed!"

Hallie laughed and rounded them up for a breakfast of hot cereal, orange juice, and scrambled eggs, and there were tears in her eyes when she met Chance's gaze, across the table. God, it was going to be hard to walk away.

Jessie wandered in from the living room, where her loom stood in a pool of wintry light pouring in through the bay windows, probably attracted by the smell of food and the sound of familiar voices. She glanced at Chance, then, more searchingly, at Hallie, who shook her head ever so slightly. *No*, was the unspoken message. *I haven't told him.*

"Morning, Chance," Jessie said cheerily, barely missing a step.

"Morning," Chance replied, rising a little, sitting down again only when Jessie had taken a seat at the table.

Hallie was content to do the cooking. That way, if nothing else, she could keep her back to them while she worked at the stove, and do her crying in relative privacy.

Everything went fairly well until after they'd dropped Jessie off at the airport in Reno, along with her bags and the large portfolio containing sketches of future designs. That was when the twins noticed that their own suitcase was in the back of the Jeep, along with a few cardboard boxes, tightly taped.

"Are we going on a trip, too?" Kiera asked innocently.

Kiley's expression was thunderous. "We're running away," she deduced. "*Again.*"

"Are we, Mommy?" Kiera asked. "We're leaving the horses, and all our friends, and the Last Chance Café?"

Hallie wanted to weep, but she'd done enough of that while she was making breakfast. Chance had noticed her red eyes, but when he'd tried to broach the subject, she'd shaken her head, and he'd given it up.

"Mommy?" Kiera prompted.

Hallie negotiated the airport exit, turned in the opposite direction of Primrose Creek when she pulled onto the highway. There was one thing she had to do before they took to the road; reclaim Lou's cashbox from its hiding place. She would need it for proof when she went to the FBI, and for a bargaining chip if Joel caught up with her first.

"Yes," she said. "We're going somewhere new."

"Where?" Kiley asked, still petulant.

Hallie blinked a few times, squinted at the green high-way signs overhead. "I don't know," she said, in all honesty. "Just away."

Kiera began to cry. "I didn't get to say good-bye to anybody!"

Hallie winced, lifted her chin a notch, gripped the steering wheel tightly. "I know," she replied, "and I'm sorry. It has to be this way."

"Why?" Kiley wailed. "I miss Jessie. I miss Chance and Madge and Evie—and who will take care of the kittens if we're gone?"

Kiera's grief reached a new and piercing pitch. "Please, Mommy," she pleaded. "Let's go home!"

Once, Hallie thought, Arizona had been home. Now, it was Primrose Creek, the place and the people, and giving all that up was almost more than she could bear. Only the very real threat to her children's lives and her own prevented her from turning around and heading for the high country again. Heading for Chance.

"We can't," she said gently, and kept driving. The twins began to sob wretchedly, and Hallie cried, too, and for many of the same reasons. Leaving Phoenix had been shattering, especially under the circumstances, but this was far worse.

13

⁓

The sun was already going down on the little town in northeastern California by the time Hallie backtracked to the place where she'd hidden Lou's cashbox, and she bit her lower lip as she drove through the open gate, wishing she'd stashed it in a locker at a bus station instead, or even rented one of those mini storage units. Mercifully, Kiera and Kiley, partly assuaged by a late lunch of Big Macs and French fries, were asleep in the backseat of the Jeep.

She drove up the hill, between rows of shadowy headstones dusted with snow, her heart wedged into the back of her throat. Suppose someone—a caretaker, or a stray mourner, for instance—had found the box? Without it, she would have no proof against Joel and the others, and no bargaining chip, either.

She shivered, tried to rein in her imagination and, for the most part, failed.

It was unlikely that Joel or anybody else had followed her here. If by some miracle he had guessed where she might hide something that important, and already found the box, he wouldn't stand around in the cold, waiting for her to show up and retrieve it. Joel was smart, methodical. He would have destroyed the evidence first thing.

And then he would come after her, to make sure she never told the story.

She drew Jessie's Jeep to a stop beside a tall monument; she'd chosen this particular grave for a personal reason—was it really only days earlier?—and the fact that it was rather elaborate, and therefore, easy for her to find again, was a bonus. The grave was also relatively isolated, and not often visited. It had a lonely look, especially as darkness gathered, standing there in the stark cylindrical glow of her headlights.

"Mommy?" It was Kiera, sleepy, confused. "Is this a . . . a graveyard?"

The girls had been asleep during the first visit, blessedly so.

"What are we doing here?" Kiley wanted to know.

Hallie had no choice but to brazen things out, see it through. "I'll explain it all later," she said, getting out of the Jeep, leaving the lights on and the engine running. "Right now, you're just going to have to trust me, okay?"

"Okay," Kiera said.

"Okay," Kiley added, with a lot less conviction.

Hallie picked her way over the rough ground to the grave site. The name O'Rourke was etched deeply into the foot of the stone. Here, her father was buried, the man she had never known, the man who had abandoned her and her mother, evidently without looking back. She couldn't remember receiving a single birthday or Christmas card from the man, and she knew for a fact there had never been any child support payments. Until her mother married Lou, finances had been nip-and-tuck.

She resisted a childish urge to give the headstone a good kick. For one thing, she might hurt her foot.

After wading through a storm of complicated emotions, she got down on one knee and began removing the small pile of rocks with which she'd covered the half-buried box. Mingled relief and regret skittered through her when she felt the metal lid, pried the chest from its hiding place.

She was still kneeling there, afraid to open the lid, when she heard the sound of a familiar engine, saw the sweep of headlights rounding the bend. She got shakily to her feet, clutching the box, and stumbled toward the Jeep. Silly, really. She didn't have a prayer of getting away, not now.

Chance's truck stopped beside the Jeep, and he jumped out, leaving the motor running and the lights on, just the way she had.

"What the hell—?" he demanded.

Hallie froze. She wasn't afraid of Chance, never that, but she would have done almost anything to prevent this confrontation. She would have no choice but to tell him what was going on, and after that, he would be in as much danger as she and the girls already were.

"You followed me!" she managed to sputter.

He stopped a foot in front of her, pushed his hat to the back of his head, wrenched it forward again, in a gesture of pure frustration. "You're damned right I followed you," was the terse reply.

"Jessie told you," Hallie lamented.

"Chance!" Kiera called, from the Jeep.

"Chance!" Kiley echoed plaintively.

The two of them sounded like shipwreck survivors, clinging to an ice floe and calling for rescue. No doubt they thought their mother had lost her mind, and Chance was probably of the same opinion.

"Jessie didn't tell me anything," Chance said. Then he waggled a finger at her. "Stay right there," he ordered. "Don't move a muscle." With that, he turned, went to the Jeep, opened the door to speak to the kids. "Everything's fine," Hallie heard him say. "We're going home. All of us."

Hallie wanted to scream with frustration, wanted just as much to go wherever Chance chose to take her. Maybe she *had* lost her mind. People caved under a lot less pressure than she'd been experiencing, since the incident at Lou's house, when she'd seen a side of her ex-husband she could never have imagined was there. She just stood there, in the gleam of Chance's truck lights, holding the box against her bosom as if it were some precious relic, and not the symbol of her own ruin.

Chance settled the girls down with a few more quiet words, then came back to Hallie. "We can do this two ways," he said reasonably. "You can resist, and I'll throw you over my shoulder and take you back to Primrose Creek in my truck, then come back and pick up Jessie's rig tomorrow. Or you can drive yourself back, with me following. What's it going to be?"

Hallie raked her lower lip with her front teeth. "That's some choice," she muttered.

"Take it or leave it," Chance replied. He wasn't going to give an inch.

"How did you know?" Hallie asked. He took her by the elbow, but gently, and steered her toward the Jeep, where the girls were waiting, their faces pressed against the same rear side window. "If Jessie didn't say anything, how did you know?"

"I stopped by the Last Chance Café for an early lunch, and Bear was in a state because you hadn't come in to wait tables. Then Doc wandered in, complaining that Jessie had let you take her to the airport when he wanted to do it, and I guessed the rest. I caught up with you just after you dropped Jessie off, and followed when you turned away from Primrose Creek instead of toward it."

"Why?" she wanted to know. Needed to know. They were standing beside the Jeep now, but the doors and windows were all closed, and she was sure the girls couldn't hear their conversation. "Why didn't you just let me go?"

He considered the question for a long time, his expression grim, there in that cold, sad, lonely place. "I don't know," he said finally. "It never occurred to me that I could."

"Now what?"

"Now we go back home. We calm the kids down, and you get a good night's sleep. Then we sit down, you and I, and we talk—really talk—until I'm clear on what the hell is going on with you."

Hallie shoved a hand through her hair, which was coming loose from its clip, and sighed. "Suppose I don't want to talk?" she challenged, but weakly. She was tired, so tired, of running away, of lying, of looking over her shoulder.

"Then I guess we'll just sit there and stare at each other until you get over it," he answered. "Now, are you okay to drive, or do you and the girls want to ride with me? The Jeep will be okay here until tomorrow."

Hallie was too frazzled to make decisions, even small ones.

Chance's smile was slight, and a little bitter. "Let's go," he said. Then he opened the back of the Jeep and removed the suitcase and the well-taped cardboard box, setting them in the back of his truck. Resigned, and strangely grateful, Hallie collected her daughters and, cashbox in hand, followed Chance.

He shut off the Jeep, locked it up, and pocketed the keys as he returned to his own rig, where Hallie and the twins were already buckled in, waiting. The girls, though wide awake, were vibrantly silent. Hallie felt like a reject from the *Jerry Springer Show;* some mother she was, dragging her kids to a graveyard, probably scarring their psyches forever.

Apparently, Kiera and Kiley felt safe, however, for they were soon asleep in the backseat of Chance's truck. Hallie hunkered low on the passenger side, the box on her lap, both hands guarding it.

Chance didn't ask questions, though Hallie knew it took a lot of restraint on his part. The reckoning would come, though, once they were back at Primrose Creek.

The climb up the curving mountain roads was almost hypnotizing, and Hallie dozed off a couple of times, lulled by the warmth of the cab, the scent and substance of Chance, beside her, the fact that her children, for the moment at least, were as safe as they could possibly be. Anyone trying to hurt them would have to get past her, and past Chance.

She was surprised and, at the same time, *not* surprised, when they took the turnoff to Chance's place, instead of Jessie's.

He parked the truck in front of the house, gathered one sleepy child in each arm, and started up the steps. Hallie followed with the cashbox, now scratched and dirty. About ten hours had passed since she'd dropped Jessie off at the airport, but it seemed like ten years.

Chance showed her to a guest room on the first floor, with an adjoining bathroom, and went back to the truck for the suitcase and box while she undressed her daughters, put them in T-shirts provided by their host, and tucked them into the large bed. For tonight, the usual brush-floss-story-prayer routine would be set aside.

Kiera and Kiley went right to sleep, to Hallie's relief. She went wearily out into the main part of the house, looking for Chance.

There was a double fireplace, opening onto the kitchen on one side, and the dining room on the other, and he'd gotten a good blaze going. He was making coffee when Hallie joined him. She'd set the cashbox in the center of the table earlier, and it was right where she'd left it, evidently undisturbed.

"I wasn't expecting you to follow us," she said.

Chance didn't turn around. He'd poured water into the coffeemaker; now, he set the carafe in place and pushed a button. "I don't imagine you were," he said. She could tell precisely nothing by his voice.

"Why did you do it?" She put the question cautiously. Softly.

"I told you," he said, turning around at last, leaning back against the kitchen counter, folding his arms across his chest. "I don't know." The crimson light of the fire danced over his form and features, lending him the aspect of a warrior, resigned to battle.

She drew the cashbox close, fished the little key out of her pocket, still tagged with Lou's cryptic "Virgin Mary" notation, and fitted it into the lock. It turned with a snap. She laid the lid back, and took out some of the pictures, the documents, the maps.

Lou had died for this stuff, she was sure of it. Tears filled her eyes, and one slipped down her right cheek. She didn't try to brush it away.

Chance took a bottle of Jack Daniel's from a cupboard and set it on the table. The whiskey was in easy reach, but he'd taken care not to invade her space. He brought cups next, and a sugar bowl. By the time he'd done that, there was enough coffee in the carafe to pour them both a dose of badly needed caffeine. He replaced the carafe, after filling both mugs, then sat down across from her.

"Do we talk," he asked, with a sort of taut humor in his voice, "or stare at each other?"

"Might as well talk," Hallie said.

Chance chuckled. "Damn," he teased. "I was looking forward to staring."

She leveled a look at him and launched into her story, starting with her conversation with Charlie Long at Lou's wake, moving on to her explorations at her stepfather's house, and Joel's arrival. His demand that she give him the box, her refusal and flight in the old truck, which had later died, two miles outside of Primrose Creek, Nevada.

When she fell silent, after talking for some fifteen minutes or so, Chance took the lid off the Jack Daniel's and poured a splash into her cup, then his own. He topped them off with fresh coffee, and sat down again.

"So," he said, after a while, "you weren't headed for Primrose Creek specifically."

She shook her head. "I was just running. We'd been on the road for a day and a half by then. I was so scared, I couldn't think straight."

"Why didn't you go to the police?"

She thumped one of the Polaroids with the tip of her index finger, hard. "See that man, making the drug buy? He *is* the police. So are a lot of the other guys. And Joel—my ex-husband—is an Assistant D.A. As you've probably figured out, he's in this thing, too, way over his head, and he's correspondingly desperate. Seems to me that my options were pretty limited."

"You could have told me. Or Jase. Or called the FBI."

"I didn't know you or Jase from Adam's best ox," she pointed out. "For all I knew, the two of you might have put your heads together, decided I was crazy, and called Joel, or the Phoenix P.D." She stopped, and tears burned behind her eyes again. "Dammit, I was frantic, scared out of my mind. I still am!"

"Nobody's going to hurt you," Chance said, with a certainty that soothed her a little. "And I can see that you're too worn out to have this conversation tonight. Hell, so am I. Get some sleep, Hallie." He studied her across the table, and she wondered, oddly, what it would be like to sit here in this warm kitchen every night, to cook here and to dream by the fire.

She bit the nail of her right index finger. "Thanks," she said.

He stood, put the Jack Daniel's back into the cupboard, set their cups in the sink. "See you in the morning," he said.

So he didn't expect her to share his bed. It was both a relief and a disappointment. She pushed back her chair, got to her feet, started putting the papers and pictures back into the cashbox.

"One thing," Chance said, his voice low.

She stopped, looked up at him. *Here it comes*, she thought.

"Don't try to take off again. Those kids have been jerked around enough."

He might as well have slapped her. "I can take care of my own children," she informed him.

He glared at her. "Right," he scoffed. "Waking up to find themselves in a graveyard in the middle of the night will be one of their fondest childhood memories, I'm sure."

Tears stung her eyes. "That was a rotten thing to say."

He sighed. "Get some sleep, Hallie. You're on the edge, and so am I. This is no time to have a sensible conversation."

She hesitated, wanting to defend herself, wanting to fight, wanting somehow to win his approval. She didn't have the energy for any of those things.

"Good night," she snapped.

"Sweet dreams," he replied, his voice flat.

~

Hallie was amazed to find herself in Chance's house, when she awakened late the next morning, alone in the bed she'd shared with her daughters, and not a couple of hundred miles down the highway, aboard a Greyhound bus. Ever since she fled Phoenix, she'd been on emotional red-alert. Even though she'd found a house at Primrose Creek, and a job, temporary arrangements, both, she'd been poised to flee every moment of every day. She was so tired.

She sat up, glanced at the window. Though there was plenty of daylight, a soft snow was falling, the flakes fat and graceful. A light knock sounded at the closed door.

"It's Chance," he said, before she could ask who was there.

"Come in," she said, against her better judgment.

He brought coffee, looked beyond excellent in his worn jeans and denim shirt. Sat down on the edge of the mattress.

"Where are the girls?" Hallie asked.

He smiled. "In my study, watching Nickelodeon," he answered. "They're fine, Hallie. They've had breakfast, and Smoke and Magic are keeping them company."

She reached for the coffee with one hand, pulled the blankets up to her chin with the other. Her eyes never left his face. "Now what?" she asked, as she had the night before.

"You get showered and dressed and eat something, and then you tell Jase what you told me. He'll take it from there."

"He's here?" Hallie swallowed. Jase was an honest cop, she knew that. Most of them were. That didn't mean his buttons couldn't be pushed, especially by other cops. He would call the Phoenix P.D., and maybe the D.A., if he hadn't done that already.

Chance took her hand, squeezed it. "He's on our side," he said.

It struck her that he'd said the word "our" when he might have said "your," but she didn't put too much stock in that. She couldn't afford to trust Chance completely, even now. There was simply too much hanging in the balance.

He smoothed her hair back from her face with one hand, and the tender ordinariness of the motion splintered her heart. "Everything's going to be all right," he told her.

"I wish I had your confidence," she replied.

He left her then, and she took her shower, put on clean jeans and a sweatshirt from the suitcase, ventured out into the kitchen. Jase was seated at the table, while Chance put the finishing touches on Hallie's breakfast.

She was surprised to find that she was hungry, and the two men allowed her to consume her poached eggs, toast, and coffee without prodding her for information. When she was finished, Chance handed her a fresh cup of coffee and took her plate away. Then he brought the cashbox down from the fireplace mantel.

Jase looked at her pointedly, through with waiting.

She launched in, drawing the box close, lifting the lid. "A few weeks ago," she said, "My stepfather was murdered."

Chance said nothing; he'd known that much. Jase leaned in, listening hard, his coffee forgotten and growing cold.

Hallie blinked back tears of grief. "Lou was a retired cop. A good one. During his career, he won every citation the department had to offer."

Chance reached out, took her hand, and she was grateful for the strength he imparted. "Go on," he said.

"About six months ago, judging by the dates on some of those documents," she went on, nodding toward the box, "he started some kind of undercover investigation, obviously not sanctioned by the police department. He stumbled onto something, Lou did, and he changed, got real edgy and secretive. I was worried, and asked him what was wrong, but he wouldn't tell me." She lowered her head, ashamed. "I was so caught up in my own life, my children and my business, that I didn't press him any further. He might be alive today if I had." She paused, gathering her thoughts, remembering. "Then—" Her voice fell away. She took a sip of coffee before going on. "Then he was killed. It was . . . terrible. The police—and my ex-husband—said it was random, a fumbled burglary, but I knew right away that it was more, and so did Charlie Long, a friend of his."

She went on slowly, relating the story as carefully, as thoroughly, as she could. Chance reached out, once or twice, stroked her hair, touched her hand, silently encouraging her to go on. It was like laying down a crushing burden; whatever happened after this, at least she wouldn't have to carry that load any farther.

Jase was all business. "Who was behind the operation?"

Chance tossed him an irritated glance, as if to say, *give her time*, but he didn't speak.

"I'm getting to that," Hallie said. She'd rehearsed the thing in her mind, over and over, during her shower, and she knew she had to tread carefully, make sure she left nothing out. "Cops," she said, and shoved the box toward him. "Some of them high-ranking. And my ex-husband, Joel Royer. He works for the D.A.'s office, in Phoenix."

Chance held her hand, stroking her knuckles with the pad of one thumb.

"A few days ago, I got up the nerve to check the news from Phoenix, on the Internet," she said. Tears slipped down her cheeks; she dashed at them with the back of her free hand. "They killed Charlie Long, like they did Lou. Only this time, they made it look like suicide."

Jase had been taking notes on a small pad of paper. "How do you know it *wasn't* suicide?"

"I don't think Charlie was the type. He wanted to bring these guys down, and see them pay for what they did to Lou. He wouldn't have checked out before the game was over."

Jase reached for the cashbox, and it was all Hallie could do not to grab it, jerk it back. He examined the contents carefully, and only then did Hallie notice the computer disk hidden at the bottom. Jase tucked it into his pocket without comment and went back to taking notes.

Chance's chair creaked as he leaned back, meanwhile, digesting all she'd said. Weighing it.

Jase was obviously not one to ruminate. He didn't even look up. "Can I use your phone, Chance? The sooner the feds are brought into this, the better."

Chance stood, crossed the room to a counter, came back with the receiver of a cordless telephone, all without saying a word.

Jase made his call with admirable dispatch, identifying himself to the agent who answered, giving a brief run-down of the situation. He listened, nodded, told the person on the other end of the line how to find Chance's place. At least, Hallie thought, he hadn't directed the FBI to the county jail, where he might have put her for safekeeping.

"If you had any part in this," Jase told her, once he'd hung up, "you'd better tell me right now."

She glared at him. "If I were one of them, what would I be doing in Primrose Creek?"

"Hiding out, maybe," Jase said, unruffled. "If you ripped them off, say, and threatened to expose them, they'd come after you."

"I knew you'd think that!" Hallie snapped back, making an effort to keep her voice down, because of the girls. "That's why I didn't come to you in the first place!"

"Take it easy," Chance told her. He was glowering at Jase. "Dammit, Jase," he said, "she's not involved, and you know it."

"I have to make sure," Jase said.

"Right now, I'm more concerned about keeping Hallie and the kids safe from these guys," Chance retorted, his jaws tight at the hinges.

Jase sighed. "You've got a point there," he agreed. His gaze rested solemnly on Hallie's face. "The FBI might want to put you and the twins in a safe house someplace, until all the dust settles."

"Hallie's staying right here with me," Chance said.

"What about the kids?" Jase asked, with a glance down at the pictures. "Can you protect them, too? There's only one of you, Chance. Looks like there might be a whole shitload of these guys."

"Them, too," Chance said stubbornly.

Jase's expression softened a little when he looked at Hallie again. "You want your children with you, I presume?" he asked.

Hallie's eyes were wet with tears. "Yes!" she cried.

Jase sighed, scratched the back of his head. "Okay by me," he said, "but keep in mind, the FBI might have a whole other plan."

"I'm not the criminal here," Hallie pointed out.

"That remains to be seen," Jase replied, rising to his feet. He fixed his gaze on Chance. "I'll be in touch," he said. He took the cashbox, and Hallie winced, though she didn't try to stop him.

"What about Jessie's Jeep?" Chance asked, standing as well. "We left it behind in the graveyard."

"Give me the keys," Jase said. "I'll send somebody to pick it up."

"Thanks," Chance said, standing next to Hallie's chair, resting one hand on her shoulder.

Jase offered a ghost of a smile. "I hope all this works out," he said quietly, and then he was gone, letting himself out the back door.

"I need to see my children," Hallie said, and stood.

Chance pointed her toward his study, and she set out. Away from the kitchen, and the fireplace, and Chance, the house felt colder, and she was shivering a little by the time she found the girls. They were sharing a bean-bag chair, absorbed in a rerun of My *Favorite Martian*.

Hallie smiled, in spite of everything, and sat down cross-legged between her children and the TV.

"Hey," she said.

They looked at her warily, no doubt bracing themselves for some new development.

"I don't want to go anywhere," Kiera said.

"Me, neither," Kiley agreed, jutting out her lower lip.

"We're staying right here, for the time being," she said.

"Then what?" Kiley asked, stealing a glance at the frenetic activity on the TV screen. Hallie reached for the remote, lying nearby, and pushed the power button.

"We need to talk," she said. Then she held out her arms. "Come here."

Somewhat grudgingly, the twins complied, snuggling from either side, like puppies.

Hallie fiddled with a lock of Kiera's hair, held Kiley close against her side.

"I'm sorry if you were scared last night," she said. "When we went to the graveyard, I mean."

"Why *did* we go there, Mommy?" Kiera asked. "It was spooky!"

Hallie kissed the top of Kiera's head, then Kiley's, and held them even closer. "I had hidden something there, after we left Phoenix, and I needed to get it back."

"That was a weird place to hide something," Kiley said.

Hallie laughed. "I guess you're right," she admitted. "Let's just say it made sense at the time."

"Are we going to stay here now, for always, with Chance?" This was Kiera.

The question lodged in Hallie's heart like an arrow. "No, sweetheart, I don't think so. We're just visiting here, until Mommy can solve some problems and make some plans."

"I'd rather stay here," Kiley insisted.

So would I, Hallie thought. "Things just aren't that simple, honey," she said.

"This is about Daddy, isn't it?" Kiera said, out of the blue.

Hallie swallowed, straightened her spine, held her children a little closer. "Yes, baby," she said. "I'm afraid so."

"Is he in trouble?" Kiley wanted to know.

"Yes," Hallie said. "He made a bad mistake."

"Is he going to jail?"

By then, Hallie was wondering if the twins had over-heard some of her conversation with Jase and Chance in the kitchen. "I think so," she said, resigned. "I'm so sorry."

They clung to her, even closer than before, silent in their misery.

She kissed them again, atop their heads, rocked them a little, the way she had when they were smaller, hum-ming softly.

"You won't leave us, will you, Mommy?" Kiera asked after a long time.

"Not ever," Hallie said. And she meant it. Whatever she had to do, she would be there for her children, as long as they needed her.

Presently, the girls relaxed, and Hallie switched the TV back on and left them to watch *Leave It to Beaver*. On the screen, Mrs. Cleaver was vacuuming the living room of her perfect black-and-white house, while wear-ing high heels, a shirtwaist dress, and pearls.

Chance was just coming in from the barn when Hallie reached the kitchen, where she'd seen him last. He'd left the rifle behind, she noticed, on its rack above the door. Did every house in Primrose Creek have one of those?

"How long do you think it will be before we hear from the FBI?" she asked nervously.

Chance took off his coat and hat, hung them on the pegs where his father, grandfather, and great-grandfather had probably hung theirs. "I don't imagine it will be too long," he answered, going to the sink, rolling up his shirt sleeves, and turning on the water so he could wash up after the morning chores.

"What's going to happen now, Chance?" she asked,

leaning one shoulder against the framework of the door to the dining room. "Between us, I mean."

"I guess that's up to you."

"Unfair," she protested. "Tell me what you want."

"I want to be able to trust you."

"If you don't trust me now, maybe you never will." She felt an infinite sadness, weighing her down. Crushing her.

He watched her for a long while as he dried his hands. "Maybe not," he agreed, at long last.

After that, it seemed to Hallie that there was nothing more to say. Without trust, their relationship wouldn't have a prayer, and if Chance couldn't believe in her, well, that was nobody's fault but her own.

"We shouldn't do this," Kiera said, watching round-eyed as her sister took the plastic cover off Chance's computer and switched it on. "We're not supposed to touch other people's things."

"I just want to tell Daddy that we love him," Kiley replied. She climbed into the desk chair and concentrated on the screen. "That's all."

Kiera drew a little closer. "We'll get in trouble," she warned, but she liked the idea of talking to her daddy, even if it was only by e-mail. Back in Phoenix, she and Kiley had sent him messages all the time, at his office, and most of the time, he'd answered, though he never said much.

Kiley was online in no time. She clicked on the little envelope-shaped icon up in the left-hand corner. A blank form appeared almost instantly, and she smiled as, using two fingers, she typed in their father's address.

14

When Hallie entered the kitchen, dressed in jeans and a long-sleeved knit shirt, hair still damp from the shower, Kiera and Kiley were seated solemnly at Chance's kitchen table. Two other chairs were occupied by strangers, a man and a woman, and though they had an official air about them, Hallie was alarmed at first.

The man stood, nodded. "Hallie O'Rourke?" he asked.

Hallie sagged against the doorframe. She was calculating the distance between herself and her daughters; on one level, she was ready to snatch them and run. On another, she was too startled to move. Her reasoning said, *These are the people from the FBI,* but the message coming from the oldest part of her brain was different. *Wrong. Something is wrong.*

"Yes," she managed to say. Only a second or so had passed since she'd stepped into the kitchen, surely, but it felt more like a lifetime.

Chance was at her side, close, but not crowding. Silent, but solidly *there.*

"I'm Agent Baker," the stranger went on, letting his hand fall back to his side. He indicated the woman, who was still seated. "And this is Agent Simms. We're with the Federal Bureau of Investigation."

A badge was produced; Hallie studied it, saw that the information was there, but couldn't take it in. It might as well have been written in Russian.

"Sheriff Stratton called our field office in Reno last night," Agent Baker prompted. He spared Hallie a brief, official smile. "According to the information he gave us, you must have quite a story to tell." He indicated an empty chair across from his own. "Won't you sit down?"

Hallie hesitated for a moment longer, then sat, perched on the edge of the seat. She didn't pull her chair up close to the table.

Chance stood behind her, hands resting on her shoulders. His touch, his presence, gave her an infusion of strength. She smiled reassuringly at her children.

"Why don't the two of you go in and watch some television?" she said.

The twins stared at her as though she'd suggested paragliding off the roof of the house. Although they were allowed to watch TV in moderation, she never encouraged the activity.

"Could we play Tetris instead?" Kiley asked. As usual, she was the first to rally. She was looking up at Chance, and Hallie vaguely recalled that there was a computer in the study, as well as a television set.

"Just don't erase my tax files," Chance said, with a nod, and the girls raced off.

Hallie looked up at him, bewildered. He was going to turn two seven-year-olds loose on his computer, without supervision? Lord, maybe the situation was more desperate than she'd imagined.

"They'll be all right," he said quietly.

Agent Simms spoke up at last. "We'd like to talk to Ms. O'Rourke in private," she said. Her smile was real, but her eyes were watchful, as though she expected someone to bolt, and was bracing herself to give chase.

Chance didn't move. "That's too bad," he said. "This is my house, and I'm staying right here."

Agent Simms, an athletic type with a rather severe haircut, raised an eyebrow. "We could take Ms. O'Rourke into custody—" she began.

Agent Baker, evidently her superior, raised a hand to silence her. He was middle-aged, barrel-shaped without being fat. "There's no need to make a big deal out of this," he said quietly. "Mr. Qualtrough, if you'd sit down, I think we would all be more comfortable."

Chance took the chair closest to Hallie's. He was still holding her hand.

Baker focused on Hallie, his gaze as penetrating as a laser beam, and simply waited.

She swallowed and, seeing no alternative, began to tell the story, starting with Lou's wake, when Charlie Long had given her the key to the cashbox, ending with her own flight to Primrose Creek. Nearly an hour had passed when she finished.

"Where is this box?" Agent Simms wanted to know, when Hallie finally fell silent, trembling a little. She had, in many ways, relived the whole ordeal in the telling of it.

Hallie's gaze stopped on Chance's face before moving on to the female agent. "Sheriff Stratton took it with him last night," she said.

Simms and Baker exchanged looks.

"I would have thought you'd know that," she said.

Chance leaned forward slightly in his chair, like a jury member tuning in to important testimony, but he didn't speak.

Agent Baker smiled another of those semi-smiles, as if his lips were glued together and he was trying to pull them apart without hurting himself too much. "Just a mix-up, I'm sure," he said. "Simms, put in a call to the sheriff, will you?"

Chance folded his arms, leaned back, resting one foot on the opposite knee, nodded when Agent Simms indicated the telephone on the nearby counter and asked, "May I?"

Hallie glanced through the window over the sink, noticed for the first time that it was still snowing. Growing up in the desert, she'd often longed for snow, imagining cozy winter days spent beside a fire, sipping tea and reading. Now, far from soothing her, the weather made her feel trapped, cut off from the rest of the world.

"He's on his way," Simms said, after a brief, monosyllabic conversation.

"Good," Agent Baker said.

Wrong, wrong, wrong, said Hallie's gut.

By the time Jase arrived, carrying the cashbox with him, however, Hallie was beginning to question her instincts where Agents Simms and Baker were concerned. They had begun to seem ordinary after Chance made a fresh pot of coffee and nuked a frozen cinnamon-and-apple cake for breakfast.

Hallie's throat was constricted, but she forced herself to nibble at her food, take an occasional sip from her coffee. For a variety of reasons, she didn't want to seem nervous, though the effort was probably too little, too late.

At last, Jase showed up, stomping snow off his boots, rapping at the glass in the back door before turning the latch and letting himself in. He carried Lou's cashbox under one arm, greeted the FBI agents with a cordial nod. Hallie wondered if he was personally acquainted with Simms and Baker, hoped he was, but she couldn't tell.

"Morning, Sheriff," Agent Baker said, ever the spokesperson. He stood and put out a hand.

Jase returned the favor. "Morning," he said.

Agent Simms was staring at the cashbox.

"Is that the evidence?" Baker asked.

Jase nodded and handed it over, just like that. Hallie wanted to protest, she'd given up so much, risked so much, to protect the pictures and documents Lou had gathered, but she refrained.

Both agents were on their feet almost immediately. "Thanks, Sheriff," Baker said. "We'll be in touch, soon as we've had a chance to look this over and run some investigations of our own."

Hallie frowned. This was it? They were just going to take the box and leave, with no talk of safe houses, or protective custody?

"Fine," Jase said, and smiled benignly. "Drive carefully in this snow. Storm's getting worse all the time."

The agents left, practically tripping over each other to get into their overcoats and be gone.

"Well," Chance drawled, giving Jase a narrow look, "*that* was easy. For them, anyway."

Jase grinned, helped himself to a mug from the cupboard, filled it with coffee, took a sip. Savored it. "I made photocopies of everything," he said, in his own good time. "And I've still got the disk."

Hallie recalled that Jase had taken a disk from the cashbox the night before, after she'd given her informal statement, and tucked it into his shirt pocket. "Have you looked at it?" she asked. She hoped whatever data the thing contained hadn't been ruined by the elements. She'd taken every care to shelter the box, when she hid it next to her father's grave, but there had been a lot of weather in the interval.

"I tried," Jase said with a sigh, "but it's protected by a password." He looked at Chance, grinned. "I gave it to Henry, over at the high school. If he can't get into that disk, nobody can. Including the FBI."

"Henry?" Hallie echoed.

"Henry," Jase confirmed. "He's a junior at Primrose High. Big future in software design." He paused. "Don't worry."

"A kid," Hallie said, worrying.

Chance cocked a thumb toward the door; the engine of the agents' car could be heard, retreating into the distance. "Are those two on the level?" he asked, putting many of Hallie's concerns into words.

"We'll see," Jase said, sounding unconcerned. "I'd better get back to town. You two sit tight right here."

Hallie let out her breath. "Isn't there anything else we can do?"

"You can get some rest," Jase said with quiet concern. "You look all done in."

Chance walked his friend out through the ever-deepening snow, and Hallie watched from the glass panel in the back door as the two men conferred. Neither of them smiled, even once.

When Chance got back, shivering because he hadn't bothered with his coat, he settled Hallie in a chair in front of the massive stone fireplace in his living room, handling her as carefully as if she were an injured bird, with tiny, brittle bones, propping her feet on a hassock, tucking a blanket around her. Then he vanished into the kitchen, returning a few minutes later with a steaming cup. His two sheepdogs, lying on the hearth, perked up their ears at his approach.

Hallie caught the scent of chicken broth, as did the dogs, no doubt, and she was profoundly touched by that homely offering. She sipped, then looked up at Chance with weary eyes. Suddenly, she felt impossibly old, ancient enough that she'd seen more grief and sorrow and warfare than God. "I'm not sick, you know," she said. "You needn't fuss."

He leaned down, resting his work-roughened, rancher's hands on the arms of her chair, his breath warm on her face. "Let me take care of you, just for a little while," he said. "Ever since the night you came into the Last Chance Café, half-frozen and scared out of your wits, I've wanted to make sure nothing ever hurt you again."

She swallowed, and her eyes burned. "I'm not one of your wounded horses," Hallie reminded Chance, very gently.

He hadn't moved, and his smile was a cocky little quirk of his lips, though she could see by the shadows in his eyes that he was afraid for her. "Most of the principles are the same," he said.

She set the mug of chicken broth aside. The twins

were still in the study, watching television. "Make love to me, Chance," Hallie said, surprising even herself with the request. "Now. Make me forget everything but the way it feels when you touch me."

He gave a sigh, lifted her feet, and sat down on the hassock. He took off her shoes, then her socks, and began to massage her arches, her toes, her insteps, her heels. It was bliss, but it wasn't what she'd asked for.

"Don't you want me?" she asked, injured.

He chuckled, shook his head, as if amazed. "Oh, I want you, all right," he answered evenly, "but if I took you to bed now, I'd be taking advantage of you. I can't do that. Besides, we're not alone, remember?"

She flushed, because she *had* forgotten, for the space of a heartbeat, about everything and everybody in the world except Chance and the way he could transport her.

She found a smile, somewhere inside, and stuck it to her mouth. It was loose on its hinges, and promptly fell away. "So take advantage of me," she said, but she was joking now, and he knew it.

He raised one of her feet to his lips, kissed her instep, and she was stunned by the jolt of need that raced through her. "Later," he said. "Right now, I want to concentrate on making sure you and the kids stay safe."

She tilted her head back, sighed, then crooned, as he continued to rub her feet. Who would have thought, she wondered, that her arches were erogenous zones? In time, she met his gaze again. "I've told you all my secrets now," she said. "How about giving up a few of yours, Mister?"

"What do you want to know?" he drawled. So help her God, if he kissed her instep again, or nibbled at one of her toes, she'd have a meltdown, right there in his living room.

Hallie squirmed a little. "Why didn't you ever get married and have a family? You seem like a pretty good catch to me."

"I'm glad you think so," he said. He spent a while considering her question; he was not a man to hurry. She'd learned that at excruciating leisure, in Jessie Shaw's spare-room bed. "I guess, after Katie and I broke up, I felt obliged to sow a few wild oats. I was pretty sorry for myself, too. Drank a lot, got into more than my share of fistfights, and slept with half the women in the county."

"You must have loved her very much," she said. "Katie, I mean."

He sighed, waggled her little toe in a small, delicious circle. Shrugged those powerful shoulders. "I thought I did, at the time," he said. "I used to lay on the floor, in the dark, and listen to old love songs on the stereo for hours." He smiled a rueful, self-deprecating little smile. "God, I must have been a pain in the ass."

She laughed, in spite of the fact that she was a woman in hiding, with no place to call home, and the future, if she had one at all, stretched before her like some primeval desert, lonely and barren. Chance, she decided, didn't have a corner on self-pity. "You must have been very young," she said.

He winced comically. "I kept it up for a long time," he said. "Until Jessie and Doc came over here one night, after I'd wrecked my fourth rig, and set me straight. That was when I went away to college. When I got back, I found out I had a knack for making a ranch pay."

"So," she said, flirting a little, whistling in the dark, "you're not only a good kisser, a hell of a lover, and a friend to horses, you're a pretty good businessman."

He grinned. "When you put it that way, it sounds impressive," he joked. "Fact is, I needed the distraction, so I put in a lot of hours." He paused, shrugged. "The land and the horses kept me pretty well occupied."

"But weren't you lonely?"

"Weren't you?" Chance countered. "Loneliness hurts, but it's not fatal."

She let her gaze stray to the framed painting hanging above the first landing of the staircase. The young man and woman in the picture were good-looking, both fair-haired and blue-eyed, and their clothing and hairstyles indicated that the portrait had been done in the late 50s or early 60s. "Is that your mother and father?" she asked.

He nodded. "I kept that painting behind some boxes, in the attic, until about a year ago. I was mad as hell that they'd gone off and left me. Does that sound crazy?"

She shook her head. "I was furious with my mother for getting sick and dying, when I needed her so much."

"What about your father?"

"Never knew the biological one," she said. She smiled, remembering happier times, when she was seven, and dancing a waltz with her stepfather at the wedding of a family friend. "Lou was my dad. A lot of men wouldn't have hung in there the way he did, after Mom died. After all, I wasn't his blood. I was a teenager with a major atti-tude and a smart mouth. He could have put me in a foster home, or looked up some distant relative and palmed me off on them, but if he ever even considered doing anything like that, he never mentioned it to me."

"He never remarried?"

Hallie shook her head. "He must have dated—he was

still a young man when Mom passed away—but if he did, he kept his own counsel." She braced an elbow against the chair arm, propped her chin in her hand, and pondered. "I should have listened to him more. Lou didn't like Joel, from the very first. Said he was a hotshot, into power instead of service. But he came to the wedding at city hall, and he was at the hospital when the twins were born, too. God, he was so proud of them, and of me. You'd think I was the first woman who ever delivered a child."

"You were married at city hall?" Chance asked, in idle surprise. He was still massaging her feet, and her skeleton was dissolving, joint by joint, bone by bone. "I would have pegged you for the whole-nine-yards kind of bride. Long white dress, big church, doves flying off into the sunset, all that."

Hallie was too worn down to hide the ghosts of the old dreams that must have shown in her eyes. "I wanted a big wedding," she admitted. "Joel said it would be a foolish extravagance."

"A thrifty guy, huh?"

"Cheap," Hallie corrected, and they both laughed.

"Drink your soup," Chance instructed. He went to the nearest window to peer out, consulting the sky. "Bad weather's rolling in for sure," he said. "I'd better check the generator, make sure it's ready to fire up."

Hallie nodded. "Need some help?"

"Just stay here," he answered.

She bit down on her lower lip. "I'm scared," she confided.

"That just shows that you're sensible," Chance answered. And then he headed for the kitchen. A few moments later, she heard the door close behind him.

Hallie stood, made her way to the study.

Kiera and Kiley were piled in the same beanbag chair, sound asleep, while the TV babbled on. Hallie switched it off, covered her children with an afghan from the leather couch, and paused as she passed the computer. The screen saver showed a cowboy on a bucking bronco.

While Chance was outside, the sky vanished behind a veil of grayish white, and the fat snowflakes caught at each other, as they fell, and joined at the edges.

Presently, Chance brought in several armloads of firewood, while Hallie made busywork in the kitchen, rooting through the pantry for spices, flour, sugar and other tools of the trade she'd been forced to abandon, along with her restaurant, and a great many of her dreams. Maybe Simms and Baker were for real, and things would be all right. Soon, she'd probably be able to go back home.

If, indeed, Phoenix *was* home. She wasn't so sure anymore.

"I like to see a woman cooking," Chance teased, dropping the wood into the box next to the kitchen fireplace. "It's old-fashioned."

She stopped, a bag of flour in the curve of one arm, and sighed. "You need to hit the supermarket," she lamented. "You don't even have saffron."

He chuckled. "There hasn't been much call for it," he said. "My specialty is chili."

She laughed, and it felt good. Very good. "You're a pretty good breakfast man, too," she said. A silence ensued, not uncomfortable, but a bit on the awkward side. "Is the generator okay?" Hallie finally asked, to break the impasse.

"Needs more gas," he answered. "I'll fill it after I put out extra feed for the horses."

Hallie tensed. Did that mean he was going to leave her and the girls alone, while he went to town to buy gasoline?

He must have read her mind. He touched her cheek with the backs of his fingers, spoke with quiet gruffness. "I'm not going anywhere," he said. "There's a tank out behind the barn."

"Oh," she said.

He smiled. "Might as well take care of it now," he said, "while I can still find my way out there and back." In less than a minute, he was gone again, and Hallie busied herself with her spur-of-the-moment culinary effort, a fancy version of chicken pot pie.

Chance had been gone for less than twenty minutes when she heard a noise outside. The fine hairs on the back of Hallie's neck stood up, even though she told herself there was nothing to worry about. It was only Chance, or maybe Jase was back. She went to the sink and peered out the window, but the glass was shrouded in vapor, and she couldn't see.

The dogs, quiet on the hearth all morning, began to bark.

"Hush," Hallie said, though she was profoundly grateful, in those moments, for any sort of company in that otherwise quiet house, canine or otherwise. Chance was nearby, but heavy snow muffled sound, even a girl from the desert knew that, and he might not have heard the car.

Footsteps sounded on the porch, booted feet, stomping off snow, and a loud knock followed. Her breath congealed in her lungs, and she was sure she was drowning in her own fear, even as she told herself she was being silly and paranoid. The dogs, hackles rising, scratched at the back door with their paws, snarling like wolves now.

"Chance!" a man's voice yelled. "Let me in, will you? I'm freezing my ass off out here!"

Hallie bit her lip. She could ignore the visitor until he went away, but he was probably a friend of Chance's, having car trouble of some sort, and if she turned him away, he might actually die of exposure, it was so cold. The dogs were making a fuss, it was true, as though confronting an intruder, but they were territorial creatures by nature, likely to bark at anyone who approached.

"Chance! Dammit, you've got to be in there—my luck just couldn't be that bad." The doorknob wriggled, but the lock was still engaged. "Shit."

Hallie tried to look through the keyhole, but all she could see was part of a blue down jacket. She watched as the jacket turned away, descended the porch steps, expanded into a whole man, with white hair and a battered leather bag in one hand. There was no sign of a vehicle and the snow was coming down so thick and fast, it had already filled in his footprints and the tracks of Chance's truck tires.

She struggled with the locks and wrenched open the door. "Wait!" she cried, as the cold buffeted the wind from her lungs.

The man turned, smiled quizzically, and came toward her. It was Jessie's friend, Hal Whitman, the veterinarian.

The intelligent kindness in the doctor's pale blue eyes reassured her. "Come in and get warm," she said. "Chance is around somewhere. He went to put gas in the generator and check the livestock."

"Well," Doc Whitman said, "I could sure use some coffee if you happen to have any handy."

Hallie closed the door behind the vet and helped him out of his coat. "Have a seat," she said. "What brings you out in weather like this?"

Doc Whitman bent to pat both dogs, who had relaxed now that they'd identified him to their satisfaction, and then went to stand near the kitchen fire, warming his hands. "I was on my way back to town from the Collier place—one of their cows got into some sweet feed and bloated right up—and I hit a patch of slick road and went straight into the ditch."

Hallie paused, coffeepot in hand. "Were you hurt?"

"Just my pride," he said, with another smile, and rocked on his heels a little as he turned his back to the blaze on the hearth. "Guess Jessie's right. I ought to think about retiring. Or at least taking on an associate, so I don't have to run from one end of the county to the other, at all hours and in every sort of weather. Thing is, I hate to let go of my practice even to a minor extent. Seems like the beginning of the end to me."

Hallie poured his coffee, offered sugar and cream, and was told that black would be fine. "Could be the beginning of the beginning," she pointed out. "There must be things you've been wanting to do, if you could just find the time."

He seemed to be musing between sips. "Could be," he allowed, after a long time. He didn't ask Hallie what she was doing at Chance's place, in the middle of a snowstorm, and she was grateful. She wasn't inclined to make explanations.

Hallie leaned back against the sink, her arms folded,

too restless to sit. What was keeping Chance? He'd been gone—she glanced at the clock—twenty-seven minutes. Her imagination was kicking in, and all the scenarios that came to mind were straight out of action-adventure movies.

"Are you all right?" Whitman asked abruptly.

Hallie dropped into a chair, covered her face with her hands and shook her head in an effort to clear away the gathering cobwebs. Before she could answer, the dogs started to bark again, eagerly this time, and then there were footsteps outside, and the door opened. Chance hurried in, shedding his hat and coat and flecks of snow as he came. Hallie's gladness bordered on exultation.

He smiled at her, then turned to the doctor. His expression was solemn. "I see you're on foot," he said. "What happened?"

"Ran off the road, down toward Jessie's," Doc said, with a jabbing motion of one thumb. "I'm fine, as you can see. If you'll just give my rig a tow with that truck of yours, I'll be on my way."

"Have you noticed that there's a blizzard brewing out there?" Chance asked.

Hallie looked from one man to the other, waited.

"I'd have to be a fool not to have noticed," Doc replied. "I just walked a mile in that mess. Damn near froze my . . . ears off. Now, before you get too comfortable, let's get out there and hook up that winch."

Chance rolled his eyes. "We'll take care of your truck tomorrow. Tonight, we're having a slumber party, right here."

"The hell we are," Doc argued. "I've got sick animals at my clinic in town, and this is my poker night. I'm going home if I have to walk the rest of the way."

"You stubborn old coot," Chance replied, disgruntled. "You ought to have better sense."

Doc glanced at Hallie, smiled, and then glowered at Chance again. "You know," he said, "with all Jessie's bragging, I never would have guessed you were so slow on the uptake. You've got a beautiful woman here. It's perfect weather for a nice fire, a little music, even some dancing. Glass or two of good wine, maybe. And you want *me* hanging around?"

Chance laughed. "Dammit, old man," he answered, "of course I don't, but that truck of yours isn't going anywhere. I'd bet money you broke an axle."

Doc swore under his breath. "I haven't missed a poker game in thirty years," he said. "If I don't show up, the boys down at the fire hall will think I'm dead for sure. Why, even if I called, they'd figure I was a kidnap victim, saying what I was told to say."

"Naw," Chance replied. "They'll want to see the body before they bring in a replacement. After all, they've made a fortune off you over the years."

Doc waggled a finger at Chance, but his eyes were bright with laughter. "That," he said, "was a low blow." He paused, and his expression was solemn. "I've got hospitalized animals to care for, Chance. They need me."

Chance looked out the window, grimaced and, with resignation, reached for the coat he'd just hung up. It was dripping melted snow onto the floor. He spoke to Hallie. "You'd better round up the kids and come along," he said.

Hallie nodded, and went to get her children. The roads were dangerous, but staying alone in that ranch house while Chance went all the way to town and back was not an option.

THE LAST CHANCE CAFÉ   269

Kiera and Kiley were delighted at the prospect of an outing.

Although visibility was near zero, they reached Doc's combination home and office at the edge of town without incident, dropping him off at his front door. After that, they stopped at the supermarket, where half the town had gathered to stock up on storm supplies. They practically collided with Katie and her daughters in the canned food aisle, and she beamed at Kiera and Kiley.

"We're having a combination pizza party and sleepover to celebrate the snow," Katie said to the twins. "How about joining us?"

Kiera and Kiley were instantly receptive to the idea, if jumping up and down and clapping their hands could be interpreted as an inclination to accept.

Hallie's gaze met Katie's, over the children's heads, and Hallie saw her friend's concern. Jase had clearly told her at least some of what was going on.

Katie took Hallie's arm and hustled her a little distance away, while Chance kept an eye on the four kids.

"Are you all right?" Katie whispered.

Hallie nodded, though she wasn't sure the answer was entirely honest. "I'm okay," she said.

"Let me take the girls," Katie pressed. "Just for tonight."

Hallie figured this was one instance where her children would be safer if she let them go, and they obviously wanted to join the party. She put her own misgivings aside. "Okay," she said. "I guess it would be all right."

Kiera and Kiley bid their mother hasty good-byes, when the time came, and left with Katie and her girls.

"They'll be okay," Chance assured her when she stood a moment too long, watching them all drive away.

The trip back to the ranch took twice as long as the one into town, and the road was more memory than reality, but Chance must have known that stretch well, because he navigated it without a hitch.

The house was cold when they went inside, and the dogs welcomed them with yips of delight. Hallie thought how strange it was that, with all her problems, and all the dangers she faced, she felt so utterly safe with this man beside her. Surely it was a sweet illusion, this sense of having stepped out of the flow of time.

He helped her out of her jacket before shedding his own coat, then went to the thermostat and cranked it up. By then, the snow was coming down so hard and so fast that Hallie doubted they'd have been able to see the barn from the back porch.

In the living room, Chance built up the fire until it roared, then he dragged a small table and two chairs into the middle of the room. Hallie watched, bemused, as he plundered a cupboard under one of the windows. When he turned around, she saw that he was holding a battered board game.

She folded her arms and arched an eyebrow. "You want to play Scrabble?" she asked. She realized she'd been hoping for another kind of game entirely, and was mildly scandalized at herself.

Chance grinned, drew back one of the chairs, and gestured for her to sit. "Loser strips to the skin," he said.

Hallie had already decided to throw the game. Win or lose, live or die, she would have this night, with this man.

15

The lights flickered as Chance led Hallie by the hand, up the stairs, along the hallway, into the bathroom, flickered again when he started water running in the shower. Warm steam billowed out into the otherwise chilly room, enveloping Hallie, as well as Chance, in what seemed like a magical mist. Within the shifting confines of that moist vapor, nothing existed except the two of them.

The first kiss was a tender exploration, careful and slow. The second had them pulling at each other's clothes, and at their own. The room went dark, and the house gave a great sigh, but the water kept running, the steam kept rising, and Chance and Hallie deepened their kiss, clinging to each other, finding their way into the shower.

They began to bathe each other in the darkness, and Hallie reveled in the sensations Chance's hands created as he stroked her with lathered hands, weighing her breasts, making them slick, sliding his grasp down over her hips, her thighs. Then he was kneeling before her, parting her, claiming her.

She stiffened with a shock of pleasure, cried out in welcoming protest, plunged her hands into his hair and held him close, and then closer still. Her body began to rock as the sweet tension mounted; she tilted her head back, closed her eyes, and gave herself up to him with a sob of ecstatic surrender.

He eased her down, until she, too, was kneeling, facing him, and then he kissed her again, feverishly, his hands kneading the soft flesh of her buttocks. The water, now tepid, poured down on them, an elemental baptism, a bonding of souls as well as bodies.

Presently, Chance lifted Hallie, lowered her again, onto him, moving smoothly, deeply, inside her. She interlaced her fingers behind his neck and groaned, leaning back to let him lave her breasts with his tongue while he continued the slow, ancient rhythm that had her climbing the peak all over again, even though she was exhausted, utterly spent from the first round.

The tempo increased until finally, their bodies locked together, they spasmed in unison for several moments, then lay curled together on the shower floor, still entwined, dazzled and struggling just to breathe. Hallie's senses remained on red-alert and, quivering with the echoes of a satisfaction too keen to be endured for long, she looked inside herself—saw the full spectrum colors of her own soul: aqua and violet, blue and red, and a few she couldn't name.

The shower water cooled, then turned cold, and still they held each other, as if sharing the same skin, oblivious to everything but the physical and spiritual communion that had consumed them both, and melded them into some new creature.

Chance rallied first; gasping, he strained to reach up, turn off the shower spigots. Then, gently, he disengaged himself from Hallie and groped his way out of the stall to snatch two large towels from the cabinet nearby. He wrapped Hallie in one, hooked the other around his waist.

Hallie was still in shock, loose-limbed and only partially present, and Chance finally lifted her to her feet. She stumbled against him, and he lifted her into his arms, carried her to his bed, dried her with brisk, tender motions, pulled one of his sweatshirts over her head, covered her with the blankets.

He was beside her before she could manage a protest that he must not, *must* not, leave her, taking her into his arms, warming her body with his own. He kissed her forehead, gave a low, raw-sounding chuckle.

"My God," he breathed, "what *was* that? I feel like I've been dropped from an airplane and then hit by a freight train."

She snuggled closer, smiled a little. "That," she answered, "was the best sex anybody, any*where* has ever had. Is it always like that with you?"

He expelled a sharp, amused breath. "Hell, I was going to ask you the same question," he said.

She ran a hand down over his chest, to his belly, and beyond. She caressed him, and he began to get hard again. "I'd put it in the firestorm category," she said.

Chance groaned. "Hallie, show a little mercy, will you?"

But Hallie was not inclined toward mercy, not then, at that moment, or there, in that place. She slipped under the covers.

By morning, the snow had stopped, but some three feet of the stuff had fallen in the night, and Hallie, wearing Chance's shirt and her own jeans, stood in the kitchen, the floor icy beneath her feet, contemplating breakfast. Chance had left the house while she was still sleeping, to start the generator, so there was electricity, though it faltered often. A lively fire was just beginning to catch on the hearth.

By now, Chance was probably feeding the horses.

She put the coffee on, peered out the window at what seemed like miles of glistening diamonds, fine as sand. Despite everything she faced, she felt her spirits rise. Her body, cherished in the night, still hummed from Chance's skillful attentions.

When he came in at last, his face was reddened with cold. "Hungry?" she asked.

He grinned, slapped his work gloves against one thigh and then laid them on a heating vent to dry. "I guess we need to eat," he conceded. "If it were up to me, though, I'd just take you right back upstairs to bed."

She felt a frisson of response—he could arouse her so easily that it was frightening—and took a step back. "Chance," she said, with quiet determination, "we have to talk. Really talk."

He slanted a glance at her, then looked away again, shoved a hand through his weather-dampened hair. "About what?" he asked, cautious.

"Sit down, and I'll explain. I've started an omelet for you, and the coffee will be ready in a couple of minutes."

He dragged back a chair and sat, watching her.

She set an empty plate before him, and silverware,

then laid a hand on his shoulder. "I have a business in Arizona, Chance," she said. "I have a home, and friends, though I admit I neglected them for a long time, while I was building the business. I have a life there."

He waited.

"When—if—this thing gets settled, and the heat is off . . ." She couldn't finish.

He did it for her. "You plan to go back."

"What else can I do?"

His jawline tightened. "You can stay here," he said. "With me." He looked away, looked back. The omelet, meanwhile, began to scorch on the stove and, reflexively, Hallie pushed the pan off the burner, turning from Chance in the process. Stiffening her spine. "Excuse me," he persisted, in a fierce whisper, "but didn't we just spend the best part of the night driving each other crazy? Was it just me, or did something special happen when we were together?"

She blinked back tears. "Sex is one thing," she said bravely, "and love is another. We strike sparks, all right, but that isn't enough, Chance. You know it isn't."

He could have turned everything around then, merely by saying that he loved her, or even that he thought he could learn to love her, but he said nothing, nothing at all. He just sat there at the table, scowling, and when she put the omelet in front of him, he pushed it away.

The telephone rang, and Chance answered, snapping, "Hello?" It was more demand than greeting.

Hallie felt a cold shimmer of fear pass through her in that instant, like a spirit met on a narrow stair.

"It's Jase," Chance said, and shoved the receiver at her.

She took it, listened, mumbled her thanks, pressed the disconnect button.

"What is it?" Chance asked.

"Joel has vanished, and so have several of his associates."

"Meaning?" He looked at his food for a long moment, picked up his fork, then laid it down again.

"What if they've found out where I am? What if some of them are on their way here to make sure I don't get a chance to testify?"

Chance gripped her hand, pulled her down onto his lap with a sigh. "I won't let anybody hurt you, Hallie," he said, and he gave the promise the weight of a sacred vow. "Or the kids."

She laid her head on his shoulder. "Are you over being mad at me?"

"No," he replied. "We've got something here, Hallie. You and me, together. The least you could do is stick around until we figure out what it is."

She shook her head, turned far enough on his lap to pick up the fork he'd laid down, and popped a bite of food into his mouth. "What we've got, Chance," she said reasonably, "is some kind of crazy sexual conflagration. It takes more."

"How are we going to know for sure, if you take off?"

She sighed, offered him another bite, which he refused by clamping his mouth tightly shut. "Maybe," she suggested carefully, knowing she was pushing the envelope, "I'll come back. Once everything is settled."

His blue eyes darkened to near-violet. "Maybe I'll be waiting," he answered, "and maybe I won't." Having said that, he raised her shirt, slipped her left breast out of her bra, and bent to tease the nipple with his tongue. "In the meantime, we still have sex."

Hallie's breath caught, and her heart skipped over at least one beat, but she reined in her emotions and kept her head. She knew she should turn away, but she couldn't. "Don't," she said, without a trace of conviction. Where was her dignity? Where was her pride?

He savored her mercilessly. "Do you really want to leave this behind?"

She whimpered, stretched involuntarily, sensual as a cat. "Chance—"

He unsnapped her jeans, put his hand inside her panties, found the center of her passion, and began making slow circles with the tips of his fingers. "Ummmm?" he asked.

Hallie's body jerked, and she parted her legs, unable to help responding. "Oh," she gasped, "this isn't fair—"

"To hell with fair," Chance murmured, and heightened his efforts. "I'm going for *good.*"

Oh, it was good, all right. Hallie strained against his hand, seeking him more and more desperately even as he tormented her. She dug her heels into the floor and raised herself to him, her head back, and he nipped at her earlobe. "Oh, *God,*" she moaned.

"Feel nice?" he taunted.

"Dammit," she choked, back arching, breathless with need, fevered. "You know it does!"

"How much more could you want, Hallie?" he drawled, and tongued the length of her neck. His voice was like gravel. "A man, a woman—it doesn't get much more real than this, does it?"

"Ooooh," she cried.

He took her over the edge, held her there, suspended, for what seemed like a small eternity, then settled her back on his lap, and zipped and snapped her jeans back up, as matter-of-factly as if they'd just shaken hands. She was trembling, lying boneless against him, when suddenly he set her on her feet, gave her a swat on the bottom, and said, "My breakfast is getting cold."

Heat surged through Hallie's system. The man had just put her through her paces, at the kitchen table, for God's sake, and now he was going to sit there and calmly eat an omelet? "What just happened here?" she demanded, setting her hands on her hips.

He chuckled. "Well," he said, "if I remember correctly—"

"That isn't what I mean," she spouted, "and you know it. I was speaking rhetorically. You were manipulating me!"

"Actually, I was manipulating your—"

She cuffed him in the back of the head. "I don't *like* being manipulated!"

He grinned. "I could have sworn you did," he countered.

"Damn you, Chance, you know perfectly well what I'm talking about, so stop trying to throw me off!"

"Are we fighting?" he asked cheerfully, chewing as he pondered the possibility. "Look out. Next thing you know, we'll be going to a movie or playing Strip Scrabble or maybe even doing laundry. It's frightening."

Hallie's frustration knew no end. Neither, apparently, did the small, sweet aftershocks that were still thrumming through her pelvis. "What, precisely, is your point?"

"Think about it," Chance said, as if she could do anything else *but* think about it. Then he calmly finished his breakfast, carried the plate to the sink, rinsed it, and set it in the dishwasher.

She crossed the room, yanked her jacket down from its peg, and flailed into it. "That does it," she said. "I'm leaving."

He leaned against the counter, folded his arms, and regarded her with something like sympathetic amusement. "Is that so? Where do you plan to go?"

"Back to Jessie's place," she informed him. "I'll walk if I have to."

"Are you out of your mind? The snow is up to your waist."

Hallie shoved a hand through her hair, which needed shaping. "After *that* little episode," she blustered, waggling her fingers in the direction of the chair where she and Chance had been sitting, "I can probably melt a path for myself."

He laughed, ambled over to her, unzipped the jacket and slid it back off her shoulders. "Stay," he said. And when he saw a protest brewing in her eyes, he spoke again, quickly. "I'm not talking about forever, okay? Just until the weather eases up, and the feds have rounded up your ex-husband."

Hallie's eyes filled with tears; she hadn't known they were coming, and so was taken utterly by surprise. "My children," she mourned. "Oh, God, Chance, what is all this going to do to Kiera and Kiley? I mean, lowlife that he is, Joel is the only father they've got. They'll have to deal with whatever happens, whatever he's done, for as long as they live. It isn't fair."

"There you go, looking for fairness again. Forget it."

He rested his forehead against hers. "They have you for a mother, Hallie, and that makes all the difference. You're strong and you're smart and you're resourceful as hell. They know you love them, and that they can count on you. Trust me, it's more than enough."

She smiled shakily. "How is it that you can piss me off one moment, and put my whole life into perspective the next?"

He kissed her nose. "It's a gift," he said, with a note of false modesty in his voice.

She laughed. "It's a curse," she countered, and stood on tiptoe to land a kiss of her own on his mouth.

"I think I need a shower," he said, with a comical leer and a lift of his eyebrows.

She took a step back. "No way," she said, but she knew her eyes were shining, and her heart had already tripped into double overdrive.

He took a step toward her. "What you need," he drawled, "is a little . . . manipulation. And I'm just the guy to handle the job, if you'll forgive the play on words."

Heat suffused her face. "Now, Chance—"

He picked her up bodily, tossed her over one shoulder, and started toward the stairs. "That's exactly what I was thinking," he said merrily. "Now."

⎯

"Maybe we shouldn't be too hasty here," muttered Selkirk, a man Joel would have preferred not to associate with, if he'd had any real choice in the matter. Nobody else was willing to handle the dirty work, and Joel wasn't sure he could manage it all on his own. "I don't like it. This is too easy. The place is too quiet, too empty. There might be feds inside, just waiting for us."

Joel was tired of delays. The feds had already been nosing around in Phoenix, thanks to Hallie. His whole life was in a state of suspended animation, and while there was no chance that it would ever be normal again, silencing Hallie would not only provide the satisfaction of revenge, it might also buy him time and maybe even make it possible to return to the States someday. If she were dead, she couldn't testify, after all.

Yes. There was a major bank account waiting for him in a small town just over the Mexican border, and a very convincing passport. Once Hallie had been dealt with, he would disappear forever.

He'd live like royalty on the amount of money he had been able to skim over the past several years. All he had to do now was follow through; the goal posts were in sight.

"Come on," he said, tired of lurking in the barn. The place smelled bad, and he'd never cared for animals. "Let's go in and take a look around."

Selkirk shook his head, but when Joel led the way out onto the moon-washed snow, hugging himself against the cold and against the task that lay ahead, the other man followed.

"Any sign of an alarm?" Joel asked, when they reached the back porch.

"There's no alarm," Selkirk said, with certainty, and rapped hard on the door.

No answer. Joel wiped off the glass and peered inside. He saw an old-fashioned kitchen, just the kind of corny setup he would have expected Hallie to wind up in.

"Outta my way," said the thug. "We gotta get this

done and get out of here. I got a real bad feeling—something ain't right."

"Trust you to get right to the heart of the matter, Selkirk," Joel snapped. " 'Something ain't right.' How long did it take you to figure that out?"

Selkirk thrust one meaty shoulder against the door; wood splintered and the lock gave way. It never ceased to amaze Joel that anybody ever felt safe anywhere, ever, without dogs, high fences, and major security systems. But then, this was the country, and folks might be a little backward.

"Anybody!" Selkirk yelled.

"Shut up," Joel snapped, shoving him.

"Hel-*lo!*" the hit man chimed derisively, his eyes glittering with dislike as he turned to Joel. "If breaking down the goddam door didn't stir the place up, yelling won't, either."

"Hallie!" Joel shouted.

The place where his ex-wife had been hiding all this time was silent, cold.

"Keep an eye out," Joel ordered, and started up the back stairs. He was sure there was no one in the house, but maybe, if he searched the place, he could find out where to start looking for Hallie and the kids. He allowed himself a brief, heartening fantasy, in which he came across the evidence Lou Waitlin had gathered, had a chance to destroy it before things went any further. Sure, the feds had been asking questions, but maybe they were just blowing smoke. Maybe they didn't actually have the proof.

Of course, he wasn't going to be that lucky. He knew that. Lord, if he'd had that stuff he'd seen Hallie looking through in Lou's backyard that day, he could turn back time, start over with little or nothing to keep him awake at night.

Upstairs, he found the room where Hallie slept almost immediately; her singular scent lingered in the chilled, wintry air, and the bed was neatly made. Hallie hadn't slept in this room recently.

He pondered that, rubbing his chin with one hand, then proceeded to go through the dresser drawers. Nothing. But then, that wasn't surprising, since he knew Hallie had left most of her belongings behind when she fled Phoenix. He had personally checked her condo, and the restaurant, too, finding everything but what he needed, the collection of damning stuff he knew Lou had hidden away. It was all in that box, of course, the one she'd refused to give him, the one she'd deemed important enough that she'd run away that day.

He might never have found *her*, for that matter, if the kids hadn't decided to e-mail him from Chance Qualtrough's computer, just to say hello. After that, it had been easy. If only the kids had contacted him earlier; it would have saved so much time and trouble.

Now, because of all the grief she'd caused, Hallie was going to suffer, big-time. He intended to make sure of that.

He moved on, into a smaller room, with twin beds, and something gentled inside him as he imagined his daughters here, sleeping, playing, reading. He leaned against the doorjamb, smacked the framework lightly with the heel of one palm, blinked back tears of frustration, fury, and sorrow. They were very young, Kiera and Kiley were, and with time and persuasion, they would forget Hallie, if not entirely, then close enough. She would be a distant memory, a specter in a dream—but not their mother. Maybe he'd find them another mother, somewhere along the way.

"Hey!" Selkirk shouted from downstairs. "Did you find anything?"

Joel turned from the sparse little room and went to the head of the stairs. "No, dammit," he replied, "and stop yelling like that. Somebody might hear."

"If you're thinking we can hide in here, and get the jump on whoever turns up first, you've been working a desk too long. The back door is in shreds, remember? That's gonna be a clue, even to a bunch of rubes like these people."

"Go outside and keep watch," Joel said, descending the front stairs, gravitating toward the computer. Selkirk remained where he was, as long as he dared, and then shuffled off through the kitchen, muttering.

Joel sat down in the chair, pulled the covers off the monitor and keyboard, and logged on. Hallie wouldn't be stupid enough to store the contents of that disk on this very computer—would she? He scanned her files, found nothing, and moved on to her e-mails.

One was particularly interesting, a missive from somebody called Katie, in the nearby burg of Primrose Creek. From what little Joel had seen of the place, it consisted of two bars, a feed store, and a greasy spoon, the Last Something-Or-Other. He opened the message.

Hallie—Don't worry about a thing. Relax and let Chance take care of you. The kids are doing well. What safer hiding place than the sheriff's house? We're on our 75th game of Candyland, and I'm losing. See you soon, Katie.

Joel sat back in the desk chair, thinking. *Let Chance*

take care of you. Who exactly was this guy? A boyfriend?

It didn't matter. If he got in the way, he'd be a dead man.

And the kids were at the Stratton place. He smiled. "What safer place indeed?" A methodical person, he covered the monitor and keyboard again before making one last swing through the house, then going outside to find Selkirk. The moon and stars were particularly bright that night, their light reflecting off the surface of the snow, and Joel peered at his watch, then raised his eyes to the barn.

"Sooner or later, somebody's going to stop by to feed those animals," he said with distaste. "We'll hide out in there until they do."

Selkirk spat to show his aversion to the idea. "You know, Royer, when I took up with you, I figured you for a class act, with a taste for the finer things in life. I never thought it would come down to sleeping in a barn."

Joel was slogging through the deep snow. He'd come to the high country from Phoenix, on impulse, and without preparing properly. He didn't have the right clothes, and his custom-made oxfords were soaked through. The hem of his Brooks Brothers overcoat dragged on the ground, and now, instead of stretching out next to some succulent senorita, on silk sheets, he could look forward to an ambience of hay and horse shit. He felt another surge of hatred for Hallie.

All her fault. All of this was her fault.

George Selkirk had always been a take-charge sort of guy, and after two hours of shivering in the hayloft, listen-

ing to Royer's snores, and to the horses snorting and fart-
ing below, he got up, pulled his Glock out of his shoulder
holster, and inspected it with a sense of fond admiration
that had never dwindled since he'd shelled out a serious
chunk of change for the thing, back when he first got into
the trade. He wasn't the extravagant type, but a man
needed good tools.

The hay rustled as he got to his feet, but Royer didn't
stir. George stood over him for almost a minute, sighting
in the Glock on his left temple. *So easy*, he thought. It
would be so damn easy to rub the bastard right out, hook
up with Royer's funds in Mexico, and spend the rest of
his life celebrating.

What stopped him was the gut-deep certainty that he
wouldn't get away with it; something would go wrong if
he tried, either here or at the border, and there was no
room for error in this little gambit. He'd learned the hard
way to listen to his instincts, way back when it would
come to him ahead of time that he shouldn't go home
until he was sure the old man had passed out for the
night. Three good beatings was all it took to learn that
lesson. Dear old Dad had committed "suicide," and the
pain was over.

He tucked the Glock away, patted it reverently
through jacket and holster, and climbed down the ladder
to the barn floor.

The second-to-last thing George Selkirk wanted was
to be caught and sent to prison—the *very* last was to die
before his time. He was still young—forty-four—and he
had a brilliant career ahead of him. So what if he was a
little tired? He'd get over that. Take a vacation or something.

The horses nickered a little as he passed on his way out, but none of them raised the alarm. He made for the house, with its gaping mouth, at the entrance to the kitchen, whistling under his breath. Mr. Young D.A. wasn't the only one who knew his way around a computer, and Royer had made some notes while he was surfing the Web, though he probably figured a dumb thug like Selkirk wouldn't notice.

Well, George Selkirk noticed plenty. And he didn't wait outside like a dog just because some suit gave the order. He'd watched Royer at work at that computer for a couple of minutes before slipping back outside to pretend he was keeping watch, like Tonto or some-goddam-body.

He lit a cigarette, drew deeply on the smoke, coughed a couple of times, and stepped over the threshold. It was cold as all get-out inside that house, but warmer than the yard had been. George liked to think he was a guy who saw the glass as half-full, not half-empty.

He took a look around, just to make sure he really had the place to himself, and then he went to the desk, sat down, and reached for a pencil. It was an old trick, but it usually worked, and this time was no exception. He laid the pencil on its side and rubbed the lead over the top of the notepad where Royer had scribbled, and an impression came through.

Sheriff: Jase Stratton. A Primrose Creek address followed. After that, Royer had written *Hallie + Chance Qualtrough*, with directions to the place. Damn if it wasn't just through those woods behind the barn, George thought, turning in the chair, as if to look through the wall. He'd never been in this godforsaken hole of a town, and he'd never be there again, but he *had* taken the time to download some information on the place. Unlike some people he could name.

He tore off the tracing he'd made, folded it, and tucked it into his pocket. Earlier, while Royer was playing dickhead spy, he'd walked around back and found a shed. Inside, among other useful items, he'd spotted an old pair of snowshoes. All he had to do was strap those on and follow his nose through the woods to the Qualtrough house, finish Royer's ex-wife off good and proper, once she'd given him the evidence, use his cell phone to summon his ride, and get the hell out of Dodge. He was being paid by somebody higher up than the Golden Boy, anyhow.

The moon was high and full, the light glittering on the snow. George, sporting the snowshoes, almost expected to see Santa's sleigh cross the sky, pulled by eight tiny reindeer. But wait, that was Christmas. It was still only October, despite the shitty weather. Might see a witch sail past instead. He chuckled. *Ma, on a broomstick,* he thought.

George continued to slog.

He didn't see the monster until it was too late. He didn't hear it, either, or smell its gamey hide. But the hairs rose on the back of his neck when he took off his snowshoes to cross a gleaming silver ribbon of a creek, using an old log for a footbridge. He stopped, right in the middle, and tuned in to his surroundings.

"Not good," he muttered. "Not good at all."

An unearthly shriek rent the frigid air, and George matched it with one of his own. The snowshoes toppled into the creek and floated away downstream, giant tennis rackets swirling on top of the water. George shuffled to the other side, hoping to God that the terrible sound had not come from that direction.

The cry sounded again, plaintive and, at the same time, fierce. George's blood froze in his veins, and he grappled for his Glock, dropped it, scrabbled for it in the snow. Before he could straighten up again, the thing was on him with a force that knocked the wind out of him; he felt its breath on his face before it went for his throat, was deafened by its snarling screams of attack, and the last thought his brain ever processed was a single word.

Lion.

—

"What was that?" Hallie asked, sitting bolt upright in bed.

"What?" Chance echoed, sounding rummy, but the .357 Magnum he'd left on the bedside table was already in his hand.

"A scream," she said. "I heard a scream."

"The cat," Chance said. He got up, pulled on his jeans, buttoned the front. "I'd better check on the horses."

Hallie tossed back the covers. "I'm going with you," she said.

He gave her a rueful grin, shook his head, and jammed his feet into his boots. Apparently, he'd finally figured out that it was useless to argue with her.

The barn was quiet, the horses fitful but not seriously disturbed. Still, Hallie had an uneasy feeling, a prickling sensation along the length of her spine. Lou had told her, long ago, to pay attention when she picked up vibes like that, and behave accordingly, and she frowned, looking around.

She stepped out into the barnyard and looked up at the sky, and a motion at the edge of her vision caught her eye. She turned and watched in horror as a cougar shot across the space between Chance's house and barn, bathed in blood and leaving a trail of crimson paw-prints in the snow.

She started to scream, swallowed the cry in the space of a heartbeat, and stared as the animal leaped the barbed wire fence and entered the pasture, there to be swallowed whole by the night.

"Chance!" she managed, sagging against the outside wall, one hand pressed to her heart.

He was there in an instant, the .357 drawn and ready. "What is it?"

She pointed to the streaks of blood in the snow. "Look," she said. It was all she could manage at the moment, but it sufficed.

Chance swore and went over to squat and inspect the blood. "The cougar must be wounded," he said, and Hallie knew he was speaking more to himself than to her. He rose to his full height, followed the gruesome prints backward a little way. "Maybe it tangled with another cat, or woke up a bear."

"Or it killed something," Hallie said. She wanted to throw up, and put her hand to her mouth, but willed herself to keep it together.

"I've never seen anything like this," Chance said, lifting his gaze toward the woods that lay between his place and Jessie's, on the other side of Primrose Creek. "If that cat made a kill, it was no rabbit, and he tore the throat out of it. Shit, he practically bathed in the blood."

Hallie shuddered, unaware of the cold. "Do you think

we should go and look?" she asked, hoping to God he'd say no, but willing to follow him anywhere if he said yes.

"Somebody will have to track that bastard at first light," he said, staring into the darkness as if he could see the retreating cat. "If it's wounded, it's ten times as dangerous as before."

"Won't it . . . just . . . die?" Hallie asked.

"Maybe," Chance said, "and maybe not. If it doesn't, and it runs across somebody's stray cattle, or a pack of kids out sleigh-riding—"

Hallie squeezed her eyes shut against the image, but it only grew more intense, more savage. Her stomach rolled at the pictures that rose in her mind.

Chance put out a hand to her. "Come on," he said, with gruff tenderness. "Let's get in out of the weather. There's nothing more we can do tonight."

All the same, when they were inside, and he'd made them both a hot toddy to take the edges off their shock, he placed a quick call to Jase's cell phone number and reported the sighting of a blood-covered mountain lion.

"Did Jase say anything about Kiera and Kiley?" Hallie asked, more anxious about the brief separation from her daughters because of the incident. She hoped Jase was at Katie's, protecting them all.

"I got his voice mail," Chance answered. They were sitting in his living room, side by side on the long leather couch, and he got up to start the fire. When he came back, he slipped an arm around her shoulders. "You really miss those two kids, don't you?"

She nodded, breathless with the force of her emotion, and stared into the blaze, her eyes hot with tears.

"They're all right," he said quietly, "but if you're worried, why don't you call Katie?"

For a moment, she actually considered the idea. Then she looked at the antique clock on the mantel piece, and saw that it was 3:25 A.M. As much as she wanted reassurance, she knew Chance was right; the girls were fine, and waking Katie, maybe waking all the kids, too, was not a viable option.

"You have a computer," she said, moments later, remembering that he'd e-mailed her at least once, while she was at Jessie's.

He nodded, indicated a doorway in the heavy log wall. "That way," he said.

"I'll try to access my messages," she told him, just in case. "It might make me feel better."

"Go ahead," he answered. "While you're doing that, I'll lock up and make us another drink. Sleep insurance." He smiled wickedly. "Or we could make love again."

"Perish the thought," Hallie said, with a weary laugh. "I'm so tired I'd never survive it."

He shrugged. "It was worth a try," he said, resigned.

She found the computer, after taking in Chance's workspace at a glance. It was tidy to a fault, as she'd expected, and there were enough books on the shelves to stock a good-size library. Normally, she would have found them irresistible but, at the moment, she was only interested in finding out if anyone had tried to contact her via the Internet.

It took a few minutes to get into her mailbox, and when she did, she found the usual sales pitches, and promptly deleted them. She was about to send her daughters a message, via Katie's e-mail address, when a thought occurred to her. She opened Recently Deleted Mail and there it was, a subject line bearing Katie's address.

"Chance," she whispered rawly. Then, as she read, her voice rose to a shout. "Chance!"

He bolted into the room, with both dogs at his heels, his face white with worry, the .357 clasped in one hand. "Hallie, what—?"

She pointed at the screen with a trembling finger. "Look. He's here, the son of a bitch. Joel is *here*, in Primrose Creek. He read this e-mail, and now he knows where my children are!"

Chance scanned the message. "Come on," he said urgently, grasping her by the hand and dragging her to her feet.

16

~

Chance paused in the kitchen, grabbed the telephone while Hallie was dragging on her coat and boots, and promptly threw the receiver against the wall, swearing under his breath. "Line's down," he said.

Hallie wanted to scream. "What about your cell phone?"

"It's in the truck. Let's go."

It was hard traveling, just getting to the barn, where Chance's truck was parked, the snow was so deep. It was stone dark out, as well, except for the starlight, which was disappearing as new clouds moved in, harbingers of another storm, perhaps even more ferocious than the last one.

Chance started the truck, racing its powerful engine a couple of times, to hurry the warm-up process along, and then slammed it into reverse, grinding his way out of the barn. Hallie snatched up the cell phone he'd left on the dashboard and saw that the battery was dead.

She opened the glove compartment, at Chance's order, and rummaged until she found the charger and plugged both it and the phone into the cigarette lighter. Hallie dialed 911, listened, and then swore in furious desperation. "It's still not working!"

Chance held the small instrument with one hand and drove with the other, the truck careening through the deep snow, fishtailing this way and that. He pressed a series of numbers with the tip of his thumb, put the device to his ear, tossed it away.

"Shit," he said. "Emergency Services must have commandeered the satellite for a while, or something. This kind of snowfall can cause all kinds of problems, even up here, where we're used to it."

"My *children!*" Hallie whispered. While she was fairly certain Joel himself wouldn't hurt Kiera and Kiley—he loved them, in his twisted way—she couldn't predict what his associates might do. After all, they'd killed Lou, and then Charlie Long, without any compunction at all.

"We'll get to them, Hallie," Chance promised, fighting the wheel with both hands now, plowing through grille-high snow. "It won't be easy, and it won't be fast, but we'll get there in time, and you have my word on that."

Hallie swallowed, hung on to the handle above the passenger door window, her feet braced against the floorboards. "Hurry," she said, quite unnecessarily.

The form of a man loomed, feet set apart, at the end of the driveway, and Hallie knew instantly who it was, despite the fact that she couldn't see his features, or even the details of his clothing.

"Joel," she said. "Dear God, that's Joel."

Chance brought the truck to a stop, not that he had any other choice, beyond running over another human being. Almost in a single motion he put the engine in neutral and reached back to wrench his rifle down from the rack that stretched across the back window.

Hallie scrabbled to grab his coat, lying almost flat against the seat, and missed. "Stay there," she heard him bark, as he left the door gaping and trudged through the knee-deep snow.

She ignored the order, of course, sat up, and fumbled to free herself from the seat belt. The door on her side had jammed, or maybe Chance had locked it somehow, and Hallie didn't bother trying to find the switch. She scooted over the seat and went out after him.

The two of them, Joel and Chance, stood out in frightening relief, in the center of a shared aura of snow-speckled light from the truck's high-beams, two man-shapes facing each other, ready to fight to the death.

Hallie slipped, fell on the ground, got up again. Just as she rounded the front of the truck, she heard shots, a staccato *plump-plump-plump* and knew, as the daughter of a cop, that Joel had gunned Chance down with a revolver.

She screamed, dropped to her knees beside Chance, who was bleeding in the snow, and only half conscious. "Take this," he said, indicating the rifle.

"Too late," Joel said, taking a handful of Hallie's hair and wrenching her to her feet. With the other, he jerked the rifle from her fingers and hurled it into the bushes, out of sight. "Looks like your cowboy ain't too quick on the draw, ma'am."

"Let me go!" Hallie shrieked, flailing. Chance was lying on the ground behind her, very probably dying, and she had no time for anything or anyone, at the moment, but him.

Joel flung her down hard, and she landed on top of Chance. She caught herself, her hands slippery with blood. "Kiss him good-bye," her ex-husband snarled. "He's as good as dead and so are you."

"I'm sorry," Hallie whispered to Chance. "Oh, God, I'm sorry." But she knew he couldn't hear her. His eyes were closed, and his breathing was shallow.

Joel dragged her to her feet again, this time by the back of her jacket. He flung her out of the glaring light and she landed on her knees in the snow. She struggled back to her feet, turned and leaped on him, claws bared, shrieking like the mountain lion she'd heard so many times.

He sent his elbow slamming into her face, and this time, when she fell, she didn't get up again. She came to, a few seconds, minutes or hours later, to find herself being carried through the woods, in the direction of Jessie's place, slung painfully over Joel's shoulder like a sack of alfalfa pellets.

On and on they went, through the deep snow and the trees. Hallie stayed inert, hoping to catch Joel by surprise when he finally put her down.

When he did, he threw her backward, beside the creek. She knew immediately that the thing she'd landed on wasn't a log or a stone, but a body. She turned, looked into a mass of gore that had once been somebody's face, and wriggled away with a little squeal of fear and revulsion.

"Good . . . God . . . what hap-happened?" she managed, sitting a few feet from the corpse, her hands back behind her, the snow seeping through her jeans. She was numb with cold and shock, and her brain was functioning at warp-turtle. A moment or two after she'd voiced the question, it all came back to her: the blood-drenched cat she'd seen earlier that evening, running between Chance's house and barn. She shuddered and tried wildly to scrub the crimson from her hands with fistfuls of snow.

Joel grabbed her wrist, wrenched her to her feet with a force that nearly pulled her shoulder out of its socket. He was seething, his eyes cold and dark, picking up reflected moonlight from the whispering waters of the creek. "You just couldn't leave things alone, could you?" he rasped.

Hallie retreated from him, rubbing her aching wrist with her free hand. "You're crazy!" she retorted. "My God, Joel, what *happened* to you? When—*how*—did you turn into this . . . this monster?"

His grin was eerie, and he was holding his revolver on her. The same gun he'd used to shoot Chance.

Chance. Her heart seized with the anguish of knowing that Chance was either dead or dying, alone on a country road, and all because of her. She put a hand to her mouth to hold back a sob.

"Maybe I was *always* a monster," Joel taunted. "Does it bother you, Hallie, to think you slept with me, bore my children, all the while never knowing who or what I was?"

"You need help," she said, and was surprised at the calm and reasonable tone she used. "Stop this, now. Don't let it go any further. Think of Kiera and Kiley, if you won't do it for yourself."

He spat into the snow. "Tell me where the disk is," he said. His face softened then, momentarily, and somehow that was even more frightening than his anger and scorn had been. "Not that I'm going to let you live, either way," he added, in a sort of mad, chanting meter. "I still have the kids, at least. I'm going to pick them up, when I've finished with you, and take them away from here. They'll forget you, in time, and this place, too."

"Joel," Hallie whispered, putting out both hands, palms forward, in a plea for reason. "Listen to yourself. You've committed *murder*. You're planning more. Do you really think a killer can be a fit parent—even if that killer is you?"

Joel wavered for the first time since the whole horror had begun, the revolver dangling from his right hand while he considered. "The disk," he reiterated. "Where is the damn disk?"

"I gave everything to the sheriff," Hallie said in an even tone that surprised her, considering that she was shaking inside. "It's over, Joel. Give yourself up. Don't you see that you're going to be on the run from the law for the rest of your life if you don't? And that means your daughters will be hunted as well, if you take them with you. What if you're caught, and they're stranded in some foreign country? Don't do this to them, Joel. It's time to stop."

"Words," Joel replied, with another scary little smile. "You always were so good with words. The thing is, I'm going to make it all up to them. Keep them safe. They'll live in a big house, with servants, and have ponies and anything else they want."

"What about a sane father, Joel? What about normal

lives? Will they have those things?" She knew she should back off, think about escaping into the trees somehow, getting back to Chance, but she couldn't seem to stop these hopeless attempts to reach Joel on some level of rationality.

He dragged the sleeve of his ruined overcoat across his mouth, like a man who has just taken a great draught of some powerful, evil potion. She saw the very fires of hell leaping in his eyes. Dear God, if he killed her, and snatched her babies from Katie, they would grow up with the devil himself for a father. They would be living with a madman.

She couldn't let that happen, no matter what she had to do to prevent it. And that included dying.

She took a step toward him. "Listen to me, Joel," she said. "I'll do anything you want me to do. I'll get the evidence back somehow, and you can destroy it."

"Where was it? We looked everywhere."

She swallowed hard. Told him about the key, the plastic Virgin Mary in Lou's storage shed. All the while, she was thinking of Chance, and of her children. Of the Strattons, too, and their girls. Chance was dying, or maybe already dead, and the others were in grave danger. If harm came to anyone else because of her, she wouldn't be able to live with the knowledge, even if somehow, miraculously, they survived this night of horror.

If it hadn't been for her children, her precious daughters, she wasn't sure she would even have *wanted* to live, not after what had happened to Chance. Had she been alone in the world, she'd surely have chosen to follow him into whatever hereafter awaited them.

"The FBI has the stuff, Joel," she reasoned. "Please—

can't you see it's over? They'll be here soon—the police, the feds, all of them."

"In for a penny," Joel said, singsong, "in for a pound." He ran his eyes over the length of her. "I'm going to shoot you now," he went on, sounding for all the world like a childhood bully outlining the rules of some sick game. "But not through the heart. I'll start with your ankles, then move on to your knees, then, finally, blow your belly open. Then, if you're still conscious, I'll shoot off your fingers, one at a time."

Was this how it had been for Lou? Had Joel—or whoever had done his dirty work—tormented him with fear before emptying five shots into his chest?

"Don't," was all she could say, and the word came out as a terrified croak.

Joel raised the pistol, aimed. Hallie closed her eyes tightly and lunged to one side after waiting as long as she dared. There was a sound in the woods; Hallie was sure the cougar was back. She heard the bullet splash into the creek, heard a loud report, a burbling cry of agonized indignation.

Lying on the ground, only a foot or so from the corpse, she opened her eyes and saw Joel on his knees, his back to her now, the snow turning crimson around him. Beyond him was Chance, a dead man walking, unsteady on his feet, his face bloodless, rifle in hand.

Joel lifted his gaze to heaven, then fell forward into the stained snow, still gripping his belly, surprised and affronted by death.

Hallie scrambled to Chance, full of joy, because he was alive and he'd saved her life, and of sorrow, because matters had come to this. Chance, despite his heroics, was badly injured. Joel was gone, and so were Lou and Charlie, and this poor remnant of a man lying on the ground, with his throat torn out and his features obliterated by blood.

Chance sagged against her. "I . . . think I need . . . an ambulance."

She supported him by standing under his right arm, using her body like a crutch. "Yes," she said simply, and somehow, moving over a bridge of dark stars, she managed to get him, and herself, back to the truck, which was still running when they reached it, after a long hike, the driver's side door hanging wide open, just as she'd left it.

Hallie shuddered, remembering all that had happened in this place, and maneuvered Chance into the seat she'd occupied earlier. He slumped, his clothes awash in blood, and closed his eyes.

Hallie got behind the wheel, closed the door with a slam, and headed for the main road into town, honking the horn intermittently as she made her painstaking way over buried roads, in case someone nearby should hear, and be able to help. She simply guessed where the ditches were. By sheer determination, luck, and stubbornness, she got as far as Doc Whitman's house, and laid on the horn until he came out, coatless and rushed.

"What the hell?" he demanded, looking past Hallie to see Chance on the other side of the truck, quite literally floating between two worlds.

"He's been shot," Hallie said. "He needs a doctor—a hospital—but we won't be able to make it that far, not in this weather."

Doc was already opening the passenger door, catching Chance in strong, wiry arms when he fell from the high seat. "Help me get him inside!" he said, and Hallie rushed to obey.

They laid Chance on a steel examining table in Doc's office and Hallie covered him with every blanket she could find while Hal Whitman used his two-way radio to summon help from Reno. A helicopter was dispatched immediately.

While they waited, Doc did his best to stop the bleeding and keep Chance breathing. He monitored his heartbeat steadily, with a stethoscope, ready to perform CPR if that was necessary. Hallie simply held Chance's bloody hand and wept.

The helicopter arrived in a surprisingly short time, despite the darkness and the snow, and landed noisily in Doc's small parking lot. The sound and the lights brought out half the town of Primrose Creek, and Jase arrived simultaneously.

"What the hell happened?" he demanded, grabbing Hallie by both shoulders and all but lifting her off the ground.

"Take it easy," Doc said sternly. "She's on our side."

Jase gave her a little shake, all the same. "Talk!" he snapped.

The flying EMTs burst in then, with a gurney, hoisted Chance onto it, hooked up an IV, and wheeled him out, all in the space of a few seconds. Hallie tried to break free and follow, but Jase held her fast.

"You can't go with them," he said. "There isn't room in the 'copter. Now, *tell me what happened.*"

Hallie began to cry. "I need to be sick," she said, as all

of it flooded back, all the blood, all the fear and the gore and the spectacular, hopeless horror.

"Better let her loose," Doc warned.

She reached the sink just in time, retched violently, over and over again. When the spate was over, Doc handed her a glass of water to rinse her mouth, and draped her gently in one of the blankets they'd used to cover Chance.

"Give her a few minutes," Doc said to Jase, shepherding her out of the exam room and into the main part of his house. He settled her in a large, comfortable recliner in the living room, which smelled of leather and pipe tobacco.

While Hallie shivered in Doc's favorite chair, despite the way he'd bundled her up, Jase sat nearby, turning his hat round and round in his fingers, waiting impatiently to grill her. Doc brought her a double shot of brandy and ordered her to drink it slowly.

She drank.

Jase and the doctor waited.

"My children," Hallie said finally.

"They're fine," Jase assured her. "Katie gave them supper and put them to bed hours ago."

She let out a long sigh of relief. "Thank God," she whispered.

Jase, obviously thinking of Chance, simply waited.

She began to talk, relaying the grim story in halting words, sparing no detail. She described their confrontation with Joel on the road, Chance's shooting, her abduction, the ravaged body sprawled beside the creek. Jase listened with no expression, and no interruptions, until she'd finished.

"Sweet God," he said then, and reached for the radio on his belt.

"I want to see my children," Hallie said, "and then Chance. I have to go to Chance."

Doc spoke gently. "You can't let those little girls see you like this, all shaken up and covered in blood, and the hospital staff won't let you near Chance. He'll be in surgery for hours, and then, God willing, the recovery room, for another long stretch."

Hallie closed her eyes, sick again, and too dizzy to stand. *This*, she thought, with a sort of crazy detachment, *must be what shock is like*. She knew she was too weak to fight her way to Chance's side, and the last thing she wanted was to give her babies any more trauma by showing up in such a state, and dragging them out of bed. They would have enough to deal with, when they learned the nearly unendurable truth about their father, and everything that had gone on.

"What . . . what can I do?"

"You can sleep," Doc said. "I'll get you some clothes, start a shower running. This couch makes out into a bed. In the morning, when you've gotten some starch back, you'll be able to function."

"I'm going to have a lot of questions for you," Jase warned her, "and so will the feds, I'm sure, so don't get any ideas about taking those kids and running off again, all right?"

He was treating her as though she were one of the criminals, but she didn't have the energy to fight anymore. She'd used the last measure, getting Chance to Doc's place. She could go no further. Besides, she knew Jase was afraid for Chance.

"I'll be around," she said.

Evidently satisfied, Jase stood up and, after exchanging a few low-volume but heated words in the hallway, with Doc, he left.

Hallie sleepwalked through her shower, put on the flannel pajamas Doc gave her, and collapsed on the hide-a-bed, which had been folded out and piled high with blankets while she was washing away Chance's blood. She saw the crimson spiral, whirling and whirling around the drain, long after her mind had shut down all but its deepest functions and faculties.

Doc shook her awake, and she came up gasping, like a swimmer gone too long without air, plunging through the surface of consciousness into the light. She blinked, and the doctor's voice led her the rest of the way into the waking world.

"Brought you some coffee," he said. "I didn't know if you took cream or sugar, so it's just black."

She stared at him, trying to read the craggy lines of his face, searching for secrets. "Chance?" she whispered rawly. "My children?"

"Your children are fine," he told her gently, steadying her grasp on the mug of hot coffee by laying his hands over hers. "I called Jessie, and she'll be here as soon as she can catch a flight."

She took a shaky sip, though she felt the caffeine spurt, with that small mouthful, into every aching, bruised muscle, resurrecting all the pain of the night before, indeed, all the unconscious suffering and sorrow, joy and celebration, handed down from one generation to the next, from before the beginning, to pulse in her own cells.

"What about Chance?"

He thought before answering. "Chance is alive," he said, after a long time. "Like I said, Jessie is on her way. As next of kin, she—"

"Oh, my God," Hallie gasped, and then her words fell over one another, coming so rapidly that she couldn't stand them upright. "Chance can't be dying. He can't. He's so strong. He walked through the woods, found me, saved me from Joel—"

Doc closed his patient blue eyes for a long moment. He'd set her coffee aside, and now his hands were resting on her shoulders, much the way Chance's had done. She couldn't bear it.

"It's been touch and go ever since Chance got out of surgery," he said. "He's flatlined a couple of times. They've managed to bring him back so far, but—"

Hallie slapped both hands over her mouth, to keep in a scream as shrill as that of any cat, prowling any jungle or forest, in any time or dimension.

"Get yourself dressed now," urged the doctor. "Jase will take us to Reno, to the hospital."

Hallie threw back the covers and bounded out of bed before she remembered that she was wearing borrowed pajamas, and that her own clothes were ruined. She looked down at them with an expression of surprised dismay that must have said it all.

"I've put out some things for you," Doc said gently, with an attempt at a smile. "Jessie keeps a few things here. Ought to fit okay."

She nodded, numb again, and hurried into the bathroom. Sure enough, Doc had laid out jeans, a blue sweater, neatly folded, and even socks and a pair of boots. No bra, no panties. Hallie barely noticed. She took a scalding hot shower, in a vain effort to drive the chill from her bones, and dressed hastily. When she'd toweled her hair dry and combed it with her fingers, barely noticing her own fierce shiner, where Joel had struck her with his elbow, she emerged in a billow of steam to find Doc and Jase seated in the living room. Doc seemed worn out, like an old washcloth gone thin in the middle, and Jase looked somber and official.

"I thought you might want to stop by our place and say hello to Kiera and Kiley," the sheriff said, "so I came by a little early."

Hallie's heart leaped at the prospect of seeing her daughters, enfolding them in her arms, holding them tightly, tightly, until their images were impressed into the very fabric of her soul. "Yes," she said. "Oh, yes."

They all trooped out, Jase leading the way, Hallie following, and Doc behind her. Jase's SUV, which bore the Sheriff's Department's star-shaped logo on both doors, was up to navigating the storm-ravaged roads, and then some. Within a few minutes, they were at Katie and Jase's house, and Hallie was dashing up the front walk to her daughters, who waited, shivering and grinning, on the porch.

"Look, Mommy!" Kiera cried, pointing to a gap where her right front tooth had been. "I lost a tooth! And the tooth fairy left a whole dollar on my pillow!"

Hallie laughed, and cried, and knelt right there on that frosty porch, hugging her babies, kissing them, drawing in their powdery scents. Celebrating the simple fact of their existence, in a world where even that could be so fleeting.

Small fingers touched the angry bruise covering Hallie's right eye. "What happened to your face, Mommy?" Kiera asked.

"I had an accident," Hallie said gently.

"I bet I lose a tooth soon, too," Kiley said, put out at coming in second, even in the tooth fairy event. "And I bet I get a *hundred* dollars!"

"I wouldn't hold my breath," Hallie advised, after giving the little girl a squeeze, and stood, sensing Jase and Doc behind her, on the step. She turned and gently shooed her daughters into the house.

Katie was in the kitchen, up to her elbows in blueberry pancake batter. She'd fried bacon, too, and started a panful of scrambled eggs. Seeing Hallie, she stopped her work and hugged her tightly.

"Thank God, you're all right," Katie said, and warmth spread through Hallie.

Hallie returned the hug, then stepped back. There were dark circles under Katie's eyes, and her skin was a waxen color. "What about you, Katie?" Hallie asked softly. "Are *you* all right?"

Tears came, but Katie smiled, and nodded her head. "I'm okay. It's Chance—"

"I know," Hallie said. "I know."

Somehow, she managed to eat part of a pancake, part of an egg, part of a slice of bacon, although she would have sworn by all that was holy that she couldn't force down so much as a bite. During the meal, she watched Katie and Jase interact with each other and their own young daughters, amid all the chaos of that Morning After.

It seemed to her that they were like bumper cars at a carnival, Jase and Katie, bouncing off whenever they encountered each other, although each of them managed to engage without a problem when talking to their children.

Hallie was saddened by what she saw, and wished she could wave a magic wand, or light candles, or *something*, and make everything all right for the Stratton family, for all of time and eternity. They were such good people.

When the time to leave approached, she took Kiera and Kiley aside, explained that Chance had been hurt very badly, and she was going to the hospital to see him. She would have to tell them about Joel, too, sooner or later, but that was going to require a lot of thinking and praying. It was so vitally important to get it right, because whatever she told them about Joel, and his death, would remain in their minds for the rest of their lives, like a mental tattoo.

The trip to Reno was long and treacherous, and none of them talked much, not Doc, not Jase, and certainly not Hallie, who had forgotten, it seemed, how to make simple small talk. Her face hurt, and so did most of the rest of her body. She sensed that Jase wanted to ask a thousand, if not a million, questions, but he was restraining himself. Probably both Doc and Katie had asked him to hold off on the interrogations until she'd had an opportunity to catch her breath. The federal agencies, she knew, would not be so obliging.

At the hospital, Hallie was out of the rig and running toward the entrance while Jase was still waiting for a State Patrol car to back out of the parking spot he'd chosen. Nobody tried to stop her.

When the elevator came, she went straight to the Intensive Care Unit.

Hallie didn't need to ask which room was Chance's, once she reached her destination; there were men in suits standing guard on either side of it. Implacable types, with brown shoes and attitude. Here, Hallie realized, was a barrier she couldn't cross, not without Jase's help.

"Ms. O'Rourke?" one of the agents asked, startling her.

She stared at him. "Yes." She was feverish with impatience and with grief. "Why are you here?"

"Just keeping an eye on things, in case somebody got through the net." He showed his badge; an unnecessary gesture, given the situation. "Special Agent Walters," he said. "FBI."

She gave the ID a desultory examination. Nodded. "What about Agents Simms and Baker? Where are they?"

Jase and Walters exchanged glances and, suddenly, Hallie felt weak in the knees. Walters caught her by the elbow, squired her to a nearby chair. "Oh, my God," she gasped, and put her head down to keep from fainting. "They were fakes. I knew something was wrong."

"They're in jail in Primrose Creek," Jase put in. "When these guys showed up, they were real surprised to find out they weren't the only game in town. Turns out the Bureau hadn't sent anybody but them. I picked up Simms and Baker at the Last Chance Café—they were having doughnuts and coffee."

Walters nodded, verifying the story. He bent to peer into Hallie's surely bloodless face. "You were with Mr. Qualtrough when this . . . unfortunate incident happened?"

"Yes," she said again. *Unfortunate incident.* It was

such an inadequate phrase, to cover a scene, a night, that had been etched into her memory in stark, slashing lines.

"Can you tell us what went on?"

She raked her upper lip with her teeth, and nodded once more. "I can," she said, "but I'm hoping you'll let me in to see Chance first."

At that moment, while the agents were still debating, Jase spoke up again.

"Let her in," the sheriff said, with no effort at diplomacy. Hallie knew about the undercurrent of strain that so often ran between regular cops and the agents they invariably referred to as "feds." Lou had regarded them as high-handed interlopers.

Agent Walters hesitated, then stepped aside in response to Jase's demand, and gestured with one hand for Hallie to enter.

When she saw Chance, lying there in an odd-looking, high-tech hospital bed, with all manner of tubes and wires affixed and implanted, she flashed on those last days of her mother's life, and a tangle of emotions rushed to the surface, stinging her eyes, making her throat ache, twisting her stomach into knots.

"Oh, Chance," she whispered.

He didn't speak, or move, or open his eyes, but somehow, Hallie sensed that he knew she was there, and he was reaching out to her. She went to his bedside, found a place on his arm where she could touch him without disturbing some tube or machine.

"I did this to you," she said, leaning over to let her forehead rest against his. "I caused it to happen. I'm so sorry, Chance. *So sorry.*"

There was no answer, either verbal or by any sort of sign, and yet she sensed a change of some sort, as if his energies were flowing into hers, and vice versa, in silent communion.

"You've got to get well," she said, when she could trust herself to speak.

"Miss?"

Hallie turned, saw a young male nurse standing at the foot of Chance's bed. "I'm sorry, but these visits have to be kept short. I'll have to ask you to step out now."

She nodded, kissed Chance's forehead, already moist with her tears, and then turned and went out into the hallway again.

"How is he?" Jase asked. He looked grim, and Hallie felt ashamed for acting as if the grief surrounding Chance's shooting was hers alone to bear. Of course Jase loved him, and so did Jessie, who would be back soon, her tour cut short, to watch and wait. Katie cared for Chance, too, and as word of the incident spread through the town of Primrose Creek, there would be plenty of sorrow to go around.

Hallie just shook her head, too choked up to speak. Jase's eyes were wet.

"Not Chance," he said, to no one in particular. "*Not Chance.*"

"We'd like to ask Miss O'Rourke some questions," Special Agent Walters put in.

"Wouldn't we all?" Jase bit out, glaring at the man.

"Everybody take it easy," Doc put in. "This is no place for head-butting. We don't want Chance picking up on a lot of drama."

Jase sagged a little. "You're right," he said.

"I'll tell you everything I can," Hallie said, and Agent Walters nodded, called on his radio for another man to replace him on guard duty, and escorted her into a nearby lounge. Jase joined them.

"From the beginning, please," the FBI agent said, and, once again, Hallie told her story.

17

The FBI interview was grueling, but Hallie saw it through, well aware that there would be a lot more of that sort of thing in the future. Until the full extent of Joel's criminal activities had been explored, and those of the men he'd associated with, all the knots untangled, her life would be a circus. She and the children might as well brace themselves for an onslaught of cops and questions and, given Joel's position in the D.A.'s office, probably a platoon of media types, too. As much as she dreaded the prospect of all that uproar, however, her primary concern was still Chance, in there in that hospital bed, holding on to his very existence by a thread. If he recovered, and that was a big if, he sure wouldn't be up to coping with a media storm, not to mention a lot of court appearances and depositions.

None of this would have happened to him, if it weren't for her.

When Agents Walters and McNullen had finished with her—it was only a temporary respite, of course—she was allowed another brief visit with Chance. His condition was unchanged.

"Why don't you let somebody here take care of that shiner?" Jase asked, when she came out of the lounge the Bureau had appropriated as a sort of office.

"What can they do?" she countered. "It will fade away in time."

Jase huffed out a sigh. He was impatient, as she was, because he couldn't *do* something, make something happen, change things for Chance, for all of them. "You still ought to have it looked at," he said. "What the hell did that bastard hit you with?"

"His elbow," Hallie answered, remembering the stunning insult, the pain of the blow. It had been worse, she thought, coming from a man she'd once loved.

"Jesus," Jase muttered, with a wincing grimace, as the elevator doors opened at the end of the hallway.

"What happened to Baker and Simms?" she asked, as a diversionary tactic and because she was curious.

"They were cops," he said, "though I hate to call them that, and lump them in with a lot of decent, hard-working law enforcement people. Part of the Phoenix operation. They're busted for all of time and eternity, and singing like the fat lady at the end of the opera."

Hallie smiled a little, and the two of them watched as a tall, elegant woman wearing a long, divided riding skirt of black suede, boots, a blouse, and a bolero jacket stepped out.

Jessie had arrived. Her hair was wound into a single silver braid, reaching past her waist, and she wore a round-brimmed hat, gently laced with snow.

Hallie could have hugged the woman, if she hadn't

been rooted to the floor. Jase strode down the corridor to greet her, embracing her for a long moment, letting himself be embraced.

"How is he?" Jessie asked, when hellos had been exchanged.

Hallie had been strong since arriving at the hospital that morning; she'd had to be, but now she wanted nothing so much as to dissolve, to simply fall apart. She held herself together tightly with both arms. "The same," she said weakly.

Just then, Doc came out of a doorway, and his and Jessie's gazes locked, causing the air in the corridor to sizzle.

"Hello, Jessie," Doc said, in the same tone he might have used if a goddess had appeared before him. "You're here."

"Of course I am, you old coot," she replied, but there were tears standing in her eyes, and she went into his arms in a graceful, practiced glide. "Did you think you were seeing things?"

Doc's hands lingered on the sides of Jessie's slender waist. Though she was seventy, at least, her spine was straight and her eyes were bright, and there was an energy about her that said she was nobody to mess with. Hallie, admiration renewed, wanted to be just like her when she grew up.

"You'll stay?" he asked. He seemed oblivious to the rest of the world, and there was such extraordinary tenderness in his blue eyes as he regarded Jessie that Hallie ached.

Jessie laid a long, slim, artist's hand to Doc's cheek. " 'Course I'll stay," she told him. "This is home, and I'm done with touring, whether my agent likes it or not." She paused. "Now. Let me see Chance."

Because she was next of kin, and had just arrived after a long journey, Jessie was admitted to Chance's room immediately, although she stayed less than a minute. When she came out, she was crying.

"What happened here?" she demanded.

Hallie didn't have another accounting in her, after what she'd been through with the FBI. She looked help-lessly at Jase, who took Jessie's elbow and steered her toward the waiting room.

"I think I can fill you in on most of the details," he said.

Hallie paced the hallway until she was allowed to visit Chance again. She felt as though he were a diver trapped in some wreckage far under the sea, and she was bringing him mouthfuls of air. When she had to leave him again, she went to the chapel, sat quietly in one of the pews, and tried to pray.

No words came, and she offered no promises. She sim-ply sat there, fingers interlocked, staring up at the multi-national tableau painted on the wall behind the altar. It seemed that every conceivable religion was represented, and all were illuminated by the same Light.

Presently, she sensed someone near, and turned just as Jessie sat down beside her and took her hand. Hallie's eyes flooded with tears; it was her fault what had hap-pened to Chance. She had expected cold fury from his friends and family, not comfort, not quiet acceptance. Together, the two women sat, saying nothing, communi-cating everything.

It was much later, in the cafeteria, where Jessie and Hallie sat across from each other, drinking tea out of foam cups, that Hallie was able to say more than a few words.

"Are you all right? This must have come as a terrible shock to you."

Jessie sighed, and fresh tears welled in her eyes. "There has been too much loss in this family," she said. "It's time we had some joy."

Hallie touched the other woman's hand. "Yes," she agreed.

"But let's talk about you, and about that hard-headed man in there, in that hospital room. He's going to make it, mark my word. We won't have it any other way." She paused, sipped her tea. "Will you be staying on at Primrose Creek?"

Hallie shook her head. "I've got a lot of fires to put out back in Phoenix," she said. Just the prospect of it all made her feel as if the very marrow in her bones had turned to liquid. "My business, some details concerning my stepfather's estate, all the stuff that's happened with Joel."

"I see," Jessie said. "I understood that you and Chance—"

Hallie let out a raspy sigh. "I'm not good for him," she said. "Look what's already happened, because of me."

"But you love him," Jessie said gently.

It was true, Hallie realized. She'd never admitted it to herself before, but that didn't change the facts of the matter. She'd fallen in love with Chance almost right away, and all the things that had happened since then, good and bad, had only served to reinforce what she felt.

She nodded slowly. "Yes," she said.

"He'll need you, when he comes out of this," Jessie went on.

"No," Hallie answered. The sentence stopped with that

one desperate barrier of a word. If she'd been able to articu-
late the rest of it, she would have said, *He needs peace, and
the time to heal. He needs his family and his friends and his
horses. My kind of trouble, he can do without.*

Jessie looked sad. "I shouldn't have said that,
shouldn't have put that kind of pressure on you. It's easy
to forget that you've been through as much as Chance
has, if not more—you're still standing, that's all. But
you're just as badly wounded."

Hallie didn't know what to say to that. She ran her
hands down the legs of her borrowed jeans—this woman's
jeans—and tried in vain to smile. The result of her effort
felt like some kind of ghoulish mask, so she let it fall away
into space. Before she had to say anything else, Evie
appeared, with a woman she introduced as her mother,
Della. Hallie had seen her a couple of times in the café.

The pair didn't scan the large room from the doorway,
the way most people would have done, but simply zeroed
in on Hallie and Jessie, at their corner table, with all the
unerring confidence of a pair of homing pigeons.

"We heard what happened," Della said, and hugged
Jessie, who stood up to greet her with genuine gladness.

Evie glanced at Hallie, full of sorrow. "We're holding a
candlelight vigil tonight," Evie announced, "in the parking lot of the Last Chance Café."

"I'll be there, if I can," Jessie said. "It depends on how
things go here, of course."

Della, a robust woman with no apparent ax to grind,
pulled Hallie to her feet and virtually slammed her
against her bosom in a matronly hug. "No wonder I saw
all that darkness around you the other day, when you
served me the chili special," she said. Like her daughter,

Della was into auras, tarot cards, and magic in general. "Poor little thing!"

Evie mellowed a little. "How are you, Hallie?" she asked, with a note of reserve. Hallie saw a flicker of cautious concern in the other woman's face. Maybe she'd noticed the shiner, though it was hard to conceive of anybody missing something like that. The bruise covered half her face.

"I'll be okay once Chance takes a turn for the better," she said. She wished she had Evie and Della's ability to see into the future, at least some of the time, then quickly called it back before some passing fairy godmother decided to grant it. If she'd known all this ahead of time—Joel and the divorce and the murders and Chance's possibly fatal injuries—well, she'd probably have stayed in bed with the covers pulled up over her head.

Evie, standing next to Hallie's chair, laid a hand on her shoulder. "I'm sorry, Hallie," she said. "I—"

Hallie covered Evie's hand with her own. "I know," she said. "I know."

Della drew up a chair and sank into it. She was wearing a black velveteen sweat suit, Hallie noticed, with a big orange pumpkin grinning, saw-toothed, on the front of the shirt. "One of my little blue-haired ladies made this for me," she said, referring, no doubt, to a customer at her beauty shop. She beamed with subdued pride. "We swapped for a color rinse and a perm. She's going to whip up a reindeer for Christmas."

Jessie smiled, and it was clear then to Hallie how much this woman had missed her friends, Primrose Creek, and being in her own house, with her things around her. "I'll bet you're talking about Audrey Moss, aren't you? She was always so clever—she was in my art class in high school."

Della beamed fondly. "Heck, Jessie, I know that," she said. "I graduated with you, remember?" She slid a glance to Hallie, indicating Evie with a nod. "Got my family started late in life," she added, in a whisper that could have been heard on the other side of the room, had anyone else been paying attention.

Maybe it was the mention of the reindeer, a fallen domino starting a chain of thoughts. "The horses," Hallie said. "And Chance's dogs—"

"Taken care of," Evie said. "Soon as word got around, the men in town organized a schedule. They're looking after Chance's livestock, and Miss Jessie's, too."

Hallie let out a breath. "I can't believe I forgot."

"I'd have been surprised if you remembered," Jessie countered gently. "A person can only manage so much trauma without shorting out their circuits, Hallie, and you're well past the normal limit."

It was balm to her, this woman's friendship and caring. Almost like having her mother with her again, for a few golden moments.

Presently, Della stood and, at her signal, Evie did, too. "We'd better get back to Primrose Creek," she said. "The Harvest Festival is tomorrow, and there's the vigil tonight. Six o'clock, if you can make it." The invitation was issued to both Hallie and Jessie, Hallie noted, with something that might have been relief.

The day that followed was unmercifully long.

Chance stayed the same.

Hallie paced, and Jessie and Doc talked earnestly on the hallway bench, sometimes clasping hands, sometimes shooting fire with their eyes. Hallie carefully filtered out the conversation and so couldn't have told anyone what was said, even though she was standing right there much of the time.

At four-thirty, Doc let it be known that they were all going back to Primrose Creek for Chance's candlelight vigil. The roads had cleared some during the day and, though Jase had had to leave earlier, understandably swamped with police business, they weren't stranded. They could all get home in the mid-size sedan Jessie had rented at the airport when she arrived.

For Hallie, leaving Chance now was like having a dressing torn from a wound, but she needed to see her children, shower and change her clothes, and, yes, she needed to join in the vigil for Chance's recovery. She needed to raise her lighted candle, with all the others, as a part of the ceremony.

The twins, safely ensconced at Katie's all day, were beside themselves with relief when she appeared, and she wondered, as she crouched to hug them, if they'd thought she was gone for good. It made her shudder to think how close she'd come to dying, to leaving her babies alone.

"We're going to light candles," Kiera told her, lisping a little through the gap left by her vanished tooth. "Is Chance gone to heaven, Mommy? Is that why we're having candles?"

Hallie's eyes stung, and she shook her head, hard. "Chance is still with us, baby," she said. "But he's sort of asleep."

"Maybe he'll see the candles," Kiley speculated gravely, "and follow the light to Primrose Creek."

Hallie could only nod.

By six o'clock, the parking lot at the Last Chance Café was full of people, bundled up in coats and scarves and stocking caps, talking among themselves. Jessie was greeted with a sort of formal affection, and Hallie, to her slight surprise, was treated like a member of the community.

Bear and Madge and Wynona served hot cider. The pastor of the Presbyterian church passed out candles, with little paper skirts around their bases, and then, standing in the bed of somebody's pickup truck, he led the crowd in an eloquent prayer. He asked for Chance's recovery, thanked God that he and Hallie had survived. He called for heavenly comfort for those who awaited word, and divine mercy for those who had set the tragedies in motion.

Hallie, who had had neither the time nor the words to explain to Kiera and Kiley that Joel was gone from their lives for good, was deeply grateful when the names of the dead were not spoken.

The air was crisp, bitingly cold, and the wavering light of the candles, as the gathering sang "Amazing Grace," was a sacred fire to Hallie. She knew that, whether Chance lived or died, she would always remember this little patch of time as a turning point. How ironic that, in the face of death, and despite all the turmoil of recent times, some mystical healing process had begun within her. She was stronger than before, battle scars notwithstanding, and places in her spirit, long since closed off and locked up, like forbidden rooms, were suddenly open to new experiences and new people.

The majesty of it took her breath away.

Madge approached, when the candles were out and the singing had stopped, and the two of them hugged tightly.

"That's some shiner," Madge said.

You ought to see the other guy, Hallie thought, but she didn't say it aloud because, after all, the "other guy" had fathered her children, and he was dead. "I haven't had one of these since I got into a scratching match on the playground in sixth grade," she said. "I won, but Tiffany Brooks put up a hell of a fight."

Madge chuckled, and her hand lingered on Hallie's arm. "How's Chance?"

Hallie sagged. "Not good," she said. "But holding on. It would mean a lot to him to know about this little ceremony tonight."

"He knows," Madge said softly, and patted Hallie's arm again.

That night, Hallie and the girls stayed at Chance's place, as did Jessie. Jessie's back door had yet to be replaced, although the crime-scene guys were finished with the inside of the house. Just as Della had said, the animals were well taken care of by an organized contingent of friends and neighbors.

Hallie slept in Chance's bed that first night, sprawled across the wide mattress, at once comforted by the familiar smell and feel of the blankets and sheets and shattered by the indescribable emptiness. When Kiera and Kiley toddled in, sometime in the darkest hours, she was grateful for the company.

Before dawn the next morning, Hallie sneaked downstairs to find Jessie already moving about in the kitchen. She was wearing a plaid flannel shirt, jeans, and barn boots, and her silver hair trailed, in a single gleaming plait, down the middle of her back. The room was warm with the scent of fresh-brewed coffee and the little fire blazing on the hearth.

"Good morning," Jessie said, as though it were an ordinary day, and Chance might pop in from doing his chores at any moment.

Hallie had both hands on the railings as she descended the last few stairs, moving with a strange awkwardness, like an invalid just out of a sick bed. "Morning," she murmured.

"I couldn't sleep," Jessie said, pouring coffee for them both. "Evidently, you're having the same problem—insomnia, I mean."

Hallie sank into a chair at the table, nodded her thanks, and closed both hands around the coffee mug, as much to warm her icy fingers as raise the brew to her mouth. "Do you think it's too early to call the hospital?"

Jessie shook her head. "You go right ahead, if that's what you need to do."

Hallie got up, made her way to the phone, and, after considerable difficulties with her memory and her awkward fingers, managed to place the call. "I'm calling to ask about Chance Qualtrough," she told the Intensive Care duty nurse, after getting past the switchboard.

The nurse sounded weary. "No real change," she said, "although his heartbeat is a bit stronger this morning."

It was an inordinately long time before Hallie could speak; her emotions kept rising up out of her depths and filling her throat, swelling her heart to the bursting point, stinging her eyes. Finally, she got out a scratchy, "Thank you," and hung up.

Jessie was watching her. Waiting.

"His heartbeat is stronger," she said. "Otherwise—"

"Nothing's changed," Jessie finished, with a sigh.

Hallie nodded.

"Sit down," Jessie ordered good-naturedly, "and finish your coffee. You look like the downside of bad news."

Hallie more fell than sat. Reached for her cup.

Jessie sat down across from her, the model of serenity and peace, and sipped from her own mug. Catching Hallie watching her with what must have been a puzzled expression, she smiled. "You're wondering how I can be so calm, aren't you?" she asked and, at Hallie's slight nod, she went on. "I'm a lot older than you are, and I've seen plenty of sickness and death in my time. I've learned one thing—that the sad times are as important as the happy ones; it's all part of the same tapestry. Why, dying is as much a cause for celebration as being born."

Hallie thought of earlier losses in her life, first her mother, then, some years later, Lou. She'd felt a lot of things, and repressed most of them, but an inclination to celebrate wasn't among them. "I guess I just don't see that," she said.

"That's because you don't really believe there's another phase of life, waiting out there Beyond. Death is just another way of being born, that's all. An entryway into a new place."

Hallie swallowed, stared into her cup. "If Chance dies, I'll never forgive myself."

"He won't die," Jessie said, with such confidence that Hallie stared at her. "Not for a long time, anyway. Chance isn't anywhere near finished with all he's got to do right here, on this earth."

"How can you be so sure?" Hallie asked. She wanted to cling to Jessie's belief, but for her, it would be wishful thinking, nothing more.

"Came to me while I was weaving one day, a long time back," Jessie said. "Lord, but I've been aching to get back to my loom."

Hallie nodded, thinking of the colorful weavings she'd seen at Jessie's. Rather than admiring the designs, or studying the mechanism of the loom itself, she'd concentrated most of her efforts on keeping the kids from touching anything they shouldn't.

"Well, when I weave wool or silk, my mind weaves, too. It uses different strands, colors and textures all its own, but it makes a picture all the same. Chance will fight his way back from this. He'll marry and father children." She looked up at the rafters supporting the roof. Sighed. "He comes from good pioneer stock, Chance does."

"Like you," Hallie said. "You're related, after all."

"We're cut from the same cloth, all right."

Hallie smiled. "I read some of Bridget Qualtrough's diary. What a woman she was. Good Lord, facing down Indians, recovering from a snakebite, trying to tame wild horses—"

"She was nineteen when she came here," Jessie said. "Already a widow, with a baby son, a younger sister, and a household retainer to support. She'd improvised a cabin of sorts when Trace showed up one day, carrying his saddle over one shoulder, bound and determined to take care of her." Jessie paused, laughed. "She was having none of that!"

Hallie grinned, picturing Chance's great-great-great-grandmother, holding her land by hard work and will-power. "What about the others?" Chance had told her some of the family history, but she knew she'd find a certain comfort in hearing it again.

"It all started back in Virginia, when old Gideon McQuarry died and left his granddaughters 2,500 acres on either side of that creek out there." She gestured with a thumb. "He was trying to reunite his family—his sons, the fathers of these four young women, died hating each other. I guess old Gideon figured they'd have to get along, those gals, living side by side on this land."

Hallie propped her chin in one hand. "What were the other three women like?" she asked.

"Well, Bridget was the eldest. Her younger sister was Skye, a pretty brown-haired thing, a tomboy. She married a man named Jake Vigil, and the two of them built a timber dynasty that stands to this day, though it's incorporated and all that. Across the creek were my people—Christy, who married Zachary Shaw, the local marshal—and Megan. She got hitched with a rancher named Webb Stratton." She sighed. "I shouldn't be surprised at the way Jase and Chance have always gone round and round about everything from religion to politics. They're McQuarrys, after all, and the McQuarrys tend to go toe-to-toe with each other and duke it out."

"So Bridget and Skye, Christy and Megan, were all feuding?"

"When they first settled down on this land, yes. They worked out their differences in time. Made some discoveries about themselves. All four of them lived to a great old age, and so did their husbands. Noah, Bridget's boy, grew up to be a senator."

"I wish I'd known them."

"You know Chance and Jase and me," Jessie answered. "That's close enough. When this snow melts away, I'll show you their graves, up there on the hill."

Hallie didn't have the heart to tell Jessie she'd probably be gone before the snow was, though she wasn't leaving until Chance opened his eyes, until she could tell him good-bye, face to face. "Thank you, Jessie," she said.

"For what?"

"A place to live. A new start. Primrose Creek changed me."

"It changes everybody," Jessie replied. "I can't take the credit. Now, let's get ourselves organized for the day ahead, shall we? I trust you want to go back to the hospital with me this morning?"

Hallie nodded. She'd take the girls to Katie, try to keep things as normal for them as possible. Sooner, rather than later, she'd have to tell them about Joel, but she was still trying to frame the tragedy in words they could comprehend, and she was getting nowhere.

"Good," Jessie said. "Well, I reckon I'll make us all some breakfast. If the children sleep awhile, we'll just keep their French toast warm in the oven." She went to the window at the sound of an engine, peered out. "There's Jim Williams, coming to tend the critters. It's nice to have neighbors at times like this."

Hallie thought of Phoenix. It was a great city, but like all densely populated areas, it was anonymous, and she was a stranger there, wandering among other strangers. She drew a deep breath, refilled her cup at the counter, and headed upstairs to shower and dress for another day of keeping watch.

"Tonight's the Harvest Festival," she told Chance, a few hours later, when she stood beside his bed. There wasn't a flicker of response, and yet she couldn't help feeling that he grasped at least some of the constant stream of words and thoughts she sent his way. "Jessie says we all have to go. Present a solid front, and all that."

Chance didn't move.

She kissed his forehead, wound a finger loosely in his hair. Tears blurred her vision. "Did you see all those candles last night, Chance? They were all for you. We were calling you back here, back home, where you belong."

The day nurse, a young black woman, slipped in on crepe-soled shoes and touched Hallie's arm to let her know it was time to step out. She delayed long enough to kiss Chance's forehead again, then turned and headed for the hallway.

Jessie and Doc were there, having another one of their spirited conversations, but as far as Hallie was concerned, they might as well have been speaking Japanese. She couldn't seem to focus enough to eavesdrop, which was, she decided, just as well.

Agent Walters was on duty again, and he touched her arm when she would have walked on by him. She'd gotten so used to ignoring Chance's guards that they seemed invisible.

"Yes?" she asked, trying to be polite.

"I just thought I'd tell you, Mrs. Royer, that although the Bureau has held off the media as long as possible, they're probably going to break through the red tape today, and they'll be all over you."

Hallie drew a breath, let it out. "I'm not 'Mrs.' anybody," she said, a little stiffly. "Joel and I were divorced well before he died, and I've been using my maiden name since I got here."

"Whatever," the fed replied, all business. "I'm just trying to warn you that you're probably in for some harassment from those folks. There's a big investigation coming up, you know. It'll be very public, there will be arrests and indictments, and I'm sorry to say you'll most likely be caught in the middle of it."

Hallie felt a headache take root at the base of her neck. Agent Walters was just doing his job, and he was right about the press. She'd left them out of the equation so far, but now she couldn't afford the luxury. If she didn't tell Kiley and Kiera what had happened to their father, they might hear it on the evening news or second-hand, on the playground. It was a risk she couldn't take.

"I'm sorry," Agent Walters said and Hallie squinted up at him.

"You sounded like you really meant that," she said.

He chuckled. "That's because I did."

She believed him. "Thanks," she said, and shoved a hand through her hair, already rehearsing, for the millionth time, what she'd say to her children. *Kiera, Kiley, I know this is hard to hear, but—*

She shook her head.

"It'll be okay," Agent Walters said.

"Will it?" she asked sadly. She hoped he was right but, for the life of her, she couldn't see how her life could ever be even remotely "all right" again, especially if Chance didn't make it. If he died, she would mourn him for the rest of her days, and blame herself every minute of that time.

It was late that afternoon, with more snow graying the

sky, that Chance first opened his eyes. Hallie happened to be leaning over him at the time, trying to memorize every plane and angle of his face, the way his hair grew, the meter of his breathing, all of it.

She gasped his name.

Laboriously, he raised one wired hand from the bed-clothes and tapped angrily at the plastic mouthpiece taped to his face.

"Nurse!" Hallie cried, exuberant, rushing out into the hall. "Jessie, Doc—Chance is awake!"

A nurse and doctor entered the room at top speed, and Jessie and Doc and Hallie all stood in a tight little knot in the hallway, waiting, holding their collective breaths.

Finally, after what seemed like forever, the doctor came out, smiling cautiously. "Mr. Qualtrough would like to see Hallie."

Jessie and Doc exchanged glances, squeezed each other's hands.

Hallie dashed back into the room, almost tripping over some of the cables in her eagerness to reach Chance's side.

They'd removed the tube going down his throat, and the nurse was injecting something into the IV bag. He smiled at Hallie, and she smiled back.

"Hi, Cowboy," she said.

His voice was a hoarse rasp, barely more than a breath, and the sentence took a long time to find its way, word by word, past his lips. "Who's taking care of the horses?"

18

Hallie smoothed Chance's hair back from his forehead, her eyes hot with happy tears. "The horses are fine," she told him. "There's a volunteer crew of neighbors and friends looking after them 'round the clock."

He sighed, relaxed visibly, then tensed again, evidently noticing the bruise on her face. "What about you? How badly did he hurt you?"

She chuckled. "Trust a cowboy to ask about his horses first," she teased. "And I'm better than okay, thank you, now that you're back in the world of the living."

He frowned. Every word he said, every breath he drew, was laborious, and Hallie knew he wasn't out of the woods yet, not by a long shot. Chance was in for a long, slow recovery, but at least he *would* recover. "Your eye looks pretty bad—"

"Just an ordinary shiner," she said, laying her fingers to his dry lips.

"I need . . . water," he said.

The nurse, who was hovering nearby, promptly provided a glass, with a bent straw. Hallie held it so Chance could take a few sips. He swallowed, laid back with a sigh, and closed his eyes.

For a moment, despite her profound conviction that he would live, Hallie was afraid he'd gone back into his coma. "Is he—?"

The nurse smiled, shook her head. "He's sleeping," she said. "That's a good thing."

Hallie nodded and went back out into the corridor, where Jessie and Doc were waiting. "He's sleeping," she said joyously.

Jessie started to weep, and Doc put an arm around her shoulders and squeezed her against his side. "Best we let him rest, then," he said. "We'll head on back to Primrose Creek and spread the news."

"I'd like to rest up for the Harvest Festival," Jessie said.

"You're amazing," Hallie said, with a smile. "All of you Primrose Creekers. You just keep going, doing what you do, no matter what comes down the road." It seemed to Hallie that a thousand years had passed since she and Chance and the rest of the community had made the preparations for the celebration, but it was right on schedule.

Jessie hugged Hallie, then held her by the shoulders as she gazed into her eyes. "That's the secret," she said. "We always go on, do what's there to be done, no matter what else is happening. When you do that, it all comes right in the end."

Hallie hoped they were right, because she had some seriously difficult tasks ahead of her. Telling the twins about Joel was first on her list.

Back in Primrose Creek, where another snow was dusting the ground, this time lightly, she went straight to

Katie's house, greeted her children, bundled them up in coats and mittens, and took them out for a walk.

The Grange Hall was bustling with final preparations for that evening's town party, but they went on past, until they came to the church at the end of the street. Hallie took the girls inside, to sit in a wash of colored light from the stained-glass windows. The quality of the reds, blues, greens, and yellows was muted by the weather, but still brilliant, as though possessed of some other source of illumination than the sun.

With one child on either side, Hallie looked up at the figure in the window, said a silent prayer, and started talking to her daughters.

"I have something to tell you," she said huskily, "and it's very hard to say."

Kiley huddled against her, Kiera clung to her arm.

"Something really bad has happened." She stopped, too choked up to go on.

"I know," Kiera said, her voice small and soft. "Chance got hurt. He has to be in the hospital."

"Yes," Hallie agreed, and bent to kiss her little girl on top of the head. "But there's something else."

"Daddy," Kiley said, with heartbreaking finality.

"Yes," Hallie said, putting an arm around both children and holding them tightly. "Your daddy's gone, babies. He made some mistakes, and some awful things happened, and he died." It was all she dared say, at the moment. The horrible details—that Joel had been planning to kill her, that Chance had fired the bullet that stopped him from accomplishing his purpose—would have to wait.

Kiera and Kiley were both silent for a long time, probably numbed by the shock of that news. Then Kiera sniffled, and began to cry, and Kiley followed suit. Hallie felt tears slipping down her own cheeks, and that was fitting. For a while, they all mourned the very different Joels they had known, Kiley and Kiera grieved for a father more imagined than real, Hallie for a man who had once shared her life.

The festival was packed with revelers, laughing, drinking soft cider and sodas, trying to win prizes, like teddy bears and homemade pies, at various booths. Della occupied an area made to look like the back of a gypsy's wagon, dressed in colorful garb and running her hands over a crystal ball.

Hallie, who had just left her listless but resilient children to have their faces painted, sat down across from Della and laid the requested fee on the table. The profits would go to Evie's school.

Della smiled mysteriously. "So," she said, in what she probably fancied to be a picturesque Romanian accent, "you vant your fortune told."

"I'd rather have a haircut," Hallie confided, teasing.

Della laughed. "You need one," she agreed, and looked into the crystal ball, waving her plump, hardworking hands in a summoning gesture. "I see an appointment here. Ten o'clock, tomorrow morning. Highlights and a trim. All for the bargain price of thirty-five dollars, plus tip."

Hallie chuckled. "I'll be there," she said.

"But *wait*," Della said, her eyes widening in the Cleopatra makeup that surrounded them. "Eeet ees like zat televishun commercial for zee Ginsu knives. There ees still more."

Hallie leaned forward, laughing a little. "What?" she asked.

Della looked up, as if surprised and a little hurt. "You're leaving us. I see you *leaving.*"

"I have things to do elsewhere, Della," Hallie said gently. "Important things."

"Then you'll come back?" Della wasn't looking at the crystal ball. She was just asking, as one ordinary mortal to another. "To Primrose Creek, I mean?"

Hallie had asked herself the same question. The truthful answer was, she couldn't be sure she would ever return. She had the press to deal with, and the Arizona court system, not to mention the feds, and she wanted to shield Chance from all that, so he could make a complete recovery. In short, he didn't need her kind of trouble.

In time, sooner, probably, rather than later, he would be ready to go on with his life. He'd meet a woman, or take up with one he already knew, marry, and have the family he wanted. "I don't know," she said, after a long time. "There are things I have to do back home. People's feelings change, when they're apart for a while."

"Not if their feelings are real." Della absorbed Hallie's reply, looking sad, then tapped the crystal ball with one fire-engine red fingernail. "Well, now, that's the future as you see it. You want to know what *I* see? You paid your money, and I'm not about to give it back."

Hallie smiled, in spite of the pain she felt, at the mere prospect of putting this place and these people behind her, for good. She shrugged. "What the heck?"

Della condensed her energies with a visible reshaping of her body, cupped her hands over the crystal ball, and drew them back with a gasp.

"What?" Hallie asked anxiously. There was, as Lou had always said, a sucker born every minute.

Della smiled smugly and sat back in her metal folding chair, which had been festooned, like the card table in front of her, in multicolored crepe paper streamers, in shades of bright red, blue and yellow. "You wouldn't believe me if I told you," she said. Then she rummaged in her purse, somewhere in the vicinity of her feet, and brought out a little notebook and a pencil. She scribbled something, covering both sides of the paper, folded it, and tucked it into one of the little donation envelopes sitting beside her business card holder. With considerable ceremony, she licked the back of the envelope, then sealed it by laying it on the table and giving it a couple of good thumps with her fist.

Hallie's eyes were wide, then narrow. "What are you up to?" she demanded.

Della's smile broadened. "Open that, six months from today, and read it. We'll see, Miss Smarty-Pants, who's where, doing what, *then*."

"Huh?" Hallie said, confounded, but she tucked the missive into her fanny pack.

"Next!" Della trumpeted.

Hallie looked behind her—there was nobody waiting—then back at Della.

"Do not forget," Della said, in a booming voice, waving her hands over the ball again. "You have an appointment at ten o'clock tomorrow morning. Wear something that buttons up the front, instead of going on over your head."

Hallie stood, a little dazed, waggled her fingers in a weak farewell, and walked away.

—

"You look . . . beautiful," Chance said, with considerable effort, when she stood at his bedside the next afternoon. "Did you do something to your hair?"

Hallie gave him a smacking kiss on the forehead. He'd been moved from the ICU to a regular private room, on the second floor, and there were a few less tubes and wires. "Thanks for noticing," she said, her eyes shining with all she felt for this man, bittersweet and hopelessly complicated as it was. "You look pretty okay yourself."

He gave a small, dismissive grunt. " 'Pretty okay'?" he echoed. "Is that the best you can do?"

She kissed him, not deeply, but sweetly, the way a sister or an aunt might do, and he registered the difference right away. She saw it in his eyes.

"You're leaving," he said.

She bit down hard on her lower lip, willed the tears thrumming in her sinuses to go no farther. "Yeah," she replied.

"Hallie," he said, "whatever needs handling, we'll handle it together, okay?" He paused, ground out the words she most—and least—wanted to hear from him. "I love you, Hallie."

She rested her forehead against his. "And I love you," she replied. For the moment, it was all she could manage.

"Then stay. Marry me. Make babies with me." He was tiring, and Hallie was painfully conscious of that. He was on the road back to full health, but it would be a long trip.

"I can't," she whispered. "Not now, anyway. Give me some time, Chance. Let me get things squared away in Phoenix."

He was going to be stubborn; she saw it in the set of his jaw and the glint in his eyes. The stress was already taxing him. "I won't wait around for you to come to your senses," he warned. "I'm tired of being alone."

He would be all right, Hallie told herself. More than all right. He had a family, and a whole town full of good friends, on his side.

"I understand," she said.

He turned his head away, stared out the window, and Hallie wondered if he saw the trees, naked of leaves, and the skiff of snow edging their branches, there in the small park beside the hospital.

"If you won't let me share your troubles, help you through them," he said, after a long time had passed, "then there's nothing left to say but good-bye."

Hallie swallowed hard. Closed her eyes for a moment. "Good-bye, Chance," she answered, when she could. Then, calling upon all her strength, which she now realized was considerable, she turned and walked out of Chance's hospital room for the last time.

~

Her condo had been tossed at least twice, once by Joel and his people, probably, and again by the authorities. With a sigh, Hallie went through it, room by room, straightening up, putting things away, vacuuming and scrubbing, sweeping and dusting. The twins watched her in worried amazement, perched on the couch in the living room like a pair of birds.

"I want to go home," Kiley said.

"This *is* home," Hallie replied, gripping the handle of the vacuum cleaner.

"No," Kiera argued. "Primrose Creek is home."

Hallie's entire spirit convulsed in a lonely ache. Maybe Kiera was right, she thought. Home, the old saying went, is where the heart is, and Hallie's heart was certainly not in Arizona. It was back in the high country of Nevada, riding around in the shirt pocket of a certain stubborn rancher. "Not anymore," she said. "Grilled cheese sandwiches?"

The twins stared at her. "What?" Kiley asked.

Hallie sighed. "Are you two hungry? Would you like sandwiches?" They'd made a lengthy visit to the supermarket that morning. Life was easier, now that she had her car again, and access to her bank accounts. Or so Hallie kept telling herself.

Kiera punched a needlepoint pillow. "No," she said. "I'm never going to eat again."

"Me, neither," agreed Kiley.

Hallie rolled her eyes heavenward. Then she put her broom away, washed her hands at the kitchen sink, and commenced slicing cheese and buttering bread and warming up a skillet. When she served the sandwiches, a few minutes later, her daughters came grudgingly to the table and ate.

"I bet the kittens miss us," Kiley said, fiddling. "The ones we left in the barn, at Jessie's place."

"They have the mama kitty to look after them," Hallie replied firmly, "and when they're big enough, Jessie will see that they have homes. She might even keep them all herself, right there in the barn."

Both the children looked relieved.

"It's almost Christmas," Kiley announced, tearing the crust off her sandwich.

"It's more than a month away," Hallie said, hoping to avoid hearing what they wanted, since she already knew. They'd told her every five minutes since she'd piled them into a rental car, with the few belongings they'd acquired during their high country odyssey, several weeks before, and brought them back to Scottsdale.

So far, she'd managed to stay one jump ahead of the press, but she'd already been informed that she would have to testify before a grand jury, and then in court as well. A great many arrests had been made; the drug-running network had been an extensive one, with money-laundering and murder thrown in for good measure, and there would be trials going on for months, maybe even years. The TV news-magazine shows were having a field day.

Just the thought of recounting it all, over and over again, in front of an assortment of juries, practically crushed her. She needed, she decided, to get back to her yoga class, and get centered. She needed to reopen her restaurant. She needed sleep and peace of mind and time with her children. And vitamins. Lots of vitamins.

Most of all, she needed Chance.

She put that last thought firmly aside, as she had a hundred times before. He wasn't going to wait for her to get her life squared away, he'd said as much. And she would be entangled in her affairs in Phoenix and Scottsdale for the foreseeable future. Better to sever all ties now, get it over with.

The telephone rang, and Kiera and Kiley knocked over their chairs leaving the table, racing to answer.

Kiera got to the counter, and the cordless phone, first.

"Hello?" she cried. Then a smile spread across her small face. "Hi, Katie. I'm fine, and so is Kiley. Yes, Mommy's here."

Hallie took the receiver, braced for bad news. Chance had suffered a reversal of some kind, she just knew it. Or he'd gone back to working with his horses too soon, and hurt himself. "Katie?"

"Hi, Hallie," her friend said. "How are you?"

"Frazzled," Hallie said, shoving a hand through her hair. "What about you?"

"Jase and I are working on our marriage. I guess the things that have been happening around here lately have put some stuff in perspective. We're going on an Alaskan cruise—we leave next week."

"That's wonderful," Hallie said, sitting down on one of the high stools at the breakfast bar, and waving away the twins, who were jumping around her like pistons in a high-speed motor, begging for the phone.

"The Bureau of Land Management guys caught that cougar," Katie went on. "Everybody breathed a sigh of relief when word got around." She sighed. "Of course there are others, in the mountains, but you don't see them often. That one must have been a rogue of some kind."

"I imagine the ranchers are celebrating," Hallie said, sending the girls back to the table by pointing one arm and making a stern face. They obeyed, but not willingly, and she slipped into the next room. "Did they kill it? The cougar, I mean?"

"In this day and age?" Katie answered. "No way. It's gone to some private reserve, to be tagged and studied. Poor thing, they'll probably harass it to death."

Hallie swallowed, waited, swallowed again. She finally found the courage to ask the question that was uppermost on her mind. "How is Chance?"

There was a note in Katie's voice that said she wouldn't have been fooled by all the tactics in the world. "He's getting out of the hospital next week. He'll be fine, Hallie. Physically, at least." She was quiet for a moment. "You broke his heart, you know."

Hallie closed her eyes. She wanted to go back to Primrose Creek, had started to go a million times. The pain of being away from him was a consuming thing, tearing her limb from limb, organ from organ, cell from cell. She wasn't living, she was merely functioning, going through the motions, an actor in a play, with a very limited grasp on her lines. But something had stopped her, and that was the memory of Chance, telling her he wouldn't wait. If she went to him, and he turned her away, she would die. "Katie—"

"Look, I'm sorry," Katie said, on a soft breath. "I shouldn't have said that, all right? It's just that you two seemed so perfect for each other."

"Obviously," Hallie said, blinking back tears, "we aren't."

"How are things going down there in Phoenix?"

Hallie glanced toward the kitchen door, beyond which her daughters were squabbling. "It's a battle," she admitted. The first night back, after the twins had gone to sleep in their frilly beds, surrounded by their many toys and closets full of fancy clothes, she'd sat down with a pad and pencil and listed all the things she had to do. She'd nearly been overwhelmed by the magnitude of it all, three weeks ago, and that feeling hadn't abated. The list grew, every day, instead of dwindling. "What about Madge? How are she and Wynona and Bear?"

"Wy and Bear bought a secondhand Harley and hit the road," Katie said, with some amusement. "Madge is fit to be tied. Threatening to sell the place, or just board it up and take off herself." Pause. "A few of us are still hoping you'll come to your senses, come home to Prim-rose Creek, and run the place yourself."

Hallie didn't say anything; her voice was stuck again, behind a sore place in her throat. If she tried to swallow, she would strangle.

Katie's voice brightened. "The townspeople special-ordered a stool as a welcome-back present for Chance," she said. "You know, for his place at the counter, down at the Last Chance? It's upholstered in saddle leather, and his name is being worked into the seat."

A chuckle got past Hallie's swelling sorrow. "He'll like that," she said.

"Yeah," Katie agreed. Sighed again. "Well, I'd better get back to work. It's story day at the bookstore."

"Right," Hallie said. "Thanks for calling."

"Keep in touch, Hallie."

Both of them knew it wouldn't happen. Their phone calls and e-mails would become few and fewer, until there was nothing left of their friendship but a memory. It was inevitable, given how busy they were, and how far apart.

Hallie said good-bye and hung up, but she stood there in the living room for a long time, alone, listening to her children argue in the kitchen, and crying for a cowboy who would have been infinitely better off if he'd never so much as heard her name.

Chance scowled at the tray of food before him, gray rice, a chunk of shoe-leather, a little heap of peas that were probably grown in a Petri dish somewhere. "I'd rather starve," he said.

"Nonsense," Jessie said, with a patience he knew was hard-won. "If you ever want to get out of this hospital, you'll have to build up a little strength."

"You could reduce this stuff to molecules and never come across a single vitamin," Chance grumbled. "How about bringing me some real food? Like a hamburger with bacon and extra cheese?"

"In your dreams," Jessie replied, arms folded, lips curved into a gentle smile.

"You said it," Chance said, and gamely took a bite of the rice. For the first few days after Hallie left, he'd done his darnedest to just go under and die, but it hadn't happened. Now, after a few of weeks of being hog-tied with wires and tubes, he just wanted to go home to Primrose Creek, work with his horses, try to grope his way, somehow, through the rest of his life.

Jessie had been leaning against the windowsill. Now, she came to sit on the edge of his bed. "How are you?" she asked. "Really?"

He laid down the fork. "I'm coping," he said. It was an overstatement, but Jessie didn't need to know that. It would only make her fret more, and she was already on overload in the worry department, when it came to him. Thank God, things had settled down a bit between Katie and Jase, or she'd be a wreck. "Looks to me like you and Doc are pretty thick these days."

She smiled. "*That* old coot," she said, fondly.

"You're crazy about him," Chance teased.

Jessie laughed. "I never could fool you," she said. Her expression turned solemn. "And you're not fooling me, either. You're pretty broken up inside, aren't you?"

He sighed, settled back on his pillows. God in heaven, he was tired of being bedridden, tired of being cheered and fretted over and just generally pestered. "I've been in this place before," he allowed, studying the ceiling, and he didn't mean the hospital.

Jessie took his hand. "When your folks died," she said.

He nodded, without looking at her. "And when Katie fell in love with Jase," he admitted, never meaning to let the words out. "Sweet Jesus, I thought nothing could hurt more than either of those things, let alone the two of them put together, but this does."

"It will pass."

"Maybe."

"You could go after her, you know. Just go to Phoenix, gather Hallie up, and bring her home to Primrose Creek, where she belongs."

"She'd never agree. She's got 'responsibilities' there."

"She's trying to do the right thing."

"The hell she is. The right thing is to marry me. She's running. She's scared shitless of what she feels for me, and what I feel for her, and she's come up with a bunch of excuses for staying away." He reached resolutely for the tray. "Running," he repeated, with scornful emphasis.

Jessie ran a thumb over his knuckles. "Maybe one of these days, Hallie will run this way," she said.

"I couldn't get that lucky," Chance replied. And he forced himself to eat.

Hallie stood in the center of Princess and the Pea, looking around, remembering. There was the table where she and Lou had celebrated her first profitable month with a prime rib dinner. There was the antique tapestry she'd bought on eBay, and there were the mismatched dishes and glasses that gave the place a French country café feeling, the crockery coffee mugs, the copper utensils.

The real estate agent, Mr. Elwyn, spun one of the stools at the short counter and looked at her closely. "Are you sure you want to sell?" he asked.

She shook her head, sniffled. She wasn't sure of anything, except that there was a broken place, in the deepest part of her heart, that was never going to heal, no matter what she did. In the weeks since she'd left Primrose Creek, she'd fended off dozens of reporters, cleaned out Lou's house, put it on the market, settled his bills, given half a dozen different depositions at the prosecutor's office.

Mr. Elwyn took in the small place in one sweeping glance. "Shouldn't have any trouble getting a good offer," he said. "This is a great location, and the notoriety alone—"

"Notoriety?" Hallie asked, with an edge to her voice.

The middle-aged man had the good grace to blush a little. "Well, you know," he said awkwardly, "any sort of publicity is valuable."

"Not to me, it isn't," she said. "I want the asking price, and not a penny less."

He nodded, put out his hand. "I sold your dad's place for top dollar, and I can sell this one."

"Thanks," Hallie said, and led the way out. The sun

was dazzlingly bright, the sky was a heartbreaking blue. It was a classic Arizona winter, drawing visitors from all over North America, and here she was, wishing for snow. She gave a rueful little smile, locked the restaurant, and headed for her car, which was parked at the curb.

"You'll be hearing from me soon," Mr. Elwyn called, as he got into his Cadillac.

Chance stood leaning against the corral fence, his arms resting on the top rail. The Winslow mare, Sugar, ambled over and nuzzled him, pushing off his hat, and he smiled. Since the shooting, since losing Hallie, he'd come to understand this horse, and all other suffering creatures, on a whole new level. Evidently, Sugar knew that.

"Think you could ride her?"

Chance turned to watch as Doc came toward him, dressed in his Sunday finest. He and Jessie were getting married that afternoon, in the Presbyterian church in town, and he looked the part of a bridegroom, all right. They were honeymooning at Jessie's place, since she'd had her fill of traveling, and there was an old-fashioned shivaree scheduled for midnight.

"Ride this mare?" Chance asked, with a note of false surprise in his voice. "In my sleep, old man. In my sleep."

Doc grinned. "Five bucks says she throws you in under a minute," he challenged.

"You're on," Chance said. He picked up his hat, hung it on a fence post, and scrambled over the fence. It hurt only a little. Sugar moved away, nickering and tossing her head. Chance approached the horse, eyes averted, one hand out.

The mare stood her ground, flared her nostrils, ducked her head.

"I'll get the saddle and bridle," Doc called.

"No need," Chance answered.

Jessie was running across the yard. "Chance Qualtrough!" she whooped. "Don't you dare—" He swung up, Indian style, and the mare quivered from withers to flanks, her hind end bunched to spring. "—get on that horse," Jessie finished, reaching the corral.

Chance leaned down, patted Sugar's sleek neck. "Easy, now," he said. "You throw me, and I'll not only have to fork over five bucks to that old fart over there by the fence, I'll wind up back in the hospital into the bargain. I don't think I can take any more of that grub they serve down there."

Sugar shuddered, blew. Chance knew she was debating whether to endure the indignation of being ridden or throw him over the barn roof. He was counting heavily on the former.

"Thirty seconds," Doc called.

Using his grasp on the animal's mane as a bridle, Chance turned the mare, walked her around in a circle. She played along, and he tipped his hat to Doc when they went by the second time, grand as Roy Rogers at a rodeo.

"Damn," Doc snapped, slapping his wristwatch as though he thought something was wrong with it. "You did it."

"Idiot," Jessie cried. It was hard to tell who she was talking to, for she simultaneously elbowed Doc hard in the side, and glared up at Chance.

He swung down, winced at the pain that seized his

midsection. "Pay up," he said, walking toward Doc with one hand out.

—

The envelope arrived the first week in April, with Katie's name above the return address. Hallie, seated beside her computer, took it from Kiera with a little smile.

"Mrs. Clarence brought it," her daughter explained. The elderly woman, who lived nearby, was a helpful soul, and often picked up Hallie's mail when she fetched her own. "It's from Katie."

Hallie peered at Kiera over the rims of her reading glasses, trying to look stern. "Reading other people's mail, are we?" she intoned.

Kiera giggled. "No, silly," she said. "It's still sealed."

Hallie made a teasing face. "So it is," she said, and slid a thumb under the flap. She hadn't heard from Katie in a long time, except for the occasional e-mail, and she wondered what had prompted her friend to send a regular letter in this age of fiber-optic communication. "Where's Kiley?"

"She's not finished with her lunch," Kiera answered. "Shall I go and tell her to hurry up?"

"No," Hallie said. "Leave her alone and mind your own business." She began to read, and to smile. Jase and Katie were expecting another baby. Doc and Jessie were married, and they'd set up housekeeping out at her place. One of Jessie's weavings had been chosen as part of an American handcrafts display, and would be on view at the White House. Evie was expanding her school. Nothing about Chance.

There was a clipping inside the envelope, and Hallie nearly threw it away before she spotted it. When she unfolded the scrap of newsprint, her eyes widened.

A classified ad, in the center of the page, had been circled in red.

For sale cheap, it read, *Last Chance Café, Primrose Creek, Nevada. No decent offer refused.* Madge's phone number followed.

"Mommy?" Kiera tugged at Hallie's sleeve. "Mommy?"

Hallie focused on her daughter's concerned face. She summoned up a smile. "What?" she asked.

"Is it bad news?"

Hallie sighed, propped an elbow on the edge of her desk, rested her forehead in the upturned palm. In the past six months, she'd done everything she could to rebuild her life. She'd survived the investigations and the scandals. She'd settled Lou's estate, and sold Princess and the Pea for a small fortune, and if she didn't want to, she'd never have to work another day. She'd also lost fifteen pounds, stopped sleeping more than two hours at a stretch, broken out in periodic cases of hives, and completely failed to decide what she wanted to do with the rest of her life.

"Mommy?" Kiera prompted.

"No, sweetheart," Hallie answered belatedly. "It's not bad news."

"What then?"

She looked down at the clipping again, bit her lip. "It's just . . . news," she said.

And for some reason, she thought of Della, and the sealed note she'd given her that long-ago night, at the Harvest Festival in Primrose Creek. Frowning, she got out of her chair, ambled into her bedroom, and dug through the purses and other paraphernalia on the top shelf of her closet until she came to the fanny pack she'd been wearing that evening. Sure enough, the envelope was inside, dog-eared and scrunched, still sealed.

She carried it to the kitchen, sat down at the table, and opened it with all the solemnity of a high priestess performing a sacred ceremony. She unfolded the paper inside, her fingers shaking a little, a smile playing on her mouth, and read.

Come home now, Della had written. *You've stayed away long enough. Too long. Your future is in Primrose Creek, with Chance Qualtrough and all the rest of us. He's waiting for you, waiting to love you, and to receive your love in return. You've done what you had to do. Now, come home.*

Hallie turned the page over.

You have money now. You have time. You need to be here, where your heart lives, and so do your children. Chance will be waiting, I promise.

19

The little bell jingled over the door of the Last Chance Café that April evening, and Chance might not have turned around, on his fancy, personalized stool, if everybody else in the room hadn't drawn in a collective breath, a sort of community gasp.

The place was crowded—it was a kind of last hurrah for the Last Chance Café, since Madge planned to close up indefinitely and do some traveling herself, instead of letting Bear and Wynona have all the fun—but all the noise and the familiar faces subsided into a kind of dim, flickering void when his gaze came to rest on Hallie.

She looked beyond good, in white jeans and a light-weight, sleeveless blouse of printed cotton. Her hair had gotten longer since he'd seen her last, and she'd pulled it up into a spunky little ponytail, high on the back of her head. Kiera and Kiley, both of them grown a foot taller, he'd have sworn, stepped back out of the odd, thrumming channel that had opened between him and Hallie.

"I heard this place was up for sale," she said, and though she must have been speaking to Madge, who was behind the counter in her usual pink waitress regalia, she never once looked away from Chance's face.

Madge said something, and Hallie slapped a hand down on the smooth, well-worn counter top, standing so close to Chance as she did so that he could feel the heat of that delectable little body of hers.

"Sold!" she said, and a round of cheers rocked the Last Chance Café.

Chance was dazed. Oh, he saw flashes of other people's faces, a sort of strobe-light effect, heard them greeting her, but he was still almost completely focused on Hallie. He wondered if he were really there, eating cherry pie and drinking coffee, or if he were at home, in bed, and all this was just a dream. God knew, he'd had several like it since Hallie went away, though they usually just included him and her, with nobody wearing clothes.

He watched, still trying to decide if he was awake, while she went over to the jukebox and dropped some coins into the slot. By the time she'd made her selections, the café had nearly emptied out, which just about cinched it, as far as Chance was concerned. This was a dream.

She crossed the room as an old Emmylou Harris ballad began to play, and put out a hand to him.

"Dance with me," she said. The words were softly spoken, but they were a command, nonetheless, not a request.

He stood, took her into his arms, knew, *knew* it was all real. She was real. Solid and warm. "What are you doing here?" he asked, but he danced, one hand resting on the small of her back, the other holding hers.

"I live here," she said. "Now that I own a business."

Madge took the kids, smiling, and sneaked out.

The conversation went on. "Yeah?" Chance asked. "*Where* are you planning to stay?"

She wriggled against him. "With you," she said. "We can get married. It's time you made an honest woman out of me."

He chuckled, unable to pretend for another second that her coming back wasn't the best damn thing that had ever happened to him. "I think we ought to do some more sinnin', ma'am," he teased, "before we go to repentin'."

She threw her head back, laughing, and he kissed her throat. They waltzed, bathed in the flashing lights of the jukebox. Some romantic must have switched off the overhead lights during the mass exodus, because the room itself was full of shifting shadows.

"You're sure you're back to stay?" Chance asked, pulling her against him at the end of the song, holding her there. "Because once we say those words, neither one of us is going anywhere. So if you won't agree to be my wife—and I'm talking right away, Hallie, not next year or the year after—we'd better just step back, both of us, right now."

She smiled. Slipped her arms around his neck. "I'll marry you," she said, "any time you say. Just set the date, Cowboy." She pulled a face. "I don't see why we can't start the honeymoon early, though."

"We've got a lot of things to talk about, Hallie, before we go to bed," Chance heard himself say. He wondered if he'd suffered an undiagnosed head injury somewhere along the line.

She tasted his mouth, took her time at it. "Like what?" she said, on a breath.

"Like whether you're really staying."

"I'm staying. I said I was."

He weighed the promise. "What about kids? I'd want some."

"Me, too," she said.

He put his hands on her hips and set her away from him, out of simple self-defense. She was a witch, casting spells, and although he knew he was already lost, he guessed he wanted the illusion of having at least some power over his own destiny. "You bought the café," he reminded her. "That'll mean putting in a lot of hours right here."

Her eyes were dreamy. "You don't want a working wife?"

He leaned in, until they were nose to nose. "I'll take you any way I can get you," he said. He swatted her shapely bottom. "And right now, I have some very innovative ways in mind."

She trembled, to his delight, and flushed a little. Her eyes were sparkling, though, and a courtesan's smile played at the corners of her mouth. "Your place," she crooned, "or mine?"

"Neither," he answered, and took her by the hand. He led her outside, hoisted her into the passenger side of his truck, got behind the wheel. Didn't even bother to see that the Last Chance was locked up. He figured it would still be there when they got back.

"Where are we going?" she asked. People honked their car horns and waved as they drove down the main street of town, and Chance hoped it wouldn't turn into a parade. The scenario unfolding in his mind called for one man, one woman, and no audience whatsoever.

"The meadow, above my place," he answered. He indicated the sky with a motion of his thumb. "Look. There's a full moon."

She offered no protest, but tossed him a come-hither look. "Madge has the girls," she said. "So I've got all night."

He chuckled. "We're going to *need* all night," he answered, and he thought he saw her give a little shiver of anticipation, out of the corner of his eye.

The meadow was blanketed by a sky full of stars and moon, and the grass smelled sweet. The air was cool, but Hallie was oblivious to such mundane matters. She stepped down off the running board, only to find herself deliciously pinned in the open doorway of Chance's truck.

He kissed her, his weight resting against her, and her bones turned to liquid and seeped into the earth at her feet, leaving her more spirit than mortal. She slid her hands up the front of his shirt and then around his neck, gave herself up, just as she had dreamed of doing for so long.

The kiss went on forever, it seemed; galaxies flared to life during that interlude, while others finished their span and went dark. Finally, slowly, Chance undid the buttons of Hallie's cotton top, spread the fabric, pulled her bra down to bare her breasts to his hands, his eyes, his mouth.

She surrendered utterly, with a little cry of welcome, tilting her head back, closing her eyes. He enjoyed her until she was sure she would die of the pleasure, and then he unsnapped her jeans, pushed them down and away. Her panties vanished soon after; he must have torn them off and flung them aside, because she never saw them again.

When he hoisted her, half-naked, onto the seat of his truck, she laid her hands on his shoulders. "Oh, God, Chance," she whispered, "I love you, and I've missed you—and this—so much."

He eased her backward onto the seat, murmuring love words of his own as he stroked her bare thighs with his strong, rancher's hands, and arranged her just so. He draped her legs over his shoulders, soothed her when she arched her back and cried out in a spasm of delight, and then burrowed through the silken veil to please her in earnest.

She stretched her arms back over her head and raised herself to him, like a sacrifice on an altar, and Chance showed her no mercy at all. He consumed her, tamed her like some wild goddess, captured and ravished in a moon-lit field, and when at last, at last, her climax came, it went on and on, endlessly, her body buckling, her heels digging into Chance's back.

Presently, he lifted her down, laid her on a blanket in the sweet grass a few feet from the truck, stretched out beside her and, after taking his maddening time, took her back over the bridge she'd just crossed, into a place where rainbows arched from star to star.

—

"What'll it be, Cowboy?" asked the saucy waitress. She might have carried off the vamp act, if she hadn't been eight and a half months pregnant. One thing was for sure, though. She was cute as hell.

Chance Qualtrough leaned over the counter, caught his wife's face between his hands, and kissed her soundly. "You tell me," he chuckled, and reached to pat her rotund belly. "What'll it be?"

She laughed, came around the end of the counter, and perched on his lap. It was late, and they had the café to themselves. "The doctor says we're having a boy," she said. "You know that. You were there when they did the sonogram."

He kissed her again, this time lingering on and around her mouth. "Sometimes those things are wrong," he said. He winked. "Come on home now, woman. You shouldn't be working this late, especially in your condition."

"You know I just supervise," she said. She gave a little whimper when he kissed the side of her neck. "Besides, it's only four o'clock in the afternoon."

"Where are Fred and the others?" Fred was the fry cook. Hallie had hired him and four waitresses when she took the place over, and still she could barely keep up with the business.

She wriggled out of his arms, tossed a coy little smile over one shoulder, and went to the window, parting the blinds with two fingers and peering out. "I sent them home early," she said. "Looks like snow."

He grinned, remembering the first time he'd ever seen Hallie, covered with snow, scared as a rabbit, and at the same time, ready to take on the whole world, two-fisted, if she had to. He figured he'd fallen in love with her way back then, though the truth of it didn't gel in his mind for quite a while after that.

"Are you happy here?" he asked, meeting her in the center of the room, where they'd practically worn a path in the linoleum with their after-hours dancing. "In Primrose Creek, I mean?" *With me,* was what he meant.

She took hold of his hand, raised it to her lips, kissed the knuckles one by one. "My life started," she said softly, "when I walked through that door right over there. Everything before that was just getting-ready."

He nodded. "So did mine," he said, and kissed her.

A strange expression crossed her face, all of a sudden, and she laid both hands to her basketball stomach. "Chance," she whispered, not afraid, but marveling. Her brown eyes were wide, luminously joyful.

"What?" he asked, too quickly. Maybe she wasn't scared, but he was. Right about then, he'd rather have dealt with a full grown grizzly than a woman in labor. Even if she *was* his woman.

"It's time," she told him, her eyes shining with love as she looked up at him. "Oh, Chance, he's coming. *The baby is coming.*"

He took a few deep breaths, centered himself, then panicked anyway. "Come on," he said, half-dragging her to the door, pulling her coat on over her arms, trying and failing to button it in front. She laughed, and the sound echoed like the peal of bells through the long corridors of his heart, empty for so long.

"Chance," she said, grasping his face between her hands. "Calm down."

How could he calm down? His son was getting ready to be born, and they were miles—forty-five minutes, at least—from the nearest hospital.

"Breathe," she said.

"I'm supposed to tell *you* to breathe," he said, half-dragging her outside to his truck. He left the café door unlocked, and all the lights on. He had a moment of déjà vu, but he couldn't place it.

She giggled as he hoisted her, with comical awkwardness, into the seat. Then he flashed briefly on the night they'd made this baby, he and Hallie, up there in the high meadow, under the stars. They'd been married a week later, and made love a million times since, in a million other places besides that one, and each time had been better than the last. For Chance, an ordinary world had turned into a place where miracles were commonplace, and dreams came true as a matter of course.

"The girls," she reminded him. He was in the process of adopting them legally, and they used the name Qualtrough. He loved them as his own, and was already bracing himself for their teen years, still almost a decade away, when he'd have to start beating the boys off with a club. He believed in being prepared.

"They're with Jessie," he said, a little short of breath, scrambling behind the wheel. "Fasten your seat belt."

She fumbled, he fastened it for her. She smiled at him.

"Breathe, Chance," she coached. *"Breathe."*

He drove down the mountain like a wild man, but a careful wild man. Hallie lay back in the seat, hands clasping her belly, now grunting, now panting, practicing the stuff they'd learned in natural childbirth class. "Am I turning you on, Cowboy?" she asked once, with a devilish little smile.

They finally reached the hospital, the same one where Chance had spent several weeks after the shooting and the subsequent surgery, but the place barely seemed familiar. All of that stuff belonged to another time, another life.

Hallie was rushed into an exam room, and her doctor was summoned. Chance stood beside her, holding her hand, when they wheeled her into the elevator on a gurney, headed for Delivery.

An hour and a half later, during which Hallie did considerable yelling and cursing, not to mention plain old screaming, their baby was born, an eight-pound boy with the lung power of an Italian opera singer. Chance, who had been present throughout, feeling faint and powerful by turns, stood there, in his green hospital garb, stunned by the scope of his good fortune, and held his son close to his chest for a long moment. Then, solemnly, guided by instinct, he raised the child to the sky, to receive a blessing.

Hallie's eyes were full of tears and smiles as he laid the infant on her chest and smoothed her hair back with his free hand. "I love you," she said. "Did I do good?"

"I love you," he replied, bent to kiss her. "And you did great." He gazed into her eyes for a long, long time. "Hallie?"

She was holding his hand, and she kissed it. "What?"

"Thank you," he said. "Thank you for coming back. Thank you for loving me. And thank you for giving me this baby."

She touched his face, too overcome with emotion to speak.

Solemnly, Jessie took down the McQuarry Bible from its new place on Chance and Hallie's bookshelf, laid it on the table beside the fireplace, and turned to the page listing births. She smiled, running her finger over the long columns, two centuries of McQuarrys, being born, marrying, living and dying. Then, making room for Chance beside her, with Hallie standing opposite, holding the baby and looking for all the world like an angel come to bide awhile on earth, Jessie dipped the pen reserved for this purpose and handed it to Chance.

Trace Qualtrough, he wrote. *Born the seventh day of January to Chance and Hallie Qualtrough.*

He added the year with a flourish, and then looked up at Hallie. When their eyes met, Jessie would have sworn the earth shifted. They were in the prime of their lives and of their love, Chance and Hallie were, and she envied them just a little, though at the same time, she was glad she was past that kind of passion. Frankly, she hadn't the strength for it.

She smiled fondly at Doc, and he smiled back. There were other kinds of passion, she reflected. Her husband might not take her breath away as often as he once had, when they were younger, stealing the moments they had together, but his touch was tender, and it brought her bliss. Her soul knew his, and was known, and rested there safely, wanted and welcome. He reached across, squeezed her hand.

New beginnings were all around. Jessie squeezed back, and smiled.

It was late, and the kids were all sound asleep, Kiera and Kiley in their room, Trace in his nursery, next door to Hallie and Chance. A wolf howled in the far distance, and Hallie Qualtrough lifted her head to listen, and something in her, something wild and wise, called back to that creature in silent acknowledgment.

Chance, just in from the barn, crossed the room and stood behind her easy chair, where she'd been curled up, reading the last of Bridget's letters and diaries, as well as those of Christy Shaw, Skye Vigil and Megan Stratton. Coming to Primrose Creek had changed those women, just as it had changed her.

Her husband began to knead her shoulders lightly. "What are you thinking?" he asked, and something inside her leaped with happiness, because she knew he really wanted to know. He would listen.

"That I've grown since I came here," she said. "I've learned to trust myself."

He leaned down, kissed the top of her head. Later, in the quiet of their room, they would make sweet, slow love, as they did nearly every night, and Hallie felt her senses quicken in anticipation of that. "I love you, lady," he said. He came around the chair, pulled her gently to her feet, sat down, and tugged her onto his lap. "Don't ever leave me."

She snuggled against him, and he covered them both with an afghan Jessie had woven as a wedding gift. "I couldn't," she said, and they sat like that, just soaking in each other's presence, for a long time. Then, languid as a cat, Hallie stretched in her husband's arms, yawned.

He chuckled. "Long day?"

"Long day," she confirmed, turning to kiss his neck. "I made an important decision, though."

He turned her on his lap, smoothed her hair tenderly

back from her face, kissed her lightly on the mouth. "What?"

"I'm going to find out as much as I can about my mother's parents, and my biological father. So everything can come full circle."

"Thus making your life complete?"

She smiled at him. "My life is already complete," she said. "I just want to solve as many mysteries as I can."

"Makes sense," he said. He began eyeing the buttons on her shirt with a look of speculation she'd long since come to recognize. Something widened inside her, and melted, preparing the way for the inevitable union of their two bodies. "I'd say my life is pretty complete, too," he told her. "Though a little nookie wouldn't go amiss."

She laughed. "Chance Qualtrough," she said, "you are insatiable."

"Where you're concerned, yes," he told her drowsily. He worked the first button, and a thrill shot through her.

"Have you forgotten that we made love this afternoon," she whispered, "in the barn?" The kids had been at school, and Jessie and Doc had been at the house, fussing over the baby like a pair of grandparents.

He chuckled. "I doubt I'll ever forget that," he said. He undid another button, kissed the bit of flesh left bare.

"Me, either," she admitted, with a soft sigh and a smile. They'd climbed into the hayloft, like a couple of kids, and despite the chill, they'd removed their clothes and made fierce, fiery love on a scratchy bed of straw. At the height of her ecstasy, Hallie had glimpsed a ghost moon, through a space between the boards of the weathered roof, and made a wish. Now, she wanted to distract Chance, prolong things a little bit. "Katie and

Jase are thinking of having another baby," she said.

Chance was not about to be distracted. He reached a finger inside her bra and began chafing her nipple to attention. "Is that so?" he drawled, concentrating on the task at hand.

Hallie groaned, stretched a little. "Oooh," she said. "Yes, it's so." She closed her eyes for a few moments, in sweet surrender, and gasped when Chance bared her and took the tip of her breast into his mouth. Her fingers entangled themselves in his hair. "Jase—oh, God, Chance—is going into ranching. Using the . . . the land he inherited."

He tongued her thoroughly before lifting his head. "I know," he replied. "Guess he's tired of the sheriff business."

Hallie pressed her husband's head back to her breast, drew in a sharp breath when he made contact. "I guess so," she murmured. "How . . . how would you feel . . . about—?"

He chuckled against the plump bounty of her flesh, teasing the hard knot of a nipple with tiny flicks of his tongue until Hallie thought she'd climax before they even got upstairs to bed. "Right now," he said, "I feel pretty damn good."

She made a whimpering sound. "Damn it, Chance," she exclaimed softly, between small, breathless gasps, "I'm trying to have a serious conversation here."

He laughed. "Oh, trust me," he said. "I'm dead serious." He tugged down the other side of her bra, so that she was bared to him, her breasts gilded in firelight.

"I want another baby," she managed to say.

"This seems like a good way to go about getting one," he said, very busy again.

Hallie eyed the bear rug on the floor in front of the fireplace, wondered if they'd make it even that far. She could think of several occasions when they hadn't, and the memories sang warm songs in her blood.

"What about the kids?" she whispered. "What if they—?"

"Sleeping," he answered, and reached up to switch off the lamp beside the chair.

The room fell into darkness, the fire glowed crimson on the hearth, sent light dancing over the soft fur of the bearskin rug.

Hallie found herself lying there, on her back, with her shirt open and her jeans and panties down around one ankle. Chance, as naked as she was, lay half covering her with his body, kissing her mouth, her eyelids, the underside of her jaw and chin.

"Do you really want another baby, Mrs. Qualtrough?" he asked, between nibbles. "We've got three kids already."

"Yes," she said, and drew in a quick, shallow breath as he encircled her navel with his tongue. "I've counted and come up with the same total." She reveled in his touch, in the warmth of the fire and the deep, cosseting softness of the rug. "I think we should have one more, at least. Trace needs a brother or sister close to his own age."

"If you say so," Chance murmured. God in heaven, he was driving her crazy. He *loved* to drive her crazy. He poised himself over her—mercifully, he had decided not to make her wait interminably the way he usually did— and she felt his hardness pressing against her, seeking entry. Seeking solace and sanction inside her.

She spread her legs to welcome him, and opened the portals of her soul as well, and he claimed her, making them one spirit, one flesh, one mind and heart. When it was over, and they lay exhausted, sweating and sated, entangled in each other's arms, Chance rested his head on her breast.

"Do you think it took?" he asked, in good time. "Or should we try again?"

Hallie laughed. "Oh," she said, "I definitely think we should try again."

"You're right," he agreed solemnly.

"But let's wait until tomorrow, okay? I've pretty much given you all I have to give, between that session in the hayloft and what we just did right here."

"That," he said, "is what you think." He got up, helped Hallie to her feet, wrapped her in the discarded afghan, and hustled her toward the stairs.

"Wait," Hallie said quickly. "Our clothes."

Chance went back, pulled on the jeans he'd shed at some point, without Hallie's noticing—she'd been preoccupied, to say the least—and snatched up the rest of their things. Hallie giggled, and they dashed for their bedroom.

The next morning, Chance was up before the sun, as usual, while Hallie lay sprawled on her belly in the middle of the bed, yearning for one more hour of sleep. Just one more hour.

It wasn't to be. She heard Kiera and Kiley scuffling in the hallway, arguing over who got to use the bathroom first, and hastily covered herself, lest her daughters decide to come in and bid her good morning.

They did precisely that. They'd grown considerably

since coming to Primrose Creek and they were now proud third graders at the local elementary school. They caught the school bus every morning, down by the mailbox, with Hallie looking on from the kitchen window, and joined her and Trace at the café in the afternoons. Chance always came to fetch them all home again in the early evening, where they helped with the chores while Hallie cooked a family supper, just for them.

Trace, a blond, blue-eyed bundle of mischief, ruled the ranch as well as the café from his collapsible playpen, and his big sisters adored him.

"Where's Trace?" they asked now, in chorus.

"Right here," Chance said, carrying the baby into the room and laying him on Hallie's chest. Trace was too busy sucking the bottle his father had fixed for him to respond to his adoring public.

Hallie kissed her son's forehead and offered yet another silent prayer of gratitude, for this baby, for these children, for this man, for this pristine land stretching around them for miles. She loved them all with an intensity that often frightened her.

Chance bent, kissed Hallie lightly on the lips. "New horse arriving today," he said.

Hallie held Trace against her chest, bottle in hand. She'd wanted to nurse him, but it hadn't seemed practical at the time, and though she sometimes regretted the decision, she was sure it had been the right one.

"Is it that little sorrel that was in the jumping accident last month?" Kiera asked. Chance had given her and Kiley each their own ponies for Christmas, and then patiently taught them to ride.

He ruffled the little girl's hair. "Sure is," he said.

"Can you make her better?"

Chance sighed. "I don't know," he replied. He was always honest, even when a little fib would have made him look like a hero. "Some horses can't be reached. The scars just run too deep. I'll do my best with her, though."

Kiera looked up at him in just the way Hallie must have looked at Lou in those early years after he married her mother, and somehow turned a broken home into a family. "Can I help? After school?"

"We'll see," Chance said, and smiled. "Go on, now. Your sister will get to the bathroom before you do if you dally too long."

Kiley let out a squeal, and ran, with Kiera, also squealing, hot on her trail.

Chance laughed and shook his head.

"You're good with them," Hallie said. "I appreciate that, Chance."

The bed gave a little as he sat down beside her, smoothed Trace's tiny head with the pad of one finger. "It's easy enough," he said. "Far as I'm concerned, they're as much my children as this little guy is."

She knew he meant it, and her eyes filled with happy tears. "How did I ever get so lucky?" she asked.

He stretched out beside her, propped on one elbow. "Well," he began, with a long sigh, "if I remember correctly, you were down to your last chance, the night you wandered into that café."

She smiled, touched his mouth with her fingertip. "*You* are my last chance," she said. "My first, last and always Chance."

He laughed. "Why, shucks, ma'am," he drawled. "You're like to turn my head, with talk like that."

Hallie scooted down a little way, so that their faces were in line with each other. "Am I, now? Well, you just turn your head this way, Cowboy, and see if I don't kiss you so hard your socks will shoot right off your feet."

He chuckled, but the sound died, between their lips, when she kissed him. The new-old electricity was there, like always, lively as the night sky on the Fourth of July.

"Oh, Lord," Chance muttered, shaking his head, as if to restore his equilibrium, when it was over. Trace lost his grip on the bottle, and whimpered, and she stuck the nipple back into his mouth. Chance, meanwhile, scrambled off the bed, looking dazed.

"Come on, " Hallie said to the baby. "Let's go downstairs, put you in your playpen, and make this crew some breakfast."

"The coffee's already on," Chance said, a little smugly, from inside their bathroom.

Hallie got up, carried the baby to his crib, changed his diapers, and headed downstairs. After settling him in a warm corner of the kitchen, she stood at the sink, washing her hands.

She was an ordinary woman, on an ordinary day, and yet, as she looked out over the snowy expanse of land, and the creek sparkling in the distance, she couldn't help marveling at the sheer magnitude of her blessings.

8/15

CPSIA information can be obtained at www.ICGtesting.com
Printed in the USA
LVOW07s1451220715

447214LV00001B/87/P